Praise for *I Owe You One*

"I love the opportunity to escape with a Sophie Kinsella book, and *I Owe You One* came just when I needed it. Fixie's story is one of missed cues, mistakes, and the realization that you can't fix someone else's mess until you fix your own—a smart lesson wrapped in a gem of a novel."
—JODI PICOULT, #1 *New York Times* bestselling author of *A Spark of Light* and *Small Great Things*

"A humorous exploration of family life, finding love and the difficulties of coming into one's own as a young professional woman . . . [Kinsella's] trademark Brit wit shines . . . and the entertaining cast of characters . . . will certainly remind readers why nineteen years after her first hit Kinsella remains one of the reigning queens of women's fiction."
—*The Washington Post*

"*I Owe You One* is another impossibly delightful story by Sophie Kinsella, a must-read for her diehard fans and new readers alike."
—*PopSugar*

"Kinsella offers another winning novel. . . . [Her] reliable mix of humor and spot-on insights into both romantic and familial relationships adds spice as Fixie finally learns to take charge and speak her mind, making this a surefire hit for Kinsella's fans."

—*Publishers Weekly*

"Kinsella again provides a delightful, irresistible romp."

—*Booklist*

"Kinsella creates a charming story full of quirky characters and laugh-out-loud dialogue. Fixie is a likable character, one readers will root for as she learns to take control of her own life. Kinsella's many fans will devour this warm and hilarious read."

—*Kirkus Reviews*

"This book is a shot of pure joy!"

—JENNY COLGAN, *New York Times* bestselling author of *The Bookshop on the Corner*

Praise for *Surprise Me*

"Well paced and . . . genuinely funny, with a likeable cast of peripheral characters . . . [Kinsella's] hold on the reader's sympathies is deft, and I found myself rooting for Dan and Sylvie."

—*The New York Times Book Review*

"Sophie Kinsella is full of surprises. . . . The British author of the chick-lit-y Shopaholic series (and other charming stand-alone titles) is still making us laugh. . . . An unexpected and wholly satisfying payoff for the devoted Kinsella fan."

—*USA Today*

"Pure fun . . . A fast-moving and entertaining story with well-rounded and endearing characters. A hilariously moving look at marriage and the power of mixing things up."

—*Kirkus Reviews*

"In her signature fashion, Kinsella brings a cast of quirky, funny characters to this new work. . . . [She] keeps the laughs coming. . . . Readers will follow the story with bated breath as the couple struggle to make their marriage right after everything they thought they knew about each other proves wrong."

—*Library Journal*

"A delightful take on the mixed blessings of marital longevity."

—*People*

"Heartfelt . . . What at first seems like a light novel about familiar woes turns into a deeper story about trust, family, and perception."

—*Publishers Weekly*

"Winsome and zesty, Kinsella's latest delivers all the hallmarks her many fans have come to expect."

—*Booklist*

"I was intrigued by the epigraph, hooked at the prologue and laughing out loud by page one. . . . Kinsella is a master at engaging storytelling, entertaining quips, and developing nuanced, interesting characters. . . . Entertaining and comical with questions we can puzzle over."

—*Bookreporter*

"Kinsella, the wickedly funny author behind *Confessions of a Shopaholic* (and its sequels), wrote a new fiction piece about Sylvie and Dan, a young married couple who are told that thanks to longer life expectancy, they could be married for another sixty-eight years. . . . So, they decide to surprise each other with gifts, gestures and the like to keep things interesting. All goes well until the surprises turn into 'shocking truths.'"

—*Dailybreak*

Praise for *My Not So Perfect Life*

"A sparkling, witty novel about social media and the stories we tell ourselves."

—*People* (Book of the Week)

"You'll relate hard and root harder for Londoner Katie, whose quarterlife crisis feels even worse thanks to the Insta-perfect people all around her."

—*Cosmopolitan*

"Something else separates this comic novel from the usual fare. . . . The soul of this book concerns female friendship and its dynamics. . . . [It] has a touch of real wisdom in its slapstick hand that will satisfy Kinsella die-hards as well as new readers."

—*The Washington Post*

"With both warm-hearted and laugh-out-loud moments, Sophie Kinsella's *My Not So Perfect Life* was a joy to read. . . . Katie is relatable, bright and quirky—you'll find yourself cheering for her from the start, even as she learns that a perfect life isn't always what it seems, or what it's cracked up to be. Themes of friendship, love and living your true life rise to the top in this must-read stand-alone romantic comedy."

—"Happily Ever After," *USA Today*

"The book is fun, as Kinsella's books are, but it delivers a strong positive message, as well. . . . Kinsella creates a solid, likable character—one that I got to know and root for throughout the book."

—Fairfield *Daily Republic*

"This one is [not only] a comic romance, but a family novel and even a business novel. . . . You'd be silly to bet against [our heroine], obviously, but the happy ending is well earned, not forced."

—*Sullivan County Democrat*

"This is a really funny and relatable story about working women, women's relationships with each other and one plucky heroine's journey. . . . A perfect pick-me-up."

—*The Parkersburg News and Sentinel*

"Many laugh-out-loud hilarious moments in this feel-good novel about social media and personal branding, and the hectic realities behind our perfect online lives."

—*Bustle*

"Pure escapist fun."

—*PopSugar*

"Katie is a winning heroine. . . . Kinsella creates characters that are well-rounded, quirky, and a complete joy to read."

—*Kirkus Reviews* (starred review)

"With her signature humor, bestselling author Kinsella explores the frequent disconnect between perception and reality in modern life. . . . Driven by Katie's witty observations and numerous missteps as she attempts to reconcile various aspects of her identity, this novel is smartly satirical and entertaining."

—*Publishers Weekly*

"Sophie Kinsella keeps her finger on the cultural pulse, while leaving me giddy with laughter. I loved it."

—JoJo Moyes

By Sophie Kinsella

I OWE YOU ONE

Sophie Kinsella

I OWE YOU ONE

A Novel

THE DIAL PRESS

NEW YORK

2019 Dial Press Trade Paperback Edition

Published in the United States by The Dial Press, an imprint of Random House, a division of Penguin Random House LLC, New York.

The Dial Press and the House colophon are registered trademarks of Penguin Random House LLC.

Originally published in hardcover in the United States by The Dial Press, an imprint of Random House, a division of Penguin Random House LLC, and in the United Kingdom by Bantam Press, an imprint of Transworld Publishers, a Penguin Random House UK Company, in 2019.

Library of Congress Cataloging-in-Publication Data
Names: Kinsella, Sophie, author.
Title: I owe you one : a novel / Sophie Kinsella.
Description: New York : The Dial Press, [2019]
Identifiers: LCCN 2018038400| ISBN 9781524799038 (paperback) | ISBN 9781524799021 (ebook) | ISBN 9781984854698 (international)
Subjects: | BISAC: FICTION / Contemporary Women.
Classification: LCC PR6073.I246 I2 2019 | DDC 823/.914—dc23
LC record available at https://lccn.loc.gov/2018038400

Printed in the United States of America on acid-free paper

randomhousebooks.com

4 6 8 9 7 5 3

Title page adapted from iStockphoto.com images

Book design by Dana Leigh Blanchette

To my friend and editor,
Joy Terekiev

I OWE YOU ONE

I OWE YOU ONE

One

*T*he trouble with me is, I can't let things go. They bug me. I see problems and I want to fix them, right here, right now. My nickname isn't Fixie for nothing.

I mean, this can be a good thing. For example, at my best friend Hannah's wedding, I got to the reception and instantly saw that only half the tables had flowers. I ran around sorting it before the rest of the guests arrived, and in her speech, Hannah thanked me for dealing with "Flowergate." So that was OK.

On the other hand, there was the time I brushed a piece of fluff off the leg of a woman sitting next to me by the pool at a spa day. I was just trying to be helpful. Only it turned out it wasn't a piece of fluff; it was a pubic hair growing halfway down her thigh. And then I made things worse by saying, "Sorry! I thought that was a piece of fluff," and she went kind of purple, and two nearby women turned to look. . . .

I shouldn't have said anything. I see that now.

Anyway. So this is my quirk. This is my flaw. Things bug me. And right now the thing that's bugging me is a Coke can. It's been left on the top shelf of the leisure section of our shop, in front of a chessboard propped up for display. Not only that, the chessboard is covered with a brown stain. Obviously someone's opened the can or dumped it down too hard and it's splattered everywhere and they haven't cleared it up. Who?

As I look around the shop with narrowed eyes, I fully suspect Greg, our senior assistant. Greg drinks some kind of beverage all day long. If he's not clutching a can, it's noxious filter coffee in an insulated cup decorated with camouflage and webbing, as though he's in the army, not working in a household store in Acton. He's always leaving it about the place, or even thrusting it at customers and saying, "Hold this a mo," while he gets a saucepan down off the display for them. I've *told* him not to.

Anyway. Not the time for recriminations. Whoever dumped that Coke can (Greg, definitely Greg), it's caused a nasty stain, just when our important visitors are about to arrive.

And, yes, I know it's on a high shelf. I know it's not obvious. I know most people would shrug it off. They'd say: "It's not a big deal. Let's get some perspective."

I've never been great at perspective.

I'm trying hard not to look at it but to focus instead on the rest of the shop, which looks gleamingly clean. A little shambolic, maybe, but then, that's the style of our all-purpose family shop. (*Family-owned since 1985*, it says on our window.) We stock a lot of different items, from knives to aprons to candlesticks, and they all need to go somewhere.

I suddenly catch sight of an old man in a mac in the kitchen section. He's reaching with a shaking hand for a plain white mug, and I hurry over to get it for him.

"Here you are," I say with a friendly smile. "I can take that to the till for you. Do you need any more mugs? Or can I help you with anything else?"

"No, thank you, love," he says in a quavering voice. "I only need the one mug."

"Is white your favorite color?" I gently press, because there's something so poignant about buying one plain white mug that I can't bear it.

"Well." His gaze roams doubtfully over the display. "I do like a brown mug."

"This one maybe?" I retrieve a brown earthenware mug that he probably discounted because it was too far out of reach. It's solid, with a nice big handle. It looks like a cozy fireside mug.

The man's eyes light up, and I think, *I knew it*. When your life is restricted, something like a mug choice becomes huge.

"It's a pound more expensive," I tell him. "It's £4.99. Is that OK?"

Because you never take anything for granted. You never assume. Dad taught me that.

"That's fine, love." He smiles back. "That's fine."

"Great! Well, come this way. . . ."

I lead him carefully down the narrow aisle, keeping my eyes fixed on danger points. Which isn't *quite* the selfless gesture it might seem—this man is a knocker-overer. You can tell as soon as you lay eyes on him. Trembling hands, uncertain gaze, shabby old trolley that he's pulling behind him . . . all the signs of a classic knocker-overer. And the last thing I need is a floor full of smashed crockery. Not with Jake's visitors arriving any moment.

I smile brightly at the man, hiding my innermost thoughts, although the very word *Jake* passing through my brain has made my stomach clench with nerves. It always happens. I think *Jake* and my stomach clenches. I'm used to it by now, although I don't know if it's normal. I don't know how other people feel about their siblings. My best friend, Hannah, hasn't got any, and it's not the kind of question you ask random people, is it? "How do your siblings make you feel? Kind of gnawed-up and anxious and wary?" But that's definitely how my brother, Jake, makes me feel. Nicole doesn't make me feel anxious, but she does make me feel gnawed-up and, quite often, like hitting something.

To sum up, neither of them makes me feel *good*.

Maybe it's because both of them are older than me and were tough acts to follow. When I started at secondary school, aged eleven, Jake was sixteen and the star of the football team. Nicole was fifteen, stunningly beautiful, and had been scouted as a model. Everyone in the school wanted to be her friend. People would say to me, in awed tones, "Is Jake Farr your *brother*? Is Nicole Farr your *sister*?"

Nicole was as drifty and vague then as she is now, but Jake dominated everything. He was focused. Bright-eyed. Quick to anger. I'll always remember the time he got in a row with Mum and went and kicked a can around the street outside, shouting swear words into the night sky. I watched him from an upstairs window, gripped and a bit terrified. I'm twenty-seven now, but you never really leave your inner eleven-year-old, do you?

And of course there are other reasons for me to feel rubbish around Jake. Tangible reasons. Financial reasons.

Which I will *not* think about now. Instead, I smile at the old man, trying to make him feel that I have all the time in the world. Like Dad would have done.

Morag rings up the price and the man gets out an old leather coin purse.

"Fifty . . ." I hear him saying as he peers at a coin. "Is that a fifty-pence piece?"

"Let's have a look, love," says Morag in her reassuring way. Morag's been with us for seven years. She was a customer first and applied when she saw an ad pinned up on a noticeboard. Now she's assistant manager and does all the buying for greeting cards—she has a brilliant eye. "No, that's a ten-pence," she says kindly to the old man. "Have you got another pound coin in there?"

My eyes swivel up to the Coke can and stained chessboard again. It doesn't matter, I tell myself. There isn't time to sort it now. And the visitors won't notice it. They're coming to show us their range of olive oils, not inspect the place. *Just ignore it, Fixie.*

Ignore it.

Oh God, but I can't. It's driving me *nuts*.

My eye keeps flicking upward to it. My fingers are doing that *thing* they do whenever I'm desperate to fix something, when some situation or other is driving me mad. They drum each other feverishly. And my feet do a weird stepping motion: *forward-across-back, forward-across-back.*

I've been like this since I was a little kid. It's bigger than me. I know it would be mad to drag a ladder out, get a bucket and water, and clean the stain up, when the visitors might arrive at any moment. I *know* this.

"Greg!" As he appears from behind the glassware section, my voice shoots out before I can stop it. "Quick! Get a step-ladder. I need to clean up that stain."

Greg looks up to where I'm pointing and gives a guilty jump as he sees the Coke can.

"That wasn't me," he says at once. "It definitely wasn't me." Then he pauses before adding, "I mean, if it was, I didn't notice."

The thing about Greg is, he's very loyal to the shop and he works really long hours, so I forgive him quite a lot.

"Doesn't matter who it was," I say briskly. "Let's just get rid of it."

"OK," Greg says, as though digesting this. "Yeah. But aren't those people about to arrive?"

"Yes, which is why we need to be *quick*. We need to *hurry*."

"OK," says Greg again, not moving a muscle. "Yeah. Got you. Where's Jake?"

This is a very good question. Jake is the one who met these olive-oil people in the first place. In a bar, apparently. He's the one who set up this meeting. And here he isn't.

But family loyalty keeps me from saying any of this aloud. Family loyalty is a big thing in my life. Maybe the biggest thing. Some people hear the Lord Jesus guiding them; I hear my dad, before he died, saying in his East End accent: *Family is it, Fixie. Family is what drives us. Family is everything.*

Family loyalty is basically our religion.

"He's always landing you in it, Jake is," Greg mutters. "You never know when he's going to turn up. Can't rely on him. We're short-staffed today too, what with your mum taking the day off."

All of this might be true, but I can hear Dad's voice in my head again: *Family first, Fixie. Protect the family in public. Have it out with them later, in private.*

"Jake does his own hours," I remind Greg. "It's all agreed."

All of us Farrs work in the shop—Mum, me, Jake, and Nicole—but only Mum and I are full-time. Jake calls himself our "consultant." He has another business of his own and he's doing an MBA online, and he pops in when he can. And Nicole is doing a yoga-instructor course Monday to Friday, so she can only come in at weekends. Which she does sometimes.

"I expect he's on his way," I add briskly. "Anyway, we've just got to deal with it. Come on! Ladder!"

As Greg drags a stepladder across the shop floor, I hurry to our back room and run some hot water into a bucket. I just need to dash up the ladder, wipe the stain away, grab the can, jump down, and clear everything before the visitors arrive. Easy.

The leisure section is a bit incongruous, surrounded as it is by tea towels and jam-making kits. But it was Dad who set it up that way, so we've never changed it. Dad loved a good board game. He always said board games are as essential to a household as spoons. Customers would come in for a kettle and leave with Monopoly too.

And ever since he died, nine years ago now, we've tried to keep the shop just as he created it. We still sell licorice allsorts. We still have a tiny hardware section. And we still stock the leisure section with games, balls, and water guns.

The thing about Dad was, he could sell anything to anyone. He was a charmer. But not a flashy, dishonest charmer; a genuine charmer. He believed in every product he sold. He wanted to make people happy. He *did* make people happy. He created a community in this little corner of West London (he called himself an "immigrant," being East End born), and it's still going. Even if the customers who really knew Dad are fewer every year.

"OK," I say, hurrying out to the shop floor with the bucket. "This won't take a sec."

I dash up the steps of the ladder and start scrubbing at the brown stain. I can see Morag below me, demonstrating a paring knife to a customer, and I resist the urge to join in the conversation. I know about knives; I've done chef training. But you can't be everywhere at once, and—

"They're here," announces Greg. "There's a car pulling into the parking space."

It was Jake who insisted we reserve our only parking spot for these olive-oil people. They'll have asked, "Do you have parking?" and he won't have wanted to say, "Only one space," because he's pretentious that way, so he'll have said airily, "Of course!" as though we've got an underground vault.

"No problem," I say breathlessly. "I'm done. All good."

I dump the cloth and the Coke can into the bucket and swiftly start descending. There. That took no time, and now it won't bug me and—

"Careful on that ladder."

I hear Greg's voice below, but he's always regaling us with stupid health-and-safety rules he's read online, so I don't alter my step or my pace until he shouts, "Stop!" sounding genuinely alarmed.

"Fixie!" Stacey yells from the till. She's another of our sales assistants and you can't miss her piercing nasal voice. "Look out!"

As my head whips round, it takes me a moment to comprehend what I've done. I've snagged my sleeve on a netball hoop, which has caught on the handle of a massive tub of bouncy balls. And now it's tipping off the shelf . . . there's nothing I can do to stop it, *shit* . . .

"Oh my *God*!"

I lift my spare hand to protect myself from a deluge of little rubber balls. They're bouncing on my head, my shoulders, all over the shop. How come we have so many of the bloody things, anyway?

As I reach the bottom of the ladder, I look around in horror. It's a miracle that nothing's been smashed. Even so, the floor is a carpet of bouncy balls.

"Quick!" I instruct Greg and Stacey. "Teamwork! Pick them up! I'll go and head off the visitors."

As I hurry toward the door, Greg and Stacey don't look anything like a team—in fact, they look like an *anti*-team. They keep bumping into each other and cursing. Greg is hastily stuffing balls down his shirtfront and in his trouser pockets and I yell, "Put them back in the *tub*!"

"I didn't even notice that Coke stain," volunteers Stacey as I pass, with one of her shrugs. "You should have left it."

"Is that helpful?" I want to retort. But I don't. For a start,

Stacey's a good worker and worth keeping on side. You just have to deal with what Mum and I call the SIMs (Stacey's Inappropriate Moments).

But of course the real reason I say nothing is that she's right. I should have left it. I just can't help fixing things. It's my flaw. It's who I am.

Two

The visitors are posh-looking. Of course they are. My brother likes hanging out with posh people. Jake has always been ambitious, ever since he was a little boy. At first he was just ambitious to be on the football team. Then, in his late teens, he started socializing with a rich crowd—and suddenly he was dissatisfied with our house and our holidays and even, one awful time, with Dad's accent. (There was another huge argument. Mum got really upset. I still remember the sound of the shouting coming through the floor from downstairs.)

He worked as an estate agent in Fulham—until about three years ago, when he started his own business—and there the poshness rubbed off on him even more. Jake likes being around blokes in brogues, with identikit haircuts and *raah* voices. Basically he resents the fact that he wasn't born in Chelsea. That he's not one of those poshos on the telly, partying with royalty and taking six holidays a year. But since he's not, he can at least spend all his time in pubs on the King's Road with guys called Rupert.

These two men, stepping out of their Range Rover, clearly come from that crowd, with their polo shirts and deck shoes and tans. I find these types a bit intimidating, to be honest, but I tell myself, *Chin up, Fixie,* and go forward to greet them. I can see one eyeing up the shop with a critical frown, and I feel a defensive prickle. OK, it's not the most beautiful shop front—it's a 1970s purpose-built structure—but the glass panes are gleaming and the display of kitchen textiles looks great. We have a pretty good amount of space for a High Street store, and we use it well. We have several display tables at the front and three aisles, and it all works.

"Hi!" the taller one greets me. "Clive Beresford. Are you Felicity?"

A lot of people hear *Fixie* and think *Felicity.* I'm used to it.

"Fixie." I smile and shake his hand. "Welcome to Farrs."

"Simon." The other guy lifts a hand as he lugs a heavy-looking box out of the Range Rover. "We found it! Good space you've got here."

"Yes." I nod. "We're lucky."

"Not exactly Notting Hill, though, is it?"

"Notting Hill?" I echo, puzzled.

"Jake said the family business was in Notting Hill."

I press my lips together. This is so Jake. Of course he said we were based in Notting Hill. He probably said Hugh Grant was a regular customer too.

"No, we're Acton," I say politely.

"But you're planning to expand into Notting Hill soon-ish?" presses Clive, as we head inside. "That's what your brother told us."

Expand into Notting Hill? That's total rubbish. I know

Jake just wanted to impress a pair of strangers at a bar. But I can hear Dad's voice in my head: *Family first, Fixie.*

"Maybe," I say pleasantly. "Who knows?" I usher them into the shop, then spread my arms around at all the saucepans, plastic storage boxes, and tablecloths. "So, this is us."

There's a short silence. I can sense this isn't what they expected. Simon is peering at a display of mason jars. Clive takes a few steps forward and looks at a Monopoly set curiously. A moment later, a red bouncy ball drops on his head.

"Ow!" He looks up. "What the—"

"Sorry!" I say quickly. "No idea how that happened!"

Shit. There must have been a stray one teetering somewhere.

"So you're looking to turn into more of a high-end deli?" Simon seems puzzled. "Do you stock any food at *all*?"

I feel another defensive prickle. I don't know what stories Jake's been telling him, but that's not my fault.

"Absolutely." I nod. "Oils, vinegars, spices, that kind of thing. Please do put your box down."

"Perfect." He dumps the box on a front display chest, which we cleared in advance. (Normally we'd go into the back room, but it's full of boxes of scented candles, which we need to unpack.) "Well, let me introduce you to what we do. We've sourced a range of olive oils which are rather special." He says it in that posh way—*raaather special.* "Have a taste."

As he speaks, both men are unpacking large bottles of olive oil from wooden boxes. Simon briskly lays out some dipping saucers and Clive produces some precut cubes of bread.

He's talking about some olive estate in Italy, but I'm not listening properly; I'm staring in horror at Greg. He's just walked into view—and his pockets are still stuffed with bouncy balls. His entire groin area looks massive and lumpy and just . . . *weird*. Why didn't he get *rid* of them?

I give him a furious eye roll, which means: "Why have you still got bouncy balls in your pockets?" Greg immediately shoots back an urgent eye roll of his own, which clearly means: "There's a good reason, believe me."

I don't believe him for a moment. Greg acts in good faith, no one doubts that, but his logic is random and unnerving. He's like a computer on its last legs that works perfectly until it suddenly decides to email your whole in-box to Venezuela.

"Would you like to have a taste?"

I abruptly realize Clive's spiel is over and he's proffering bread cubes and oil.

As I dip and taste, I'm thinking: *Typical Jake, setting up this meeting on the one day that Mum isn't in the shop.* What does he think, that he can get this past her beady eye? That she won't notice? Mum notices everything. Every sale, every refund, every email. *Everything.*

Suddenly I notice that the two posh guys keep shooting surreptitious glances at Greg's bulging groin area. I mean, I don't blame them. It's a pretty disturbing sight.

"Excuse Greg's strange-looking appearance," I say with a relaxed laugh. "He doesn't normally look like that! It's just that he—"

"Hormone disorder," Greg cuts me off with an impassive nod, and I nearly choke on my bread. Why . . . What does he even mean by . . . *Hormone disorder?* "Nasty," Greg adds meaningfully.

I'm used to Greg's idiosyncrasies, but sometimes he silences even me.

"Funny story," Greg adds, encouraged by the attention. "My brother was born with only half a pancreas. And my mum, she's got this manky kidney—"

"Thanks, Greg!" I interrupt desperately. "Thanks for . . . Thanks."

The two smart guys look even more appalled, and Greg shoots me a self-satisfied look which I know means, "Saved things there, didn't I?"

For about the hundredth time I wonder if we could send Greg on a course. A course on Not Being Greg.

"Anyway!" I say as Greg heads off. "These olive oils are amazing." I'm not just being polite; it's true. They're rich and aromatic and delicious, especially the dark-green peppery one. "How much would they retail for?"

"The prices are all laid out here," says Simon, handing me a printed document. I scan the figures—and nearly fall over flat. Usually I'm pretty cool in situations like this, but I hear myself gasping, *"Ninety-five pounds?"*

"Obviously this is very much a luxury, high-end product," says Clive smoothly. "As we explained, it's a very special estate, and the process is unique—"

"But no one's going to spend ninety-five quid on a bottle of oil!" I almost want to laugh. "Not in this shop. Sorry."

"But when you open in Notting Hill?" chimes in Simon. "Very different market. We think 'The Notting Hill Family Deli' is a great name, by the way."

I try to hide my shock. The *what*? Our shop is called Farrs. It was named Farrs by our dad, whose name was Michael Farr, and it's never going to be called anything else.

"This is the olive oil we stock." Greg's voice takes us all by surprise, and he places a bottle of oil on the table. "Costs £5.99." His prominent gray eyes survey the two posh guys. "Just saying."

"Yes," says Simon, after a pause. "Well, of course, that's a rather different product from ours. Not to be rude, but if you both have a taste, you'll notice the difference in quality of the cheaper oil. May I?"

I notice how skillfully he's drawn Greg into the conversation. Now he's pouring out our £5.99 oil and dipping cubes of bread into it. As I taste, I can see what he means. Our oil tastes thinner in comparison.

But you have to know your customers. You have to know their limits. I'm about to tell Simon that our customers are a practical, pragmatic lot and there's not a chance in hell they'll spend ninety-five quid on oil, when the door opens and I turn to see Jake striding in.

He's an impressive sight. Always is. He's got Dad's firm jaw and Dad's twinkling eyes and he's dressed in really nice clothes. Posh estate-agent clothes. Navy blazer, tie, shiny expensive shoes. Cuff links.

And at the very sight of him, I feel a rush of familiar feelings attacking me, like flapping ravens. *Inadequate. Guilty. Inferior. Rubbish.*

This is nothing new. My big brother always brings these feelings out in me, and why shouldn't he? If I believe in anything as much as *family first*, it's *be fair*. I'm always fair and truthful, however painful it is.

And the painful truth is that Jake is the success and I'm the failure. He's the one who started an import-export business without a penny from anyone else. He's the one who made a mint on some brand of nude seamless knickers that he sold to a discount store. He's the one who has the flash car and the business cards and the (nearly) MBA.

I'm the one who took a loan from Mum ("our inheritance," Jake always calls it) and tried to set up a catering business and failed. And who still hasn't paid the money back.

I'm not the black sheep of the family. That would be glamorous and interesting. I'm just the stupid dumb sheep who still has a stash of dark-green aprons under the bed, all embroidered with my logo: *Farr's Food*. (I sold everything else, but I couldn't get rid of those.) And whenever I'm around Jake, I feel even more stupid and dumb. Like, *literally* dumb. Because I barely ever open my mouth, and when I do, I start to stammer.

I have opinions; I have ideas. I really do. When I'm managing the store alone—or alongside Mum—I can tell people what to do. I can assert myself. But around Jake, and even sometimes Nicole, I think twice before I venture my thoughts. Because the unsaid message hanging in the air is: "Well, what would you know? Your business went bust."

The only one who makes me feel like none of it matters and I'm still worth something is Mum. If it weren't for her, I don't know how I'd have coped.

"Guys!" Jake greets the visitors. "You're here already! *Ciao*."

Ciao. This is how he talks with them. We grew up in the same family, but I can't imagine ever being the type of person who says *ciao*.

"Jake!" Clive claps him on the back. "My man."

"Call this Notting Hill?" joshes Simon, shaking Jake's hand. "This is bloody Acton!"

"It's just the start of the empire," says Jake, with a broad grin—then he darts me the tiniest of looks, which I can read completely. It means, "I'm assuming you haven't dumped me in it?"

I shoot back a corresponding look, which says, "The Notting Hill Family Deli?" But now he's blanking me.

Jake often blanks me when he's with his smart friends. He's probably worried I'll expose some of the fibs I've heard him tell. I'd never do that—*family first*—but I do notice when he's fudging the truth about things. Like where he went to school (he calls himself a "grammar school boy," but it was a comp). And references to our "little place in the country." I have no idea which "little place" that would be— maybe the old privy at the end of Mum's garden?

"So these are the famous oils!" Jake exclaims. "*Fantastico!*"

"You have to come and see the estate, Jake," says Simon enthusiastically. "Absolutely stunning."

"Love to," Jake drawls. "I adore that part of the world."

I don't remember Jake ever going to Italy in his life, although obviously I'm not going to point this out.

"You know it costs ninety-five quid a bottle?" I say tentatively to Jake. "I don't think our customers can afford that, can they?"

I see Jake flinch in irritation and I know why. He doesn't want to be reminded of our practical, price-conscious customers. He wants nonexistent millionaire customers.

"But if you're going high end, this is where the market is." Clive taps the bottle. "The taste is phenomenal, I'm sure Fixie will agree?"

"It's great," I say. "It's delicious. I'm just . . . you know. Will our customers appreciate it?"

Sure enough, my voice has started shaking. I'm asking questions instead of making statements. Jake's presence has that effect on me. And I hate myself for it, because it makes me sound uncertain, when I'm not—I'm *not*.

"They'll learn to appreciate it." Jake brushes me off. "We'll have tasting evenings, that kind of thing. . . ." He addresses Clive and Simon. "We'll definitely make an order, guys, it's just a question of how much."

I feel a shaft of panic. We can't make an order on the spot, especially in Mum's absence.

"Jake, maybe we should talk about this first?" I venture.

"Nothing to talk about," he shoots back, his eyes clearly telling me: "Shut up."

Oh God. Even though the ravens are batting their wings in my face, I have to persevere. For Mum.

"I just . . ." My voice is wavering again and I clear my throat. "Our customers come here for sensible, value-for-money products. They don't buy luxury food items."

"Well, maybe we have to *educate* them," snaps Jake. "Teach them. Get their mediocre taste buds used to finer flavors." He grabs a cube of bread, scoops up some of the £5.99 oil, and puts it in his mouth before anyone can say anything. "I mean, this is sublime," he says in muffled tones as he chews. "It's on a whole different level. It's nutty, it's rich . . . you can *taste* the quality. . . . Guys, what can I say, congratulations. I'm seriously impressed."

He holds out a hand, but neither Simon nor Clive takes it. They seem too stunned to move.

"So, which one was that?" says Jake, finally finishing his mouthful. "Was it the most expensive?"

There's silence. I can't look at anyone. Every *fiber* of me is cringing for Jake.

But, kudos to the posh: They have impeccable manners. Not a flicker runs over Clive's face as he immediately, deftly, saves the situation.

"I'm not *quite* sure which one that was?" he says to Simon, his brow wrinkled.

"I'm not sure either." Simon swiftly takes his cue. "I think the dishes have been mixed up maybe, so—"

"Probably our fault for bringing so many."

"Absolutely," chimes in Simon. "They all start to taste the same!"

They're being so kind to Jake, while he's totally oblivious, that I want to say, "Thank you, posh guys. Thank you for being so nice to my brother when he doesn't even know it."

But of course I don't. Simon and Clive glance at each other and tacitly seem to agree to wrap up. We all keep smiling and chatting as they pack their stuff and suggest that we have a chat and they'll be in touch.

As they drive away from the front of the shop, Jake and I both draw breath to speak—but he gets in first.

"Well done, Fixie," he says, looking annoyed. "You scared them away. Nice work."

"Look, Jake, I'm sorry," I begin, then curse myself for apologizing. *Why* do I always do that? "I just . . . I really think—"

"I know what you think," he cuts me off dismissively. "But *I'm* the one trying to be strategic about the future of the shop here. Bigger. Better. High-end. Profitable."

"Yes, but ninety-five quid for one bottle of olive oil, Jake," I appeal to him. "You can't be serious."

"Why not?" he snaps. "Harrods stock it."

I don't even know what to say to this. *Harrods?*

I'm aware of Greg glancing our way, and I hastily paste on a smile. Dad would *kill* us for airing family disputes on the shop floor.

"Jakey?" I turn to see Leila, Jake's girlfriend, coming into the store, wearing an adorable yellow full-skirted dress and sunglasses on her head. Leila always reminds me of Bambi. She has long spindly legs and she wears high wedged sandals that clip-clop like hooves and she peers at the world through her long eyelashes as though she's not sure if it's about to shoot her. She's very sweet and I can't possibly argue with Jake in front of her.

Not just because she's sweet, but because *family first*. Leila isn't family. Not actual family. Not yet. She's been going out with Jake for three years—they met in a club—and I've never seen them argue. Leila doesn't seem the arguing type, although she must get angry with Jake sometimes? She's never mentioned it, though. In fact, she once said to me, "Jake's a real softie, isn't he?" and I nearly fell over backward. Jake? A *softie*?

"Hi, Leila," I say, kissing her. She's as thin and tiny as a child; in fact, I'm amazed she can hold all those glossy carrier bags. "Been shopping?"

"I've been treating the missus," says Jake loftily. "We got Mum's present too."

Jake always calls Leila "the missus," although they're not even engaged. I sometimes wonder if she minds, but then, I've never known Leila to mind about anything. Once, Jake arrived at the shop for a family meeting and it was only after an hour that we realized he'd left Leila in the car to watch out for traffic wardens. She wasn't annoyed at all; she'd just been sitting scrolling through her phone, humming to herself. When Mum exclaimed, "Jake! How could you leave Leila like that?" he shrugged and said, "She offered."

Now Leila dangles a shiny Christian Dior shopping bag at me and I inspect it with a small pang. I can't afford to buy Mum Christian Dior perfume. Still. She likes Sanctuary stuff too, which is what I bought her. And now just the thought of Mum is calming me down. I don't need to worry about any of this, of course—Mum will sort it out. She'll talk to Jake in that firm, calm way she has. She won't let him order silly-money olive oil.

Mum runs the family, the home, the business . . . basically everything. She's our CEO. Our anchor. When Dad suddenly died of a heart attack, it was like something exploded in her. It was as if all the negative energy of her grief circled round into a determination that this *wouldn't* destroy the business, or the family, or anything. She's powered us all through the last nine years, *and* she's learned Zumba *and* no one makes flaky pastry like she does. She's amazing. She says she channels Dad in everything she does and that he talks to her every night. Which sounds weird—but I believe her.

She's normally in this shop from dawn to dusk. The only reason she's not here now is it's her birthday party this evening and she wanted the day off to cook. And, yes, some women of her age—or any age—would let other people cook *for them* on their birthday. Not Mum. She's made sausage rolls, Waldorf salad, and apple pie every August 2 since I can remember. It's tradition. We're big on tradition, we Farrs.

"By the way, I sorted out your car-repair bill for you," Jake says to Leila. "I rang the guy. I said, 'You've been messing my girlfriend around. Try again.' He backed down on everything."

"Jake!" gasps Leila. "You're my hero!"

"And then I think you should upgrade," Jake adds carelessly. "Let's get you a newer model. We'll look at the weekend."

"Oh, Jakey." Leila's eyes glow, and she turns to me. "Isn't he the sweetest?"

"Er . . . yes." I smile feebly at her. "Totally."

At this moment, Morag and her customer—a middle-aged woman—come up to the till. Immediately Jake switches into top customer-service mode, beaming at her and asking, "Did you find everything you need? Ah, a paring knife. Now, I'm afraid I *will* have to ask a delicate question: Are you over eighteen?"

The woman giggles and blushes, and even I crack a smile. Jake's pretty charming when he wants to be. As she leaves we all say, "Goodbye," several times, and smile until the door closes. Then Jake gets his car keys out of his pocket and starts swinging them round his finger, the way he's done ever since he first got a car.

I know what I want to say to him. It's almost as if I can see the words forming in front of me in a thought bubble. Articulate, passionate words about the business. About what we do. About Dad. But somehow I can't seem to get the words out of the thought bubble and into the air.

Jake's face is distant and I know better than to interrupt him. Leila is poised like me, waiting, her eyebrows anxiously winged together.

She's so pretty, Leila. Pretty and gentle and never judges anyone. The thing she takes most seriously in life is manicures, because that's her business and her passion. But she doesn't even blink at my tatty nails, let alone sneer at them. She just accepts everyone for who they are, Jake included.

Finally, Jake stops swinging the keys and comes to. I have no idea what kinds of thoughts have been transfixing him. Even though I grew up with him, I really don't understand Jake very well.

"We'll head over to the house, then," he says. "Help Mum out."

By "Help Mum out" I know he means, "Get myself a beer and turn on Sky Sports," but I don't challenge him.

"OK," I say. "See you there."

Our house is only ten minutes' walk from the shop; sometimes it feels like one is an extension of the other. And I'm turning back to sort out a display of table mats which has gone wonky when Leila says, "What are you going to wear, Fixie?" in excited tones, as if we're going to the school prom.

"Dunno," I say, puzzled. "A dress, I suppose. Nothing special."

It's Mum's birthday party. It'll be friends and neighbors and Uncle Ned. I mean, I want to look nice, but it's not exactly the Grand Embassy Ball.

"Oh, right." Leila seems perplexed. "So you're not going to . . ."

"Not what . . ."

"I just thought, because . . ."

She trails off meaningfully, as though I'll know exactly what she's talking about.

"Because *what*?" I peer at her, and Leila suddenly swivels on her clippy-cloppy heel to Jake.

"Jakey!" she says, in her version of a reproving tone. (Basically still an adoring simper.) "Haven't you told her?"

"Oh, that. Right." Jake rolls his eyes and glances at me. "Ryan's back."

What?

I stare at him, frozen. I can't speak, because my lungs have seized up, but my brain has already started analyzing the word *back* like a relentless computer program. *Back.* What does *back* mean? Back to the UK? Back home? Back to me?

No, not back to me, *obviously* not back to me—

"He's back in the country," elaborates Leila, her eyes soft with empathy. "It never worked out with that American girl. He's coming to the party. And he was asking after you."

Three

I don't know how many times a heart can be broken, but mine's been shattered again and again, and every single time by Ryan Chalker.

Not that he'd know it. I've been pretty good at concealing my feelings (I think). But the truth is, I've been in love with Ryan pretty much solidly since I was ten years old and he was fifteen and I came across him and Jake with a group of boys in Burger King. I was instantly fixated on him. How could you *not* be fixated on him, with that blond hair, that profile, that glow?

By the time I joined secondary school, Ryan and Jake were best friends and Ryan used to hang around our house every weekend, cracking jokes and flirting with Mum. Unlike every other boy in that year, he had flawless skin. He knew how to style his hair. He could make our school uniform look sexy—*that's* how hot he was.

He had money too. Everyone whispered about it. Some relative had left him a small fortune. He always hosted parties and he got a car for his seventeenth. A convertible. I'm twenty-seven years old and I'm sure I'll never own a convertible. Ryan and Jake used to drive around London in it, roof down, music blaring, like a couple of rock stars. In fact, it was Ryan who introduced Jake to that posh, flash, hard-partying set. The pair of them used to get into the kind of clubs that you read about in tabloids, and they'd boast about it at our house the next day. When I was old enough, Mum let me go out with Jake and Ryan sometimes, and I felt like I'd won the lottery. There was such a buzz around them, and suddenly I was part of it too.

Ryan could be genuinely kind too. I'll always remember one evening when we went to the cinema. I'd just broken up with a boy called Jason, and a bunch of his friends were behind us. They started to laugh at me and jeer, and Ryan whipped round before anyone else could and lashed into them. People heard about it at school the next day, and everyone was saying, "Ryan loves Fixie!"

Of course I laughed along. I treated it like a joke. But inside, I was smitten. I felt as if we were connected now. I kept thinking, *Surely we'll end up together? Surely it's meant to be?*

There were so many moments over the years when I thought I had a chance. The time in Pizza Express when he kissed me lingeringly on greeting me. The time he squeezed my thigh. The time he asked if I was single at the moment. Dad's funeral, when he sat with me for a while at the reception and let me talk on endlessly about Dad. At my twenty-first birthday party he sang a karaoke version of "I Don't Want to Miss a Thing," straight to me, while my heart fluttered like a manic butterfly and I thought, *Yes, yes, this is it.* . . . But that night he went off with a girl called Tamara. Over the years I watched and secretly wept as he dated what seemed like every girl in West London and never looked my way.

Then, five years ago, he moved to L.A. to be a movie producer. An actual *movie producer*. You couldn't pick a more glamorous or unattainable job. I've still got the business card he gave me before he left, with an abstract logo and an address on Wilshire Boulevard.

It would have been easier to forget him if he'd disappeared forever—but he didn't. He flew back to London all the time and he always came to see Jake, in a blast of light and excitement. His wavy blond hair was permanently sun-bleached. He had endless stories of celebrities. He'd casually say "Tom," and I'd think, *Tom? Who does he mean, Tom?* And then I'd suddenly realize he meant Tom Cruise and my heart would be gripped and I'd think, *Oh my God, I know someone who knows Tom Cruise?*

Meanwhile, I went out with other guys; of course I did. But Ryan was lodged in my heart. And then last year, a full *sixteen years* after I first met him, he arrived at Jake's birthday drinks really drunk and unhappy—I never got the full story, but it was something about a studio executive playing him around.

I'm a good listener, so I let him slag off this guy and nodded and said sympathetic things. At last he ran out of steam, and I could see him looking at me. Like, really looking at me. As though he'd only just realized I was an actual grown-up woman. He said, "You know, I've always fancied you, Fixie. You're so genuine. You're so bloody refreshing." Then he added, as though puzzled, "Why have we never got it together?"

My heart was hammering, but for once in my life I managed to play it cool. I just looked at him and left it a moment, and then said, "Well."

And he gave me one of his lazy smiles, and said, "Well."

Oh my *God,* it was amazing. We left about three minutes later. He took me back to the flat where he was staying and we spent the night fulfilling every teenage fantasy I'd ever had, and then some. My brain kept screaming, *It's happening! I'm with Ryan! It's actually happening!* For ten solid days I was in a trance of delight.

And then he went back to L.A.

I mean, of course he went back to L.A. What did I expect, that he was going to propose?

(I'm not going to answer that. Not even in my own head. Because I might give away my most pathetic fantasy of all: that we'd be one of those pairs of lovers who were "meant to be" all their lives and finally realized it and never left each other's sides again.)

As he left for his flight that gray April morning, he kissed me with what looked like genuine regret and said, "You've been so good for me, Fixie." As if I were a juice fast or a series of TED Talks.

I said, as lightly as I could, "I hope you come and see me again." Which wasn't quite true. I *actually* hoped he'd suddenly exclaim, "Now I realize the truth! Fixie my darling, I can't live without you and I want you to get on this plane with me *now*."

Anyway. Astonishingly enough, that didn't happen.

Then I heard from Jake that he'd got a new girlfriend in L.A. called Ariana and they had rows all the time, but it was pretty serious. I looked at them on Facebook a few times. (OK, all the time.) I wrote casual, friendly texts to him, then deleted them. And all the while I pretended I was fine with it. To Mum, Jake, everybody. Because what other option did I have?

But it was all lies. I never reconciled myself to having lost him. I still secretly, crazily, hoped.

And now he's back. The words are thudding through my head like a drumbeat—*he's back, he's back*—while I stand in Anna's Accessories like a starstruck fourteen-year-old, frantically trying out hair clips. As though choosing exactly the right hair decoration will somehow magically make Ryan fall in love with me.

I couldn't cope with going straight home from the shop. What if he was there already, lounging on the sofa, ready to catch me out with his irresistible smile? I needed time. I needed to prepare. So at 5:00 P.M. I told Greg to close up and headed to the High Street. I bought myself a new lipstick. And now I'm standing in front of a display rack, trying to transform my appearance beyond belief with a £3.99 diamanté hair clip. Or maybe I should go for a flower.

Glittery hairband?

I know this is all displacement. I can't even contemplate the momentousness of seeing Ryan again, so instead I'm fixating on an irrelevant detail which nobody else will even notice. Story of my life.

At last I gather up two beaded hair clips, some diamanté hair grips, and a pair of dangling gold earrings for good luck. I pay for them and head out to the balmy street. Mum will be laying out the table by now. Stacking the paper cups.

Wrapping knives and forks in napkins. But even so, I need more time. I need to get my head straight.

On impulse, I duck into Café Allegro, which is our family's favorite local café. I buy a bag of coffee beans for Mum's cappuccino machine—we're always running out, and Café Allegro does the best ones—then order a mint tea and go sit by the window. I'm trying to think exactly how to greet Ryan. What vibe to give off. *Not* gushy or needy, but self-possessed and alluring.

With a sigh, I retrieve my Anna's Accessories bag, take out the two beaded clips, and hold them up against my hair, squinting into my hand mirror. Neither looks remotely alluring. I try the gold earrings against my ears and wince. Oh God. Terrible. I might take them back.

Suddenly I notice a guy opposite me, watching in slight amusement over his laptop, and at once I flush. What am I doing? I would never normally start trying on hair clips in a coffee shop. I've lost all sense of propriety.

As I shove the clips and earrings back in the bag, a drip of water lands on the table, and I look up. Now I think about it, there's been a steady stream of drips from the ceiling ever since I sat down, only they've been landing in a bucket on the floor.

A barista is nearby, giving a hot sandwich to a customer, and I attract her attention as she turns to go.

"Hi, the ceiling's leaking." I point upward and she follows my gaze briefly, then shrugs.

"Yeah. We put a bucket down."

"But it's dripping on the table too."

As I study the ceiling, I can see two sources of drips and a patch of damp. That whole area of ceiling looks very un-healthy. I glance at the guy opposite to see if he's noticed, but he's on his mobile phone and seems totally preoccupied.

"Yes," he's saying, in a voice which crackles with educa-tion and polish. "I know, Bill, but—"

Nice suit, I notice. Glossy, expensive shoes.

"They're doing building work on the floor above." The barista seems supremely unconcerned. "We've called them. You can move seats if you like."

I should have wondered why this window seat was empty, when the rest of the coffee shop is full. I look around to see if there's another available seat, but there isn't.

Well, I'm not fussy. I can put up with a few drips. I'll be leaving soon, anyway.

"It's OK," I say. "Just thought I'd let you know. You might need to get another bucket."

The barista shrugs again, with a look I recognize—it's the famous "I'm going off shift so what do I care?" look—and heads back to the counter.

"Strewth!" the guy opposite suddenly exclaims. His voice has risen and he's making exasperated gestures with his hand.

The word *strewth* makes me smile inside. That's a word Dad used to use. I don't often hear it anymore.

"You know what?" he's saying now. "I'm sick of these in-tellectual types with their six degrees from Cambridge." He listens for a bit, then says, "It should *not* be this hard to fill a junior-level position. It should *not*. But everyone Chloe finds for me . . . I know. You'd think. But all they want to do is tell me their clever theories that they learned at uni. They don't want to *work*."

He leans forward, takes his cup for a gulp of coffee, and meets eyes with me briefly. I can't help smiling, because even though he doesn't know it, I'm hearing my dad again.

On the face of it, this man is nothing like my dad. My dad was a weather-beaten former market trader. This guy is a thirty-something professional in a posh tie. But I'm hearing exactly the same note of energy; the same pragmatism; the same impatience with clever-clever know-it-alls. Dad had no time for theories either. "Get on and do it," he'd say.

"All I want is to hire someone bright and savvy and tough who knows how the world works," the guy is saying now, thrusting a hand through his frondy hair. "Someone who's been *in* the world, hasn't just written a dissertation about it. They don't even need a bloody degree! They need some sense! Sense!"

He's lean and energetic-looking, with an end-of-summer tan. Deep-brown hair, lighter where the sun's caught it. As he reaches for his coffee again, the fronds cast shadows over his face. His cheekbones are two long, strong planes. His eyes are . . . can't quite tell. Mid-brown or hazel, I think, peering surreptitiously at him. Then the light catches them and I see a tinge of green. They're woodland eyes.

It's a thing of mine, classifying eyes. Mine are double espresso. Ryan's are Californian sky. Mum's are deep-sea blue. And this guy's are woodland eyes.

"I know," he says more calmly, his ire apparently vanished. "So I'm having another meeting with Chloe next week. I'm sure she's really looking forward to it." His mouth curves into a sudden, infectious smile.

He can laugh at himself. That's one up on Dad, who was

the sweetest, most softhearted person in the world but didn't really *get* the concept of banter or laughing at yourself. You could never have sent Dad an irreverent, jokey birthday card. He would have just been hurt or offended.

"Oh. That." The guy shifts on his chair. "Look, I'm sorry." He passes a hand through his hair again, but this time he doesn't look dynamic; he looks upset. "I'm just . . . It's not happening. You know Briony, she gets ahead of herself, so . . . no. No home gym, not for now. Tanya's designs were great, she's very talented, but . . . Yeah. I'll pay her for her time, of course. . . . No, *not* with dinner," he adds firmly. "With a proper invoice. I insist." He nods a few times. "OK. I'll see you soon. Cheers."

The wry blade of humor is back in his voice—but as he puts his phone away, he stares out of the window as though trying to rebalance himself. It's weird, but I feel like I know this guy. Like, I *get* him. If we weren't two uptight British people in a London coffee shop, maybe I'd strike up conversation with him.

But we are. And that's just not what you do.

So I do that traditional London thing of pretending I didn't hear a word of his phone call and staring carefully into midair in a way that won't attract his gaze. The guy starts typing at his laptop and I glance at my watch—5:45 P.M. I should go soon.

My phone buzzes with a text and I reach for it, madly hoping it's Jake saying: **Ryan's here.** Or, even better, Ryan texting me himself. But it's not, of course; it's Hannah, replying to the text I sent her earlier. I quickly scan her words:

Ryan's back? I thought he was in L.A.

Unable to stop smiling, I type a quick reply:

He was!!! But he's here and he's unattached and he was asking about me!!!!

I press SEND, then instantly realize my error. I've put too many exclamation marks. Hannah will see them as warning signs. She'll be on the phone within half a minute.

I've been friends with Hannah since we were eleven and both elected as class monitors. At once we knew we'd found kindred spirits. We're both organized. We both love lists. We both get things done. Although, to be fair, Hannah gets things done *even more* efficiently than I do. She never procrastinates or finds an excuse. Whatever the task is, she does it straightaway, whether it's her tax form or cleaning out her fridge or telling a guy that she didn't like the way he kissed, on their very first date. (Fair play to him, he took it on the chin. He said, "How *do* you like to be kissed, then?" And she showed him. And now they're married.)

She's the most levelheaded, straight-talking person I know. She works as an actuary and she starts Christmas shopping in July and . . . here we go. Her name's popping up on my screen. Knew it.

"Hi, Hannah." I answer my phone casually, as though I don't know why she's calling. "How are you?"

"Ryan, huh?" she says, ignoring my greeting. "What happened to that girl in L.A.?"

"Apparently it's over." I try to speak calmly, although a voice inside me is singing, *It's over! It's over!*

"Hmm." She doesn't sound convinced. "Fixie, I thought you were over him. *Finally*."

I don't blame her for that emphasis on *finally*. I've been spilling my heart to Hannah about Ryan pretty much since the first day we met. When we were eighteen I used to drag her around endless London pubs, just in the hope of bumping into him. She used to call it the Ryan Route. And it would be fair to say that last spring, after Ryan went back to Hollywood, every other conversation we had was about him.

OK, every conversation.

"I am!" I lower my voice so the whole coffee shop doesn't hear. "But apparently he was asking after me." Just the thought of Ryan asking after me makes me feel giddy, but I force myself to sound matter-of-fact. "So that's interesting. That's all. Just interesting."

"Hmm," says Hannah again. "Has he texted you himself or anything?"

"No. But maybe he wants to surprise me."

"Hmm," says Hannah for a third time. "Fixie, you do remember that he lives in L.A.?"

"I know," I say.

"And your whole life is your family shop."

"I know."

"So there's no prospect of you actually getting together," Hannah carries on relentlessly. "Like having a relationship or anything. It's not going to happen."

"Stop spelling stuff out!" I hiss crossly, turning toward the window for extra privacy. "You always have to spell things out!"

Not for the first time, I wish I had a flaky, romantic best

friend, who would say, "Oh wow, Ryan's back! You two are *meant* for each other!" and help me choose what outfit to wear.

Nicole's quite flaky and romantic, I suppose. But then, she's not really interested in my life.

"I'm spelling things out because I *know* you," says Hannah. "And what I worry is that deep down you're still hoping for some sort of miracle."

There's silence. I'm not going to say, "Don't be ridiculous," because there's no point lying to your best friend.

"It's like . . . a ten percent hope," I say at last, watching a traffic warden on the prowl. "It's harmless."

"It's not harmless," Hannah contradicts me with energy. "It means you don't even *look* at any other men. There are nice men out there, you know, Fixie. Good men."

I know why she's saying that. It's because she tried to set me up with this actuary mate of hers last month, and I wasn't into him. I mean, he was nice. He was just so *earnest*.

"I get it," Hannah continues. "Ryan's good-looking and glamorous and whatever. But are you going to give up on finding a proper guy just for ten minutes with Mr. Hollywood?"

"No, of course not," I say after a pause, even though the phrase *ten minutes with Mr. Hollywood* has instantly flashed me back to Ryan and me in bed last year, and just the memory is making me damp behind the knees.

"I think you need to draw a line and move on," says Hannah. I imagine her at her desk, briskly drawing a line under a column of numbers with a ruler and then turning the page, no problem.

But then, Hannah was always immune to Ryan's charms. In the sixth form she dated all the guys in the A-level physics set, one by one, and ended up with Tim, the second-cleverest one. (She was the cleverest.) They were together all through sixth form, broke up, went to uni and dated other people, then got back together again and married. His kissing has improved a lot since that first date, apparently. They both have good jobs and they're trying for a baby and they're basically sorted.

"So what am I supposed to do?" I say, a bit snippily, because I know she has a point and I resent it, even though I love her for caring enough to call me up and lecture me. "What if he's there tonight, and—"

I break off. I don't want to say it out loud, because I'll jinx it.

"You mean, what if he's all hot and sexy and wants to carry on where you left off last year?"

"I guess."

"Well." Hannah is silent for a few moments. "Here's the thing: Can you sleep with him and *not* get upset when he goes back to L.A.? Be honest."

"Yes," I say robustly. "Of course. Sex is just sex."

"No, it's not!" says Hannah with an incredulous laugh. "Not for you. Not with Ryan. He'll mess you up somehow, I know it. You'll end up weeping on my shoulder."

"Well, maybe I don't care," I say defiantly.

"You're saying the sex is so good, it's worth it even if you *do* end up weeping on my shoulder?" says Hannah, who always likes to analyze everything into equations.

"Pretty much." I have a sudden memory of Ryan's L.A.-tanned body entwined with mine. "Yes."

"Fine," says Hannah, and I can hear the rueful eye roll in her voice. "I'll buy the tissues."

"He might not even come," I point out. "This whole conversation might have been for nothing."

"Well, I'll see you later," says Hannah. "With or without Ryan."

I ring off and stare morosely out the window. Now I've said it, I realize of course that's the most likely scenario. Ryan must have a million more-glamorous events to be at tonight than Mum's party. He won't turn up at all. I'll have bought all these hair clips for nothing.

"Hi, Briony." The guy across the table is answering his phone, and I glance round. "Oh, you've spoken to Tanya. Right. So— No, that's not what—" He seems to be trying to get a word in. "Listen, Briony—" He breaks off, looking beleaguered. "Sweetheart, I'm not trying to ruin— No, we did *not* agree anything."

Ha. Well, at least it's not just me with the messed-up love life.

"Is that what you think!" he's exclaiming now. "Can I remind you that this is *my* flat, for *me* to—" He lifts his eyes and suddenly seems to become aware that I'm listening. I quickly look away, but even so, he gets to his feet.

"Excuse me," he says politely to me. "I'm just stepping out to take a phone call. Could you watch my laptop?"

"Sure." I nod and watch him threading his way between the tables, already back on the phone, saying, "I never promised anything! It was *your* idea—"

I sip my mint tea and glance at the laptop a couple of times. It's a MacBook. He's left it closed, with a stack of glossy folders next to it. I tilt my head slightly and read the top one. *ESIM: Forward-Looking Investment Opportunities*. I've never heard of ESIM—not really my thing—but then, investment funds aren't really my thing either.

People who invest money in funds and shares and all that are like a foreign country to me. In the Farr family there are three things you do with money. You spend it, you put it back into the business, or you start another business. You don't trust a guy in a suit and a posh tie with a glossy folder that probably cost a tenner to produce.

There's nothing else interesting about the guy's laptop, so I sip my drink and run my mind over my outfit options for tonight. And I'm just wondering where my blue lace top has got to, when something in my mind tweaks. Alarm bells have started to ring. Something's wrong.

Something's happening.

Or something's about to happen.

My brain can't even articulate what it is properly, but my sixth sense is kicking in. I have to act. Now.

Quick, Fixie. Go.

Before I've even thought clearly what's happening, I'm diving across the table, like a rugby champion scoring a try, cradling the guy's laptop. And, a split second later, a whole section of the ceiling crashes down on top of me, in a gush of plaster and water.

"Argh!"

"Oh my God!"

"Help!"

"Is it an *attack*?"

"Help that girl!"

The screams around me are a din in my head. I can feel someone pulling at me, saying, "Get away from there!" But I'm so worried about the laptop getting wet that I won't move from my rigid protective position until I feel paper towels being thrust at me. The water has finally stopped cascading, but plaster is still falling in bits from above, and as I raise my head at last, I see a freaked-out audience of customers watching me.

"I thought you were dead!" says a teenage girl so tearfully I can't help laughing—and this seems to set off everyone else:

"I saw that water dripping! I knew this would happen."

"You could have been killed, innit!"

"You need to sue. That's not right, ceilings falling down."

A moment ago we were all strangers in a coffee shop, studiously ignoring each other. Now it's as though we're best friends. An elderly guy holds out his hand and says, "I'll hold your computer while you get dry, dear." But I don't want to give it up, so I awkwardly mop myself with one hand, thinking, *Of all the days, of all the days* . . .

"What the *hell*?"

It's the guy. He's come back into the coffee shop, and he's staring at me, his mouth open. Gradually the excited comments die down and the coffee shop falls silent. Everyone's watching the pair of us expectantly.

"Oh, hi," I say, speaking for the first time since I was drenched. "Here's your laptop. I hope it isn't wet."

I hold it out—it isn't wet at all—and the guy steps forward to take it. He's looking from me to the ravaged ceiling to the puddles of water and plaster, with increasing disbelief. "What *happened*?"

"There was a slight ceiling incident," I say, trying to downplay it. But like a Greek chorus, all the other customers eagerly start filling him in.

"The ceiling fell in."

"She dived across the table. Like lightning!"

"She saved your computer. No question. It would have been ruined."

"Ladies and gentlemen." A barista raps on the counter to gain our attention. "Apologies. Due to a health-and-safety incident, we are closing the coffee shop. Please come to the counter for a takeaway cup and complimentary cookie."

There's a surge toward the counter and the most senior-looking barista of them all comes up to me, her brow crumpled.

"Madam, we would like to apologize for your discomfort," she says. "We would like to present you with this fifty-pound voucher and hope that you will not . . ." She clears her throat. "We will be glad to pay for the dry-cleaning of your clothes."

She's looking at me beseechingly and I suddenly realize what she's driving at.

"Don't worry," I say, rolling my eyes. "I'm not going to *sue*. But I wouldn't mind another mint tea."

The barista visibly relaxes and hurries off to make it. Meanwhile, the guy in the suit has been scrolling through his laptop. Now he looks up at me with a stricken expression. "I don't know how to thank you. You've saved my life."

"Not your *life*."

"OK, you've saved my bacon. It's not just the computer—that would have been bad enough. But the stuff on the computer. Stuff I should have backed up." He closes his eyes briefly, shaking his head as though in disbelief. "What a lesson."

"Well," I say, "these things happen. Lucky I was there."

"Lucky for me," he says slowly, closing the laptop and surveying me properly. The late sun is full on his face now. His eyes are so green and woodlandy, I find myself thinking briefly of deer in dappled forest glades; leafy branches; peaty scents. Then I blink—and I'm back in the coffee shop. "It wasn't lucky for you," the guy is saying. "You're a mess and your hair's wet. All on my account. I feel terrible."

"It wasn't on your account," I say, embarrassed under his gaze. My T-shirt feels wet, I suddenly register. But how wet? Wet-T-shirt-contest-level wet? Is *that* why the whole coffee shop was staring at me? Because my T-shirt is, in fact, transparent?

"The ceiling fell in," I continue, folding my arms casually across my chest. "I got wet. Nothing to do with you."

"But would you have dived in that direction if you hadn't promised to look after my laptop?" he counters at once. "Of course not. You obviously have very quick reactions. You would have dived out of harm's way."

"Well, whatever." I shrug it off.

"Not whatever." He shakes his head firmly. "I'm indebted to you. Can I . . . I don't know. Buy you a coffee?"

"No, thanks."

"A muffin?" He squints at the display. "The double chocolate chip one looks good."

"No!" I laugh. "Really."

"What about . . . can I buy you dinner?"

"I'm not sure Briony would appreciate it," I can't resist saying. "Sorry, I overheard you talking."

A wry smile comes across his face and he says, "*Touché.*"

"Anyway, it was nice to meet you," I say, taking my mint tea from the barista. "But I'd better get going."

"There must be something I can do to thank you," he insists.

"No, really, nothing," I say, equally firmly. "I'm fine."

I smile politely, then turn and head toward the door. And I'm nearly there when I hear him shout, "Wait!" so loudly that I swivel back. "Don't go," he adds. "Please. Just . . . hold on. I have something for you."

I'm so intrigued, I take a few steps back into the coffee shop. He's standing at the counter with a cardboard coffee sleeve and a pen, and he's writing something.

"I always pay off my debts," he says at last, coming toward me. "Always." He holds out the sleeve and I see that he's written on it:

I owe you one.

Redeemable in perpetuity.

As I watch, he signs it underneath—a scribbly signature I can't quite make out—and puts the date.

"If you ever want a favor," he says, looking up. "Something I can do for you. Anything at all." He reaches in his pocket, pulls out a business card, and then looks around, frowning. "I need a paper clip . . . or any kind of clip. . . ."

"Here." I put down my cup, reach into my Anna's Accessories bag, and pull out a diamanté hair grip.

"Perfect." He affixes the business card to the coffee sleeve with the hair grip. "This is me. Sebastian Marlowe."

"I'm Fixie Farr," I reply.

"Fixie." He nods gravely and extends a hand. "How do you do?" We shake hands, then Sebastian proffers the coffee-sleeve IOU.

"Please take it. I'm serious."

"I can see." My mouth can't help twitching. "Well, if I need any 'forward-looking investment opportunities,' I'll let you know."

My tone is a little mocking, but he doesn't pick up on it—in fact, his green eyes light up.

"Yes! Please do! If that's the case, we can set up a meeting; I'd be delighted to give you some advice—"

"It's not the case," I cut him off. "Far from it. But I appreciate the offer."

Belatedly, he seems to realize I was teasing him, and his face flickers with a smile.

"Something you actually need, then." He's still holding the coffee sleeve out to me, and at last I take it.

"OK. Thank you."

To humor him, I put the coffee sleeve into my bag and pat it. "There we are. Safe and sound. And now I really must be going. I have a family party I need to get back for."

"You think I'm joking," he says, watching as I pick up my cup. "But I'm not. I owe you one, Fixie Farr. Remember that."

"Oh, I will!" I say, and flash him a last, cheerful smile, not meaning a word of it. "Absolutely. I really will."

Four

Ryan isn't at the house yet. Nor Jake.

As soon as I get inside, I sidle to the sitting room and glance through the door crack, ready to dart away. If they were anywhere they'd be there, sitting on the sofa, swigging beers. But they're not. I'm safe.

I head toward the kitchen at the back, passing Nicole en route. She's photographing a paper garland hanging from the wall. I guess it's a party decoration, although our house barely needs any more embellishment. Over the years, Mum has covered every wall with family photos, collages, and box frames full of mementos. She's really artistic, Mum, and so is Nicole, but that gene totally missed me out, just like the supermodel-looks gene. Both Jake and I inherited Dad's dark-hair dark-eyes combo, which I guess you could call "striking." But Nicole is heart-stoppingly beautiful, even if she never did quite make it as a model. The line of her jaw, the turquoise of her eyes, her slanty eyebrows . . . it all adds up to something magical. Even *I* want to stare at her all day, and I'm her sister.

"Hi, Nicole," I greet her, and Nicole nods, squinting at her phone. Although she's married, she's living here for a few months, because her husband, Drew, has gone to work in Abu Dhabi for six months, setting up a computer system for some multinational, and Nicole refused to go.

"*Abu Dhabi?*" she said, as though that was all the reason she needed. "*Abu Dhabi?*" Then she added, as the clincher: "What about my yoga?"

So Drew left for Abu Dhabi and they've sublet their flat and Nicole is back in the family house for a bit. The fridge is full of probiotic yogurt, and her strandy ethnic necklaces are all over the place where she leaves them, and every morning I hear her podcast telling her soothingly not to judge herself, while pipe music plays.

I know Nicole's finding it tougher than she thought, Drew being away, because she sighs a lot and peers at her phone and tells everyone she meets how she's got separation anxiety. I feel sorry for Drew too. He phones us on the landline whenever he can't reach Nicole on her mobile and often ends up talking to Mum or me. I've heard all about the vicious heat and his insomnia and the in-office battles he's having with someone called Baz. The last time he phoned he sounded quite poorly, so Mum and I ended up googling illnesses and sending him links.

He and Nicole were only together for a year before they got married, and he works pretty hard in IT, so I didn't know Drew *that* well at the wedding last year. But I've spoken to him so much on the phone since he's been away, I've got to know him far better. He's got a great sense of humor and I can see why Nicole married him. Although I can't see why she hasn't gone to Abu Dhabi with him. They must have yoga courses there, surely?

"Oh, Nicole, did you get my message?" I say, remembering. "I spoke to Drew last night and apparently it's *not* malaria."

"Oh, good," says Nicole absently. "Isn't this great?" she says with more animation, holding up her garland. "I'm putting it on Pinterest. It's like, it's . . ."

I wait for her to finish—then realize that she has. Nicole quite often drifts away into blankness while you wait there politely.

"Amazing," I say. "Where's Jake?"

"Haven't seen him."

"But he said he was on his way to the house to help Mum, what, two hours ago?"

Nicole shrugs and takes another photo of her garland.

"So who *has* been helping Mum?" I know I sound accusing, although the truth is, I feel defensive. I should have come home to help Mum, not gone shopping, let alone stopped at a coffee shop.

"I have!" says Nicole, sounding injured. "I've been doing decorations!"

"Right," I say carefully. "But I meant the food and tidying up and everything?"

"I need an artistic outlet, OK? I'm coping with a lot of stress right now, Fixie." Nicole shoots me a baleful look. "My husband's on the other side of the world, in case you'd forgotten. I'm experiencing separation anxiety. I need to look after myself."

"Well, I know, but—"

"My yoga teacher says if I don't find ways to self-care, I

might end up with *mental-health issues*." She throws the phrase out like a trump card.

"Right," I say after a pause. "OK. Er . . . sorry."

I hurry on to the kitchen and push the door open to find Mum bent over the work top, just as I guessed she would be. She's still in her apron and jeans, her graying hair pulled into a scrunchie, laboring over a sheet of pink sugar paste with a plastic cutter. She has a smear of icing on her earlobe and her usual daytime makeup look—i.e., none.

Has she taken some time out, washed her hair, or applied a face mask? No, of course she hasn't. I shouldn't think she's planned what to wear either. The challenge with Mum's birthday party every year is getting her to actually *go to the party*.

"Hi, Mum!" I greet her, but she cuts me off, her brow creased with concentration. She's naturally beautiful, Mum, with high strong cheekbones and a thin vibrant face. You can see where Nicole got it from. "Can I help?"

"Shh! Wait!"

All her attention is on crafting a peony out of sugar paste. Painstakingly, she winds the cutout shape into a flower and attaches a green sugar-paste leaf.

"Beautiful." I applaud.

"It works, doesn't it?" Mum pops the peony on a frosted cupcake, then taps the plastic cutter. "This is good. Well priced too. I think we should stock it."

Mum is never knowingly under-tasked. Right now not only is she preparing cupcakes for her own birthday party, she's simultaneously trying out a product for the shop. Mum would never stock a product unless she believed in it. So every pan, every food storage container, every fancy culinary gadget has to pass the Mum Test. Does it work? Is it good value? Will our customers actually use it?

"Vanessa will love this," she adds.

"Definitely." I nod, smiling at the thought of Vanessa, with her patchwork waistcoats and red raincoat and boundless enthusiasm. Vanessa is one of our most regular customers and a member of the Cake Club, which we run every Tuesday evening. Morag does demonstrations at a portable cooking station and everyone shows off their own efforts. We've got a customer board in the shop, filled with photos of cakes, plus an Instagram page. It's one of the things that makes Farrs so special: our community.

"I'll take over in here," I say now, seizing my chance while Mum has paused. "You go and get ready."

She looks up for the first time—and her face drops.

"Fixie, what happened to you? The weather's not *that* bad?" She glances out the window at the light summer rain, which began as I was walking home.

"No! I just had a little accident. It's fine."

"She looks awful, doesn't she?" says Nicole, drifting in.

"Mum," I try again. "Why don't you go and get ready? Have a nice bath. Relax for a bit."

"I'll just make two more of these," says Mum, rolling out more sugar paste.

"OK, well, I'll nip up and sort out my hair," I say. "I'll be super-quick."

"Then maybe you could make me a coffee, darling?" says Mum to Nicole. "If you're not doing anything else?"

"Oh." Nicole wrinkles her nose dubiously. "Coffee. You know I can't do the machine."

It was Jake who bought Mum her cappuccino machine as a present last Christmas. It's quite technical, but you *can* get to know it if you try. Nicole, though, seems pathologically unable to. She peers at it and says, "What does it mean, *Empty drip tray?*" and you explain it and show her three times, but she still doesn't get it. So in the end you do it yourself.

"I'll do it," I say hurriedly, and reach for a mug.

"Hi, Mum." Jake breezes into the kitchen, wafting aftershave and beer. "Happy birthday." He plants a kiss on her cheek and presents her with the Christian Dior bag.

"Darling!" Mum's eyes have widened at the glossy bag. "You shouldn't!"

When most people say, "You shouldn't," they really mean, "You should," but not Mum. She gets twitchy when people spend money on her, especially us, her children. Of course she's touched—but she's anxious too, because she thinks it's needless.

Mum thinks a lot of things in this world are needless. She rarely wears makeup. She never travels abroad. In fact, she hardly ever takes a holiday. She never reads the paper. I'm not sure she even votes. (She says she does, but I think she's fibbing so we won't lecture her.)

The only websites she ever visits are craft suppliers, cooking stores, and gadget sites. She watches *EastEnders,* she manages Farrs, she goes to her Zumba class; that's it. Sometimes I've suggested that she take a trip abroad or visit a country-house spa. But she gives me this kind little smile and says, "That's for other people, love."

As for another man, forget it. She hasn't looked at another man or been on a single date since Dad died. She says he's still with her and she still talks to him and she doesn't need anyone else. When Jake once tried to sign her up to some "silver years" dating site, she got quite angry, which is unlike her.

"Jake, *you* make the coffee for Mum," says Nicole. "Where's Leila?"

"I sent her off to buy some more beer," replies Jake, whereupon I have a sudden image of poor Leila lugging ten crates of beer along the street in her skinny arms. And I wasn't going to ask, but before I can stop them the words spill out:

"Is Ryan here?"

My voice is husky and I flush as everyone turns to look at me. I would never have mentioned Ryan—but I suddenly got worried he might appear in the kitchen. I've still got pipe water all over my hair and I'm wearing my work jeans and basically I'd have to hide in the fridge.

"Not yet." Jake runs his eyes over me. "Jeez, is that your party look? Drowned weasel?" At once Nicole bursts into laughter.

"Oh God, Fixie, you *do* look like a drowned weasel."

"A ceiling fell on me!" I say defensively. "It wasn't my fault!"

"Darling, you go up and take a shower and you'll look lovely," says Mum in that soothing way she has. Soothing with an edge of steel, enough to warn off Jake and Nicole.

Mum's like one of those dressage riders on TV. She

changes her voice an iota and we all obey her instantly, like trained Olympic horses. Even Jake.

"Are you OK, Fixie?" asks Nicole, looking abashed. "Sorry, I didn't realize."

"Fixie, I didn't mean it," says Jake. "You go and get ready. Take your time. I'll hold the fort here."

He sounds so charming, I'm mollified. Jake *can* be really nice when he wants to.

"OK." I pick up my bag of hair clips. "I'll go and have a shower. Mum, why don't you come up too now? We could pick out an outfit for you."

"In a moment," says Mum absently as she shapes another peony.

I'll be in a better position to chivy Mum into her party clothes when I'm ready myself, I decide. I sprint upstairs, rip off my damp jeans and T-shirt, and quickly take a shower in our tiny old-fashioned cubicle.

I haven't always lived at home—I shared with Hannah for a while. She bought a flat in Hammersmith and said I *had* to live there too and she would subsidize the rent with her ridiculously large salary. But then she and Tim got more serious and I felt awkward, lurking around every evening.

Then my company went bust and everything had to change, anyway. Mum was the one who said, "Lots of girls your age are still at home, love," and made me feel OK about moving back for a while. To be honest, I was just really grateful to have that option.

I stand on the landing to dry my hair, wrapped in a towel, because there's more space and a big mirror. And I'm pausing between blasts when a sound catches my attention from downstairs. It's Jake, talking.

Our house isn't huge, and the walls and floors are pretty thin. So although I can't hear exactly *what* Jake is saying in the kitchen, I can pick up on *how* he's saying it. He's talking on and on, and nobody's interrupting him, and I suddenly feel suspicious. I hurry downstairs, still in my towel, and now I can hear Jake properly, saying in his smoothest drawl, "As I say, it's an amazing opportunity, and the oil tastes out of this *world*. But I don't want to bother you with the details, Mum; you're busy enough. So shall I just put in an order? Ten bottles?"

What?

I'm breathing furiously as I reach the bottom of the stairs. He deliberately got me out of the way; he deliberately chose a moment when Mum was distracted. . . .

Shit. I've dropped my towel.

I hastily wrap it around myself again and approach the kitchen.

"Mum!" As I burst in, my chest is rising and falling. "About this olive oil . . ." The ravens are flapping around me, but I'm trying desperately to ignore them. "I've already talked to Jake, and I . . . I really don't think . . ."

Oh God, my voice has gone wobbly again. My courage has disintegrated. I *loathe* myself.

"It's nothing to do with you, Fixie," says Jake, glowering at me.

"Yes, it is." I glare back at him.

"Jake. Fixie." Mum's calm voice cuts through the atmosphere. "You know I'd never order a new product without seeing the details. Show me, Jake."

"It's your party!" Jake is obviously trying to sound jovial. "You don't want to see all that right now—"

"I do, love," she says pleasantly. "Hand it over."

"Right. OK," says Jake at last. He hands Mum a sheaf of papers and we both stand waiting while she flicks through them. I see her reach the price list and I see her eyes snap in shock.

"Too expensive, love," she says, and hands the papers back to Jake. "Way too expensive. Not for us."

"They're aspirational," begins Jake. "They're a different *kind* of product." But Mum shakes her head.

"Our aspirational is a bottle of edible glitter. Not this."

"Mum, don't set your sights so low," says Jake cajolingly. "People buy this kind of stuff! They really do. At Harrods—"

"Maybe they sell all sorts at Harrods," Mum cuts him off calmly. "But put olive oil on our shelves for a hundred pounds and it won't just not sell, it'll upset people. It'll offend them."

Now she says it, I realize she's right. I can see Vanessa striding through the shop, brandishing a bottle, saying, "You're charging a hundred pounds for this? That's daylight robbery!"

"But—"

"No, Jake." Mum interrupts him as crisply as she did when he was ten and using grown-up bad words. "Enough. My answer's no. Your dad would have said the same."

When Mum invokes Dad, that really is the end of the discussion. Jake shoots me a look, as though this is all *my* fault, but I don't care. I just feel relieved. And foolish. How did I ever think that Jake would hoodwink Mum? She's Mum. She runs the ship.

"I'll go and finish my hair," I say, and Mum looks up. She runs her eyes up and down me and I don't know what she sees, but she suddenly gives me one of her special, warm, encouraging smiles.

Whenever Mum smiles, lines appear all over her face. They stretch like sunrays from her eyes; they score her cheeks and mark out her forehead in deep creases. Grief brought extra lines to her face. I saw it happen. And maybe some people think the lines are ugly, but I see love and life in every one of them.

"Why don't you ask Nicole to do it with her special curler?" she says, and shoots Nicole a look.

"Oh," says Nicole indifferently, looking up from her phone. "OK, fine, I'll do it. Come upstairs."

I know Mum wishes that Nicole and I were closer. She'd love us to be "there for each other," like sisters in movies: hugging and confiding in each other and all that.

I mean, I try to be close to Nicole. I do. But it's a bit like oil trying to be close to water. We just don't *take*.

"And, Jake," says Mum, as he reaches into the fridge for a beer, "before you have that, could you help me arrange these cupcakes? Mind you don't mess up the icing, though."

"Right," says Jake, looking unenthusiastic as he puts down the beer, and I hide a smile. No one else could get Jake to put off drinking beer in order to arrange cupcakes. But then, no one else is Mum.

Five

*N*icole's room is like an Instagram page come to life. Everywhere you look there's a photo of her, or a poster with a saying on it, or some styled accessory. I linger by the black-and-white montage of her wedding pictures and yet again sigh inwardly at how effortlessly lovely she is. What is it like to wake up every morning and be Nicole?

In all the photos, Drew is gazing at Nicole as though he can't believe his luck. He's tall and nice-looking, with thick brown hair and a frank, open face—but he's not in Nicole's league, looks-wise. Even his mum would admit that. I turn to the shot that they sent out with their thank-you cards. They're under a tree and Drew looks besotted, while Nicole looks . . .

Well. Affectionate. She definitely looks affectionate.

I've never really got a handle on Nicole's relationship with Drew, but then, that's Nicole. She doesn't talk about stuff. She doesn't confide in anyone, even Mum. If anyone confronts her or tries to dig deeper, she just slides away and changes the subject or looks blank.

She met Drew through a friend, and at first he was going

to help her with a new digital lifestyle company. He used to come over and they'd get quite animated about it and we'd all make suggestions. Then Nicole went off the idea, but by that time they were going out together, and then, fairly soon, they were engaged. I think Mum was concerned it was too quick—but on the other hand, Drew seemed nice and stable and well meaning . . . and the wedding was *amazing*.

I turn away from the montage and look at some new cushions on the bed. They've all got embroidered slogans, like *Love Yourself* and *Me Time* and a big one which says, *You can't pour from an empty cup: Take care of yourself first.*

Nicole is lighting a series of scented candles in glasses, and they've got slogans printed on them too: *Love. Spirit. Compassion.*

"I'm all about compassion right now," says Nicole seriously, following my gaze. "Compassion feeds the soul. Compassion is what makes us *human*."

I blink at Nicole, trying to hide my surprise. Compassion? I've never heard her talk like this before.

"I totally agree!" I say eagerly, as she reaches into a low drawer for her curling wand. "You know, I often think we could do more at the shop to help people. Like, have a senior citizens' cooking group or something?"

Maybe we *can* be close sisters after all, I'm thinking. Maybe we can start a joint community project and really bond. . . . But as Nicole sits back up again, she shoots me a blank look.

"It's not about the *shop*," she says pityingly. "You and Mum are obsessed by that stupid shop."

That stupid shop? I feel a tweak of indignation. That stupid shop which is paying for the roof over her head? Which paid for her wedding?

I don't say anything, though, because I'm trying to be positive and bonding.

"Compassion is about *yourself*," Nicole continues wisely. "It's about your journey. It's about: What is your light and how do you make it shine?"

"Right," I say, slightly baffled. "I was just thinking that some of our older customers might be a bit lonely. . . ."

Nicole isn't even listening, I realize.

"Compassion is actually very much a Buddhist concept," she informs me, plugging in the curling wand. "*If your compassion does not include yourself, it is incomplete.* That's a quote from Buddha. You should get into Buddhism, Fixie. It's like . . ."

I wait for her to tell me what it's like, then realize she's finished.

"Maybe I will," I say, nodding. "Absolutely."

"My yoga teacher, Anita, says affirmations are crucial for me right now," Nicole adds. "It's important for me to boost my endorphins, because I'm pretty vulnerable, with Drew away." She eyes me seriously. "I could spiral."

"Right," I say hastily. "Awful. Poor you."

"Anita says I've got to prioritize myself," Nicole carries on. "Take care of myself. You know? It's always about other people, but sometimes you have to say, 'Sod other people; it's about *me*. I *deserve* it.' Sit there."

Nicole nods at a chair and I take a seat. She brushes out my hair, sprays it with something from a bottle, then starts winding it round the curling wand.

I notice a book on the dressing table called *Your Animal Psychological Self,* and Nicole follows my gaze as she creates a tightly curled ringlet.

"I've got into psychological profiles too," she says. "I'm a Dragonfly. I'll give you a questionnaire. You should, like, rearrange your whole life according to . . ." She trails off and stares critically at a second ringlet. "Your hair doesn't really *shine,* does it?"

"No," I admit. "It doesn't."

My hair is the same length as Nicole's—shoulder-blade level. But while hers ripples and glows with a combination of highlights and natural brilliance, mine just *hangs.* Nicole blasts my head with more spray and pulls my hair so tight that tears come to my eyes.

"You know Ryan's got a girlfriend?" she says. "Ariana. I mean, I don't know what you're expecting, Fixie, but—"

"Leila says they've split up," I say, too quickly.

"Really?" Nicole makes a skeptical face and releases another ringlet. "I follow Ariana on Instagram. She's amazing. She's all about compassion too. Compassion through cuisine."

"Right." I try to sound more nonchalant. "Well, they're over now, so—"

"Look, this is her." To my dismay, Nicole thrusts her phone into my field of vision. "She's so inspirational. I commented on her pomegranate salad once, and she replied to me."

"Don't!" I want to wail. "Don't show me pictures of Ryan's girlfriend, or ex-girlfriend, or whatever she is!" But that would sound insecure, so I keep my mouth shut. I know Nicole isn't *trying* to torment me; she just doesn't think about other people much. She's scrolling through the photos now, presumably searching for her own comment. Short of closing my eyes, I can't escape, so I gaze morosely at the blond Californian vision in front of me, doing yoga, cooking, and rollerblading in tiny shorts.

I've seen Ariana's Instagram page before. Well, of course I have. I keep following her, then un-following her, then following her again. She probably thinks I'm a nutjob, if she's ever noticed me, which she won't have done because she has 26.6 thousand followers.

"Here we are." Nicole finally stops on a photo of Ariana wearing a pink crop top and leggings, standing in an arabesque pose, holding out a big salad to the camera.

"I mean, is she exercising or cooking or what?" I say at last.

"Both," says Nicole. "It's her new thing. She cooks and works out all at once."

"Right," I say, trying not to fixate on Ariana's white teeth and perfect rounded butt. "Well. You know. Good for her."

As Nicole releases another ringlet, her phone bleeps and she reaches for it. "Oh," she says, frowning at a message. "I have to go." She puts the curling wand down and reaches for her bag. "Sorry," she adds as an afterthought. "Julie from my yoga class is at the tube station. I said I'd meet her, because she's never been here before."

"You're going *now*?" I say in horror. "But what about my hair?"

"I've started you off," says Nicole. "You can finish it yourself."

"No, I can't!"

I catch my reflection in the mirror and wince. Half my head is a ringletty mass of curls. The rest is lying flat and dispirited, like a girl who hasn't been asked to dance.

"Please finish it off," I beg. "It won't take long."

"But Julie's *waiting*," says Nicole. "She's *there*."

"She could find the way, surely—"

"That's not the point!" Nicole seems offended. "Fixie, you could be a little less selfish. My husband is halfway across the world, OK? This is a really difficult time for me."

Her phone buzzes with a call and she lifts it to her ear. "Oh, hi, Drew," she says irritably. "I'm in the middle of something, yeah? I'll call you back."

She rings off and glowers at me again. "Friendship is vital for my endorphin levels right now. And you want me to stay here and fix your *hair*?"

Now she puts it like that, I suddenly feel shallow.

"Sorry," I say humbly. "I'm sure I can finish it off myself. You go."

"*Thank* you," says Nicole in pointed tones. "And blow the candles out when you leave. Otherwise, like . . ." She trails off in her vague way.

"I will," I say hastily. "And thanks!"

As she heads out of the room, I pick up the wand. I wind some hair around it, trying—unsuccessfully—not to burn my fingers, then release it and stare at my hair in dismay.

I've made it curl *backward* somehow. It looks totally weird.

I try one more time—burning my fingers again—then give up. I can't sit here struggling with a hair wand when

Mum's doing all the work. I'll shove my hair in a clip. It'll be fine.

I switch off the wand, blow out the candles, straighten a plaque which says, BELIEVE YOU CAN AND YOU'RE HALFWAY THERE, then leave the room. I go to my bedroom, grab one of my new hair clips, and wind my hair in a knot. I put on my shortest black dress, because Ryan once said to me, "Great legs." I do my makeup as quickly as I can and peer at myself, trying not to think how pale and English I look compared to Ariana.

Then I hear a noise from Mum's room and turn away from the mirror, impatient with staring at myself. Enough brooding. I'll go and see if Mum needs any help.

Mum only has two smart dresses and she never goes shopping. ("Not for me, love.") But she's so slim, she can't help looking lovely in her trusty blue linen shift and matching heels from the charity shop. She's sitting in front of her kidney-shaped dressing table and I perch on the bed, passing makeup to her out of my makeup bag. (Mum's had the same No. 7 palette forever, and all the good colors have worn away.)

"Tell me about the day," she says, as she squirts foundation onto her fingers.

"Oh, it was pretty good. A couple came in this morning to stock their whole kitchen. They bought *everything*."

"Excellent!" Mum's eyes sparkle with the fire she always gets when we make a good sale.

"Only I had to get rid of Greg," I add. "He kept asking

them how often they cook at home and what they make. You know, quizzing them about risotto. He was trying to be helpful, but it freaked them out."

"Poor Greg." Mum shakes her head ruefully. "He does try."

"And then Jake brought round his olive-oil people. . . . You know, he has all these really grand ideas, Mum," I say, feeling a knot of tension rise. "He wants to open a branch in Notting Hill. He wants to rename the shop the Notting Hill Family Deli; can you believe it? We're not even a deli!"

I'm expecting Mum to be as wounded by this idea as I am. But she just nods thoughtfully and says, "That'll never happen. You know Jake. He needs his little schemes. Always has done." She glances at me and smiles. "Don't worry, Fixie. I'll have a word."

She sounds so easy and unruffled, the knot in my stomach starts to unclench. Mum is magic like that. She's like one of those therapists who know where all the pressure points are. A word here, a hug there, and everything eases. Sitting here with her, I feel like all the threat has melted away. Our shop will never be anything but Farrs. And Jake will never get his stupid pretentious schemes past Mum.

"Ryan's coming tonight, I hear?" says Mum, brushing shadow vaguely onto her eyelids with the air of someone who really doesn't care how it comes out. It's not that she can't do makeup—she used to do mine perfectly when I competed in junior skating competitions. Eye shadow, glitter, the works. But when it's herself, she hardly bothers.

"Yes." I try to sound casual. "Apparently he is. I wonder what brings him to the UK."

"Fixie, darling . . ." Mum hesitates, brush in hand. "Be careful. I know he hurt you last year."

Not Mum too.

"He didn't!" My voice shoots out before I can stop it. "God! I mean, I wasn't *hurt*. We had a thing, we ended . . . no big deal."

Mum looks so unconvinced, I don't know why I bother.

"I know Ryan's always been there in your life," she says, applying highlighter. "And we're all fond of him. But there are lots of other men in the world, love."

"I know," I say, although a voice in my brain is instantly protesting, *Yes, but not like Ryan.*

"He may be nice-looking," Mum continues resolutely, "and he may be a big success in Hollywood, but when it comes to emotional matters, he's always been a bit—" She breaks off and her face creases in thought. "Oh, love, my head's not working. What's the word you all use? Crumbly."

"*Crumbly?*" I stare at her before it hits me. "You mean *flaky?*"

"Flaky!" Mum meets my eye and starts to laugh. "Yes! Flaky."

I can't help dissolving into giggles too, even as I'm thinking: *So maybe Ryan has been a bit flaky. People change, don't they?*

"Anyway." Clearly Mum considers the lecture over. She closes up the highlighter and surveys herself without great interest. "Will we do?"

"Mascara?" I suggest.

"Oh, love. So fiddly. I leave that for other people."

"Hi, Fixie! Hi, Joanne!" We both turn to see Hannah

standing in the doorway, wearing an amazing clingy red dress. Hannah has the most sexy wardrobe in the world, which she says compensates for having the least sexy job in the world. When she tells people what she does, they goggle at her and say, "You're an *actuary*?"

"Hiya!" I go to give her a hug. "I didn't hear the doorbell."

"Nicole was on her way out and she let me in," says Hannah. "There's a few guests here too, came in with me. They've all arrived early to help."

This is typical of Mum's friends. Maybe in some circles you arrive fashionably late. In Mum's circle, you pop along early and ask if there's anything you can do. All the women will be rolling up their sleeves and fighting over who should carry the vol-au-vents through. All the men will be drinking beers and smoking and telling each other what a great guy Mike was.

"Tim's on his way," adds Hannah, and I quickly say, "Great!"

I'm always careful to sound enthusiastic when we discuss Tim. He's a good, solid, loyal guy. He's got the same kind of logical brain as Hannah's. But he's missing her empathy. He always pursues the conversation a bit too far and says tactless things without even realizing.

I'll always remember him saying, "But, Fixie, presumably you simply didn't revise hard enough," when I failed an English test at school. Who *talks* like that? (Tim, that's who.)

Hannah doesn't mind, though. She says she likes the fact he's straightforward and doesn't play games. (I can't actually imagine Tim playing a game, except some super-high-IQ contest in which he'd keep correcting his competitor.)

"Did you get yourself a drink, love?" says Mum to Hannah, and Hannah waves back a glass at her.

"Grapefruit juice."

"Ah." Mum nods wisely. We both know all about Hannah's regime for conceiving. She and Tim have been trying for four months, and Hannah is already a total expert on maternity-leave rights, cribs, and breast-feeding counselors. She's also read a million books on child-rearing and has decided to bring up her children as Danish-French hybrids. Apparently then they'll be super-relaxed, stylish, *and* eat their vegetables. (I said once, "Why not bring them up British?" and she stared at me and said, *"British?"* like I was nuts.)

"OK, so how can I help?" she says now. "What needs doing? Let's break it down."

Let's break it down is Hannah's favorite phrase in the world. Give her any job, from a client report to washing her hair, and she'll break it down into smaller tasks. Her Christmas to-do list has 926 entries, beginning with *Order wrapping paper* on Boxing Day.

"We're fine, love," says Mum fondly—Mum, who was once given a color-coded organizational calendar by Hannah for her birthday and used it to doodle on during phone calls. Mum really isn't into systems. She runs the shop out of a hardback notebook, where she writes cryptic messages like *Forks—68* or just *Greg?* and always knows what she meant.

The doorbell rings, and my stomach lurches. Oh God, is that— It might be—

"I'll go!" I say before I can stop myself. I'm aware of Mum and Hannah exchanging looks, but I ignore this and hurry downstairs, nearly tripping on my heels, rehearsing my greeting.

Hi, Ryan.

Well, hello, Ryan.

Hello, stranger.

But as I approach the front door my heart sinks. I can already see gray hair through the wavy glass, and as I swing the door open, a familiar cantankerous, raspy voice greets me.

"Come on, come on, don't keep me on the doorstep!"

Great. It's Uncle Ned.

An hour later Ryan still hasn't arrived and I'd quite like to stab Uncle Ned.

I pretty much always want to stab Uncle Ned at every family gathering. But I have to smile politely at him, because he's Dad's brother and the only one left of that bit of the family. More to the point, Mum gets upset if we slag him off.

We're all in the sitting room by now and there's quite a crowd of Mum's friends, chatting away. Music is playing, people are greedily eating sausage rolls, and smoke is hazing the air, because Mum's never believed in the whole "smoke outside" thing. Dad used to smoke inside, so even though she's not a smoker herself, she almost encourages it.

"Shop doing well, then, Joanne?" asks Uncle Ned.

"Not bad." Mum smiles back over her glass of Cava. "Not at all bad."

"Well, I'm not surprised," Uncle Ned declaims. "Mike was a master at what he did. He set you up for life, Joanne."

"He did." Mum nods with a misty fondness. "He lives on in the shop; that's how I see it."

"He had a *knack*," Uncle Ned explains to Mum's friend Pippa, even though I'm sure Pippa knows as much about the shop as he does. "He knew what people wanted, you see? Clever man. And now Joanne can simply carry on in the same pattern."

I'm bristling inside. I know Dad set up the shop, but what's Uncle Ned saying? That Mum's been coasting along these last nine years?

"Bob's very helpful," adds Mum, gesturing at Bob, our financial manager, who is hovering over the buffet table with an anxious look on his face. He reaches for a little sausage, reconsiders, peers doubtfully at a quiche, then takes two crisps and places them on his plate. (Bob Stringer: Most Cautious Man in the World.)

"Bob!" says Uncle Ned as though this makes everything plain. "Fine man, Bob! Bob keeps you going."

I feel another dart of indignation. Bob's helpful—of course he is—but he doesn't "keep us going."

"Bob's great," I say. "But Mum's in charge—"

"Every organization needs a 'Man of the House,'" Uncle Ned cuts me off. "A Man of the House," he repeats, with weighty emphasis. "And since poor Mike left us . . ." He pats Mum's hand. "You've coped marvelously, Joanne."

I can see Mum flinching slightly at the hand-pat, but even so, she doesn't confront him. And although I'm seething, nor do I. I've tried in the past, and it doesn't achieve anything; it only upsets Mum.

I got really angry last Christmas, when Uncle Ned started patronizing Mum yet again during lunch. This time, I challenged him. He instantly got red-faced and *after-all-I've-done-for-you*, and Mum soothed the situation by telling him I didn't mean it.

Even then I didn't give up. I dragged Mum, still wearing her paper hat, into the kitchen and listed all the ways he'd talked her down, finishing up with: "How can you just sit there, Mum? You're a strong woman! You're the boss of . . . everything!"

I was hoping to stir her up, but it didn't happen. She listened, wincing a little, but then said, "Ah, he doesn't really mean it, love. What does it matter? He's been there for me when it counts, your uncle."

"Yes, but—"

"He helped me sort out the new lease after your father died, remember? I was in such a state, and Ned stepped in to negotiate. I've always been grateful for that."

"I know he did, but—"

"He got very good terms for us," she carried on resolutely. "He beat them down. There's more to Ned than meets the eye. He's not perfect, of course he's not, but who is? We've all got our funny little habits."

Personally, I wouldn't call being a total misogynist a "funny little habit." But in the end I gave up, because it was Christmas, and who wants to upset their mum at Christmas?

And since then I've stopped trying to make the point. For her own reasons, Mum wants to preserve Uncle Ned in her head in the best possible light. She doesn't want to fall out with him. She's such a strong woman in so many ways—but this is her total blind spot.

And I know why. It's because Uncle Ned is family. He's the only bit of Dad she's got left. And she values that more than most things.

"How's the dating going, Ned?" she says now, changing the subject in that easy way of hers. Uncle Ned got divorced recently, for the third time. I have no idea what any woman sees in him, but the world's a mysterious place.

"Oh, Joanne, these girls." He shakes his head. "Nice-enough looking, some of them, but they *talk* so much. I need to take ruddy earplugs with me."

Yet again, I wonder how he can be Dad's brother. Dad was old-fashioned in some ways—he believed his role was to be the provider and he didn't like bad language—but he respected Mum. He respected women.

Mum once told me after a few drinks that Uncle Ned took after my granddad, who could be a "difficult man." But then she wouldn't reveal any more. And I never really got to know my granddad before he died. So as far as I'm concerned, Uncle Ned is just one of those unsolvable family mysteries, like "Whatever happened to the key to the shed?"

"You'll find someone," says Mum peaceably. "And how's the fishing going?"

Nooo! Not fishing. When Uncle Ned gets going on fishing, he can last for hours.

"Well," says Uncle Ned. "I was down at the river the other day— Ah, Jake!" He breaks off as Jake joins the group. "How's business, m'boy?"

Thank God. Saved from a six-hour anecdote about a trout.

"Pretty good, Uncle Ned." Jake gives Uncle Ned his flashy smile. "Got a few interesting deals coming my way, as it happens. I've been at the Global Finance Conference at Olympia this week; have you ever been to it?"

Of course Uncle Ned hasn't been to it. He used to work for an insurance company, but he was an office administrator in the Woking branch. I'm not sure he ever made it to head office, let alone any global finance conference. But he'd never admit that.

"Those were the days, m'boy," he says, as though he were there every year. "Dealmaking and drinking and all the rest of it." He gives a throaty laugh. "What happens at conference stays at conference, eh, Jake?"

"Amen to that!" says Jake, lifting his glass.

They're such a couple of phonies. I know Jake only went to that conference because a friend of his had an extra pass.

"We had some times, back at the firm," says Uncle Ned, blowing out smoke. "The stories I could tell you . . ." He makes an expansive gesture with his cigarette and knocks a glass off the sideboard, where it was resting. It crashes to the floor, breaking into bits, and he frowns in annoyance. "Damn it," he adds. "One of you girls had better clear that up."

One of you girls? I instantly prickle again, but Mum steps in, putting a hand on Nicole's arm. "Love," she says. "Would you mind?"

"And the MBA?" says Uncle Ned to Jake. "Going well?"

"Excellent," says Jake emphatically. "It'll open so many doors."

"Nothing like letters after your name," affirms Uncle Ned.

They carry on talking about qualifications and opportunities, but I'm not listening. I'm watching Nicole clear up the glass. She's hopeless. She's got a broom but she's pushing it aimlessly at the bits of glass, spreading them around the floor, staring at her phone. Can't she look at what she's doing? She's sweeping shards all over the place. This is *glass*. Someone could get *hurt*.

My fingers are drumming in that way they do. My feet have started pacing: *forward-across-back, forward-across-back*. I can't stand it any longer.

"I'll do it," I say in a sudden gasp, and grab the broom from her. "We'll need to wrap this glass up in paper." I reach for an empty breadbasket and start picking up fragments with my fingertips.

"Oh, Fixie, you are brilliant," says Nicole vaguely. "You always know how to do things."

I was going to ask her to find some old newspaper, but she's already started tapping at her phone, so I carry on with my task. I'm craning my head to spot the shards of glinting glass on the wood-effect floor and wrapping them in an old *Radio Times,* when I hear Tim's voice booming above me, "*Ryan's* back?"

I hadn't realized Tim had arrived at the party, so I stand up and say, "Hi, Tim!" But Tim doesn't seem to hear. He stares at me with his bullet eyes, his dark hair plastered across his forehead, then says, "So are you two an item again? You and Ryan?"

Trust bloody Tim to put me on the spot in front of everyone.

"No!" I say brightly. "I mean, not *no*, like, it's totally unthinkable, but . . ."

"So you're thinking about it?" supplies Tim.

"No!" I almost squeak.

"Yes, you are," contradicts Nicole, looking up from her phone. "You were talking about it with Mum."

Thanks a lot, Nicole, I think viciously. What I could really do with is for the conversation to move on, but Tim persists:

"How long were you two together for?"

"No time." I try to laugh it off. "Ten days. Nothing. And I mean, he lives in L.A., so . . ."

"Yeah." Tim nods slowly. "I mean, L.A. It's a different standard, isn't it? The women, I mean. They *do* things. To their lips, their boobs . . . plus they don't age," he adds, warming to his topic. "You're a whole year older than when you last saw Ryan. In L.A. years, that's what? A decade?"

"So I'm an old crone now?" I say. I'm trying to find this funny, but Tim has this way of pursuing a subject relentlessly, like a terrier, not noticing that you're bleeding from the neck. Normally Hannah steps in tactfully, but I can't see her. Where *is* she?

Then, as though in answer to my question, the doorbell rings and Hannah's voice comes from the hall: "I'll get it!" There's a pause, then her voice comes again, like a clarion: "Oh wow, Ryan! Welcome back!"

I can feel eyes all around the room bouncing toward me with curiosity. In horror, I suddenly realize how I look, standing here with a broom in my hand and no chance to refresh my lip gloss even, and *oh my God, here he is.*

He's in the doorway. His tan, sun-bleached wavy hair, and

cool frayed T-shirt are like nothing else in this room. As he walks up to me, a hush falls over the party. As for me, I can't even breathe. I'm desperately thinking: *Stay cool, Fixie; do NOT get any hopes up. . . .*

But, God, he's beautiful. He *glows*.

"Hi, Fixie," he says, his California-blue eyes locking on to mine, a lazy smile slowly spreading. "I've missed you."

As everyone watches in silence, he unclips my hair with a sexy gesture, letting it fall around my shoulders.

"No, don't!" I want to cry out, but it's too late. As my hair drops down, half curled, half straight, Ryan blinks at it, startled—and no wonder. I can see my reflection in the mirror, and I look totally weird.

My face flames, and behind me someone stifles a snort of laughter. *Great.* I've been waiting a whole year to see Ryan and this is how I greet him. With freaky hair.

But before I can even draw breath to explain, Ryan lifts both hands to cup my face. He looks at me for a few silent seconds, then kisses me, hard. As though he doesn't care about the hair; as though he isn't interested in anyone else. Through a kind of humming in my ears, I hear Nicole exclaim, "Oh!" and Tim saying, "Bloody hell!"

At last we draw apart. I'm aware that the whole room is watching us, and I muster every fiber in my body to address him nonchalantly.

"Welcome back, Ryan. So how long is it for this time? A day?"

Ryan surveys me silently for a moment, his mouth twitching as though with some little joke. Then he says, "Actually, I'm back."

"I can see that." I match his light, bantering tone.

"No, I'm *back*." His eyes flick around the room again, aware of our audience. "I'm done with L.A. Finished with it. Back for good."

He's—*what*?

I stare at him, blood thundering through my head. My brain can't quite process his words. Or believe them. For *good*? He's back here for *good*? Desperately I try to find a cool, witty reply, but my mouth won't work properly.

"I'd better get you a drink, then," I manage at last, and Ryan's eyes crinkle as though he knows exactly how stunned I am.

"Yeah," he says, and kisses my hand. "You better had."

I head to the drinks table, trying to gather myself. I never dreamed he'd come back to the UK for good. I never even *contemplated* it.

And as I grab a beer out of the ice bucket, a giddy joy starts to infuse me. Miracles don't come true; I know they don't. But just this once—this magical one-off time—one did.

Six

*T*he party goes on, as it does every year. I know I should be helping Mum with the profiteroles. I know I should be clearing plates. But for once in my life I'm thinking: *Let Nicole do it. Let Jake do it. Let anyone else do it.* Because Ryan wants to talk to me, and that sweeps everything else away.

We're alone in the tiny back room overlooking the garden. It's stuffed with furniture that we moved out of the sitting room for the party—we're sitting on the floor awkwardly between two sofas—but I don't think either of us cares. We're transfixed, in our own private bubble. Ryan has been talking for about an hour and I've been listening in a state of shock, because he's not saying anything I expected.

Every other time Ryan has come home, all we've heard about L.A. is the glamour. The excitement. The celebrities. But now he's telling me real stuff. Painful stuff. He doesn't look like old Ryan; he looks battered. World-weary. Kind of like he's had it.

And the more he talks, the more I realize what he's telling me is: He *has* had it. He's done with L.A. I have no idea how he can have sunk so quickly from "My best friend is Tom

Cruise" to this place, but the way he's talking now, he never wants to see L.A. again.

"Everyone there is two-faced," he keeps saying. "Every single bastard."

I haven't quite followed his tale of woe—there are two people in it called Aaron, which doesn't help—but what I've picked up is that he went into business with a couple of guys, but nobody did what they'd promised to, and now he's out of money.

"You burn through the stuff," he says bleakly. "Everyone wants to discuss work over Japanese food or on a boat. The one-upmanship. It's insane."

"But when you say, 'out of money,'" I venture, tentatively, "you don't mean . . ."

"I'm out, Fixie." He spreads his hands. "Broke. Nowhere to live, even."

"Shit," I breathe out.

There's a nasty feeling in my stomach. How can Ryan Chalker be broke? I'm remembering him and Jake, aged seventeen, riding around in that convertible. He had money. He *had* it. How can you just lose it all?

"So, what will you . . . where . . ."

"I'm staying with Jake right now. Your brother's great. But then . . ." He shakes his head and his blond waves glimmer in the evening sun. "It's hard. When you had a dream and you tried your utmost best and it didn't work out."

"I know," I say fervently. "I know exactly what you mean."

Hearing all this is bringing back painful stabbings in my heart. I'm remembering my pile of dark-green aprons under the bed. I'm remembering the drenching mortification of failure.

"I've had exactly the same experience," I say, staring at the carpet. "You know I started that catering business? I did a load of work for this married couple called the Smithsons. They had a PR agency and they threw all these dinners for their clients, but they never paid me, and suddenly I was in debt and it was . . ." I try to compose myself. "I'd bought top-class organic filet steak, and I'd paid my staff, and they'd eaten it all, but I never got any money out of them. . . ."

Despite my best efforts, my voice is wobbling. I don't often talk about the Smithsons, because it makes me feel like such a fool. Even worse, it makes me feel ashamed, because I didn't listen to Mum. She knows about small businesses, she knows the risks, and she tried to warn me. She tried to ask me practical questions about invoicing and cash flow. But I so desperately wanted everything to be great that I glossed over the answers.

I'll never make that mistake again. I'll never gloss; I'll never cross my fingers and hope; I'll never do business based on sweet talk and promises and handshakes. If anything good came out of the whole thing, it's that I learned. I became more savvy.

"There were other issues too." I exhale. "It was a bad financial climate. I pitched too high-end. It was harder to crack the market than I realized. But the Smithsons didn't help."

"Didn't you sue?" says Ryan, looking interested. "Could you get some money out of them now?"

I shake my head. "They went bankrupt."

It was like the last toxic ace up their sleeve. After they'd ignored all my invoices, all my emails, even my visits in person to their office, they filed for bankruptcy. I'm in a list of creditors on a computer somewhere. And I couldn't afford to carry on. I couldn't get any more credit and I definitely wasn't turning to Mum again. Farr's Food was over.

That's when I made the decision to channel all my energies into the shop instead. Because I do love it and it's our family legacy and it plays to my strengths. I even sometimes use my chef training when I advise customers on cooking products. And if I ever think wistfully about my catering dreams, then I remind myself: *I had my chance.*

"No one understands except people who have been through it," I say. "No one."

"Exactly." Ryan's eyes burn intently into mine. "They don't get it. Fixie, you're like the only person who understands properly."

My heart swoops inside—*I'm the only person who understands Ryan?*—but somehow I manage not to melt.

"I broke up with my girlfriend," he adds abruptly. "You find out about people." He rubs his face, as though trying to rid himself of memories. "I tried so hard. I wanted to talk it through. . . . But girls like that, they're shallow. It's not about who you are as a person; it's about what can you do for them? How much can you spend on them? How can you help their career? As soon as she realized I was in trouble"—he clicks his fingers—"it was over."

"She sounds awful!" I say hotly, and he shoots me a grateful half smile.

"So . . . what now?" I ask. "What are you going to do?"

"God knows. But it's got to be something *different*, you know?" says Ryan emphatically. "No more fucking smoke and mirrors. Real people. Real work. Roll up my sleeves and get on with it."

"You could do anything!" I say. "The experience you've had . . . it's amazing!"

Ryan shrugs. "Well, I know my shit, let's say that."

"So you just have to choose what to do," I offer encouragingly. "Find a new line of work. I mean, I suppose you might need to go down a few rungs on the ladder to begin with. . . ."

"Of course." Ryan smiles wryly. "I can't expect to go in at CEO level." He gazes into the distance for a few moments, then adds in a low voice, "If I've learned one thing from all this, Fixie, it's how to be humble."

I feel yet another huge wash of affection for him. He's the same as me. Chastened and pounded by experience . . . but not beaten. *Never* beaten.

"Good for you," I say in heartfelt tones. "It's really brave, to start again. I know exactly how you feel."

I sip my drink, trying to think of career options for Ryan and surreptitiously checking out his pumped-up shoulders. If he looked good last year, he looks phenomenal this year. His arms are huge and muscled. His skin is smooth. He looks like an advert for healthy L.A. living.

"So what next?" I venture. "And is there anything I can do to help?"

"Just talking to you helps." Ryan raises his blue eyes to mine, and my stomach squeezes a little. "I guess my next move is, contact some headhunters."

"Headhunters!" I seize on the word. "Of course. Oh my

God, they'll love you. I mean, you've dealt with huge Hollywood companies. You could do anything! They'd be lucky to have you!"

"Oh, Fixie." Ryan surveys me, his eyes crinkling up in a wry smile. "You make a guy feel good, you know that?"

"Well," I say breathlessly. "It's just what I think."

I'm half-hoping Ryan will lean forward and kiss me, but he doesn't; he stands up and turns toward the dresser laden with trophies. We hardly ever use this room, so I've got used to the trophies being ignored. Disregarded by everyone except Mum. But now Ryan's studying each one with fascination.

"I'd forgotten about your ice-skating," he says. "That must have been a big dream for you too. What happened there?"

"Oh, that." I feel a familiar painful twinge. "God. Whatever. Didn't work out." I get to my feet and reluctantly follow his gaze.

"But, look! You were good. I never knew why you gave up." He's picked up a framed photo of me in an aquamarine skating dress, aged thirteen, one leg held above my head as I glide across the ice.

"Oh, just lost interest, I suppose," I say with a feeble smile, and look away.

Seeing that photo brings back a rush of bad feelings, because that was the day it all changed. I'd practiced my junior free program for months. The whole family had come to watch, to cheer me on.

If I close my eyes, I'm back at the rink again, the place that felt like home for so many years. I can recall the crisp chilled air. The silky finish of my outfit. And Jake, in a filthy mood, standing mutinously as Mum fussed around me and took photos. He was angry because Mum had found him secretly drinking in his room and stopped his allowance. And he took it out on me. When he came over to me, I thought he was going to say, "Good luck." I was totally unprepared for what happened.

"How many hours?" he said into my ear. "How many fucking hours have I sat and watched you slide around? Mum's obsessed, Dad goes along with it, but what about me and Nicole? You've ruined our lives, you know that?"

And before I could even draw breath, he walked off, leaving me trembling in shock.

I could blame him for my fall that day. I could say he put me off. And there would be some truth in it. As I skated out onto the ice, my legs were quivering. I'd never, not *once,* seen my skating as anything but positive. I'd always thought Jake and Nicole were proud of me. Just like Mum always told me they were.

But now Jake's point of view was all I could see. Mum's attention sucked up. Money spent on lessons and costumes. All the spotlight focused on me. It was all painfully clear. So I was off my game, not concentrating, and I fell. Badly.

Afterward, everyone told me not to worry—*never mind, you nailed the jump in practice, and you'll nail it again next time.* My heart wasn't in it, though. I gave up skating completely within three months, despite my coach, Jimmy, trying to talk me back into it.

I can't only blame Jake. It was me. My personality. The best skaters are natural performers. They see the audience and blossom. They wouldn't care if their brother was jealous—it'd spur them on. They'd approach their jumps thinking, *Fuck you!* and reach even greater heights. After Jake landed his bombshell on me, I approached every jump thinking, *I'm sorry.*

The trouble is, *I'm sorry* doesn't power anything. It drags you down. By the end, I could barely get my feet off the ice.

"Do you still skate?" asks Ryan, and I flinch before I can stop myself.

"No," I say flatly, then realize I sound too abrupt. "I went back to it in my year off," I amend. "I didn't compete or anything; I qualified as a skating coach and taught beginners."

"I expect you're sick of ice rinks." He laughs.

"Yes," I agree, although it isn't true. I still love ice rinks. I go to Somerset House every year when they put on the skating. I watch all the people swishing round the ice—or falling, most of them—and I love the sight. I just don't need to join in.

I take the photo from Ryan's hand and cast around for a new subject—but before I can think of one, Jake strides in, holding a beer. "Here you are!" he says, almost accusingly.

"Have you been helping out Mum?" I ask, but Jake ignores me. He sees the photo in my hand and rolls his eyes.

"Showing off your past glories, Fixie? You should have *seen* her fall on her bum," he adds to Ryan with a bark of laughter. "Classic. Wish I'd recorded it."

"I don't believe it," says Ryan, twinkling at me. "I bet you never fell on your bum."

Silently, I put the photo back on the dresser. I've never mentioned that day to Jake. We've never revisited that conversation. Does he even *know* what an impact he had on me?

Anyway. You move on.

"Hey!" I say, as a new idea seizes me. "Ryan, you could

work at the shop with us for a bit. Learn the retail trade. We could teach you everything! And then you could move on to something, you know, bigger."

I'm trying to sound as though this is simply a reasonable career suggestion, although my heart has seized up in delirious hope. It's the perfect solution! I'd see him every day . . . he'd feel like part of the family. . . .

"Ah, I'm not sure about that." Ryan wrinkles his suntanned nose. "Might be awkward, working for you guys. Jake, mate, didn't you bring me a beer?"

I force myself to keep smiling, determined he won't see my disappointment. Why would he think it would be awkward? It wouldn't be awkward! But there's no point pressing the idea. If he doesn't want to work at the shop, he doesn't.

"Have you been helping Mum?" I ask Jake again. "Or has Nicole?"

"Jeez, Fixie." He rolls his eyes. "Get off my case. I haven't even *seen* Mum."

Now that Jake is in here, the magical, transfixing bubble we were in has burst. And suddenly I feel guilty. I've dodged all the work. I've forgotten about the party. I've forgotten about everything except Ryan and me.

"I'll go and see if Mum needs anything," I say. "You know what she's like. She'll be back in the kitchen."

I'm not being totally noble here. I'm feeling the need of Mum's calming presence. Jake unnerves me, and I was already unnerved enough by Ryan. I need an injection of Mum's calm, loving, steadying voice. I want her to say something that makes me smile, so I can take a step back from life and see it all in perspective.

I head out and glance into the sitting room, where the guests have given up standing. They're perched all over, on chairs and even the floor, chatting and smoking and still nibbling food. But sure enough, Mum isn't anywhere to be seen. I *knew* it.

"Mum?" I call, as I stride down the corridor toward the back of the house. "Mum, are you there?"

I see a familiar flash of blue linen through the ajar kitchen door, but it's in the wrong place somehow. I pick up speed, frowning as my brain tries to process the sight. There's something not right, but I can't work out—

"Mum?" I push the door right open—and my heart freezes in horror.

Mum is collapsed over the table, motionless. Her piping bag is still in her hand; her straggly hair is all over her face. "Mum?" My voice is strangled in alarm. *"Mum?"*

I push her shoulder gently but she doesn't respond—and now terror is ripping through my guts.

"Mum? *Help!*" I yell through the door, frantically patting her cheeks, trying to work out if she's even breathing. I can't feel a pulse, but then, I don't know how to feel for a pulse; I should have done first-aid lessons. . . .

"Mum, please wake up, please. . . . *Help!* Someone please HELP!" I yell again, my voice hoarse, tears of fright springing from my eyes. "HELP!"

Footsteps are thudding along the corridor. I grab for my phone with fumbling, panicky fingers, feeling totally surreal. I've never dialed 999 in my life and I've always wondered what it must feel like. Now I know. It's the scariest thing in the world.

Seven

When everything happens at once, it's hard to process. It's hard not to go around with a bewildered look and your brain only half engaged, because the rest of it is crying out, *What's happening? What's happening?*

First Ryan arrived out of the blue, which was enough to be dealing with. Then Mum collapsed and I thought my world had caved in. And then we got to the hospital and she was OK, and that was kind of shocking in its relief.

Except of course she wasn't really OK. She isn't really OK. As it turns out, she hasn't been OK for ages.

She'd never even mentioned she'd been having chest pains, which is *so bloody Mum*. I wanted to scream when it came out. All this time, she'd had a dodgy heart and she'd never let on? A lot of her trouble comes down to smoking, they've said. She used to smoke, and of course Dad was on thirty a day. But then there's the fact that she works fourteen-hour days in the shop. Still. At her age.

Make changes is the phrase every single medical profession used during those few days that Mum was in hospital. *Make changes to your life.* When Mum replied, "I'm not changing what I do! I love what I do!" they just reiterated it.

You need to make changes. But this time they looked at us—Nicole and me—as they said it. They gave *us* the job of changing Mum. (And Jake too, I guess, except he wasn't there much of the time. He had meetings to be at, apparently.)

Now it's two weeks after the party. And if it were up to Nicole and me, even with our best efforts, I'm not sure anything would have changed very much. But that's irrelevant now. Because last Friday, a brand-new thing hit us, like a juggernaut: Mum's sister, Karen, came to stay.

We don't even *know* Aunty Karen. She might be our aunt, but she's lived in Spain for twenty-seven years. She never comes back to the UK, because it's "too bloody cold." She doesn't do email, because it's a "pain in the neck." She didn't come to Nicole's wedding, because she was having a "procedure." But she's here now. And not only has Mum changed, the whole *house* has changed.

She burst into the house like a suntanned whirlwind, dragging a bright-pink wheelie case, her hair in a highlighted, straggly blond ponytail.

"I'm here!" she cried to Mum, who was sitting on the sofa. "Don't you worry! I'll take care of things! Now, first things first: flowers for the invalid."

We all watched, a bit gobsmacked, as she produced a bunch of bright-red fake flowers from her bag, like a magician. "I don't do fresh flowers," she added. "Waste of bloody money. Put these in a vase, just as good, and you can use them again." She thrust the plastic flowers at me, then she peered at Mum and shook her head. "Oh, Joanne. Bloody hell. Look at you. Look at your lines. I know I'm lined"—she poked at her suntanned, crinkly face—"but these are from *fun*. Look at you, working yourself into an early grave! That's got to stop. If you can't enjoy yourself, what's the point of life? I'm taking you *away*."

At first, I didn't even know what Aunty Karen meant by "away." Then I realized she meant away to Spain. Then I thought, *Yes! Of* course *Mum should have a holiday*. Then I thought, *Mum will never have a holiday. No way. She won't go.*

But I'd reckoned without Aunty Karen. Somehow she's got sway over Mum. She can talk her into things no one else can. Like, she told Mum she *had* to have gel nails, *had* to— and Mum listened meekly and let her apply them. How many times has Leila offered to do Mum's nails without getting anywhere?

And now she's talked Mum into coming back to Spain with her. Mum, who hasn't been on a plane since before she was married. The doctors have okayed it. (I phoned up the consultant especially, to be extra sure.) Mum's bought a new swimsuit and a hat and a one-way ticket. She doesn't know how long she's going for, but it'll be at least six weeks. It was Aunty Karen who insisted on six weeks. She said short holidays are stressful. She said Mum would never properly relax otherwise. She said they might go to Paris too and she barely knew her own sister and it was about bloody time.

Which is great. It's *so* great. Mum deserves some time to relax and see the world and get to know her sister properly again. When she told me she'd be gone for six weeks, if not more, I flung my arms around her and said, "Mum, that's amazing! How exciting!"

"It's a long time to be away," she said with a nervous laugh. But I instantly shook my head and said, "You need it. And, anyway, it'll fly by!"

Today we're having a meeting to talk about how we're going to manage the shop. Jake and Nicole have both promised to give more time to it. (It's turned out that Nicole's yoga course isn't quite as "full-time" as she's been making out.) We've upped Stacey's hours and reworked the shifts so that everything is covered. Still, it'll be weird with Mum away.

We've cleared the oak gateleg dining table that we only use at Christmas and we're sitting round it with cups of coffee: Nicole, Jake, me, and Mum, whose appearance keeps making me draw breath. She's now an unfamiliar biscuity color and has sparkly blue earrings dangling from her lobes. Aunty Karen talked her into the fake tan last night—and the earrings appeared this morning as a "little pressie."

The chair at the end with the big wooden arms is empty. That's still Dad's chair, even after all these years. No one would ever sit in it, but no one ever moves it either. It's like we still respect Dad and his position in the family, even though he's gone.

"Here we are!" Aunty Karen plonks a bowl of pink marshmallows on the table, and we all blink at her. "You didn't know you needed those, did you?" she exclaims triumphantly as she sits down and pops one into her mouth, and we all stare at them, a bit baffled.

This is what Aunty Karen says every time she brings something new into the house—which is every single day. From fake flowers to bowls of sweets everywhere to plug-in air fresheners, she's constantly "improving" the place with things which aren't really *us*. And each time, she cries, "You didn't know you needed that, did you?" But she's so bright and breezy and bossy, no one objects.

Jake eyes the marshmallows with disfavor, then pushes them away slightly and turns to Mum.

"Right," he says. "So. Mum. You're off to Spain."

"*Hola!*" puts in Nicole brightly. "*Por favor, signor.*"

"*Por favor-e,*" corrects Jake.

"No, it's not." Nicole rolls her eyes. "It's *por favor.*"

"It's *por favor,*" Aunty Karen confirms. "But don't bother with any of that nonsense," she adds to Mum. "Miguel down the beach, he pretends he only speaks Spanish. Load of rubbish. Just speak English, nice and loud."

"Really?" Mum looks taken aback. "But if he's Spanish—"

"Oh, he can speak English well enough when he wants to," says Aunty Karen scoffingly. "I've heard him at the karaoke bar. He does Adele, Pet Shop Boys . . . what else?" She thinks. "Wham! Lots of Wham! . . ."

"Could we get back on track?" says Jake, his smile a little fixed. "Not that this isn't fascinating."

"Yes. We should. Because I have something to announce—no, to ask you all. It's rather . . ." Mum glances at Aunty Karen, who clearly knows what she's about to say. For an instant I feel shut out—Mum's been talking to Aunty Karen before us? But then that thought is swept away as Mum looks round the table at us and says, "I've had an offer on the shop."

What?

There's a startled silence. Jake's eyebrows have shot up. Nicole murmurs, "Wow." As for me, I'm beyond shock. An offer? For Farrs? Who would buy Farrs? *We're* Farrs.

"We don't want to sell," I blurt out before I can stop myself. "Do we?"

"Well," says Mum. "That's the question. I'm not as young as I was, and things have . . . changed."

"Your mum needs a rest," puts in Aunty Karen. "And it's good money."

"How much?" demands Jake, and Mum slides a piece of paper into the middle of the table.

It's never even occurred to me to think how much Farrs might be worth. But it's a lot. We all stare at it silently, and I can sense our brains are reconfiguring the facts of our lives.

"Your mum could retire. Put her feet up. Buy a little place in Spain near me," says Aunty Karen.

"But this is so weird. How come you've had an offer *now*?" I stare at Mum, suddenly stricken. "Oh God, this isn't some kind of ambulance chaser, is it?"

"No!" Mum laughs. "Love, the truth is, we've had offers to sell all the time over the years. Never wanted to, before. But after everything that's happened . . ."

I look at the piece of paper again, my brain doing new sums. Yes, it's a lot of money, but if that means the end of Farrs, of our incomes, of our jobs . . . then it doesn't seem that much after all.

"Do you *want* to sell?" I ask Mum. I'm trying my hardest to sound neutral. Pragmatic. Supportive. All those grown-up things. But even so, I can feel my eyes glistening as the idea really hits me.

Sell? Our beloved Farrs? *Dad's* beloved Farrs?

I look up, and as she sees my expression, Mum's guard drops.

"Oh, Fixie," she says, and reaches a hand across the table to squeeze mine. "Of course I don't want to. But I don't want to burden you children either. If I'm going to step back, what then? Running Farrs is hard. It's full-time. It's got to be what *you* want to do. Not just for me. Or for Dad."

She's blinking too now, and her cheeks are rosy. I think Mum and I are the only ones in the family who feel Dad's presence every time we step into that shop. Jake only sees money. And Nicole sees . . . I have no idea what Nicole sees. Unicorns, probably.

"I want to do it," I say without hesitation. "I don't want to give up. Mum, go to Spain and don't worry. We'll run the business. Won't we?" I look at Jake and Nicole, trying to get their support.

"I agree," says Jake, to my surprise. "I think Farrs has great potential." He jabs the piece of paper. "I mean, this is all very well, but we could double that figure. Treble it."

"What about you, Nicole?" says Mum, turning to her, and Nicole shrugs.

"If you wanted to sell, I'd be, like . . . fair enough," she says in her drifty, absent way. "But if you *don't* want to, then, like . . ."

We all wait for her to finish her sentence—then realize she *has* finished her sentence.

"Well," says Mum, and her cheeks are even rosier. "I have to say, I'm relieved. I don't want to sell Farrs. It's a good outfit, though I say so myself."

"This is a bird in the hand, though," says Aunty Karen, picking up the paper and brandishing it. "This is solid cash. Security. If you don't sell now, you might regret it."

"If Mum *does* sell now, she might regret it," counters Jake. "You know what I think?" He looks around the table, his face animated. "This is an opportunity to take our small family business to the next level. Turbocharge it. We've got the name, the premises, the online presence . . . I mean, the sky's the limit. But we need to think big." He pounds a fist into his palm. "Rebrand. Focus. Maybe we need to hire a consultant. I know some guys; I could bring them in, hear what they have to say. Shall I set that up?"

I gape at him. How have we got onto hiring a consultant? How much would that cost? And what does that mean anyway, "turbocharge"?

"Don't worry about that, Jake," says Mum in that quiet, firm way of hers. "Just keep the place from falling down while I'm away, and we can think about all your ideas when I get back. Now, let me run through a few stock issues."

She starts to talk about suppliers, but I can't concentrate. I'm suddenly feeling anxious. It's as though the situation is hitting me properly for the first time. Mum will be away. I'll be running the shop with Nicole and Jake. How's *that* going to work out?

I half-listen as Mum hands round a list of reminders which she's handwritten and photocopied. But I'm mostly worrying about Jake. What if he makes some stupid decision and I can't stop him? I can see Mum glancing at me as though reading my thoughts—and I hastily smile back. My top priority is not worrying her.

At last we finish, and as we get up from the table, Mum draws me aside. The others have already headed into the kitchen, so we're alone.

"Fixie," she says gently. "Love. I know you're worried about . . ." She hesitates. "Well. Let's say it. Jake."

Her words feel like they're prodding something hidden and sore.

"You know," I say, looking away, not wanting to admit the truth. "He's just a bit . . ."

"I know. He gets his exciting ideas into his head, and he can't be put off. I do understand." Mum squeezes my arm reassuringly. "But I'm not going to leave you in the lurch. I've got a solution for while I'm away which I think will help."

"Oh!" I say in huge relief. "Wow. What is it?"

I should have known Mum would have a plan up her sleeve. Maybe we'll have daily Skype calls with her in Spain. Or maybe she's hired some new brilliant member of staff. Or a new computer system that Jake can't get round.

"Uncle Ned," says Mum with a beam.

My stomach drops like a stone. Uncle Ned? Uncle Ned is the solution?

"Right," I manage, in a strangled voice, which Mum takes as a sign of approval.

"I've spoken to him and he's promised to keep an eye on things while I'm away," she says happily. "He's got a good business head. We can trust him."

I don't even know what to say. *Uncle Ned?*

"He's so good to us," adds Mum fondly. "I know he'll be a comfort."

"He's not good to me!" I want to wail. "And he won't be a comfort!"

"It's an idea," I say at last, trying to sound calm and reasonable. "Definitely. But I'm just wondering—is Uncle Ned the right person?"

"You know how helpful he was over the lease when Dad died," Mum reminds me. "I'll feel happier if he's here to support you."

I want to yelp with frustration. OK, maybe he did help with the lease—but that was nine years ago. What's he done since?

"I know you don't like some of the old-fashioned things he says," adds Mum, pinkening. "And nor do I, for that matter. But he's family, love, and he cares about Farrs. That's what counts."

There's a light in her eyes—the determined light that appears when she talks about family. She's made up her mind. And I can't say anything to worry her. So I smile my most cheery smile and say, "Well, I'm sure it'll all work out. The *most* important thing is that you have a fantastic break. You look so glamorous already!"

I reach out to touch her dangling, sparkling earrings, incongruous against her graying workaday hair. (Aunty Karen's hairdresser in Spain has already been booked.)

"It's hard to go away and leave you all!" says Mum, with a little laugh, and I can see traces of anxiety appearing in her face. "Harder than I thought. Even now I'm wondering . . . do I actually want to do this?"

Oh God. She can't backtrack now.

"Yes!" I say firmly. "You do! We'll be fine."

"Just don't lose the shop, Fixie. Or let the family break up." Mum gives the same odd little laugh.

I think she's only half joking. I think she has secret deep-down worries, like I do. "You're the glue," she adds. "You can keep everyone together."

I can *what?* I almost want to laugh, because she's so wrong. *Mum's* the glue of this family. She leads us all. She unites us all. Without her we're just three disparate siblings.

But I don't give away my real thoughts for a nanosecond. I need to bolster up Mum before she decides not to go away after all and do a sixteen-hour shift at the shop instead.

"Mum, listen," I say, with as much confidence as I can muster. "When you get back, we'll be sitting around that very table to celebrate." I gesture at the gateleg oak table. "The shop will be in great shape. And we'll be a happy family. I promise."

Eight

After Mum and Aunty Karen have left the next afternoon, everything feels flat. Jake and Leila disappear off to the pub and I decide to make a Bolognese for supper, because that's what Mum would do. But even as I'm cooking, it isn't the same. I'm not filling the house with the same magical, Mum-like atmosphere. I don't feel warm or cozy or reassured.

To be honest, it's not just because Mum's gone that I feel so flat. It's that I haven't heard from or seen Ryan since the party. Not a visit, not a phone call, just a single text: **Sorry about your mum.**

The day after the party, he went to Sonning to visit his family, and then it was as if he'd disappeared into a black hole. He didn't reply to any of my texts. A couple of times Jake said, "Ryan says hi," and that was the sum total of our communication. To be honest, I didn't mind too much. He wasn't the priority; Mum was. But now I can't help thinking: *What happened?*

I stare at the pan dispiritedly and give it a stir—then turn it off. I'll pop out for some ice cream. You can't go wrong with Ben & Jerry's when you need a pick-me-up.

As I'm hurrying along the High Street, I see a guy with

frondy hair walking ahead of me, with a brisk determined stride. At once I think, *Is that the guy from the coffee shop?* Followed by, *No, don't be silly, it can't be.*

Odd that my mind has instantly gone there, though. And even odder that I'm faintly blushing. What's that about? I haven't even *thought* about him since that day.

Well, OK, maybe I have, once or twice. Just his eyes. There was something about his eyes. I've found myself picturing them now and then—that flecked, leafy green-brown color.

The man ahead of me stops to consult his phone and I catch sight of his face—and it is him! It's Sebastian . . . whatever he's called. He glances up and sees me approaching— and at once his face creases into a smile of recognition.

"Oh, hello!" he says.

"Hi!" I come to a halt. "How are you?" I meet his woodlandy gaze—then quickly look away again before I overdo the eye contact.

"Good! Just waiting for a cab." He gestures at his phone, and I see the map of a cab-company app.

"Back in Acton!" I say. "Or are you local?"

"No. I've been here for . . ." He hesitates. "A thing."

"Oh, right," I say politely, because it's none of my business—and it feels as though the conversation should perhaps end there. But Sebastian's face is animated; his brow is creasing up; he seems like he wants to share his thoughts.

"As it happens, I've been consulting 'the skiing workout guru,'" he suddenly says, making quote marks with his fingers. "Did you know that *the* skiing workout guru lives in Acton?"

"No," I say, smiling. "I didn't even know *the* skiing work-out guru existed." I nearly add, "I've never skied in my life," but I can tell Sebastian is on a roll.

"Nor did I, till my girlfriend gave me two vouchers for my birthday and insisted I go to see him. So I went. Twice."

"Right. And how was he?"

"Absolute rubbish!" exclaims Sebastian indignantly. "I'm offended by how rubbish he was. I'm shocked!"

His outrage is so comical, I break into laughter—although I can tell there's genuine grievance there too.

"How was he rubbish?" I can't help asking.

"The first session, all he did was describe how he won a bronze in Vancouver. Today he described how he just missed a bronze in Sochi. I could have got that off Wikipedia in five minutes, if I were interested, which I'm not."

I can't help laughing again. "What about exercises?"

"He revealed the insightful information that lunges are a good idea and suggested I come back twice a week for the next six months."

"What a rip-off!" I say in heartfelt tones.

"Exactly!" exclaims Sebastian. "I'm glad you agree. I'm sorry, I just had to get that off my chest." He glances at the map on his phone and I see an icon of a cab coming up the High Street. "Anyway, enough of that. How's life been treating you?"

I open my mouth to say, "Fine," but it doesn't seem honest, somehow.

"Actually, my mum's been in hospital," I say instead.

"Oh no." He looks up from his phone in dismay. "And here I am going on . . . Is there anything I can do?"

This is such a kind, ludicrous instinct that I can't help smiling again. What on earth could he do?

"It's fine. She's better. She's off on holiday."

"Oh good," he says—and he really seems to mean it. At that moment a minicab pulls up and he signals to the driver. "This is me," he says. "Nice to see you again."

"Bye," I say, as he opens the car door. "I'm sorry Acton hasn't been kind to you. Collapsing ceilings and dodgy work-out gurus. We must do better."

"Wouldn't have missed it," he says with a grin. "Acton has a place in my heart."

"We do have an *amazing* Thai restaurant here," I say. "If you're into Thai food."

"I love Thai food." His eyes crinkle at me. "Thanks for the tip. Oh, and remember." He pauses, his hand on the car door. "I still owe you one. I'm serious. You haven't forgotten?"

"Of course not!" I say. "How could I?"

I watch as the cab drives off, still smiling at his good-humored outrage—then head on my way.

The little exchange has buoyed my spirits, but as I get back to the house I start to feel flat again. I reheat the pasta sauce, inhaling the delicious scent, then put on *The Archers,* because that's what Mum would do too—but it feels fake. I don't listen to *The Archers,* so I don't know who any of the characters are.

"Hey, Fixie." Nicole wanders into the kitchen, interrupting my thoughts. I'm hoping she's going to offer to help, but she doesn't even seem to have noticed that I'm cooking. She leans against the counter, picks up the chunk of Parmesan I was about to grate, and starts to nibble it. "So I've had a great idea," she says thoughtfully. "I think we should have yoga at the shop."

"Yoga?" I echo. "What do you mean? Like . . . a yoga section?"

"Yoga *sessions*," she says, as though it's obvious. "We should run sessions in the evenings. I could do them."

I put my wooden spoon down on Mum's bunny-rabbit ceramic spoon rest (£6.99, bestseller at Easter) and peer at her to see if she's joking. But she meets my gaze with a full-on Nicole-taking-herself-seriously expression. The thing about Nicole is, she's all vague and wafty until she wants something, whereupon she can suddenly become quite gimlety and focused.

"Nicole, we're a shop," I say carefully. "We sell saucepans. We don't do yoga."

"We have the Cake Club," she counters.

"Yes, but that's a selling event. We sell cake tins and stuff. It enhances our business."

"Loads of shops do all sorts of evening events," she responds. "It would build up the clientele."

"But *where*?"

I'm picturing the shop, trying to imagine even *two* people putting down yoga mats, and I'm failing.

"We'd have to move a few things," she says breezily. "Get rid of a couple of displays."

"Every night? And then put them back?"

"Of course not!" She rolls her eyes. "Permanently. There's

too much stock, anyway. Even Mum says so. It's over-crowded."

"We can't get rid of whole displays of stock to make space for yoga lessons!" I say in horror.

"Well, that's your opinion," says Nicole calmly.

"What about the cleaners? They start at six P.M. When would they get in?"

Nicole stares at me blankly as though she never even realized the shop gets cleaned every night.

Oh my God. She *didn't* realize the shop gets cleaned, did she? She lives on another *planet*.

"We'd sort it," she says at last with a shrug. "Like we do on Cake Club night."

"OK," I say, trying to be positive. "Well, would you sell any stock?"

"We'd be doing *yoga*," says Nicole, frowning. "Not *selling* things."

"But—"

"You're *trying* to find problems, Fixie," she adds.

"So Mum only left, what"—I look at my watch—"four hours ago. And already you want to change things."

"You should be more open-minded!" retaliates Nicole. "I bet if I rang Mum now, she'd love the idea."

"She would not!" I say hotly. I feel so sure of myself, I almost want to dial Mum's number and prove it. But of course I won't.

"You should do yoga yourself." Nicole eyes me dispassionately. "Your breathing is really shallow. Look." She points at my chest. "It's stressing you out."

I want to retort, "It's not my *breathing* that's stressing me out!" But the thought of Mum stops me. She'd be really upset to think that within hours of her departure, we were arguing about the shop. So somehow I force myself to take a deep breath.

"Well, this is what the family meetings are for," I say as reasonably as I can. "We'll put it on the agenda and discuss it."

Uncle Ned and Jake will never go for yoga classes. It'll all be fine.

"Could you do the spaghetti?" I add, and Nicole replies, "Sure," in an absent tone. She wanders to the larder, now engrossed in her phone, gets out the spaghetti packet, and stands motionless for a bit while I count out forks.

"Nicole?" I prompt her.

"Oh. Yeah." She gets out a saucepan and puts it on the hob, then peers at the spaghetti. "How much, do you think?"

"Well, there's going to be four of us."

"Right," says Nicole, still peering at the packet. "The thing is, I never know with spaghetti."

"Well, you know. It's basically a clump for each person."

I text Leila—**Supper in about 10**—and lay out water glasses. Then I glance at Nicole. She's taken out a bunch of spaghetti and is looking at it, her brow wrinkled. For God's sake. She hasn't even put the water on.

I fill the pan with water, add salt, whack up the heat on the hob, and take the spaghetti from Nicole's hands.

"I'll do it," I say. "You know we've actually got a spaghetti measurer? You know we stock them in the shop?"

I show her the spoon with the special hole in it, and she opens her eyes wide and says, "No way. I never knew that was for measuring spaghetti! You're so good at all that, Fixie."

As I start to measure out the spaghetti into the boiling water, she wafts out of the kitchen without asking if she can do anything else to help, bumping into Leila on the way.

"Fixie!" says Leila in excitement. "*Guess* who's here." She hurries forward and smooths down my hair, then produces a lip gloss from nowhere and slicks it across my lips.

"Huh?" I stare at her in puzzlement.

"*Ryan!*" she whispers.

"*What?*" I feel my eyes widen. But before I can say anything else, I hear Jake saying, "Come on in, we'll have some grub." And I force myself to leave it a full five seconds before I swivel round to see Ryan. Here. In our kitchen.

He's as tall and blond and dazzling as ever. His easy smile has gone, though. His face is tired-looking and there's a crease in his brow.

"Hi, Fixie," he says vacantly. "All right?"

"Here." Jake is already pouring him a glass of wine. "Drown your sorrows, mate. Ryan's eating with us," he adds to me.

"Right," I manage. "Lovely!"

My stomach is flipping over. My thoughts are on a circular loop: *He's here! Where's he been? Why does he look so down? Why hasn't he texted? Is he with someone else? He's here!*

"I hope you like spaghetti," I say in bright, fake tones.

"Yeah," Ryan says, and takes a gulp of wine. "Great." He stares into the distance for a moment or two, then seems to see me for the first time. "Hey. Let me say hello properly."

He comes over and kisses me on the mouth.

"Sorry I haven't been in touch," he murmurs. "I know you've had it hard with your mum in hospital and everything. Thought you wouldn't want me in your way."

"Oh," I say, a bit disconcerted. "Right."

"I know what it's like when people barge in," he adds. "I didn't want to intrude. I thought: Give them some space."

I have a couple of replies at the tip of my tongue: "It wouldn't have been intruding." Or: "You could at least have texted." I suddenly recall Sebastian's instant kind response: "Is there anything I can do?" And he doesn't even *know* me.

But then . . . everyone's different. People don't know how to react to things. Especially medical emergencies. Hannah came along to the hospital and sat with me in the ward and googled everything the doctor said . . . but that's her.

I must be giving away some of what I'm thinking, because Ryan is scanning my face closely.

"I didn't know what to do," he says, looking stricken. "I guess I panicked. I drew away. But that was wrong, wasn't it? You think I'm a total shit now."

"No!" I say quickly. "Of course not! It's been fine, really. And Mum's gone off on holiday, so . . . all good." I smile to reassure him—but he still looks despairing.

"Everything's so messed up right now," he says. "So messed up."

He drains his glass, leans against the wall, and heaves a huge, heavy sigh.

"Oh, Ryan," says Leila sympathetically. "It'll all work out."

"What's up?" I say anxiously.

"Headhunters." Ryan shakes his head.

The spaghetti suddenly boils over and I hastily grab the pan. I want to hear more about this, but I also want the spaghetti to be al dente.

"Sit down, everyone," I say. "I'll dole this out. Jake, can you get Nicole?"

"I'll help," says Leila, reaching for the plates.

We serve out the food and Jake fills everyone's wineglass, and Nicole slides into her chair, and as I look around the table, I feel a small tweak of pride. Here we are, anyway, eating together as a family. We will be OK with Mum away, we *will*.

"So what happened with the headhunters?" I say warily to Ryan, and Leila winces.

"Five years' experience in the film industry," says Ryan blankly. "I mean, you'd think . . ." He forks spaghetti into his mouth. "No, I don't have any experience in fucking . . . *widgets*. No, I don't have any professional qualifications. No, I'm not . . . what is it, digitally literate." He gulps his wine. "But I have experience. I know about deals. I know about people. Doesn't that count for *anything*?"

"Haven't they found anything at all for you?" I venture.

"Oh, they talk the talk. They say, 'Yeah, we can place you straightaway, a talented guy like you, no problem!' But you know where they want to place me?"

"Um . . . no."

"A call center."

"A *call center*?" I echo, aghast.

"It's a bloody insult," chimes in Jake hotly, and I feel a kind of warmth that for once we're agreeing on something.

"What kind of call center?" I ask, because I can't get my head round this at all.

"Selling . . ." He pauses, his spaghetti quivering on his fork. "I don't even know what it was. Some weird insurance. No salary, just commission. I didn't stay to find out. So then at the next headhunter I go, 'Look, no call centers,' and they say, 'No problem. We'll find you something.' It's bollocks. They've got nothing."

"It's tough." Jake grimaces. "Most companies are shedding people at the moment, not taking them on."

"So what are you going to do?" I say anxiously.

"Who knows?" He's silent awhile, absently chewing. "At least in L.A. . . . . I *get* L.A. I know I've messed up there, but at least . . . You get to know a place, for better or for worse. You understand how it works. Whereas starting again in London . . . I dunno. London's changed. It's brutal."

It takes me a moment to understand what he's saying.

"You can't go back to L.A.!" I say in dismay. "You said you never wanted to see the place again!"

"I can't carry on like this, though, can I? I can't keep on camping at Jake's."

"It's no sweat!" says Jake, but Ryan shakes his head.

"What about your mum?" says Nicole. "Could you stay with her?"

"Not really." He looks even more bleak. "Not with my stepdad there. We don't get on. It's hard. Mum and I used to be so close, you know?"

I feel a huge wash of sympathy for him. I can't *imagine* what it would be like if Mum married someone we didn't get on with. I'm also longing to say, "Move in here! There's plenty of room!" But that might be too pushy.

"You'll find something!" I say encouragingly. "There are other headhunters . . . there must be loads of opportunities. You said you were willing to start at a more junior level—"

"Yeah, I told them that. I said, 'What about fast-track schemes, whatever?' And they go, 'Well, are you a graduate?'"

There's a prickly silence around the table, broken by Nicole saying with vague interest, "Oh, that's right. I forgot you dropped out of uni, Ryan."

Typical Nicole to spell out what we're all thinking. Although, actually, I'd also forgotten that Ryan dropped out. It's so long ago now, and it didn't seem to matter, once he was in Hollywood, being the big success. But I guess it matters if you want to join a graduate scheme.

"Maybe you could finish your degree?" I suggest warily, even though I'm fairly sure that's the last thing he wants to do.

"Sod that," Ryan says vehemently. "Either people understand what I have to offer or forget it."

There's such a miserable edge to his voice, I wince. It must be hard. I mean, rejection is hard whoever you are—but he's Ryan Chalker! At school, he was the One. Maybe he wasn't on the school council, or top at math, but he was still the One. Coolest boy. Golden boy. He had "success story" written all over him. So how can he be in this situation? Can't these headhunters *see* his star quality? I feel so sorry for him. And I don't blame him for lashing out. He's like a wounded lion.

After we've finished eating, Nicole disappears upstairs to watch her Netflix show. Leila goes to get Jake's cigarettes out of the car and I clear the plates, preoccupied. I want to solve this. A job. What job could Ryan get? I scrape the plates and stack the dishwasher, thinking: *A job . . . a job . . . a job . . .*

And then it comes to me. Oh my God! I *have* heard about a job recently. In Café Allegro. That conversation Sebastian was having, before the ceiling fell in.

As I close the dishwasher, I'm trying frantically to remember everything I overheard. He wanted someone bright and savvy and tough . . . someone with experience of the world. . . . He didn't care about degrees. . . . Yes! It couldn't be more perfect!

"Ryan!" I exclaim in excitement. "I've remembered, I heard about a job the other day. Exactly the kind of thing you want. You don't need any qualifications, you just need some sense. . . ."

"What job?" says Jake with a laugh. "Flipping burgers?"

"It's investment management," I say, ignoring Jake. "It's this company who are sick of clever-clever people. They want savvy people who've been in the real world. Well, that's you!"

"Investment management?" Jake stares at me, flabbergasted. "How do you know anything about investment management?"

"I happened to hear about it." I address Ryan. "What do you think?"

"You're sweet to try," he says without even turning his head. "But that's, like, the most competitive field going. There's no way an investment manager's going to give me a job. I've got no degree, no experience—"

"They don't care about that. If I find out the name of the company, we can look them up. There'll be an application form. I'm sure you'd be in with a chance—"

"Fixie, stop!" Ryan lifts a hand, sounding almost angry. "Do you *know* the level of competition out there? Math graduates? Clever kids who can code and all that?"

"You don't understand!" I say eagerly. "I overheard the guy talking. I got the inside scoop! They don't *want* people with a million degrees. Look, I'll get the name of the company and you can google them."

I hurry into the hall and reach into my bag. The coffee-cup sleeve is still there, the business card still pinned to it with my Anna's Accessories hair grip. I carry them both into the kitchen, reading out the name of the company.

"Ethical Sense Investment Management. ESIM. There you go." I reach for my laptop, type the name into Google, and a moment later I'm looking at a familiar frondy-haired face. *Sebastian Marlowe. Founder and CEO.*

"They're based in Farringdon." I scan the opening paragraph. "*Ethically led investment.*"

"What the fuck is *that*?" Jake snorts.

"Don't you *want* something a bit ethical, for a change?" I say to Ryan, ignoring Jake. "Anyway, look, here's the job!" I've already clicked on *Vacancies* and found it: Trainee Researcher. *"Applications are still being accepted for this post,"* I read out loud. *"Trainee candidates are likely to have a business or finance degree; however, this is not necessary. An appropriate background in business will be taken into account.* You see?"

"Trainee." Ryan wrinkles his nose. "Like, *intern*?"

"You'll be fine, mate." Jake gives a short laugh. "Mine's a flat white, and be quick about it."

"It's not an internship," I say hastily. "But, I mean, you'll have to be trained, won't you?"

"Paying how much?" Ryan frowns at the screen.

"Does that matter?" I say. "It's a foot in the door, isn't it? I think it sounds really exciting!"

There's silence for a few moments. I was hoping Ryan's face would break into a joyful smile or he might even hug me. But he's still reading the job description, his brow furrowed.

"Dunno," he says at last. "I dunno. I need a proper job, not some crummy internship. I mean, in L.A. I *employed* interns."

"Yes, but—" I break off awkwardly.

I don't want to rub salt in his wounds. He doesn't need reminding that he can't afford to employ anyone now. I know exactly what that feels like. For about a month after my catering company failed, I'd wake up and had forgotten. Then the truth came crashing in on me again, and every time it was horrible.

"What's this?" Ryan reaches curiously for the coffee-cup sleeve and reads the writing on it. *"I owe you one. Redeemable in perpetuity."* He looks up. "What does *that* mean?"

"Oh." For some weird reason, I find myself blushing. "It doesn't mean anything."

"Whose signature is that?" Ryan peers at the scribbly words.

"Yeah, what is this?" Jake takes the coffee-cup sleeve from Ryan and scans it, frowning. "Who owes you one?"

"He does," I admit, a bit reluctantly. "The guy."

"What guy?"

"The CEO guy."

"*Him?*" Ryan jerks an incredulous thumb at Sebastian, still looking at us from the laptop screen. "How come? What happened?"

"I saved his laptop."

"How?" Both of them are agog by now.

"It was nothing!" I say, trying to play it down. "There was this gush of water and I grabbed it. He said I'd saved his bacon. He tried to buy me a coffee, but I didn't want it, so he wrote me this IOU. But it's a joke," I add for emphasis. "It's not *serious* or anything."

Ryan doesn't seem to be listening.

"You saved his bacon," he's saying slowly. "So now he owes you a favor. Like maybe . . . giving a job to someone. A proper job. With proper money."

I stare at Ryan, as it gradually dawns on me what he's suggesting. He can't mean— He *couldn't* mean—

"Yes!" Jake joins in, his face animated. "Do it!"

"Do what?"

"Claim your IOU. Go and see the guy. Get Ryan a job. And make sure the salary's decent."

"I can't do that!" I say, shocked. "I don't even know him!

He's a stranger! I mean, I did bump into him tonight, actually," I add, for the sake of accuracy. "But I don't *know* him. . . ."

"It's not about knowing him, it's about your rights. He owes you one!" Jake jabs at the coffee-cup sleeve. "Says it here."

"He doesn't owe me *that*! All I did was save his laptop from getting wet. It was a tiny favor."

"You don't know that," counters Jake at once. "You don't know what was on that laptop. You could have saved him thousands of pounds."

"Hundreds of thousands," puts in Ryan. "You might have saved his whole company, for all you know."

"You probably did." Jake nods firmly. "You probably saved him millions and he tries to palm you off with a cappuccino. Cheapskate."

"Look . . ." I exhale, trying to stay calm. "It wasn't like that. And I can't go waltzing into some guy's office and say, 'You owe me one, so give Ryan a job.' " I turn to Ryan. "Why don't you apply properly? You have great experience, a great CV—"

"Oh, give me a break!" Ryan erupts. "I'll never get this job! Not a chance. No one'll read my CV and think, *Yes! This is the guy we want to do our ethical trading shit.*"

"They might!"

Ryan shakes his head, staring at the table. Then his eyes rise to meet mine and I can see the pain in them. A bleak, humiliated pain that I recognize.

"I'm going back to L.A.," he says, and turns to Jake. "Sorry, mate, we'll have to put our plans on hold."

"No!" I say in dismay. "You can't go!"

"I don't have anything here." Ryan speaks evenly, but there's a bubbling, self-hating anger in his voice.

"You could! You might! Look, maybe I . . ." I check myself.

"You what?" Ryan tilts his head, suddenly alert.

"I . . ."

Oh God, oh *God*. I take a swig of wine, playing for time, trying to understand my own contradictory brain process. A moment ago it seemed *unthinkable*, the idea of claiming that IOU, actually going and claiming it. The very thought made me shudder. It was unpalatable. Grasping. Just . . . no way. Never.

But now my thoughts are swinging the other way. Am I being too precious? Maybe I *did* save Sebastian millions of pounds. Maybe he *does* owe me something proper. Something big.

Besides which, Ryan would be a great employee. He's so bright and experienced. He's been through such a lot. He deserves a chance—and what he says is true: He might not get through the application process. It's brutal out there. And if I don't do something, he'll disappear back to L.A. before we've even had a chance to . . .

Anyway, Sebastian can always say no. This last thought bolsters my confidence. He can always say no.

"I'll do it," I say in a rush, and take another swig of wine before I can change my mind.

"You," says Ryan, "are a star." And he leans over to kiss me in a way that makes my head sing. "An absolute star, Fixie. To Fixie." He lifts his wineglass and my cheeks glow.

"What's going on?" says Leila, coming into the kitchen, clutching Jake's cigarettes.

"Fixie's got Ryan a job!" says Jake, and he grins at me, a proper affectionate grin.

"Fixie!" exclaims Leila. "You're brilliant!"

"Isn't she?" says Ryan, his arm around my shoulders.

I feel warm and radiant, basking in all this approval. It's so unfamiliar. It's so *lovely*. Ryan leans over to kiss me again—and this time his hand creeps up my thigh—and any remaining doubts I had are swept away. I'll get Ryan a job, he'll love me for it, Jake will be impressed . . . everyone will be happy!

After I've finished clearing up the kitchen, we watch TV for a while—but I can't concentrate. I'm too aware of Ryan sitting next to me on the sofa, his thigh brushing against mine, his arm draped around my shoulders. Are we really back on? Properly?

"OK, we're off," says Jake as the show ends, and Leila immediately gets to her feet. "Coming, Ryan?"

"Not yet." Ryan gives my arm an invisible squeeze. "I'll hang out here a bit longer. That's OK, isn't it, Fixie?"

"Fine," I say, my voice a little thick. "Yeah. Why not?"

I don't know how I'm managing to sound so calm when my brain is shrieking, *He's staying! It's happening!*

Should I quickly take a shower?

No. Do *not* leave his side.

Oh God, it's been over a year. Do I even remember what I'm *doing*?

"Fair enough." Jake raises his eyebrows at the pair of us, and Leila comes over to kiss me goodbye, her eyes dancing with excitement as she glances at Ryan and back at me.

"Fixie, you look lovely," she murmurs in my ear. "But let me quickly . . . your parting . . ." I feel her tugging at my hair. The next moment she's got the lip gloss out again and she's smearing it on my lips. She's giving me a *touch-up*?

"Thanks, Leila." I can't help smiling, and she clasps my hand fervently as though to say, "Good luck."

And then they've gone and it's the two of us. At last. There's a breathless, silent beat—then Ryan leans over to kiss me properly, deeply, his hand cradling my head. I can feel my whole body responding. Remembering. *God,* I've missed him.

I hadn't realized how desperate I was. Two tiny tears are leaking out of the corners of my eyes and I quickly blink them away, because I don't want Ryan to think I'm getting all serious or anything. I'm not. It's just I thought this might never happen again. Ever.

I keep catching my breath, because he's even hotter than he was before. He's so pumped up. His biceps are about *twice* the size they were last year. I run a hand over his broad, rock-hard chest and feel a wash of lust so strong, I can hardly breathe. But somehow I murmur, "Shall we go upstairs?" and he nods and leads me out of the room.

"How big is your bed?" he asks teasingly as we go up the stairs, and I realize he's never been to my bedroom before. Last year, he was staying in an empty flat in Canary Wharf that belonged to some movie friend of his. We spent all the time there, on the luxurious super-king.

Well, mine isn't super-king, but at least I changed the linen yesterday.

"It's big enough." I smile as I pull him into the room and we tumble onto my bed. We're kissing and rolling back and forth and Ryan is unbuttoning my shirt, and I'm trying to unbutton his at the same time. Our fingers keep getting tangled up and at last I start giggling.

"OK," says Ryan, sitting up, giving me a mock-serious look. "Enough. One at a time."

He takes off his shirt and I suck in breath at the sight of his tanned, rippled torso. He looks *phenomenal*. I can see him checking out his own reflection in the mirror opposite, and I say admiringly, "You've been working out."

"Yeah." He nods matter-of-factly. "I bench a hundred kilograms every day."

"Right," I say, hoping I sound suitably impressed. "Amazing!"

I'm a bit hazy about benching levels, but that sounds enormous. I've got a pair of weights, but they're only five kilograms each. How does he even lift one hundred up in the air? Does he have help? I'm about to ask, "Do you have help?" when I realize that might not be the thing to say.

"Amazing!" I say again instead. "You look so hot."

"You look hotter," says Ryan, slowly pulling off my shirt. "God, I've missed you, Fixie. You should have come out to L.A. with me. Maybe everything would have been different."

I blink at him in shock. I should have *come out to L.A.*? He never said anything about coming out to L.A. I would have been there like a shot.

"I don't remember being invited," I say, making sure I sound light and jokey.

"I should never have let you go." He shakes his head. "That was my big mistake. You and me, we're good." His hands are running over me tenderly. "We're just *good*, you know what I mean?"

I want to cry out, "Yes! I do know what you mean! Of course I do!"

But thankfully I'm not quite that uncool. Not quite.

"Well, we're together now," I say, my voice husky. "Let's just enjoy . . . the moment."

I pull him playfully backward onto the bed. And he's leaning in to kiss me, when he stops.

"What's that?" he says curiously, peering over my shoulder. I follow his gaze and freeze dead in horror. *Shit*. How can I have been so *stupid*?

The thing with bedrooms is, you get used to them. You get used to your faded lampshade and your creaky wardrobe door and the stack of books in the corner. You stop noticing them. And you also stop noticing your pile of school memorabilia on the window seat, topped with a framed photo of . . . guess who?

"Is that *me*?" Now Ryan is leaning over and grabbing the photo, in fascination.

"Oh, right!" I try to laugh casually. "Yes, maybe! I've still got all this old school stuff. . . ."

I'm expecting him to comment on me having a framed photo of him, but he doesn't; he silently peers at the image. It's a picture I took once of him and Jake, leaning against the school fence. (I cropped Jake out.) Ryan's smiling, his school tie askew and his sleeves rolled up. His hair is gleaming. He looks golden. Perfect.

"I had no definition in those days," he says at last with a frown. "I was a skinny bastard."

"You were gorgeous," I contradict him, and run a hand over his back, but he doesn't seem to notice. He's reaching for an old DVD labeled *Jake's Park Picnic*.

Oh *God*.

"Is that our Park Picnic?" he says incredulously, taking the DVD out of its box. "Is this a video of it?"

"Er . . . yes," I admit. "I filmed the football match and stuff."

The Park Picnic is a tradition at our school—all the leavers head there after their final classes and there's a football game and they all drink beer and make a mess and residents write to the local paper and say it's a disgrace. I wasn't even supposed to be there, but I snuck along with Hannah and filmed it. Well, I filmed Ryan, mostly. I didn't know if I'd ever see him again.

"The football match." His eyes light up. "I remember that. Let's put it on."

It takes me a moment to realize he's looking at my TV. He means right *now*? Is he *joking*?

No. He doesn't seem to be.

Well, I guess we can put sex on hold for a bit. It's not like I'm desperate. (I *am*. I *am* desperate.)

I load the DVD and we wait for a few silent moments— then suddenly we're looking at a sunny day, fourteen years ago. The park is crowded with kids lolling on the grass, swigging beer, and playing football. Some of the guys are barechested, like Ryan, who's playing football, beer in hand, laughing and joking and looking like what he is: the golden boy of the school.

I remember filming him, creeping forward to the sidelines of the football game with my video camera, borrowed from Mum. And watching it later, over and over.

"Oh, Fixie," says Ryan, with a massive sigh. "How did we end up here?"

I glance at him and my heart sinks slightly. His brow is knotted in a morose expression which I recognize from drunken evenings out with Jake. It's the why-am-I-so-bloody-old look, which swiftly leads to the what-happened-to-my-life speech.

I mean, fair enough, I think those things too; everyone does. But we didn't come up here to think about how crap life is. We came up to *have sex*.

"I'm *glad* we're here," I say encouragingly. "We're together . . . you're going to have a great job . . . it's all going to work out."

"You think?" His eyes don't move from the screen, from his young, lithe, carefree self.

"Of course! You're Ryan Chalker!" I say, trying to impress this on him. "You know, just the *name* Ryan Chalker used to give me goosebumps. I used to see you coming down the corridor and nearly faint. And not only me. Every girl in the school felt the same. Every *person* in the school. You must know everyone had a crush on you, even the teachers."

Ryan's brow has relaxed as I've been speaking, and his hand wanders toward my thigh again.

"So what did you think about me?" he asks idly. "I mean, what was it you liked?"

"Oh God, everything! Like, your hair and your laugh, and you were so fit . . ."

"Not as fit as I am now. I didn't even work out back then." He starts kissing me again, with more purpose, then murmurs into my ear, "What else did you think?"

"I thought you were like a rock star. I thought if you asked me out I would *die*," I say honestly, and Ryan gives a soft laugh.

"What else?" he says, pulling me toward him.

This is turning him on, I suddenly realize. OK, quick, say some more.

"I used to think, *Oh my God, it's Ryan! He's the sexiest guy in the school!* And all I wanted to do was kiss you, but you never even noticed me because you were, like, Ryan the Sex God."

"What else?" His breath is coming quicker now. He's pulling off my underwear. I can tell he means business.

"I used to hitch up my school skirt whenever you were nearby," I improvise hastily. "And I used to watch you play basketball and . . . er . . . you were so gorgeous, I wished you were bouncing *me*, not the ball. . . ."

No, wait. What am I saying? This is gibberish. But Ryan doesn't seem to mind.

"What else?" he gasps as he enters me.

OK, it's nearly impossible, trying to summon up sexy stuff to say while Ryan is driving rhythmically into me. My mind doesn't want to work; it wants to surrender to sensation. But I must keep talking.

"That time we all went to the beach," I manage, "you looked so hot, everyone fancied you. . . ."

"What else?"

"You were so sexy . . . everything about you was amazing. . . ." My mind goes blank. "Er . . . you had really cool sunglasses. . . ."

"What about my car?" he pants, his face contorted.

"Yes!" I exclaim, grateful for the idea. "Your car! Of course. I used to love your car. It was so hot and sleek and . . . and long. And hot," I repeat for good measure. "And . . . and hard . . ." I'm racking my brain for another good word. "And throbbing," I say in sudden inspiration. "It was such a . . . a throbbing car."

"Oh my *God*!" Ryan explodes with a roar and collapses on me like a deadweight.

I don't dare to move for what feels like half an hour.

"Bloody hell," says Ryan at last, and heaves off me.

"Yes," I say faintly, because I'm fairly sure I agree with "Bloody hell," whatever he meant by it.

For a few moments we're both quiet. Ryan is staring up at the ceiling and he suddenly sighs.

"You're good for me, Fixie," he says. "Have I ever told you that before?"

"Yes." I can't help smiling. "A couple of times."

"There's been too much bullshit in my life. I need you to get me through the craziness. You know?" He turns to face me directly. "That's what I need. You."

His blue eyes are unguarded. His face is earnest. He's

playing lovingly with a strand of my hair. And I feel myself melting all over again, because Ryan needs me. Not a girl in L.A. with a perfect figure, but *me*.

"The world's a hard place," I say, groping for something meaningful to say. "But we can get through it together."

"Amen to that," says Ryan.

He leans over to kiss me on the nose, then gets up, wraps a towel around himself, and heads out to our family bathroom, while I lie on the bed, still a bit stunned.

It's happened! We've had sex. We're together! (I think.) I'm good for him. And he's *definitely* good for me.

OK. So now we need to *stay* together.

And, yes, I know I'm overthinking. I should enjoy the moment. I should lie here and relax and savor the fact that Ryan and I have got together. Nothing more, nothing less.

But I'm me. I'm Fixie. I can't help it: Already my mind is roaming ahead with urgency.

I can't bear to lose him like last time. He needs to stay in London. We need time together. We need to have a chance to mesh, to bond, to hang out, to let ourselves turn into a proper couple. But he won't stay unless I get him this job. Everything depends on that one factor—*everything*.

And as I lie there, listening to Ryan operate our dodgy shower, I start to feel serious qualms. I can't believe my entire future happiness rests on a scribbled promise on a coffee-cup sleeve.

What if it doesn't work? What if the job's been filled already?

Or what if Sebastian says the coffee sleeve was just a joke and he didn't really mean it?

He repeated his offer earlier tonight, I remind myself. And he didn't look as though he was joking. But what if he was? What if he has a very dry sense of humor?

Or what if he says the coffee sleeve *wasn't* just a joke and he *did* really mean it and they *are* still hiring . . . but even so, the answer's no?

Well. Then I'll have to persuade him. That's all.

Nine

*M*y legs don't often shake. Like, actually physically tremble. But as I turn into Clerkenwell Road, I feel as though they might suddenly give way and leave me sitting in the gutter.

I'm wearing clothes that seemed suitable for a meeting with an investment manager: a fitted skirt and shirt plus a trench coat borrowed from Nicole, from her brief stint as a City PA. It's too hot in this August weather, but it feels right. A pair of high-heeled shoes are pinching my toes. And as I tap along, I feel a bit surreal. Am I really doing this? Am I going to claim a job, worth tens of thousands of pounds, based on a scribble on a coffee-cup sleeve?

ESIM has been based in this street for two years. Before that, they were round the corner. And before that they were in Sebastian Marlowe's flat in Islington, and he used to make the team pasta every Friday night. I read that in an article in *MoneyWeek*.

I've read quite a lot about the company, in fact. I've found out exactly what ESIM does (invests in companies and funds for institutions and individuals). I know what their aim is (to help clients build portfolios with a commitment to high ethical, social, and environmental standards). I've looked up what Sebastian Marlowe does (runs it, basically).

After I'd learned all that, I had this random impulse and looked up Sebastian Marlowe on YouTube. And what I found wasn't what I expected. At least, I don't know what I expected. But it wasn't a video clip of him standing up at some big shareholders' meeting, berating the board on executive pay.

The title was "Sebastian Marlowe takes Roffey Read board to task." He stood there, holding a microphone, his frondy hair waving around as he spoke in a measured way about how unfair it was that Sir Keith Barrowdine was due to receive a pay package of £8.9 million when his lowest-paid workers scraped by on the minimum wage. Then he started on about how this once-noble company used to house its workers in cottages and feel responsibility for their quality of life, and how many people on the board today had the slightest idea of where their lowest-paid workers were housed? (He got applause for that bit.) Then he asked, was it a coincidence that so many of the lowest-paid workers were women? Then he said he represented a large number of investors who all felt the same way and the board was clinging on to old, toxic habits and it should watch out.

I mean, it was quite stirring stuff.

I looked through YouTube, and there were a couple more videos, with him saying similar things at different meetings. And then I found an interview with him in the *Financial Times,* all about how he started his company.

It said he'd lost all his family at an early age. His dad died when he was ten, then his mum when he was eighteen, and then his older brother, James, got knocked off his bike two years ago. But rather than these personal tragedies crushing him, it said, they had taught him a love of life and a passion for justice. It said his colleagues described him as cheerful, well adjusted, and compassionate, and there was even a photo of him, captioned *The Clerkenwell Crusader.*

Which should all make me feel better, because he's clearly a good person. But actually it makes me feel worse. Because here I am, coming to finagle a job out of him. OK, not finagle, exactly. But it feels a bit like that. A bit underhanded. A bit *grabby.*

Or . . . is it?

Ever since I decided to do this, four days ago, my mind has been swinging back and forth. *Be fair,* I keep thinking. That's the maxim I try to live my life by. But what's fair? One minute I think I *am* being fair. I'm totally within my rights. He owes me this. The next minute I think: *Oh my God, what am I doing? I save his laptop and in return he gives my boyfriend a job? I mean, is that justice?*

But then, he did insist he wanted to repay me, didn't he?

And maybe I *did* save him millions of pounds.

Anyway, whatever. I'm doing it. I've got an appointment in five minutes. And the thought that's powering me along is: Ryan needs this. Which means I need it too.

I've left Ryan waiting at a Starbucks round the corner. Before I went, he wrapped his arms around me and said, "It all begins here. A whole new start. Fingers crossed, eh, Fixie?"

"Fingers crossed." I nodded, breathless with nerves.

Then he smiled and said, "I know you can do it."

His blue eyes were fixed on mine in a way that I've dreamed of for *years*. I didn't overreact—I just smiled back and said, "Hope so!" But inside, I felt a kind of explosion of love. After so much yearning, here was Ryan, with me. Relying on me. In partnership with me. All the things I've so desperately wished for.

As I walk along, peering up at the office buildings, my mind rewinds over the last few days. I've seen Ryan every day, round at our house—and something's really changed between us, in a good way. Our vibe. Our *connection*. He's confided in me. Asked my advice. He always gravitates toward me—putting an arm along my shoulders or pulling me onto his knee. It feels as if we're closer than we ever have been before.

But the question that circles my mind constantly is: Do we have a viable future together? And the answer lies right here, in the office of Sebastian Marlowe.

I push the door open, take the stairs to the first floor, and there it is. A reception desk with ESIM printed in green letters on white. I can see an open-plan space with people sitting at computers and hear the hum of conversation coming from behind a door. The receptionist is a motherly middle-aged woman, and she smiles at me in a warm, friendly way.

"Hello," I begin, as confidently as I can. "I'm Fixie Farr. I have an appointment with Sebastian Marlowe."

"Of course," she says. "He's expecting you. Would you like a cup of coffee?"

"Yes, please. That would be lovely."

I'm expecting to be directed to a seating area, when a door straight ahead of me flies open—and there he is. Taller than I remember. Frondy hair shining in a little shaft of sunshine. Woodland eyes gleaming at me. An open, friendly smile.

"Hello," he says. "You came."

"I did." I can't help smiling back.

"Well, come on in!" He gestures at his door and I follow him into an office which instantly makes me feel relaxed. I don't know if it's the bright modern art or the battered leather sofa, but it feels human, despite the three computers. There's a bookshelf lining a wall and a couple of plants and a worn antique rug. The whole place feels homey.

"I'll get us some coffee," says Sebastian. "If you'd like coffee?" His brow creases. "Or I think we can run to herbal tea. . . ."

"Coffee would be great," I say. "But your receptionist said she'd get me some."

"I'm sure she did." He smiles again in that friendly way. "But she's twisted her ankle and she's supposed to be taking it easy, not that she ever obeys orders. You don't mind, do you?"

"Of course not."

As he strides out of the room, I wander over to the bookshelf. Like the rest of the room, it's pretty characterful, with books on business, novels, and ethnic-looking sculptures. The top shelf is empty apart from two modern vases, and as I survey them, I feel a familiar sensation creeping over me. The left-hand one is crooked, and I'm already itching to straighten it.

It's not my business, I tell myself firmly. *Not my vases. Not my problem. Look away.*

Oh God. But I can't look away. My fingers have started doing their *thing,* drumming against each other. How can you live with crooked vases? Doesn't he notice? Doesn't it irritate him? As I gaze at the offending vase, my feet start their stepping motion: *forward-across-back, forward-across-back*. It would be so easy to fix. It would only take a moment. In fact—

I can't bear it anymore. I *have* to straighten it. I step forward and raise a hand, and as I'm pushing it into place, I hear Sebastian's voice behind me: "Those vases haven't been touched since my grandmother placed them there, just before she died."

What? *What?*

I whip round, aghast, to see Sebastian behind me, holding two cups of coffee.

"Oh my God. Sebastian, I'm so sorry!" I say in a flurry. "I should never have— It's just, it was crooked and driving me mad, and I had to fix it. That's my flaw," I add shamefacedly. "I always have to fix things, and then I end up making everything worse, but—"

"I may not have been *entirely* serious," he cuts me off, midstream. "My flaw is: I like to wind people up. Sorry. And by the way, do call me Seb." He shoots me a mischievous grin and I can't help laughing, even though my heart is still thudding in delayed panic. What if that had been true, about the grandmother?

Or what if it had been the grandmother's *ashes*? I flinch as the horrifying thought strikes me. What if I'd come into his office, a total stranger, and messed with a memorial to a beloved relative?

"You seem worried," says Seb, eyeing me curiously.

"I was just thinking, what if that was your granny's ashes?" I blurt out before I can stop myself.

"Ah." He nods. "Yes, that would be awkward. Thankfully, my granny's ashes are safely interred in a churchyard."

It's my cue to sit down, but somehow I can't stop talking. I don't know what's wrong with me.

"We scattered my dad's ashes at sea," I hear myself saying. "It was a disaster. We threw them toward the waves, but it was so windy, they blew back in our faces, and Mum was batting at them, saying, 'You get in the sea, Mike, you obstinate sod; you know it's where you want to be,' and then this dog came running up—" I break off. "Sorry. Not relevant."

His whole family died, I remember, in a horrifying rush. And I'm standing here talking about ashes. *Shut up, Fixie.*

"Well," says Seb after a pause. "Shall we begin?"

"Yes! Sorry. Let's . . . yes."

Why did I even have to touch that vase? I'm thinking as he ushers me into a chair. I feel so angry with myself. Can't I *learn*? Can't I *change*?

Yes, I resolve. I *can* change. And I'm going to. The next time something bugs me, unless it's super-important and vital, I'm leaving it. I am *leaving* it.

"I must hear, though," Seb adds as he sits down. "What happened with the dog?"

"You don't want to know." I roll my eyes expressively and he smiles—the open, boyish smile I remember from the coffee shop. Then silence falls and he regards me expectantly.

It's time to say what I'm here to say. But I still feel rattled. I need a moment to compose myself.

"I like your office," I say.

"Oh, good," he says. "I'm glad."

"Some offices seem to say, 'Be afraid,'" I blabber on desperately. "But this one seems to say . . ." I cast around for inspiration. "It says, 'Let's get on with things; this is going to be great.'"

"Ha!" Seb seems delighted by my analysis. "I like that."

I sip my coffee, playing for time, and Seb sips his too, and there's one of those expectant, silent beats.

Come on, Fixie. Say it. Just say it.

"So anyway, I'm here to claim my IOU," I say in the lightest manner that I can.

"Great!" He looks genuinely pleased. "I hoped you were."

A tiny part of me relaxes. So he hasn't forgotten about it. And he doesn't seem offended. On the other hand, he hasn't heard what I want yet.

"OK. So." I take a sip of coffee, once more playing for time. "First of all . . . I have to ask you something. Were you serious?"

"Of course I was serious!" he says, sounding surprised. "I made you a genuine offer. I'm indebted to you and I want to pay you back for your kindness in any way that I can. Have you still got the coffee sleeve?" His mouth curves into an amused smile.

"Of course!" I produce it from my bag. "You'd better check it."

He reaches over, takes it from me, and gives it a mock-serious examination. "Yes," he says at last. "I hereby pronounce this to be authentic." He pushes it back across the desk, then faces me squarely. "So, what can I do for you?"

His eyes suddenly light up. "Did you want to take me up on the investment advice? Because—"

"No. Something else." My stomach is churning hard, but I have to press on. "Something . . ." I swallow. "A different thing."

Oh God, come on. Say it.

"Of course. Anything at all. What? Not a chocolate chip muffin, after all?" he adds with another laugh.

"No, not a chocolate chip muffin," I say, digging my nails into my palm, willing myself to say it. "Not a chocolate chip muffin." I force myself to look up and meet his gaze. "A job."

"A *job*?" I see the shock pass over his face before he can dissemble. "Sorry," he adds hastily as he notices my expression. "I don't mean to sound . . . I just didn't . . . A job. Wow. OK."

As he's speaking, I can see his brain working. I can see the cogs whirring. I don't need to point out, "You said 'anything at all.'" He's pointing it out to himself.

"I know it's big," I say quickly. "I mean, it's really big. But I thought . . . maybe we can help each other? I overheard you talking in the coffee shop, saying that you couldn't find the right person to fill a junior position. You need someone dynamic, who's been in the real world, who doesn't mind working hard, someone who wants to learn, someone who *isn't* the typical graduate . . . someone different."

As I'm talking, I can see his expression changing from wary to eager. He leans forward, gazing at me as though for the first time.

"Yes," he says emphatically, as I come to a finish. "Yes.

Yes! And I'm sorry I reacted the way I did—because what am I thinking? You'd be a perfect fit for us! I've already seen how you react in a crisis. I've seen how quick and forward-thinking you are. You're bright, you're positive, you're honest. . . ." His gaze flashes toward the vases, then glints teasingly at me. "You *clearly* have great attention to detail. . . . Basically I can say, without any further ado, we'd love to have you on the team. We'll need to talk about pay, of course. . . ."

My face is growing red. Shit. *Shit*. I need to stop this.

"Wait!" I cut off his surge of enthusiasm midstream. "No! That isn't . . . I'm sorry. I should have . . . You don't understand." I rub my face awkwardly. "Sorry, this is my fault. I thought I'd said . . ."

"Said what?"

"It's not for me. The job, I mean."

"Not for you?" he says blankly. "But—"

"I'm claiming the job on behalf of someone else. A . . . a friend." I clear my throat, trying to sound confident. "I'm transferring the debt."

The light in his eyes has faded away. For a few moments he's silent—then he says, "But I wanted to repay *you*, not someone else."

"It will be repaying me! Honestly it will. I really want to do this person a favor."

His gaze moves to the cardboard coffee-cup sleeve lying on the desk. Again I can see he's thinking hard. "Does our agreement allow for transfer?" he says carefully.

"Why not?" I say robustly, because I anticipated he might say this. "Every other kind of debt can be passed on. There's a *market* in debt, after all."

"Maybe there is," he says wryly. "That's not necessarily a good thing."

"Well, anyway. That's . . . that's what I'd like. Please."

There's silence. Seb's eyes have darkened a few shades. He picks up a stapler and starts fiddling with it, as though trying to delay his decision.

"You want me to give a job to a total stranger," he says at last.

"I'm a total stranger," I counter. "And you were hiring me a moment ago, weren't you?"

"You're not a stranger! At least—" He stops himself mid-flow, as though confused by his own thoughts, and I suddenly wonder if he feels the same way I did in the coffee shop. I heard him talking on the phone and I thought, *I get you.* Maybe he thinks that about me.

I mean, some people are like that. You instantly relate to them. Whereas others you bash away at for ages, but you'll never understand them, not in a million years. (Uncle Ned.)

"So, who is it?" I can tell Seb's trying to be positive and fair-minded. "Does she have any investment experience?"

"It's not a she; it's a he."

"Ah." Seb's face changes again, in some infinitesimal way. "Well . . . does he?"

"No. But isn't that the point? You said you want someone with experience of the world. Well, no one's got more experience than Ryan! He's started his own business, he's battled his way through Hollywood—"

"Hollywood!" Seb sounds astonished.

"He tried to make it there as a producer, but he found it

so dishonest. So *slippery*. He'd love to apply all his business principles to something more worthwhile—and what you do is worthwhile. I've seen you on YouTube," I add. "It's so inspiring, how you give all those company directors a hard time about their pay."

"Well." Seb shrugs. "It's what I believe in."

"And so does Ryan!" I say quickly. "He wants to make a difference to the world. Like you."

I'm hoping I've said enough to persuade him, but Seb shakes his head.

"I'm afraid I'm having trouble processing this," he says. "A Hollywood producer wants to take on a junior role at an ethical-investment firm? A low-salaried, unglamorous research role? Excuse my skepticism, but—"

"He's not a Hollywood producer anymore," I cut in bluntly. "He lost everything. He's had a terrible time and he knows he needs to start again from the bottom, but he's willing to work, to learn, to roll his sleeves up and get his hands dirty. . . . I mean, should he be punished because he tried and failed?" I lean forward, my voice rising passionately. "He's so talented, he has so much to offer . . . but he feels washed up. Most people wouldn't even give him a chance. But maybe you could be that person. You could change his life forever. And maybe that would be worthwhile too."

There's silence as Seb digests my words.

"You're a good advocate," he says at last. "Have you ever thought of going into law?"

"I can't spell," I say honestly, and Seb throws back his head in laughter.

"Well, you've sold me. Do I get to meet . . . Ryan, is it?"

"He's waiting round the corner," I say eagerly. "He's got his CV with him. I'll text him to come here, shall I?"

I send the text and there's a slightly awkward silence. Seb says, "I'll make some more coffee," and gets up from his desk.

He's gone for a while and I can hear him talking in a distant room. I don't try to catch what he's saying and I clamp my hands by my sides before I can straighten any more precious vases.

I'm feeling a touch jittery about Seb and Ryan meeting. I hope Ryan is open with Seb. I hope he doesn't get defensive and try to show off in that way he does sometimes. I hope he shows the real, thoughtful Ryan. The bruised, humble Ryan who's learned some tough lessons and wants to start again, however much work it takes. The Ryan I know.

As Seb comes back in, I jump. "He should be here any minute," I say.

"Great." Seb smiles, but it's not with the warmth he had before, and there's another awkward beat.

I'm desperately longing for Ryan to appear—and when at last he steps in through the door, my heart catches. With his blond hair and tan he looks like a movie star, and he greets Seb with a dazzling smile, lifting his hand for a high five. When Seb doesn't respond but extends his hand for a traditional, businesslike handshake, Ryan doesn't flicker. He simply shakes Seb's hand as though that's what he meant to do all along.

"So you're the mystery man," he greets Seb, in that charming way he has.

"I might say the same of you," replies Seb pleasantly. I can

see he's determined to be positive, and I feel a wave of gratitude toward him. He could have chucked me out, but here he
is, giving Ryan a chance. "Fixie tells me you're interested in
our junior research role."

"Oh, this is all down to Fixie." Ryan laughs. "She saved
your company or whatever, so I guess you owe her some serious payback."

I wince inside and hastily chime in, "I never said that!"

"Well, I'd be glad to have a chat," says Seb. "You've been
working in Hollywood, I understand?"

"Hollywood." Ryan winces. "Have you ever been there?
Don't. It's full of two-faced, double-crossing snakes. This
time a month ago I was sitting in the Chateau Marmont—
you know the Chateau Marmont?"

"I don't, I'm afraid," says Seb politely.

I can't help cringing. I wish Ryan wouldn't name-drop. I
mean, I understand it—he's defensive and he can't help com-
pensating. But he doesn't need to. I glance at Seb, hoping
he'll understand that Ryan's just insecure.

"Well, it all fell into place," says Ryan. "I understood my
life, just like that." He snaps his fingers. "I was in the wrong
city, wrong country, wrong career. I had two options. Grind
my way on . . . or cut my losses." He spreads his arms and
addresses Seb directly. "So here I am and I need to start again.
Whatever it takes."

"I see." Seb seems to be taking this in. "And you really
think ethical investment is the right area for you?"

There's silence. Ryan's blue eyes are flickering to Seb and
to me and around the office as though he's weighing up what
to say.

"Look," he says finally. "I don't know. I don't know all the answers. I thought film producing was for me. I was wrong. All I can say is, if you can give me a chance, if you can help me back on that ladder . . . then I'll pay you back, I'll work my ass off, and I'll appreciate it forever."

He sounds so passionate, so humble, that I want to cheer. *This* is the Ryan I love—the honest, heartfelt Ryan who's had some knocks but won't give up.

Sebastian's face has softened during Ryan's speech. Now he looks as though he has real sympathy for him.

"Knock-backs happen to everyone," he says. "And I should imagine Hollywood isn't the most straightforward place. Good for you, for wanting to start again. I mean, there'll be a lot for you to learn. . . ."

"I'm happy to learn," says Ryan emphatically. "I *want* to learn. And you know what? Maybe some of what I picked up in the film world can help you too."

Seb is silent a moment, eyeing Ryan up and down. Then he seems to come to a decision. "I'm going to bring in my head of research, Alison, if you don't mind," he says. "I'm sure she'd love to meet you."

"I'll be going, then," I say hastily. "You need to talk properly about . . . everything. Have a great chat. And thank you," I add to Seb. "Thank you so much." On impulse, I pick up the coffee-cup sleeve from where it's still lying on the desk. I grab a pen and write *Paid,* followed by the date. "More than," I say, as I give it to him. "*More* than paid."

"Well, thank you." Seb's eyes crinkle as he reads it. "I appreciate it."

"See you later," says Ryan to me. "We're meeting at Six

Folds Place, yeah? Are you a member of Six Folds Place?" he adds to Seb. "The private members' club?"

"No," says Seb. "That kind of thing isn't really my scene."

"Fair enough," says Ryan quickly. "It's all pretty fake."

"But Thai food *is*." Sebastian's eyes light up and he turns to me. "I was wondering if you could give the details of that restaurant you mentioned?"

"Of course!" I say.

His business card is still attached to the coffee sleeve, with his mobile number on it, so I quickly text him the contact details for the restaurant. I know I'm not the one being interviewed here—but even so, I feel like the more helpful I am, the better for Ryan.

"Thanks," says Sebastian, smiling at me. "Well, I guess I'll go and get Alison. Bye, Fixie."

"Bye," I say, and shake his hand, feeling suddenly shy. "And thanks again. Thanks so much."

As Seb heads out of the room, I glance up at Ryan, feeling a burst of joy. He's got a job! He's staying in London!

"You did it!" I whisper.

"*You* did it." He grins at me, glances around to check we're still alone, then pulls me in for a kiss. And I close my eyes for a moment, letting myself relax for the first time in days. No more worries! Ryan's here for good!

And I don't want to be needy. I don't want to say, "What does this mean for us?" in some pushy way, before we've even left the office. But on the other hand, why else did I make all this effort?

"So I guess things are . . . different now?" I venture. "For us? Now that you're staying?"

I feel a beat of fear that Ryan will say, "What do you mean?" or "We need to talk," or something else utterly crushing. But he doesn't. Instead, he gently cups my face with his hands, his eyes shining with an exhilaration that mirrors mine.

"I guess they are, Fixie," he says, and I can hear the happiness in his voice too. "I guess they are."

Ten

I've been to 6 Folds Place a few times with Jake, and it's really, *really* expensive. Even the doormen look expensive, all chiseled and handsome and dressed in dark-gray polo necks with intimidating expressions that seem to say, "Are you sure you belong here, because you don't look like it to us, now fuck off home."

I mean, they have a point. I don't belong here. My £19.99 shoes certainly don't belong here. But this place is Jake's spiritual home and he's invited me, so the doormen are stuck with me. (*And* my shoes.)

I know Jake and Leila are inside already, but I haven't gone in yet. I'm standing on the pavement, texting Ryan, blissfully lost in our stream of messages.

Everything's going so wonderfully, I can't quite believe it.

I hadn't heard anything from him all afternoon, so I texted him a few minutes ago: **Hope interview went well!** A moment or two later he replied:

Great!

So I texted him again: **Fantastic! You'll be boss before you know it!**

And I was going to leave it there. But then I thought, maybe it's easier to address the situation by text than face-to-face? Maybe I should say the things I want to say? So I plucked up all my courage and typed:

What now?

In case he didn't understand what I meant, I sent a quick follow-up:

Where are you going to live now that you have a job? Because the offer's open to come to mine.

I sent it, then worried that I was being too pushy. So I sent a quick additional text:

Only if you want to.

There was silence for a while. I stared at the screen breathlessly, my heart thudding, my fingers clenching the phone, waiting . . . waiting . . .

And then it happened! The miracle! He replied:

Totally. Awesome. Let's make it happen. Soon!

That's what he actually wrote. I've read it about twenty times, to make sure. He wants to move in with me. Ryan Chalker wants to move in with me!

I mean, in some ways it's no surprise. I've felt like we're on a more stable footing ever since he said he wished I'd come back to L.A. with him. Even so, I hadn't realized quite how tense I was, how fearful that I was misreading everything. But the evidence is here in my phone. In black-and-white. He wants to commit. He wants to take things to the next level. He wants everything I want!

I should go into the club—I'm already late—but I can't bear to break off our correspondence, even though I know he's on the way here. My fingers are moving speedily over the keys as I pour my heart out:

> Ryan, this is the beginning of something amazing. A whole new life. You and me. I'll stand by you as you forge your new career. I'll help you any way I can. You can bring all your stuff over anytime and we'll celebrate properly!!

I send the text, then I can't resist adding a P.S.:

> I'm so happy!!!!

Finally I compose another text, with no words but lots of emojis of champagne glasses clinking and little houses and love hearts.

I love emojis. They just, like, *say* it.

At last I put my phone away and head toward the entrance, beaming at the most intimidating doorman. No one can cast me down. No one can puncture my bubble of joy. Ryan wants to move in with me! He wants intimacy. He wants stability. He wants it soon. He actually typed that word: **Soon!**

As I enter the bar, I breathe a contented sigh and wave at Leila, who is looking ravishing in a silk cream dress and Louis Vuitton logo pumps. I'm in the same old black dress I always wear, but I've cracked open the satin knickers I got in my stocking at Christmas. So that's something.

I head over to where she's sitting with Jake, marveling anew at how amazing this place is. The carpet has a luxury softness. The chairs are heavy and stylish and sleek. The lighting glows and sparkles all around the place. The bar is made of copper. And the drinks are about fifteen quid each. Which slightly makes me want to faint—*fifteen quid for one glassful of something?*—except that Jake's already said he's paying tonight. I mean, fair enough. It's his choice to come here. But I'd be as happy with a bottle of pinot grigio at home. (And I think Leila would too.)

As I kiss them both, I see there's a bottle of champagne on the table already, and Jake pours me a glass. We clink glasses, then Jake and Leila resume their conversation about some sofa that Jake saw in the Conran Shop.

"I'm ordering it," he says. "That leather is like butter. You can go and look at it if you like, but I'm ordering it."

"We could look online for a more reasonable one," Leila ventures, but Jake scowls.

"I'm not buying some knockoff. We're having the real thing."

I've never even been into the Conran Shop, so I can't comment. Instead, I lean back and soak up the atmosphere. Music is pulsing through the air—and even that sounds bespoke and special, as if there's some band that only plays for millionaires in private members' clubs. Everything here is designed to make you feel relaxed and happy.

I'd be relaxed and happy wherever I was, to be honest. I'm more than happy—I'm euphoric. I can't stop looking down at the string of messages on my phone. *Ryan wants to live with me, Ryan wants to live with me . . .*

And then, suddenly, there he is, threading his way between the tables. I try to stay cool, but my heart has seized up. Every single woman in the place is turning to look at the blond guy with the easy stride and the tan and the Hollywood teeth, and he's walking toward *me*.

Plus he's holding flowers. Never in my wildest dreams did I imagine *flowers*.

He hands me the bouquet—stylish lilies in green waxed paper—says, "Fixie, you're a star," and kisses me.

"*You're* the star," I say, lifting a careless hand to cradle his head and murmur something soft in his ear, like intimate lovers do, although it doesn't quite work because he's already moving away to greet the others.

"Ryan!" Leila squeaks. "Yay!"

"Well done, mate." Jake high-fives Ryan, then glances disparagingly at the champagne bottle already open. "I think we need something a bit special to celebrate this." He clicks his fingers to summon a waiter, which makes me wince, because why would you do that? It's so rude. But clicking fingers is very Jake.

"A bottle of Cristal," he says grandly, and I tell myself not even to *glance* down at how much it costs, because I really will have a seizure.

"Remember when we were in the sixth form?" Jake says to Ryan. "The day we finished our exams and you blew two hundred quid on a bottle of Krug and we drank it in your garden? Well, here's my thank-you."

I remember that day too, although I don't mention it. Jake had promised me he'd tell me where they were celebrating, so I could go along too, but he never did. Then he got home all red-faced and slurry, and for the rest of the summer he talked about how he'd drunk a two-hundred-quid bottle of Krug. He even used it as a chat-up line. And it actually worked on some girls.

The waiter pours the Cristal into fresh glasses and we toast Ryan. As I sip, questions silently rack up in my mind, one by one. Does Jake really like posh champagne? Can he actually tell the difference? Can anyone? Doesn't he see the price of this and feel faint?

I don't know anything about Jake's finances, only that he's doing "well." Sometimes I think maybe he's a million-aire, he's just never told us.

"So," I say softly to Ryan as he sits next to me. "Big day. You were brilliant."

"I knew it!" says Leila, patting Ryan on the knee. "I said to Jakey, 'I know Ryan will get this.'"

"It just shows," I say eagerly. "You *can* turn your life around, however hard it seems, if you're willing to be flexible and humble and put in the hard work."

"Hard work!" Jake guffaws. "Hear that, Ryan? Hey," he adds, spotting some well-dressed guy at the bar. "That's Ed. You should meet Ed," he adds to Ryan, getting to his feet. "Come and say hello."

He doesn't suggest that Leila or I come to say hello, and to be fair I'm quite happy not to. So I sit, sipping my drink, watching Ryan charm Jake's friends.

"Yeah," I can hear him saying. "I've moved from produc-ing into investment; seemed like a good idea. Yeah, follow the money!" He gives an easy laugh, his face glowing, and lifts his glass in a toast.

I can't believe the transformation in him. He's radiant. Ebullient. Confident. If he was like a wounded lion a few days ago, that's all forgotten. Now he's the king of the jungle. The golden boy again.

And I brought it about. Me, Fixie.

"Yeah, well, they loved me at the interview. . . ." he's saying. "And of course I slipped them a tenner. . . ."

Jake's friends laugh, and I smile into my drink. I'm about to suggest to Leila that we go up and join the boys, when my phone buzzes. I get it out of my bag, planning to turn it off—but it's Mum calling. Mum!

"Hey, Mum!" I say into my phone. "Hang on a minute, I can't talk in here. . . ." As I rise to my feet, I gesture to Leila that I'm popping outside, and she nods easily.

I haven't spoken to Mum once since she left. She texted when she arrived, to let us know she was safe, but I haven't actually heard her voice. And as I hurry through the bar to the lobby, I realize I'm longing to talk to her.

"Mum!" I exclaim, as soon as I can talk. "How's it going?"

"Oh, Fixie." Her familiar tones flow into my ear. "It's lovely! I *wish* you were here!"

She says it with no irony at all. She's never done holidays, Mum. She probably doesn't even *know* that that's the clichéd phrase.

"Are you having a good time, then?" I say, smiling, wishing I could see her face.

"It's so warm!" she exclaims in astonishment, as though she was expecting the south of Spain to be a bit nippy. "We're right by the beach. I've been swimming every day. Good thing I bought that swimsuit. And the food's lovely—we're eating lots of seafood, although Karen does always order too much sangria. . . ."

As she talks on, I lean against a wall, imagining her plunging into the Mediterranean and soaking up the sun and drinking sangria with her sister. I'm thinking, *This is what she should have done years ago.*

". . . and how's the shop going?"

Mum's words bring me back to the present with a guilty twinge. I haven't really been focusing on the shop. I've been focusing on Ryan.

"It's fine!" I say automatically. "All good!"

"Ned sent me an email. He said you're having your first meeting tomorrow?"

"That's right."

"And everything's going OK with Jake and Nicole?"

It crosses my mind to tell her about Nicole's yoga plans— but no. It would worry her. I'll sort it myself.

"Everything's fine," I say reassuringly. "Couldn't be better!"

We talk for a bit longer, then Mum says she'd better go and I head back to the bar, biting my lip. Now that Ryan's future is sorted, I need to give some attention to the shop.

Ryan's still holding court at the bar and doesn't notice me at first. I wait until there's a lull in the conversation and then tap him on the arm.

"Oh, hi!" he exclaims, turning toward me. "Come and meet these guys."

"No, actually, if you don't mind, I'm going to slip away," I add apologetically. "It's the first big family meeting about the shop tomorrow. I want to prepare some stuff."

"Oh, OK," says Ryan, nodding. "Fair enough."

"See you later, then." I squeeze his arm. "Have fun!"

"Later?" He stares at me blankly. "What do you mean, later?"

"Well . . . I thought you'd be coming back to mine?" I say, equally blankly.

"Fixie." Ryan exhales with an astonished laugh. "Fixie, Fixie. What are you saying, that we should *move in* together?"

For a moment I can't speak. His words won't compute in my brain. Is he joking? Of course I think we should move in together. We were just *talking* about moving in together. But now he's sounding incredulous.

As I stare at him dumbly, wondering if I misheard, Ryan sighs and pulls me aside, away from the group.

"This is great, you and me," he says gently, pointing from his chest to mine and back again. "It's lovely. But moving in together would be the *worst* thing we could do. We need to take things slowly. Step by step."

Words are scrambling in my brain. Nothing makes sense.

"But your text," I say stupidly.

"My text?"

"About the future! Just now! I asked you and you said—" I fumble for my phone so I can read out the words exactly. "You said, **Totally. Awesome. Let's make it happen. Soon!**"

"Well, yeah." He laughs. "I *do* want to be boss soon."

Boss?

Boss?

Oh my God. I'm frozen in utter dismay as realization hits. He was replying to *that* text?

"Right, but my *other* text?" I manage, trying to sound light. "What did you . . . ? I mean, did you think . . . ?"

"What other text?" He looks puzzled. "The last text I got from you was about being the boss. Why, what did you say?"

He didn't get my text? All of my blissful happiness is based on a *misunderstanding*?

"What did you say?" asks Ryan again, and my stomach lurches in horror. *He cannot know what I said.*

"Nothing!" My voice finally bursts out in a desperate squeak. "No. I didn't say anything. Nothing. Doesn't matter."

My head is boiling. I think I want to die.

"I mean, you do get my point?" says Ryan kindly. "We've only been together for, like, five minutes. It would be ridiculous to move in together."

"God yes! Ridiculous!" I emit a shrill, fake laugh. "Believe me, moving in together is the *last* thing I want. The *last*. Although you did say you wished I'd come back with you to L.A.," I add, before I can stop myself.

Ryan looks utterly astonished.

"Fixie, L.A. is—" He breaks off as though he can't even find a word for what L.A. is. "Look, Fixie." He faces me, straight on. "I want to take us seriously. *Seriously.*"

"So do I!" I say, feeling totally confused.

"So we take it little by little, yeah?" He squints at his phone. "Hang on. Some texts are coming in now. Are they the ones you sent before?"

No. Nooo. They're arriving *now*?

"Don't read those!" My voice shoots up still higher in

panic. "They're nothing! I was just randomly chatting. . . . It was boring. . . . Actually, why don't I delete them?"

My heart thumping, I grab Ryan's phone out of his hand. Ignoring his startled look, I start frantically pressing DELETE. I'm cringing as I read my own words:

Where are you going to live now that you have a job? Because . . .

Deleted.

Ryan, this is the beginning of something amazing . . .

Deleted.

A whole new life. You and me.

Deleted.

I'm so happy!!!!

Deleted.
And all the emojis: Deleted. All gone.

As I hand Ryan his phone back, I smile as brightly as I can—but inside I'm kind of crushed. I mean, he's right. Of course he's right. I don't know what I was thinking. Long term, it's more sensible to take things slowly.

It's just . . .

I mean, you can't help wishing for things, can you?

"So, I'll see you . . . sometime!" I force myself to sound light and casual, as if I don't mind when I see him at all. As if it's no big deal. As if perhaps we won't even bother to see each other at all.

"I'll text you," says Ryan. "We'll get together soon. And thanks for today, babe."

He kisses me lightly, and I hesitate, suddenly desperate to stay. But I've already said I'm leaving and it would seem uncool to change my mind. I pick up my flowers, and as I walk out of the bar, I decide I will find five positive things about the situation.

1. *He still wants to be with me.*

2. *He didn't see my mortifying texts.*

3. *He bought me flowers.*

4.

5.

Well, anyway. Three is plenty. Plenty.

Eleven

*U*ncle Ned has booked a table at a restaurant for our meeting. It's a place called Rules, in Covent Garden, all red plush and dark wood and food like oysters and venison. As I read the menu, I can't help gasping inwardly at the prices.

"Wow," I say. "This is quite . . . grand. We normally have meetings at the shop and Mum brings sandwiches."

"Your mother likes to play things down," says Uncle Ned kindly. "It's her little affectation. But what I say is: If you mean business, then *mean* business." He lifts his gin and tonic in a toasting gesture.

"Right," I say, after a pause, because I don't want to start the evening off by arguing. But I don't get it at all. Why have we come to some luxury restaurant just to talk about the shop? My motto would be: If you mean business, then spend your money on the business, not on expensive meals.

Jake and Nicole seem happy enough, though, ordering pâté and even lobster. When we've all ordered, Uncle Ned clears his throat in a grandiose way and says, "Before we begin on this little joint endeavor, please be assured, I am merely here to facilitate. *Facilitate*, d'you see?" He looks around with slightly bloodshot eyes. "You won't want to listen to an old buffer like me. That's understood. I'm simply here to make sure you don't run the ship aground. Oh, the Chablis, I think," he adds to the wine waiter, then turns to Jake. "By the way, I take it you have a company credit card on you?"

"Oh, absolutely," says Jake at once. "I'll sort it out. All on the company."

"Good lad," says Uncle Ned, taking a gulp of his gin and tonic. "Good lad. Now, as I say, I'm here to help. To listen. To advise."

To drink gin at our expense, I think, but then immediately feel bad. Mum trusts Uncle Ned, so I should really try to as well. *He negotiated the lease,* I remind myself. *He must have a good business head. Be open-minded.*

"Right, well, why don't I start?" says Jake briskly. "I have a lot of ideas for the shop."

"I have a lot of ideas too," chimes in Nicole at once. "Loads."

"I mean, it can't stay as it is," adds Jake.

"Definitely not," affirms Nicole.

I look at them both, disconcerted. Does the shop need changing *that* much? It's a healthy business. Mum left us in charge to run it, not to transform it.

"I don't have *that* many ideas," I say. "I mean, I have a few."

"Well, let's listen to your few, Fixie," says Uncle Ned in generous tones. "Get those out of the way, as it were."

Out of the way? He sounds so patronizing I want to retort, "One good idea is worth a hundred bad ones!" Or at least blow him away with a really impressive speech.

But it's happening to me again. The sight of Jake rolling his eyes at Nicole is sapping my confidence. The ravens are flapping. My lips are trembling. As I open my mouth, my lungs seem to be working at half capacity. My voice is tiny and uncertain.

"I think we could streamline the stock. Maybe get rid of the leisure section?" I add hesitantly. "And confectionery. We only stock licorice allsorts. It makes no sense."

"Dad and I were the only ones who ever liked licorice all-sorts," muses Nicole. "He always used to say . . ."

I wait to see if Nicole is going to continue. Then, as it's plain that she's not, I take a deep breath and resume.

"I think we could lose hardware too. I know Dad loved all those sections, but they're looking out-of-date and they're the poorest performers. I think we should focus on kitchen-ware and craft. The customers love gadgets; they love advising each other and sharing their results. And everyone knows they can trust Farrs. We could make that our message: *You can trust Farrs.*"

My confidence is building as I talk; my voice is growing stronger. I'm actually enjoying sharing my thoughts.

"You know Vanessa, the customer who wears the red mac?" I continue. "Well, she recently won some big baking competition, and all her equipment was from Farrs. She came straight round to tell Mum. It was brilliant! And baking is a growing market. I have some figures, if you want to look. . . ." I get out the page of research I printed last night and put it on the table. "I think we can capitalize on this, but we need to stay on top of it. We need to follow all the TV cookery shows. Offer exactly the right equipment at the right time. And the stock should be refreshed more often. Some products sit on our shelves for years. We've got to stop that."

I'm hoping some of these ideas might spark comment— but no one says a word or looks at my research.

"Anyway," I continue, undeterred, "I think we should focus on our core business and build on the best qualities of Farrs: Trustworthiness. Value. Practical help. All the things that Dad cared about. All the things that Mum is. All the things that we are."

I look around the table, hoping I'll see the warmth I feel mirrored in my siblings' faces. Maybe we could even lift a glass to our parents. But Jake is frowning and Nicole looks lost in a daydream.

"Finished?" says Jake, as soon as I come to a halt.

"Well . . . yes," I say. "What do you think?"

"Honestly?" says Jake.

"Yes, honestly."

"I think, jeez, this is exactly the problem." He slaps a hand onto the table. "Could you think any smaller? Could you be any more parochial? Vanessa in her bloody red mac, for fuck's sake." He shakes his head incredulously. "We need as- piration. High-end. Strategic partnerships with big brands."

"We already stock big brands," I point out.

"What, 'Cake-tins-for-old-biddies-dot-com'?" says Jake scornfully. "I'm talking *lifestyle*. I'm talking *luxury*. The whole place needs a bloody reboot. Now, I met a guy at Ascot last year, works for Hannay watches. I got his card. He's someone we could do business with. I mean, we'd have to pull out all the stops to get the deal. . . ."

"Hannay watches?" I say disbelievingly. "Are you joking? Don't they cost like a thousand pounds?"

"We sell clocks," retorts Jake. "It's a natural extension." He turns to Uncle Ned. "You wouldn't *believe* the margins."

"Jake, we sell kitchen clocks," I try to point out. "None of them is above the thirty-pound price point."

But Jake isn't listening; he's pulling a brochure out of his briefcase.

"Here's another guy I've been sweet-talking recently," he says. "Comes from Prague. We've had a few dinners, went to the casino the other night."

"Work hard, play hard, eh?" puts in Uncle Ned with a chuckle.

My mouth has fallen open a little. The *casino*? When Mum and I source new suppliers, it's at trade fairs or over coffee in the back room. Not at casinos.

"Anyway, he owns a stationery company," says Jake importantly. "High-end. Gilt-edged. Wonderful. I think if we did the right deal, we could become his exclusive West London stockist."

"Good work!" applauds Uncle Ned. "It's all about networking, eh, Jake?"

I flip through the brochure, trying not to flinch. This is the weirdest stationery I've ever seen. There's a lot of gilt and bizarre colors and cards decorated with malevolent-looking mermaids. I can't see a single one of our customers wanting to buy this stuff.

"Jake," I say. "Our customers like jolly cards with jokes on them. Or Cath Kidston notecards. They're practical, sensible—"

"Exactly!" he erupts in frustration. "That's the problem!"

"Our customers are the *problem*?" I stare at him.

"London is full of glamorous, rich, international spenders," Jake says, almost fiercely. "Financiers. Lawyers. Hedgies. Why aren't *they* in Farrs?"

"Actually, Vanessa's a High Court judge," I tell him—but he's not listening.

"We need to move with the times," he says tetchily. "London is the city of the international playboy. *That's* who we need to attract."

International playboys?

I don't know what to say. I have a sudden vision of a line of international playboys in Dolce & Gabbana suits browsing our saucepans, and I bite my lip.

"We need to be forward-thinking," Jake is declaiming. "We need to turn ourselves around."

"I agree," says Nicole surprisingly, and we all turn to look at her. "Like my yoga. We're going to start a mind-body-spirit area," she tells Uncle Ned. "Evening classes. And maybe like herbal . . . you know . . ." She breaks off and we all wait politely, before realizing this is another drifty unfinished Nicole sentence.

"Nicole," I say quickly, "I know you mentioned this before, but I don't think it's practical." I turn to Jake. "Nicole wants to get rid of lots of stock so there's room for yoga classes. But we need that stock, so I don't think—"

"I think it's a good idea," Jake cuts across me. "Yoga will attract the right crowd. Pilates, yummy mummies, all that."

"A *good* idea?" I stare at him in horror. I was counting on him to nix it. "But we don't have the floor space!"

"We can get rid of some of the displays," Jake says. "All those plastic boxes, for a start." He shudders. "They're fucking depressing."

"We could sell yoga mats," says Nicole. "And yoga blocks. And yoga . . ." She waves her hands around as though words are superfluous.

"Jake, people *come* to us for food storage," I say desperately. "They know we have a good range." I feel like I'm going a bit mad here. Do Jake and Nicole actually *know* our business? "Uncle Ned, what do you think?" I say. I can't believe I'm actually appealing to Uncle Ned, but I don't have much choice.

"I think leisure is a growth area," says Uncle Ned sagely. "Yoga is very much of the times, not that I would know much about it!" He gives a hearty laugh. "What I *would* add is, if you're going to consider leisure pursuits, then consider fishing."

"*Fishing?*" My mouth drops open. What is he on about?

"There's money to be made in fishing." He eyes us all significantly. "Fishing equipment. Very popular. On the rise. Just my tuppennyworth."

I'm speechless. Is that Uncle Ned's "good business head" talking?

"Fishing," chimes in Jake thoughtfully. "I mean, it's the right image. The royal family fish."

The royal family?

"Jake," I say, trying to stay calm. "What have the royal family got to do with us?"

"I'm trying to be fucking *aspirational*," Jake snaps. "I'm trying to turn our brand around. Look at Burberry. Look at . . ."

Two waiters are approaching our table with plates, and Jake breaks off. He shakes out his napkin and scowls at me and I feel my confidence ebbing away.

"How's your own business going?" Uncle Ned asks Jake as the waiters put down our plates, and Jake gives a secretive grin.

"I'm about to make a killing on manufactured diamonds. Earrings, necklaces, all that. It's the next big thing."

"Manufactured diamonds!" Uncle Ned looks impressed. "Now, *that* sounds like the future."

Oh my God. *Please* don't suggest that Farrs should start stocking diamond jewelry.

I must be strong, I tell myself firmly. I mustn't be unnerved. I must say what I think. So when all the food has been served and wine poured out, I look around the table, screwing up courage to speak.

"I think maybe the problem is, we're not all on the same page," I say. "It's like we all think Farrs is a different thing. Maybe we need, I don't know, a mission statement?"

"*Yes,*" says Jake firmly. "That's the first sensible thing you've said."

"I've got some paper," says Nicole, hauling a notebook from her bag, with *Dream Believe Do* on the cover. "Let's all write down our ideas and, you know . . ."

She hands each of us a torn-out page and Jake summons a waiter, who gets us some pens.

"No, no!" says Uncle Ned with a laugh as Nicole tries to pass him one. "I'm simply here to facilitate." He spreads potted shrimp onto toast and takes a huge bite. "But you go ahead!" he adds, his mouth full. "Very good idea. Very good idea."

There's silence as we all eat and write. Jake finishes in about thirty seconds, Nicole seems to be writing an essay, and I keep crossing out words and starting again. But at last I'm done and I look up to see everyone staring at me.

"Sorry," I say. "I just wanted to . . ." I glance anxiously down at my page. "It's quite hard, isn't it?"

"No it's not," says Jake at once. "It's easy. It's obvious."

"Oh," I say, feeling inadequate. "Well, it wasn't obvious to me. I mean, I know what I think, but trying to express it . . ."

"You're not really a writer," says Nicole pityingly. "I've always loved creative writing."

"Well, let's go round the table," says Uncle Ned, like a headmaster at assembly. "Fixie, you start."

"OK," I say nervously. *The mission of Farrs is to sell sensible products at sensible prices, in a community of warmth and helpfulness.*

I raise my eyes to see Jake peering at me incredulously.

"Sensible?" he echoes. *"Sensible?"*

"It's a bit boring," says Nicole kindly.

"It's fucking mind-numbing!" exclaims Jake. " 'Sensible products,' " he says mockingly, making a hideous face. " 'I'd like to buy some sensible products, please.' How is *that* sexy?"

"I wasn't trying to be sexy," I say defensively. "I was trying to represent our values—"

"Our values?" Jake cuts me off. "Our values are, one,

make money, and, two, make money. You want to hear my mission statement?" He pauses for effect, then declaims, "Power. Profit. Potential."

"Ah, now, *that's* punchy," says Uncle Ned admiringly. "Say it again?"

"Power. Profit. Potential," repeats Jake, looking delighted with himself. "Says what it needs to say."

"I don't agree," says Nicole, shaking her head. "It's not all about power and profit. It's about atmosphere."

"Exactly!" I say in relief.

"It's about vibe," carries on Nicole. "It's about . . . who *are* we? I'll read you what I wrote, shall I?" She lifts up her page and clears her throat. "*Welcome to Farrs, your gateway to serenity. As you walk in through our portals, your shoulders drop. You feel yourself relax. You're on a journey. But where? Look around. See the possibilities. See a new you. See the dreams that you can achieve. Don't sell yourself short . . . but know that you can be that person!*" She's speaking with more and more emphasis. "*You can have it all. You can find peace. With the help of Farrs, you can break those barriers and climb those mountains. So near . . . so Farrs.*"

There's silence, broken by Jake giving a sudden snort of laughter.

"Sorry, Nicole," he says. "But that is gibberish."

"It's not gibberish!" says Nicole hotly. "It's inspirational! What do you think, Fixie?"

"I think it's got a really good message," I say carefully. "Only, is it a mission statement? It sounds more like, you know, the brochure to a spa."

"You're so *narrow*," says Nicole, eyeing me with disapproval. "Both of you. That's your trouble. You have such tricky personality types. I wouldn't be surprised if you're an Adder," she says to Jake. "And that's not good, by the way."

"Bring it on," says Jake unrepentantly. He hisses at her across the table, and I can't help smiling.

"That's one of my other ideas," adds Nicole, looking offended. "I want to profile everyone in the company. Then we can use people's skills better. It'll add real value. And I want to major on Instagram," she adds. "We don't do enough."

"OK, *that* makes sense," says Jake with grudging approval.

"Yes!" I say, relieved to find a point of agreement at last. "We could do far more with baking tips, we could share photos of customers' cakes. . . ."

"Always with the bloody homespun, aren't you, Fixie?" says Jake impatiently. "Instagram isn't about a few old ladies' Swiss rolls."

"It is!" I say. "It's about community and connection! What do you think, Nicole?" I lean toward Nicole, trying to engage her, but her eyes are absent.

"I think we need a face of Farrs," she says. "It was you mentioning Burberry made me think of it, Jake. Remember when Emma Watson was the face of Burberry? She was everywhere."

"Burberry," echoes Jake with a loving sigh. "*Awesome* brand."

"And the face of Farrs should definitely be me," Nicole adds. "Because I *have* been a model." She looks around as though daring any of us to point out that she only ever did one shoot, for the local paper. "We could take photos of me in store. In fact, I'm happy to take over social media. That can be my area."

"I'll focus on partnerships," Jake chimes in at once. "Build up connections with some aspirational names." He drains his glass and looks around. "Shall we get some more wine?"

"And you, Fixie?" says Uncle Ned. "What will you focus on?"

I stare at him, thoughts swirling furiously round my head. I want to say, "None of you get it! You don't understand what Farrs is!"

But who will listen to me? No one except Mum. And I'm not bothering her with this; I'm *not*.

"Fixie, you're so good in store," says Nicole kindly. "You're great with customers. You should focus on, like, sales and stock and running the staff and all that."

"OK," I say. "OK. But, listen, why don't you two come into the shop? Actually come in and see the customers and, you know, remind yourselves of what it's like?"

"Yeah," says Jake thoughtfully. "That's not a bad idea. What about tomorrow morning first thing?"

"I could do that." Nicole nods.

"The only thing is, Bob's coming in for a meeting," I say, consulting my phone.

Bob is a rock. He runs all the payroll, collates sales fig- ures, discusses big financial decisions with Mum, deals with the accountant, and basically helps with everything to do with money. Their partnership works well for Mum, because when she's being asked to spend money she doesn't want to, she says, "That's a good idea, but I'll have to ask Bob." And everyone knows that Bob is as adventurous as a pair of elasticated beige trousers. (Which also happens to be what he wears.)

"All the better," says Jake. "I haven't talked to old Bob for ages. It'll be useful to touch base with him."

"Great!" I say eagerly. "I'll text the staff to come in early."

"I'll pop along too," says Uncle Ned. "Don't want to neglect my duties!"

"Perfect," I say. "Can't wait."

I pick up my spoon and return to my soup, trying to feel optimistic. Once Jake and Nicole really look at the shop, really remember it, really *think* about it . . . surely they'll understand. After all, we're siblings. We're Farrs. We're family.

The next morning I get to the shop extra early. I hurry around, wiping surfaces, adjusting displays, and smoothing tea towels. I feel like a nervous parent—proud and protective all at once. I want Jake and Nicole to feel the way I do about Farrs. I want them to *get* it.

I pause by the wipe-clean oilcloths and stroke them fondly. They've been such a winner—we've already reordered three times. They're all in cool Scandi prints which our customers love. As I'm standing there, admiring the designs, I remember the night Mum and I sat with the catalog, choosing them. We both knew they'd sell, we *knew*.

"Morning, Fixie." Stacey's nasal voice greets me and I swing round. I need to talk to Stacey quickly before anyone arrives. "What's the big deal?" she adds sulkily, sweeping her bleached-blond hair back with silver-painted nails. "Why did we have to come in early?"

"My brother and sister are coming in," I say. "We wanted to have a quick meeting before we open. But there's another thing I need to talk to you about first. A sensitive matter."

"What?" says Stacey discouragingly. "Can I get a coffee?"

"No. This won't take long." I beckon her aside, even though there's no one else in the shop, and lower my voice. "Stacey, you mustn't give sex tips to customers."

"I don't," says Stacey seamlessly.

I breathe out and remind myself that Stacey's basic default position is denial. I once said, "Stacey, you can't leave now," and she said, "I wasn't," even though she was halfway through the door with her coat on.

"You do," I say patiently. "I heard you with that girl yesterday afternoon. Talking about . . ." I lower my voice still further. "Clips? Clamps?"

"Oh, that." Stacey rolls her eyes dismissively. "That just came up in conversation."

"In conversation?" I stare at her. "What kind of conversation?"

"I was explaining the product," she says, unperturbed. "Like we're supposed to."

"Those clips are for sealing plastic bags!" I hiss. "They're for kitchen use! Not for . . ."

There's silence. I'm not finishing that sentence. Not out loud.

"Nipples," says Stacey.

"Shhh!" I bat my hands at her.

"You think everyone who buys those clips is using them

on plastic bags?" she says dispassionately, chewing her gum, and my mind ranges swiftly over our customers.

"Ninety-nine percent, yes," I say firmly.

"Fifty percent, if that," she counters. "What about the spatulas?" She eyes me meaningfully. "You think every spatula purchase is an innocent spatula purchase?"

I gaze at her, my mind boggling. What on earth is going through Stacey's head every time she rings up a sale?

"Look, Stacey," I say at last, "you can imagine what you like. But you can't discuss any of this with customers. It's totally inappropriate."

"*Fine.*" She rolls her eyes again, as though making a huge concession. "I sold two Dysons yesterday," she adds. "One for a mum, one for her daughter. Talked them into it. The mum's recently moved house. Divorce. She's coming back to kit out her whole kitchen."

This is the thing with Stacey. The minute you're thinking she's gone too far, she pulls a rabbit out of the hat.

"Well, that's great," I say. "Brilliant work." I can hear a commotion behind me and turn to see Uncle Ned, Greg, Jake, and Nicole, all arriving together. Nicole is talking to Greg intently about something as he gazes at her, lovestruck. (Greg's always had a bit of a thing for Nicole.) Meanwhile, Uncle Ned is peering around as though he's never been here before. To be fair, it's been a while.

"Welcome to Farrs, Uncle Ned!" I say. "Do you know Stacey? And Greg?"

"Ah yes," says Uncle Ned as he looks around. "Very good, very good."

"I was wondering if we could turn the temperature up,"

Nicole is saying earnestly to Greg. "Then we could do *hot* yoga."

"Hot. Yeah." Greg gulps, his gaze fixed adoringly on Nicole. "Hot sounds good."

"What's that?" I say, suddenly noticing the wheelie case that Nicole is dragging.

"Makeup for the Instagram shoot," she says. "Next time I'll hire a makeup artist."

A *makeup artist*? I'm about to reply when Uncle Ned taps me on the arm.

"Now, Fixie," he says, gesturing at the leisure section. "*This* is where you could introduce a fishing department. Rods, nets, waders . . ."

"Er . . . maybe," I say diplomatically.

"Jesus, this place," says Jake, coming toward us, a scowl on his face. "It gets more low-rent every time I see it. What's *that*?" He lifts a packet and peers at it disparagingly.

"Muslins for making jams and jellies," I tell him.

"Jams and jellies?" he echoes in tones of utmost scorn. "Who the hell makes jams and jellies?"

"Our customers do! It's a really popular hobby—"

"So, is everyone here?" Jake cuts me off without even listening. "All the staff? Because I think we should have a word."

"Hi, Morag!" I wave as Morag comes in through the door. "OK, we're all here," I say to Jake. "At least, everyone who works today. Christine's on the other shift, and—"

"Whatever," says Jake impatiently. "Let's begin. Right." He raises his voice. "Gather round, people. As you know, my siblings and I are running the show while my mother's away, and we want change. Wholesale change." He thumps a fist into his palm and I see Stacey's eyes widen. "This place needs a boot up the backside. We want upselling. We want cross-selling. We want profiteering."

I open my mouth to protest—does he actually know what *profiteering* means?—but Jake's on a roll.

"This is a game changer, guys," he's saying. "This is where the rubber hits the road. We want to turn this place into a must-have, high-end, desirable store. Where tastemakers come. Where the beautiful people hang out. The Abercrombie and Fitch of lifestyle stores. And that's the image I want you all to project. Stylish. Hip. Sexy."

"Sexy?" says Morag, looking alarmed.

"Yes, sexy," snaps Jake. "On-trend. Modern. With it."

I can see his eyes ranging over the assembled staff with increasing dissatisfaction. Greg is gazing gormlessly at Nicole with his bulgy gray eyes. Stacey is leaning against a display, chewing gum. Morag is still bundled up in her sensible padded coat, her gray hair rumpled from the breeze. To be fair, you wouldn't walk into the store and think, *Wow, what a hip and sexy staff*.

"My turn! Let *me* say something now." Nicole gives Jake a little shove, and he scowls but lets her take the floor.

"I'm excited," Nicole begins. "Who's excited?"

There's a baffled silence, then Greg says, "Me!" in a throaty voice, and Nicole beams at him.

"There are so many possibilities here. The sky's the limit. But are you all maximizing your potential?" She eyes Morag, who shuffles backward nervously. "I want to help with that, with the use of specialized psychological profiling and teamwork. Let's use your personal qualities. Let's achieve more, letting our imaginations lead us." She makes a broad, sweeping gesture, nearly knocking a jug off the shelf behind her. "Let's use Instagram. Let's use mindfulness. Let's make change. Let's climb that mountain. Because we can do it. Together."

She breaks off into an even more baffled silence. I can see Stacey mouthing *What the fuck?* to Greg, and I should reprimand her, I suppose, but the truth is I feel exactly the same. What is my sister *on* about?

"Right!" I say, as it becomes clear Nicole has finished. "Well, thanks, Nicole, for that . . . er . . . inspiration. I think that's it for speeches," I add, "but basically we're looking at how to improve the store, so any ideas you have, please share them. Thank you!"

"Wait!" comes Uncle Ned's voice, as the staff begin to disperse. "I may be an old buffer . . ." He laughs self-consciously. "But I *have* been asked to keep an eye on this outfit, and I *have* learned a few tricks along the way. . . ." He gives another stagy chuckle.

"Absolutely, Uncle Ned," I say politely. "Please go ahead. For those of you who don't know Uncle Ned," I add, "he was Dad's brother and has a lot of experience in business. Uncle Ned, what are your ideas?"

"Well, I must echo Jake. It's all about appearance. *Appearance,* d'you see?" He wags a roguish finger. "My first impression is this: You girls should be wearing more-attractive costumes. A pretty blouse and heels—*that's* what customers want. Let's see more lipstick, perfume . . . let's see some flirting with the customers. . . ."

My face feels paralyzed. He's saying this? To the staff? *Aloud?*

"Sorry!" I gasp, finally finding my voice. "Let me clarify what my uncle is saying, to avoid any . . . uh . . . misinterpretation. By 'heels' he meant 'any heel appropriate for your general foot health.' And by 'lipstick' he meant 'lipstick is optional for employees. Male *or* female,'" I add hurriedly. "And by 'flirting with the customers,' he meant . . . 'cordial relations with customers are advised.'"

Uncle Ned looks outraged by my interruption, but too bad. *Family first* is trumped by *Don't get sued*.

"So, that's it!" I conclude breathlessly. "Again, thank you, everyone! That's all. Let's open up."

"You *should* wear lipstick," I hear Stacey saying to Morag as they head to the main entrance to open up. "Or, like, lip gloss. Or, like, lip pencil. Or, like . . ."

"Uncle Ned, I'm sorry I interrupted you," I say. "But you can't tell the staff they have to flirt with the customers. We'll get in trouble."

"Oh, all this 'health and safety' nonsense," says Uncle Ned impatiently. "I haven't the time for it!"

"It isn't health and safety," I say, trying even harder to remain polite. "Telling a staff member they have to flirt with the customers is basically, you know, sexual harassment."

Uncle Ned peers at me for an uncomprehending moment, then makes a harrumphing noise, turns away, and picks up a basket.

"Might as well pick up a few things while I'm here," he says. "Now, where can I find an iron?"

Uncle Ned heads off in the direction of the laundry section, and Nicole produces a sheaf of papers from her bag.

"Here's your psychological-profile questionnaire," she says, handing one to Greg. "It's scientifically based on, like, research, so . . ." She trails off.

"*You are invited to a party,*" Greg reads aloud. "*Do you attend?* Depends on the party," he says after a moment's thought. "If it's a Dungeons and Dragons party, I'm there. If it's a stag do, I'm there. If it's a garden party with old ladies in fancy dresses, I'm not there. If it's a—"

"It's just a party," Nicole cuts him off. "A great, fun party. The issue is, do you want to go? It's a simple question. Party or no party?"

Morag and Stacey have returned to the group by now, and we all wait for Greg to answer. He thinks for a while longer, his brow deeply furrowed, then looks up. "Is there booze?"

"Yes!" says Nicole, clearly losing her patience. "There is. Look, don't overthink it. Just write. I'm pretty sure you're an Owl," she says as she hands Morag a questionnaire. "And you're probably a Lynx," she adds to Greg. "Which means you need to work with a Fox."

"D'you think I'm a Fox?" queries Stacey, taking her questionnaire.

"No," says Nicole. "Definitely not. You're more of an Albatross."

"Then who's Greg supposed to work with?" Stacey opens her eyes wide, with that faux-innocent look she has. "I'm only wondering, because it's all so scientific and we haven't got any Foxes," she adds blithely. "Should we hire one?"

For a moment Nicole looks caught out, then she makes a sound of annoyance.

"Just do the questionnaires," she says. "I'm going to do some Instagramming. Greg, you can help."

As Nicole leads Greg down one of the aisles, Jake looks around the shop critically.

"We need to redo this place," he says. "It needs a total refit. We should have better flooring, spotlights, some awesome artwork—" He breaks off, staring at the shop door in horror. "Give me strength," he breathes. "Who is *that* repulsive wreck?"

"That's not a repulsive wreck!" I say indignantly as I follow his gaze. "That's Sheila!"

OK, so maybe Sheila isn't one of the "beautiful people." She's overweight and shabby, with her woolen hat and ancient carrier bags. But she's a regular. She's one of us. She waves at me cheerfully and heads to the back, where I know she'll spend hours examining cake liners and piping bags.

"She has to go," says Jake firmly. "She's not a good look."

"She's a customer, not a look!" I retort, but Jake's not listening.

"We need to redo the whole place," he says again, prodding at one of our functional shelves. "We should hire an interior designer."

I feel a familiar tweak of anxiety. Why does Jake always have to be so *grand*?

"I don't think we've got the funds for that," I say.

"How do you know?" he shoots back.

"Well, I don't *know*, but—"

"You know how ridiculously cautious Mum is. I'm sure

we've got a big cash reserve." Jake eyes Sheila again with distaste. "She looks like a bloody tramp."

"Well, let's introduce a dress code, shall we?" I say with a flash of sarcasm I don't usually dare use with Jake.

"Yes," says Jake with emphasis. "That is actually not a bad idea. Ah, Bob!" he adds, looking over my shoulder. "Just the man."

I turn to see Bob entering the store, in his sensible slacks and jacket, looking slightly confused at Jake greeting him.

"Hi, Bob," I say. "My brother and sister are in store today."

"I want to talk to you about money," says Jake without any preamble. "Can we go somewhere? The back room?"

He sweeps Bob off, and I look around the store to check that all is as it should be. Uncle Ned is still roaming the aisles, filling a basket with items. He's got an iron, a teapot, and one of our wipe-clean tablecloths, and I feel a sudden warmth that he's supporting us so generously.

Then, as my gaze sweeps round, I blink, disconcerted. Nicole has taken off her coat and is in tight jeans with a very revealing crop top. She's draping herself over a rack of saucepans and instructing Greg to take photos of her with her phone, while her opened-up wheelie case blocks the entire aisle.

"I need to look sexy," she says, playing with her hair. "Do I look sexy?"

"Yeah," says Greg in a strangled tone. "Yeah, you do."

"Can you see the saucepans?" I say, hurrying over. "Can you see any products in the shot?"

"It's not *about* saucepans," says Nicole, rolling her eyes. "It's about who's the face of Farrs?"

I'm about to reply when I see two women in jeans and cardigans coming in. I wait for Morag to greet them, but she's sitting on a stool, frowning bewilderedly over her questionnaire. She hasn't even *noticed* the customers. I'm about to go and greet them myself, when Stacey comes sidling up.

"I just asked your uncle if he wanted me to start ringing up his purchases," she begins. "But he said he doesn't have to pay anything because he's a temporary director?"

"He *what*?" I say, before I can stop myself.

"That's what he said." Stacey shrugs. "Reckons it's all a freebie. He's having me on, right?"

I stare at her dumbly. We've always done a friends-and-family discount of 20 percent. We haven't said, "Help yourself to anything in the shop."

Family first, I'm reminding myself frantically. I can't criticize Uncle Ned to Stacey, even though I'm secretly thinking, *How* dare *he?*

"Um . . . well . . ." I say, playing for time. "We haven't worked out *all* the details. . . ." As I'm speaking, I watch the two women in cardigans approach the display of pans where Nicole is posing. They peer round Nicole at the pans for a few moments, then one of them says, "Excuse me? Can I have a look?"

"Sorry, I'm in the middle of a photo shoot," replies Nicole impatiently.

"Oh," says one of the women, looking discomfited. "Well, could we just—"

"It *is* quite important," Nicole cuts her off. "Could you go and look at something else first?"

My jaw sags in horror. That's a *customer*! I'm about to hurry over and say to Nicole, "What do you think you're doing?" when I see Uncle Ned behind me.

"I'll just take a few more bits and pieces," he says happily, reaching for an eggcup. "Now, Fixie, do you stock such a thing as a toast rack?"

"Um, Uncle Ned, about the friends-and-family dis-count—" I begin, but I'm cut off by Jake striding back onto the shop floor.

"The whole place clearly needs a rethink," he's saying air-ily to Bob, who looks a bit freaked out. "I think the priority has got to be a hardwood floor, don't you?"

A hardwood floor? A priority?

"Greg!" Nicole suddenly screeches. "Not like *that*. Don't you know *anything* about Instagram?"

"*You fancy the guy next door . . .*" Morag is reading aloud from her questionnaire, looking utterly perplexed. "*What do you do about it? One: Look him up on Tinder. . . .*"

Blood is thumping through my temples as I look from Morag, peering at her questionnaire, to Nicole, who's try-ing to balance a saucepan on her outstretched fingers while Greg takes a photo. I turn to gaze at Uncle Ned, still contentedly filling his basket up with our stuff, and then Jake, who is now talking to Bob about the "Ralph Lauren look."

I don't know where to start.

I think I'm going a bit mad.

"Hey, Fixie," comes Stacey's sardonic voice in my ear. "I

know they're your family and all." She pauses and leans closer. "But they're shit."

For a flustered moment I don't know how to respond.

"No, they're not!" I retort at last, trying to sound convinced. "That's totally . . . They're . . ." I wince as Nicole drops the saucepan with a clatter and exclaims, "Oh, it's dented now! Greg, get another one."

"Look at them," says Stacey, unmoved. "They don't know anything about Farrs. All I'm saying is . . . you better watch out."

When I get home that evening, I'm bone-weary. It's been exhausting trying to wrangle each member of the family in turn. Uncle Ned was "offended to the core" that I'd thought he was trying to purloin goods for free. "Naturally" he'd only meant a 40 percent discount.

So then I had to explain that our discount is 20 percent. Whereupon his mouth curled up and he put back the teapot and the tablecloth.

Greg and Morag finally completed their psychological questionnaires, then vigorously disputed the results. Morag, in particular, was highly offended to be told she was a Goat. It didn't help that Nicole started her spiel by saying, "The Goat is what we call a *negative* personality, so you might want to work on your positive qualities, Morag."

Morag went all pink and huffy, but Nicole didn't even notice. Meanwhile, Greg had looked all the profiles up online and decided he wanted to be a Lion. But Nicole said he couldn't be a Lion, he was the *opposite* of a Lion. So he answered the whole questionnaire again with different answers but he still wasn't a Lion, he was a Pony. Whereupon he sulked for the rest of the day.

I'm sure all this personality stuff makes sense with a trained, tactful person doing it. But Nicole isn't trained *or* tactful. All she's achieved is to upset people. Only of course I couldn't say anything negative in public, so I filled one out myself and listened while Nicole explained it to me. I can't even remember what I was—maybe a Panda? (Stacey refused to do hers. She said, "I know which personality I am already. I'm Stroppy Bitch.")

Then we tried to look at how Nicole's yoga class was going to work and nearly had a massive row in public, because all she kept saying was, "You promised me space, Fixie, you promised me space," but didn't seem to have any idea where the space should come from. We compromised in the end by getting rid of the leisure section, reducing the baking section, and halving the glassware, but it's not ideal.

At least I managed to talk Jake out of booking hardwood-flooring companies to come and quote next week. But I gave in over the "relaunch." He wants to throw a party and invite "cool people" and "influencers" and "put Farrs on the map."

I mean, whatever. If he can get some cool people to come along to Farrs, then good luck to him.

I dump my bag and jacket in the hall, head to the kitchen, and stop in delight. Ryan is sitting at the table, drinking a beer, watching the news on our tiny TV, and scrolling down his phone. He looks so at home, I feel a bubble of joy expand inside me. He's here! I honestly thought—

Well, I didn't know what to think. He was so casual when

we said goodbye the other night, I was afraid he might already be moving on. So somehow, these last two days, I've forced myself *not* to text him constantly but to play it cool. Wait for him to make the next move. And it's worked!

"Hi!" I say. I'm trying to sound casual, but my voice is giddy with relief. "Didn't expect you tonight."

"Nicole let me in," he says, standing up. "I thought you'd get back earlier."

"We had a crisis over a damaged delivery," I say apologetically. "It tied me up."

"No biggie." He smiles. "You're here now."

He pulls me into his arms and I close my eyes, almost swooning as our mouths meet. I hadn't realized how desperate I was for him. The touch of him, the scent of him . . . the *himness* of him.

It's been so long since I had a proper boyfriend. Not that I would admit this to him.

"So how's it going?" I draw back and survey his face. "How's the job?"

The only two texts I've sent Ryan were wishing him luck with the job and then asking how his first day had gone. He didn't reply to either, but I figured he was super-busy.

"It's great!" His face creases into a smile. "Couldn't be better."

"Fantastic!" I say in delight. "So you like the work?"

"Love it," he says emphatically. "And I think I'll be good at it, you know? I'm not saying I'm an expert, but I get what they're trying to do. What *we're* trying to do," he corrects himself, a little self-consciously, and I give him another hug. This is all even better than I hoped.

"I'm so happy," I murmur against his shoulder. "I really hoped it would work out. And is Seb a good boss?"

I ask it more for form's sake than anything else, and I'm surprised when Ryan stiffens slightly.

"He's fine," he says after a pause. "He's OK."

"Only OK?" I feel a tad disappointed. I don't know why, but I assumed Seb would be a brilliant boss.

"No, he's great," Ryan backtracks. "He's fine. All good." He flashes a smile and I automatically return it—but I'm still preoccupied.

"So, what's the issue?" I can't help probing.

"Nothing." Ryan brushes it off. "I shouldn't have said anything. He's great."

"But . . . ?" I persist. I know there's a "but," and I *have* to know what it is.

"OK." Ryan exhales. "Well, I guess there's a bit of tension."

"*Tension?*" I stare at him. "Why would there be tension?"

"It's tricky." Ryan hesitates as though marshaling his words. "Thing is, people in the office are coming to me. Asking my opinion. And Seb doesn't like it." Ryan winces. "I think he's threatened."

"Why would Seb be threatened by you?" I say, astonished. "He set up his own investment company. You don't know anything about investment. How can you be a threat?"

I have a flashback to Seb in his office. His open manner. His laugh. He doesn't seem like he would be threatened by anyone. He seems like the type who would be interested in all viewpoints.

"I agree!" Ryan exclaims, nodding vigorously. "I'm a beginner! But here's the thing: I knew a lot of people in the States. Entrepreneurs, tech companies, environmental out-fits . . . I picked stuff up. And the guys want to hear it. All except Seb. He's a nice guy but closed-minded. He likes his 'process.' "

I'm silent for a moment, digesting this. This isn't what I imagined of Seb—but then, I've only had a few conversa-tions with him, I remind myself. I've never seen him in a work situation. Maybe he's more cautious and set in his ways than he appears.

"We had a big meeting yesterday," Ryan continues. "Who ends up taking it? Me. They're talking about tech. I let them have their say, but then I'm like, 'Have you even *been* to San Francisco? Have you met the guys at the cutting edge? Be-cause I have. I know their names. I've swum in their fucking *pools*.' "

"Wow," I breathe. "That sounds amazing!"

"I was telling them about tech start-ups they hadn't even heard of." Ryan nods. "They were writing it all down. Lap-ping it up."

"So what's the problem?"

"Seb," says Ryan, rolling his eyes. "Didn't like it."

"How could he not like it?" I say, perplexed. "You're only sharing information."

"He's a control freak." Ryan shrugs. "He's like, 'Stay in your box, Ryan.' But I don't stay in boxes. Sorry, but that's who I am."

His California-blue eyes are shining and he's brimming over with energy. I have a sudden vision of him taking a boardroom by storm. Blowing everyone away with his charisma and insider knowledge. Of course he's made an impact, how could he not? And maybe he's right—maybe Seb doesn't like it.

"Well, it's early days," I say at last. "I'd tread carefully if I were you. Be tactful."

"Oh, I am." Ryan nods again. "And you know what, I'm not complaining. It's all good. The main thing is, I'm in work, and that's down to *you*."

He looks so radiant, I can't help beaming back.

"I'm so proud of you," I say, gazing up at him. "They're lucky to have you!"

"Fixie," he says affectionately, and kisses my nose. "Every guy needs a Fixie, you know that?"

"I've missed you," I murmur, running my hands down his back.

"Mmm, me too," he says, but he doesn't kiss me again. He's looking at his phone over my shoulder, I realize.

I mean, fair enough. People can look at phones. It's not against the law.

I move my hands still lower and caress him, trying to make my meaning plain. I've been *longing* for Ryan. All I want to do is go upstairs and reunite properly and forget everything else. But Ryan doesn't respond.

"Hmm," he says vaguely—then he focuses on me as though for the first time. "You know what? I'm ravenous. And I've got a stack of washing in the hall. Jake and Leila's machine is bust."

"Oh," I say, halted. "Well, I'll put that on here. And let's eat. We've got some steak," I add, opening the fridge and peering in. "Does that sound good?"

"Awesome," says Ryan, wandering out. "Tell me when it's ready. I'll find something on telly."

As I get the frying pan from its rack, I don't know exactly how to feel. Deep down, I was hoping that Ryan would sweep me upstairs at once and ravish me. And even more deep down—like, *fathoms* down—I was hoping he might say something like, "Fixie, I love you." Or: "Fixie, I've always loved you, it's always been you, have you never realized that?"

No, stop it. Let's not aim too high.

Anyway, this is better than rushing off for instant sex the minute I set foot inside the door. It's *far* better.

Isn't it?

Yes, I tell myself firmly. It's definitely better. Because he wants to be with me for me. Not simply for sex but *as a person*.

The TV comes on in the other room, and the familiar sound fills me with a sudden wave of warmth. Of course this is better. Of *course* it is! Here we are, a proper domesticated couple, making supper and asking about each other's day. It's what I always wanted. Coziness. Intimacy. We may not live together, but it's as good as.

As I start to peel a potato, I find myself humming happily. There was Mum, saying Ryan was flaky. And Hannah, saying it would never last. But they were both wrong. He's here! With me! All the troubles of the day are starting to recede, even Uncle Ned. The point is, if you have someone to come home to, nothing's that bad, and now I have Ryan to come home to. My teenage self still can't quite believe it, but it's true! Ryan Chalker is here and he's mine.

Twelve

A month later, Mum is in Paris. I can't quite believe it, but she is. She's posted a million pictures of herself and Aunty Karen on her new Facebook page. (Mum? *Facebook?*) There are shots of Mum at the Eiffel Tower, Mum sitting at a pavement-café table, and Mum with Aunty Karen in white robes at a spa. (Mum? A *spa?*)

As I say, it's unbelievable. Although, to be fair, there's a lot about life at the moment that I can't quite believe. I can't believe that Ryan and I are still together as a couple, in a solid domestic routine that makes me want to hug myself with joy. He comes round at least twice a week and I cook for him and we watch telly and it's lovely. It's low-key. It's mellow. All the things I never dared to dream that Ryan and I might be.

Nor can I believe that we're hosting a party tonight at Farrs to "reposition" ourselves—Jake's word, not mine—for which he's hired a red carpet and a photographer and a DJ and a bouncer. (A *bouncer?*)

But above all, I can't believe what Hannah is telling me about her and Tim. This can't be right; it *can't.*

We're in the back room at Farrs, touching up our makeup

together. Jake has renamed the room "Backstage" for tonight and has equipped it with three bottles of champagne,
one of which Hannah immediately opened.

"He just announced it," she's saying miserably, taking a
gulp. "He sat down on the sofa and said, 'I don't want a baby
anymore.'"

"How can he not want a baby anymore?" I say, incredulous. "Your whole *life* has been about trying for a baby."

"I know! He says he's changed his mind. He says he's allowed to change his mind and he doesn't have to explain it.
What kind of person says that?"

Tim, I silently answer.

"Maybe he's just having a wobble," I say. "Take him out
to supper, have a glass of wine, and talk it through."

"Yeah, maybe." She looks doleful. "I dunno. We're not
getting on too well."

"Really? Why not?"

"It's my fault." Hannah hesitates. "I've been off my game.
We had a big row at the weekend. I . . . I put my foot in it. I
upset him."

"How?" I can't help asking. Tim is basically made of Tef-
lon. I can't even *imagine* Hannah upsetting him.

"It's kind of mortifying." She stares into her glass.

"What?" I say, agog. "Hannah, come on. What?"

"We were at this dinner party," says Hannah reluctantly.
"The talk turned to male circumcision and sex. I'd been
working since six A.M., by the way," she adds defensively.
"My brain was fried. I couldn't think straight."

"I'm not going to judge you!" I exclaim. "What did you
say?"

"OK." She breathes out. "So everyone was discussing whether circumcision affects sex. And I said to Tim, across the table, 'Well, you're not circumcised, are you, babe? And it doesn't make *you* any less sensitive.'"

"What's wrong with that?" I say, puzzled. "I mean, it's a bit indiscreet. . . ."

"You don't understand." Hannah shakes her head wildly. "He looked at me with this horrible flat look, and he said, 'But, Hannah, I *am* circumcised.'"

"Oh my God!" I clap my hand over my mouth. "*Is* he?"

"Yes! He is! He always has been! I don't know what happened. I must have had a brain-freeze."

"Shit!" I quell a sudden terrible urge to laugh. *I mustn't laugh.*

"It was *so* embarrassing." Hannah screws up her face in agony. "The whole table heard. They were like, 'How can you not know if your own husband is circumcised or not? Have you never even *noticed*?' They teased us all evening. And Tim . . ." She pauses. "He didn't take it very well."

"Huh," I say, regaining control of myself. "That's understandable."

"I know. I mean, what he should have done was say nothing. How would anyone have known? I told him that afterward. I said, 'Why did you even open your mouth?' But it didn't help."

"Right," I say, a bit lost for words. "Well—"

"How could I forget my own husband's *penis*?" Hannah's voice rises in agitation. "His *penis*?"

"Er . . ." I peer at her strained face. "Hannah, don't take this the wrong way, but is there any chance you're pregnant already? You might have got . . . I dunno. Pregnancy tension or whatever?"

"No! I haven't got pregnancy tension; I've got trying-for-pregnancy tension!" Hannah erupts. "It's turning me into a madwoman! How do people *do* it?"

"I have no idea," I admit. "Look, try to forget about it. You'll pull through. Tim and you are solid."

"Yes." Hannah seems to calm down a bit. "Maybe. Anyway, this is your evening. Let's not talk about me anymore. It looks amazing out there!" She gestures toward the shop floor.

The place has been transformed for the party. Jake closed early and brought in a team of removers. They've packed away about half the stock, got rid of the display tables, put up lights and a bar for drinks. A DJ has set up speakers and a laptop. There are also massive posters everywhere, with Nicole's face blown up huge and MEET THE FACE OF FARRS printed at the bottom.

I mean, to be fair, it *does* look amazing. It just doesn't look much like a shop. Let alone our shop.

"So, who's coming tonight?" inquires Hannah.

"Up to Jake." I spread my hands. "This is his thing. He says it's a 'curated' guest list."

"Oh, *curated*," says Hannah, and shoots me a sardonic look, which I return.

Hannah is the only person to whom I will ever be disloyal about the family, because basically she *is* family. So she knows what I think of Jake. And all Jake's ideas.

"He went through the customer database," I tell her, lowering my voice. "And he chose all the ones with posh post codes."

"Posh post codes!" echoes Hannah incredulously. "What counts as posh?"

"God knows. And he's got an 'influencer' coming. This YouTube girl called Kitten Smith. And the local press. And we've all got to look 'glamorous and sophisticated.' Jake gave all the staff a lecture today. Poor Morag looked totally freaked out."

"Well, you look very glamorous and sophisticated," says Hannah loyally, and I roll my eyes with a grin. I went to get a blow-dry this afternoon, but no way was I splashing out on a new dress, so I'm in the dark green shift I wore to be Nicole's bridesmaid. "What does your mum think?" Hannah adds. "Isn't this costing a fortune?"

"Mum's OK with it," I say with a shrug. "She says it's Jake's thing and it's harmless enough."

I try not to give away my sense of betrayal. I phoned Mum up two weeks ago because I was worried about all Jake's grandiose party plans. I wanted her to agree with me and tell him to rein it in—but she said, "Ah, love, I'm sure he knows what he's doing," in her easy way. And I didn't want to press it and cause stress and ruin her holiday. So here we are.

"There's a red carpet when you come in," says Hannah, her mouth twitching. "A red carpet."

"I know," I say. "Jake says it's for 'VIP photo opportunities.'" I meet her eye and bite my lip and suddenly I can feel giggles rising up. It all seems so ridiculous. Although maybe Mum's right—maybe Jake understands promotion in a way we don't.

"He's given the shop a total makeover," I add. "Him and

Nicole. They insisted. They want it all to look more 'cool.' You know Nicole's started yoga classes?"

"I got her email." Hannah nods. "To be honest, I thought, *Why would you do yoga at* Farrs?"

"Exactly! But she's got about six friends who do it, and she keeps moving the front displays and it's been *so* disruptive. She and Jake have cut the food storage department by half, and they've lost the jam-making department completely, and Jake's brought in these really expensive garden lanterns that his friend imports. I mean, garden lanterns when we don't have a garden department!" My voice rises with indignation. "Why are we stocking them but not the full range of storage containers?"

"I know," says Hannah sympathetically, and I belatedly remember that I ranted to her about this a few days ago. "But there's nothing you can do about that now, is there? Try to forget about it, Fix. Enjoy the evening." She tops up my glass. "Is Ryan coming?"

"As soon as he finishes at work," I say with a nod.

"And how's it going?" She raises her eyebrows meaningfully.

"His work, you mean? Or us?"

"Both," she says. "Everything."

"Well, *we're* great," I say firmly. "We're like an old married couple."

And it's true: I've felt really close to Ryan these last weeks. It's all so natural and lovely. I've come to expect his presence in the house, once, twice, or even three times a week. And our relationship is . . .

Well.

I mean, it's a *bit* different from the way I imagined. We don't have *quite* as much sex as I thought we would. There was that one time, when we first got together, and since then it's been . . . I guess the word would be *sporadic*. Or maybe *intermittent*. Five times in total is what it boils down to. In a month.

But what that says to me is that Ryan needs to be nurtured. He needs to heal. He's been through a very tough, humiliating time, so his libido has inevitably gone down. It's totally normal. (I googled it.) And the last thing I must do is make him sensitive or self-conscious about it. So I haven't even *mentioned* it. I've just looked after him in the most unconditional, supportive way I know. Good home-cooked food, lots of hugs, lots of listening.

"And his job?" inquires Hannah.

"Patchy," I admit. "Not straightforward. He's having power struggles in the office."

"Power struggles?" Hannah opens her eyes wide. "Already?"

"Don't repeat this," I say quietly, "but the boss—that guy I met—is jealous of Ryan. He *said* he wanted someone with experience of the world—but when it came to it, he didn't. He wanted the same old thing: a young, wide-eyed intern he could push around and not be threatened by. It's a shame."

I've been really disappointed in Seb. It just shows: You can be completely wrong about someone. Apparently he's insisted that Ryan stop attending some of the meetings he was going to—which makes no sense, because how's Ryan supposed to learn the business? Ryan's theory is that Seb now bitterly regrets hiring, as Ryan puts it, "a man, not a boy." Especially as the rest of the company love Ryan and keep asking his opinion.

"Hmm." Hannah thinks about this. "Can't Ryan keep his head down?"

"He does. As much as he can. But, you know, he's Ryan." I spread my hands. "If he thinks someone's going to make a bad decision, he'll tell them so."

As I speak, I feel a little glow of pride. It's exactly *because* Ryan won't keep his head down that he's such a remarkable guy. He says he can see at least ten ways in which ESIM is going wrong. He says he's not going to rest until he makes his case, and already people are cornering him, asking his advice. He reckons Seb is a nice guy but doesn't know how to manage people, and the company has grown too fast, too soon. "It's all over the shop," he keeps saying, shaking his head. "All over the shop. They've got no idea."

He talks quite a bit about someone called Erica, who is apparently the oldest and most experienced person on the team. She's a massive fan of Ryan's. She reckons he's much more a natural leader than Seb and could run things in a heartbeat. But Seb essentially owns the company, so there's not much chance of things changing.

At first I found it dizzying, the way Ryan was already talking about leading. But I've gradually got used to him, to his huge ambition. He sees the world as a place to conquer. When he tells me how he made it through Hollywood, it's like listening to an SAS commander talking about a campaign. And, yes, he crashed and burned—but isn't that the same with any success story? Great leaders fail, learn, pick themselves up, start over, and reach even greater heights.

"Anyway, he'll work it out," I conclude. "He gets on with a lot of the team, at least. They go out together and play pool, like, three times a week. It's nice."

"Well, here's to it all working out," says Hannah, and we're clinking glasses when in come Morag, Greg, and Stacey.

My jaw drops at the sight of them. They're all in party clothes, but none is what I would call "glamorous and sophisticated." Morag is in the most lurid, shiny purple dress I've ever seen, with shoulder pads and a peplum. As she moves, it turns blue under the lights. It's hideous. Where did she even *get* it from, the Flammable Dress Shop?

Stacey is in a dress which essentially consists of a set of black lace underwear with black chiffon draped over the top. And Greg is in what he probably thinks is a "sharp" suit, with gelled hair. He's wearing white socks and pointy shoes and looks like he's going to a 1950s party.

"Hannah!" Morag greets her like an old friend, which in fact she is. Everyone at Farrs knows Hannah. "Lovely to see you! Although, should you be drinking?" Her eyes fall on Hannah's glass reprovingly.

"Tim doesn't want a baby anymore," announces Stacey. "He's changed his mind. Just like that."

"Stacey!" I gasp. "That's private!"

"Couldn't help overhearing," she says unrepentantly, clearly meaning: "Couldn't help listening in on your conversation." "Bummer," she adds to Hannah.

"Has he found out he's already got a kid, then?" says Greg

sympathetically. "And he doesn't want another one because, you know, child support?"

"No!" exclaims Hannah as though stung. "Of course not."

"Happens," says Greg with a shrug. "Happened to a mate of mine on *The Jeremy Kyle Show*. He got a free DNA test out of it, though. So, you know, not all bad. Funny story," he adds, reminiscing. "They messed up on his expenses. He ended up ten quid up. Result!"

"I'm *sure* that's not what's up with Tim," I say hurriedly, seeing Hannah's frozen expression. "And as I say, it's a private matter, so could we all—"

"I say divorce him," says Stacey to Hannah, ignoring me. "And sleep with all his friends. Then, when he's an emotional wreck, find *another* friend—maybe his very *best* friend, the one he thought would never betray him—and sleep with her."

"Her?" Hannah's eyes widen.

"Her." Stacey nods without a flicker. "And you better be good."

"Stacey, love, I don't think that's the way at all," puts in Morag. "Why not bake Tim a nice cake?" she adds to Hannah. "A Victoria sponge, or a nice carrot cake . . . He may have a gluten allergy!" Her eyes suddenly light up. "That may explain everything."

"Morag, I don't think a gluten allergy makes you decide against fatherhood," I can't help saying. "I don't think that's how it works."

"It could be irritating his insides," she replies, unmoved. "These allergies can wreak havoc, love."

"I say hypnotize him," says Greg, and we all turn to stare at him.

"*Hypnotize* him?" echoes Hannah.

"I've been doing a course." Greg gives her a knowing look. "Specialist military techniques. Give me twenty-four hours; I can strip him down until he has no personality left and you can start again."

"Right," says Hannah after a pause. "Well, maybe."

"Don't resist it," says Greg, his eyes bulging at her. "You've got to let *me* help *you*." He gestures meaningfully with his hands. "Let *me* help *you*."

"Is the party starting yet?" says Hannah desperately.

"Exactly!" I say. "We should get out there and greet people. Come on."

I usher everyone out and survey the shop floor. It looks totally alien. Music is thudding through speakers, and two waitresses are taking round trays of champagne. Some people have arrived, but I don't recognize any of them. They look like Jake's estate-agent friends.

Near the entrance is a five-foot-long "red carpet," with a VIP rope and a backdrop screen covered in printed stars. Nicole is on the red carpet, looking totally at home, posing for a photographer with a blond girl who must be Kitten Smith. They're both in long dresses, and Nicole is throwing her hair around and doing lots of fake laughing with her arm around the blond girl's waist.

"Look," I say to Stacey, feeling a quickening of excitement in spite of myself. "It's Kitten Smith."

"Oh yeah," says Stacey, shooting her an unimpressed look. "How much did Jake pay her to come?"

"*Pay* her?" I stare at Stacey.

"Well, she wouldn't have done it for free, would she?" Stacey rolls her eyes.

"Right. Of course not!" I say hastily, trying not to sound as naïve as I feel. It never *occurred* to me that Jake was shelling out on this YouTuber. I thought he'd got her interested in Farrs somehow.

How much did he pay?

As I'm watching, two girls in glitzy-looking dresses come through the door and Jake kisses them both with loud exclamations. I have no idea who they are. I have no idea who anyone is. I know I need to go and mingle, but they all look terrifying. I decide I'll finish my drink, get another one, and *then* go and mingle.

Jake looks in his element, I can't help noticing. He's handing out drinks and cracking jokes, all loud and confident. I keep hearing the phrase "Notting Hill" in conversation, which makes me prickle suspiciously, but I'm trying to give him the benefit of the doubt.

I drain my glass, fill it up again, and am about to approach the glitziest, most-frightening-looking girl, when I see a welcome sight coming in through the door. It's Vanessa! She's dressed up smartly in a navy suit, but she's as smiley and familiar as ever.

Finally! An actual customer! I hurry over and find myself kissing her on both cheeks, which is not what I'd normally do but I'm picking up habits from Jake.

"Vanessa! Welcome!" I grab a glass of champagne from a waitress and give it to her.

"Well, isn't this nice?" says Vanessa pleasantly, looking

around. "Very smart. What's it in aid of? I couldn't quite work it out, from the invitation."

"Oh . . . a revamp," I say vaguely. "Relaunch."

"That's what I told the others." Vanessa nods. "They're on their way. We met in the pub first, actually, but I'm pressed for time, so I thought I'd hurry along."

"The others?" I say, not following.

"The Cake Club!" says Vanessa with a friendly laugh. "They didn't seem to know anything about it. I had to send out a round-robin email. You really need to look at your mailing list, Fixie."

"You did *what*?" I stare at her.

"But they'll be along any moment," she says cheerfully. "Ah, look, there's Sheila now."

Sheila? My head whips round. Oh my God. Sheila.

I'm sure Sheila wasn't on Jake's curated guest list, what with her being a "repulsive wreck." But after what looks like an altercation with the bouncer, she firmly pushes her way in. She takes off her shabby mac to reveal a crumpled, tent-like dress and her usual furry boots. I can see her peering around, searching for a familiar face—then she spots Nicole on the red carpet.

"Nicole!" she exclaims, and shuffles onto the red carpet to join Nicole and Kitten Smith. "Don't you look nice? Who's this? A new salesgirl? Are we doing photos?"

I glance over at Jake and feel a convulsion of laughter. His face. His *face*! He breaks away from the group of smart people he's with and heads swiftly toward the red carpet.

"*Delighted* to see you," he says smoothly to Sheila. "Absolutely *delighted*. But may I suggest—" He breaks off as the door opens and six more members of the Cake Club pile in, sweeping past the bouncer, all wearing anoraks and sensible shoes.

"Ooh, look!" Brenda exclaims, peering around. "Doesn't it all look strange?"

"Morag!" calls another woman whose name I don't know. "I brought oatmeal cookies. Where shall I put them?" She brandishes a plastic box, and I see Jake flinch in horror.

"Girls!" calls Sheila, waving vigorously from the red carpet. "Here! We're doing photos. Young man," she says to the local photographer. "Would you do a group shot? Come on, Cake Club! Nicole, you don't mind moving, do you? Morag, join us!"

As Sheila literally elbows Nicole off the red carpet, my stomach is hurting from trying not to laugh. Within thirty seconds, the red carpet is full of middle-aged women in sensible coats, all beaming and waving at the camera. The smart guests are peering at them in surprise. Jake looks like he wants to throw up. I can hear Nicole ranting to Kitten Smith about how she's the face of Farrs and this is all so unprofessional.

At that moment, I hear a voice in my ear. "Love, I wondered if you had another mug? Same as before, the brown one."

I whip round and bite my lip. It's my friend the old shuffly man with the shopping trolley. Of course it is.

"Hello!" I say. "We're not really open, but I'm sure I can get you a mug."

"I saw the lights on," he says conversationally, looking around. "Serving drinks, are you?"

"Here you are." I pour him out a glass of champagne. "Enjoy."

I hurry off and find a brown earthenware mug in the stock room. I wrap it in tissue, then return, take the old man's money, and pack his new mug safely in his shopping trolley. The tills aren't open, but I'll sort it all out tomorrow.

"Would you like some more champagne?" I ask. "And a canapé? Or a cookie?"

"Well." His rheumy eyes brighten as he looks at his nearly empty glass. "A drop more of this would be grand. . . ."

"Excuse me." Jake's stentorian voice interrupts us. "Do you have an invitation?" He doesn't even wait for the old man to answer. "No. You don't. So could you kindly leave?"

To my horror, he takes the old man by the elbow and starts to escort him, quite roughly, to the door.

"Jake!" I exclaim. "Jake, stop it!"

"This is a private event," Jake says to the old man, ignoring me. "The shop will be open during normal hours tomorrow. Thank you so much."

He turns back from dispatching the old man, and I feel a flare of rage.

"Fixie, can I see you for a minute?" says Jake in ominous tones, and I glare back at him.

"Yes," I snap, and follow him to the back room. He slams the door and we stare at each other for a silent ten seconds. I'm forming furious, outraged phrases. I can see them now, flashing in their thought bubble, red and angry.

How dare you? That was a customer and he deserved respect! Who do you think you are? What would Dad say?

I draw breath, telling myself that this time I'll do it; this time I'll really have my say. But as I look up at Jake's intimidating face, it happens again. My nerve collapses. The ravens have started flapping around me.

"Are you *deliberately* trying to sabotage our relaunch, Fixie?" he says, in his sarcastic, biting way. "I assume it was you who invited the anorak brigade, not to mention your homeless friend?"

"He's not homeless!" I retort, as strongly as I can manage. "And even if he were, he's a customer! And I think . . ." I swallow. "I just think . . ."

My words have ground to a halt. I *hate* myself right now. I can't shout. I can't assert myself. I can't say the things I want to say.

"What?" demands Jake.

"I . . . I don't think you should have treated him like that," I stutter at last.

"Oh, you don't?" Jake snaps back. "Well, *I* don't think you should have invited all and bloody sundry to what was supposed to be a professional event."

"I didn't invite anyone!" I say. "It was Vanessa!" But Jake isn't listening. He sweeps back out to the party and after a few seconds I follow, my cheeks burning. I'm thinking I might go and drown my sorrows with a cookie, when I see Leila waving at me.

"Leila!" I exclaim in relief, because if there's anyone who will cheer your soul it's Leila. She's wearing a silver dress with a tulle skirt and looks like some sort of sprite.

"Fixie!" she says, and hugs me. "Thank goodness! I told Ryan you must be here somewhere. . . ."

"Ryan?" My heart lifts. "Is he here?"

"He's here." Leila bites her lip and lowers her voice. "He's drunk."

"Drunk?" I stare at her.

"It's not good." Leila looks anxious. "Fixie, you need to know something; he—" She breaks off as Ryan himself appears, holding two glasses of champagne. His eyes are blood-shot and he surveys us all with a morose gaze.

"Hi!" I say, kissing him. "Is everything . . . Are you . . ." My words trail away and I glance uncertainly at Leila, who winces. "What's up?"

"Bastard fired me," says Ryan, so lightly that at first I think I must have misheard.

"What?"

Ryan gives me a humorless smile and lifts his glass in a mock toast. "You heard me, Fixie. Bastard fired me. I've lost my job."

Shock is too small a word for what I'm feeling right now. I'm beyond shocked. I'm stunned. Ryan's lost his *job*?

We've commandeered the back room. I've forgotten about the party. All I can think about is Ryan.

"I just don't *get* it," I say, sinking into a chair opposite Ryan. "It makes no sense. How exactly did it happen?"

"Seb called me in and said it 'wasn't working out.'" Ryan shrugs. "That was it. The end. Finished."

"But *why*?"

"I think you know why," he says wryly.

I lean forward, surveying Ryan's face, registering his calm, resigned expression.

"Seb was threatened by you," I say. "Is that it?"

"Let's just say, I saw it coming," says Ryan, and takes a slug of his drink. "He's right, it wasn't working out. It wasn't working out for *him*."

"Because you were competition," I say bluntly, and Ryan nods his head in assent.

My cloud of shock is starting to fade away and anger is rising in its place. It's so unfair. It's monstrous. Why couldn't they work together? Why did Seb have to see Ryan as a threat? He promises him a chance, then dumps him? It's just *wrong*.

"You know, I wouldn't mind," Ryan says, leaning back and looking pensively at the ceiling. "Only I gave a good few weeks to that place. I could have used that time to job-hunt. Truth is, he was never planning to employ me permanently. He was never going to keep me on. He only did it as a favor to you. Payback. Whatever."

Everything seems so clear now. Seb was never going to take Ryan seriously as an employee. The whole thing was like a game, and I should never, ever have kick-started it.

"I wish I'd never claimed that stupid IOU," I say passionately, getting to my feet. "I wish I'd never set eyes on him in the first place."

"You weren't to know." Ryan shrugs again. "I just wish he'd been honest in the first place. He takes all my ideas, wrings me dry, and kicks me out. Still, what's done is done."

"So what will you do?"

"You know, Fixie . . . I have no idea. When a guy hits rock bottom, it's like, what are the options?"

Ryan seems so resigned. So crushed. But I'm not resigned

or crushed. I'm crackling with indignation. My fingers are drumming relentlessly. My feet are doing their thing: *forward-across-back, forward-across-back*. I can't stay here. I can't let Seb Marlowe get away with it. Who does he think he is?

Drawing myself up short, I suddenly recall the vow I made to myself in Seb's office. I wasn't going to try to fix stuff anymore, not unless it was super-important and vital.

But then, what's this if not super-important and vital?

Abruptly, I reach for my bag and coat.

"I'll be back in a while," I say. "Stay at mine tonight. We'll sort all this out."

As I stride through the party, I feel grim and determined. "I have to go," I say to Hannah. "Can you tell Jake?"

"Well, sure," she says, looking surprised. "But what—"

"I have to fix a thing," I say succinctly, and march out.

I stride to the tube station, travel all the way to Farringdon, and get out, feeling stony and unforgiving. Within a few minutes I'm at the ESIM building and I glance up as I approach, feeling suddenly foolish. I rushed out in such a blaze of indignation, I didn't think about what time it was. Maybe no one's there and I've wasted my time. . . .

But there are lights on. A few, at least.

My heart pumping, I press the buzzer and someone—not sure who—lets me in. I rise up in the lift and emerge, all ready to say, "I'd like to see the CEO, *please*," in my most cutting tones—but he's there. It's him. Seb. He's waiting for the lift, looking fairly astonished to see me.

"It's you," he says. "I thought—"

"Hi," I say curtly. "I wanted to see you. If that's convenient?"

There's a short silence. Seb's pleasant gaze doesn't waver, but I can sense his brain is working.

"Sure," he says at last. "Come on in."

As I follow him to his office, I notice he's looking slightly rumpled, as though he's spent too long at work, and his brown frondy hair is askew.

I fight an urge to put it straight. That would not be appropriate. Anyway, I need to focus. I need to come in fighting.

His office is warm and inviting, just like it was before. The coffee-cup sleeve is still on his desk, I notice, and I feel a pang of indignation. Some favor. Some favor that was.

"So," he says as we sit down, and from his wary tone I sense he knows exactly why I'm here. It seems only about five minutes ago that I was here with Ryan, feeling so joyful that everything was working out. The memory fuels my rage, and I take a deep breath.

"I simply wanted to say," I begin in my most castigating tones, "that I think when you enter into an agreement with someone you should do it in good faith. That's all. You should have honest intentions."

"I agree," says Seb after a pause.

"Oh, you *agree*," I say sarcastically.

I know sarcasm is the lowest form of wit, but I've never actually known what that means, and I don't care. Low is fine. Low is good.

"Yes," says Seb steadily. "I agree."

"Well, I *don't*," I shoot back—then instantly realize that's wrong. It's his fault. He's flustering me. "I mean, I *do*," I amend. "I *do* agree. But that's not how you've treated Ryan. It's a travesty! Just because he's a man of the world, you can't cope with him? Just because he has ambition and vision and knowledge in areas you don't? Were you so threatened you couldn't find a way to make it work? Or is he right and you never intended to keep him on at all?"

As I break off, I'm breathing hard. I'm expecting Seb to spring to some feeble defense, but he's staring at me as though I'm talking gibberish.

"What?" he says at last.

"What do you mean, 'what'?" I say, incensed. "I heard all about it! I *know* you blocked Ryan from coming to meetings. I *know* the staff were asking his advice. I *know* he could see all the flaws in your company. He's got charisma and experience and you couldn't cope! So you get rid of him!"

"Oh my God," says Seb. "Oh my God." He gets up, running his hands through his hair, walks to the window, and gives a weird laugh. "OK, where do I start? Do you know the disruption that Ryan Chalker has caused to this company? Do you know how obtuse, how stupid . . . how *inane* he is? If I had to hear one more anecdote about some tech guy in a pool in L.A. . . . I was going to go bonkers!" He wheels round, his face animated. "I didn't ban him from meetings— the staff did! They petitioned me! He wouldn't bloody shut *up*!"

"Maybe you didn't listen properly!" I say defensively. "He has massive experience—"

"In what?" says Seb incredulously. "Eating lunch at Nobu? Because that's all he ever talked about."

"OK," I say tightly. "Well, you were clearly never going to give him a chance. He was right. You never even *tried* to make it work."

"I didn't *try?*" Seb sounds outraged. "Here's what I did. I gave him a mentor. I gave him advice. I sent him on training days. I discussed financial exams with him. And what does he do? Mock our ethos. Derail every meeting he goes to. Name-drop us all to death, fail to complete a single one of the assignments I actually gave him . . . and start sleeping with not one but two members of my staff! Not one, but *two!*" He clutches his hair. "It's been turmoil here! One found out about the other; we've had tears at meetings—" He stops and peers at me. "Wait. You've gone very pale. Are you OK?"

I'm staring back at him, my head thudding. Did he just say—

He didn't— He couldn't have—

"Wh-what do you mean?" I say at last. "Sleeping with who? Who do you mean?"

"I don't think it's relevant who they were," says Seb, eyeing me curiously. "I've been too indiscreet already."

"I don't believe you." My voice shakes. "I don't believe you."

"You don't *believe* me? Why on earth wouldn't you—" Seb sounds incredulous—then his face suddenly changes. "Oh strewth. Are you and Ryan . . . You're not—" He breaks off, looking agonized. "He said he was single. He told the whole office he was a single guy. I would *never* have . . . I'm sorry. That was . . ."

He stops again, as though he doesn't know how to finish, and there's silence.

My eyes are hot. My gaze is flitting around the office. I can't look at him. I'm thinking: *He's lying. He's lying.*

But I'm also thinking: *Why would he lie? Why would he lie?*

I'm remembering all the times Ryan was "too tired" for sex. And how understanding I was. How I made him lamb hot pot and rubbed his back and thought, *Give it time.*

Have I been the biggest, stupidest fool in the world? Did I want the famous Ryan Chalker so badly, I blinded myself to the facts?

"Can I just ask a question?" I manage at last. "Do your staff play pool together three times a week?"

"Three times a *week*?" Seb seems taken aback. "No! Not that I know of. Maybe once a month. Why?"

"No reason." I swallow hard. I'm trying to stay composed, even as everything comes crashing down inside me. Ryan wasn't playing pool. He was with other women. Maybe that Erica he kept talking about. He never wanted to be cozy and intimate and domesticated. I was a free meal and a back rub twice a week.

At last, Seb moves forward a step. I shoot a glance at him and see a troubled, earnest gaze.

"I'm sorry," he says. "But that man is . . . He's not good. In my opinion. How long have you known him?"

"All my life," I retort roughly. "Since I was ten."

"Ah." His face crinkles in an expression I can't read.

"We were only in a casual thing," I say quickly. "It was no big deal. So."

But it's far too little, far too late. I can tell from Seb's face that he knows I'm devastated. His woodland eyes are alive with sympathy. His brow is furrowed with pity for me. I can't stand it.

"Anyway. Clearly Ryan and you didn't work out professionally. Which is a shame. Thank you for explaining it all to me." I gather my coat and bag with trembling hands.

"Fixie, I'm so sorry." Seb is watching me. "I didn't mean— I had no idea—"

"Of course not!" My voice is shrill. "And that's not why—I simply wanted to find out what had gone wrong professionally with you and Ryan. I was simply interested. You did me a favor, and it went wrong so—" I break off as a new thought hits me. "You did me a favor," I repeat more slowly. "You hired Ryan. And your company suffered as a result. So now I owe *you* one."

"Don't be ridiculous," says Seb with a short laugh. "You don't owe me anything."

"I do."

"You don't! Fixie, we're even."

I can sense his eyes trying to meet mine, his smile trying to lighten things, but I can't be lightened. I'm heavy and sad and there are tears gathering behind my eyes.

I grab the coffee sleeve, not meeting his eye, and take a pen from his desk. Underneath the *Paid* I wrote before, I scribble some new words:

I owe you one and I'll never be able to pay you back. So. Sorry about that.

I sign it, then drop the pen down.

"Bye," I say, and I turn and go. I can hear Seb saying something else, calling something, but I don't stop to listen. I need to leave.

By the time I get back to Acton, I feel exhausted. I've tried out every phrase in my head, every accusation. I feel as though I've had about six rows with Ryan already.

I'm already mentally batting away the patronizing response that I know will come my way. He'll try to look all surprised, like I'm being possessive and unreasonable. He'll say, "Fixie, I *said* we shouldn't rush things, remember?" The thought makes my heart pump with outrage. Not rushing things is *not* the same as sleeping with two other women on the side. It is *not*.

When I think how I believed his version of everything, how I rationalized everything he said and did, I feel warm with stupidity. But he was so *convincing*.

Wasn't he?

Or maybe I just wanted to believe him, a little voice says in my head. *Maybe I ignored what I didn't want to see.* Painful realizations are filling my head, one after another, till I close my eyes to escape them. I can't think about all my mistakes now. It is what it is.

The party is pretty much over as I burst back into the shop. None of the staff are left, nor Hannah. Leila is sitting on a chair, scrolling through her phone, and Jake is talking to some jowly guy in a pink shirt, but I can't see Ryan anywhere.

"Oh, Fixie," says Leila, looking up. "*There* you are."

"Where's Ryan?" I demand, and Leila opens her eyes wide in astonishment.

"Didn't he tell you? Hasn't he texted? He's gone."

"Gone where?"

"He went to catch a train. He's staying with his cousin in . . . Leicester?" She crinkles her brow. "Something like that. The Midlands, anyway. He says there are more opportunities for him outside London."

"The *Midlands*?" I stare at her. This makes no sense. He can't have just *left*.

"I said to him, 'What about Fixie?' but he said you'd understand and you'd talked about it and everything." Leila looks innocently at me. "He said you'd be OK."

We'd *talked* about it? That's what he said? But that's—

And suddenly I can't believe I've fallen for anything Ryan's said, ever. He's just a lie machine. That's what he is, and it's taken me this long to work it out.

"He was in a real mood," adds Leila regretfully. "He kept saying there was nothing for him in London anymore. He was telling us all about losing his job. You know, that Seb guy sounds *awful*." She surveys me with her doe-like mascaraed eyes. "You've met him, haven't you?"

I stare at her, barely hearing the question. I'm still a bit dazed. Ryan has lied about everything and now he's gone and I don't even get to have it out with him. My pent-up rage and humiliation have nowhere to go except right back into my heart.

"What's he like?" Leila persists, and I blink at her, coming to. "Is he as bad as Ryan says? Because he sounds like a monster!"

I flash back to Seb in his office. Gazing at me with those troubled eyes, understanding everything. His tactful words. His hair askew. His remorse at having upset me. Trying to cheer me up. Telling me we're even.

I'm suddenly gripped by a wish. *I wish . . . I wish . . .*

But I can't finish the thought. I don't quite know what I wish. Just that things weren't like this.

"Seb?" I say at last, and exhale long and hard. "He's not that bad. No. He's . . . he's not that bad."

Thirteen

Two weeks later Mum is in St. Tropez with Aunty Karen. She keeps sending me long texts about the marina and the boats and the sunshine, and I know I should send her a proper reply—but I can't face it. Once I start typing to Mum, everything will pour out, and I'll start sniveling all over my keyboard.

So instead I'm zapping her lots of smiley faces and emojis of shiny suns and sailboats and dodging the truth altogether. (Maybe that's what emojis were invented for in the first place, and I've just been using them wrong. They're not there to convey thoughts in a fun way; they're there to *lie to your mum*.)

I've also sent three texts to Ryan. One very dignified and calm. One a tad less dignified and less calm. One totally desperate and shameless, trying to give him an opportunity to prove he *isn't* as bad as I think.

Then I made the even bigger mistake of showing my texts to Hannah and she recoiled in horror. She threatened to come and confiscate my phone at night when I was asleep. She said she had a spare key and she'd creep through the house if need be. And I thought, *Actually, she might*. So I stopped.

And Ryan never replied to any of them. Nor left me a voicemail or an email, nor any messages at the shop. Nor a letter. (I mean, clearly he wasn't going to write me a letter; I don't know *why* I asked the postman if he'd dropped any envelopes.) But it's fine, because I'm a strong-minded person and my strategy is: Simply stop thinking about him.

Well, I'm still *thinking* about him, obviously. Now and then. The name *Ryan* does pass through my thoughts; how could it not? But then, there are plenty of other things to think about right now. Like the fact that Jake still hasn't produced a budget for the relaunch party, so I still don't know how much he spent on it. And the fact that Nicole canceled Cake Club last night without telling me, so she could hold a mind-body-spirit talk in the store, and I've already had four irate emails. And the most pressing fact of all: that I've promised Hannah I'll have a chat with Tim about trying for a baby. She wants me to find out why he changed his mind and, if possible, change it back.

Change it back? *Me?* How am I supposed to change Tim's mind back? How am I even supposed to bring up the subject? I've known Tim a long time, but family planning is definitely *not* the kind of conversation topic we normally cover.

Hannah sounded so pleading, though, I found myself promising I'd have a go. She told me she'd bring him into the shop one day after work and I should "engage him in conversation about babies." Only it should seem "natural."

"I don't want him to know I've spoken to you," she said

adamantly. "I want him to think he's changed his mind back independently. OK?"

"Er . . . right," I said. "Of course. Sure."

I thought I'd have some time to prepare, but it's the next day, and here they are already, at 5:30 p.m. Hannah must have made Tim leave work early, I realize. And left work early herself. Clearly this is a high priority.

Oh God. So, no pressure, then.

"Hi, Hannah; hi, Tim!" I greet them, trying to sound natural. "What a surprise to see you!"

"Hi, Fixie!" replies Hannah stiltedly. "Yes, it was a spontaneous decision to come. I'm going to look at blenders for a birthday present. You keep Tim company." And she strides off to the back of the shop without a backward look. Tim and I are alone. It's my cue.

Shit. I should have planned this. What the *hell* am I going to say about babies?

"So!" I begin brightly. "How are you, Tim?"

"Good, thanks," he says in that flat way of his. "How about you?"

"Yes, all fine, all good." I nod a few times, frantically racking my brain. "Er . . . babies are great, aren't they?"

Shit. That just came out.

"What?" Tim peers at me with a suspicious frown. "What do you mean?"

"Oh, nothing!" I say hastily. "I was only thinking about it because . . . um . . . we had a baby in the shop today. It was so cute. And I thought, *That's the future. That's the next generation. Let's keep this planet in good shape, for the kids.*"

Wait. Somehow I've diverted onto an environmental talk.

"What kids?" says Tim, looking confused.

"Kids!" I say desperately. "You know, kids!"

I can see Hannah peering out from behind the blender display, raising her eyebrows questioningly, and abruptly I come to a decision. There's no point being subtle with Tim. You have to bludgeon him.

"Listen, Tim," I say in a low, firm voice. "Hannah wants a baby. Why have you changed your mind? You've really upset her. And, by the way, she *mustn't* know we're having this conversation."

Immediately Tim's face closes up. "It's my business," he says, looking away.

"It's Hannah's business too," I point out. "Don't you want to have a family? Don't you want to be a father?"

"I don't know, OK?" Tim's face is tight and kind of upset-looking. I'm definitely pressing his buttons.

"You'd agreed that it *was* what you wanted," I persist. "What changed your mind? *Something* must have changed your mind."

I can see Tim's face working with some sort of emotion, and I wait breathlessly.

"I didn't know what it involved!" he suddenly bursts out. "Do *you* know what having a baby involves?"

I want to make a hilarious joke about how his contribution isn't exactly tough, but I'm sensing it's not the moment.

"Like what?"

"It's a nightmare!" he says, looking beleaguered. "It's endless!"

"What do you mean?" I stare at him.

"Check baby carrier for weak seams. Visit nurseries. Research safety of car seats. Literacy. Organic paint. La Mars. Annabel Karmel. Flashcards."

As this stream of gibberish comes out of his mouth, he's counting items off on his fingers. I wonder for an instant if he's having some sort of breakdown.

"Tim," I say carefully, "what are you *talking* about?"

"Don't tell Hannah I said any of this," he says, hastily lowering his voice. "Promise me. But she's just . . . It's all . . . I can't do it."

I'm thoroughly baffled. This conversation has gone so off-piste, I don't know what to say next. And now here comes Hannah, clutching her blender, looking at me expectantly.

"Hi!" I say, my voice high and awkward. "So, Tim and I were chatting about . . . things. . . ."

There's a long, prickly silence. I can sense both Hannah and Tim trying to convey urgent silent messages to me.

"So!" I say again, avoiding both their gazes. "I'll ring that up. . . ." I take Hannah's payment and hand her the blender. "I'll . . . er . . . call you later, shall I?"

"Shall we have supper?" says Hannah eagerly.

"Can't." I pull a regretful face. "I've got Leila's birthday-drinks thing at Six Folds Place. But we'll talk." I nod. "We'll talk."

As Hannah and Tim leave, I breathe out. I need to decode all that. I need to work out what I'm going to say to Hannah. And look up what "La Mars" means. Or was it "Le Mahs"?

I'm about to type it into my phone when Bob comes out of the back room in his anorak to go home, and I smile at him.

"Hi, Bob. Everything OK? We're not going bust yet?"

This is Mum's little joke. She says it every time she sees Bob, so I'm keeping up the tradition.

"Not quite yet!" Bob replies with his customary little laugh. But I notice his fingers are tugging at his cuffs, as they always do when he wants to venture something awkward. "Just working through the invoices for the relaunch party," he adds. "That DJ was an expensive chap, wasn't he?" He laughs again—but he sounds anxious.

I remind myself that Bob is the most cautious man in the world and doesn't know anything about DJs or marketing or parties. Even so, I can't help feeling my own corresponding stab of anxiety. I suddenly want to confide in him. I want to wail, "Bob, I know exactly how you feel! We didn't even *need* a DJ! And I don't know what that party was for, anyway! It's not like anything about the shop has changed, sales haven't gone up, there aren't any new customers . . . it was pointless!"

But *family first*.

"I think all these marketing things help," I say at last. "You know. Profile and everything."

"Ah," says Bob. His mild brown eyes meet mine and I feel sure he understands everything but would never open his mouth because he's too discreet and loyal and agreeable.

"Have all the invoices come in?" I ask. "Do we know what the total budget was?"

Mum okayed the party, I remind myself. There was nothing I could do to stop it. And, anyway, it's not going to be a *problem*. It's not going to *bankrupt* us. It was only a party.

"Not yet," says Bob. "Not everything."

"Well, keep me posted," I say.

"Of course," he replies with a nod.

He turns to leave and I watch him with a sigh. Now I need to go and get ready for Leila's birthday drinks, even though the last thing I feel like is going to 6 Folds Place. The idea of dressing up feels exhausting. Let alone making conversation with Jake's posh friends about sailing (not a clue) and makes of car (not a clue). But I promised Leila, and she's such a sweetheart, I can't let her down.

Anyway, there'll be free drinks there, I remind myself as I reach for my makeup bag. Free champagne. Or cocktails, maybe. In the mood I'm in, I could do with one.

It's cocktails. It's strong, tangy, limy cocktails in martini glasses, and I seize one greedily. I have no idea what it is, only that I want to drink it. I close my eyes and glug it down and, oh my God, *bliss*. I haven't had anything to eat all day and the alcohol hits my bloodstream like a drug.

Well, it is a drug, in fact. Ha.

I open my eyes and look around for someone to share this thought with, but there's no one I really want to approach. Leila greeted me affectionately when I arrived but then went off to the ladies' with two of her beautician friends. Jake is talking loudly to three guys in suits about his manufactured-diamonds deal. Apparently there's been a holdup in Asia.

"I mean, this is international shipping for you," he keeps saying in a show-offy way. "This is the reality of global trade, know what I mean?"

I have nothing to offer on the subject of global trade, so I take another cocktail. I could drink these all night, I think with each delicious gulp. In fact, I *will* drink them all night.

Our little party area is roped off, but there are plenty of other people around the place, sitting at tables and standing at the bar. They're not in Leila's party, just members of 6 Folds Place out for the evening. There's a group of girls sitting at a table to my left, and I keep glancing at them, because that's the table we had last time. That's where I was sitting when Ryan brought me that bouquet of lilies and kissed me and I thought . . . I really thought . . .

A familiar stabbing pain hits me and I swivel away, grabbing yet another cocktail. Every icy swig numbs a bad feeling. The humiliation. The self-reproach. The worst thing is, everyone tried to tell me. Hannah, Mum, even Tim in his own way. They all sensed the truth about Ryan—although Hannah has told me several times during the past two miserable weeks that she had no idea he was *that* bad. Not *that* bad.

I don't know if that's supposed to cheer me up or not.

As I drain my glass, I suddenly see Nicole standing on the other side of Jake. I hadn't noticed her before. She's looking stunning in a short white fringed dress and tossing her carefully styled hair back as she talks to some tall guy. I can hear her saying, "Yeah, I'm actually suffering from separation anxiety, you know? I really have to self-care?"

I can't face talking to her. I can't face talking to Jake. What is *wrong* with me that I don't want to talk to my own family? In slight despair I put down my empty glass. I pick up another full one, wondering if four cocktails is somehow

against the law. And then I stiffen. Oh my God, oh my *God*.
It can't be.

But it is. It's Seb. He's sitting at a table some distance
away, dressed in an elegant understated jacket. And he's with
a girl. A tall, confident-looking blond girl with a blunt chin-
length haircut and a good manicure and a bright-green body-
con dress. She looks like she could be a TV presenter. Is that
his girlfriend? What's her name again?

I rack my brain feverishly until it comes to me: *Briony*.
Exactly. She sent him to the skiing workout guru. And there
was some issue about a home gym. Is that her?

As Seb looks up to attract a waiter, I hastily hide behind a
group of Jake's friends. I don't want him to see me. *Why's he
here, anyway?* I think, almost accusingly. He told Ryan this
wasn't his scene. He shouldn't be such a hypocrite.

More to the point: What am I going to do now?

From my hiding place I peer at him again. He's leaning
forward now, his elbows on the table. He's talking earnestly,
as though he's trying hard to get something across. And Briony is . . .

She's snapping at him, I realize. She looks quite vicious.
God, I wish I could lip-read. What's she saying?

Now he's replying. . . . She's interrupting. . . . They're
having a row, I realize in astonishment. They're actually having a row! Somehow I thought Seb wasn't the type to have
rows. Especially not in the middle of a club.

As I watch in fascination, Briony's face twists. She spits
out a whole series of words at Seb and pushes her chair back.
She flings a pashmina around her shoulders and grabs her
bag. She looks kind of magnificent, I can't help thinking, in

a scary-monster sort of way. She's so glossy. She's so self-possessed. She fires some final comment at Seb and strides out, and I exhale. That was intense. And I wasn't even in it.

My brain is swirling with alcohol. The lights are starting to blur and I'm swaying a little. Maybe I drank those cocktails a bit too quickly. Even so, as Seb gets up from his chair, I feel suddenly alert. Hang on. Where's he going? Which way is he walking?

Shit. He's coming in this direction, toward the bar. *Shit.*

OK, quick, I need to face *away* from him. *Away.* This is crucial. *Away.* I look around for a solution and spy Nicole, who is on her own, talking on the phone.

"Drew, I have to go," I hear her say. She rings off and takes a sip of her drink, staring ahead. Her jaw is tight and her eyes are narrowed and she looks quite stressed.

Yowser, I think hazily. *Did she and Drew have a row?*

"Hi, Nicole!" I say, stumbling over to her. "We never talk. Let's talk. Is everything OK?"

At once she turns a defensive gaze on me. "Of course it is," she says. "Why wouldn't it be?"

Typical. I wish just *once* Nicole would engage and we could have an actual conversation.

I glance over my shoulder. Seb is at the bar. He's ordering a drink. Whiskey, looks like.

"You know, Drew adores you," I say to Nicole. "I'm sure he does. Like, *this* much." I extend my arms wide, tottering on my heels. "*This* much."

"You look drunk, Fixie." She eyes me suspiciously.

"I'm not," I assure her. "Not at all. Not drunk," I add for emphasis.

"You *are* drunk!" She stares at me. "How many drinks have you had?"

"Ten," I say defiantly, taking a swig of cocktail. Surreptitiously I turn to check out Seb again, thinking I must be safe. But to my horror he's turned away from the bar and his eyes meet mine. His face jerks in surprise and I quickly whip my head back round, my heart thudding.

He didn't recognize me, I tell myself. Of course he didn't. He couldn't have, not in that fleeting moment. Even so, I decide to move behind Nicole so that I'm concealed. Then, in sudden inspiration, I crouch down. OK, this is good. She's completely blocking me. Also, it's quite comfortable, down here on my heels. The room is whirling less. It's relaxing. Parties should have more crouching.

"What the hell are you doing?" demands Nicole.

"Shhh!" I say. "Don't move!"

I can't see Seb. I can't see anything but the shifting light on Nicole's white fringed dress in front of my eyes. It's kind of mesmerizing, especially given that my brain seems to be doing a 360 rotation every thirty seconds.

"Look, there's sushi," Nicole announces suddenly. "I'm getting some." And to my dismay, she moves away, leaving me totally exposed.

"Wait!" I cry. "Nicole! Come back!"

I try to get to my feet, but I'm stuck. What is wrong with my knees? Why won't they *work*? Stupid knees. Stupid cocktails.

"Fixie?" As I hear Seb's incredulous voice, my stomach drops. I force myself to raise my head. And there he is, standing in front of me, holding his glass and looking astonished.

He doesn't have to look *so* surprised. It's a free country.

"Oh," I say with dignity. "Yes. Hello. I was just crouching here."

"So I see."

There's silence, and I attempt to rise gracefully to my feet like a swan, but it really isn't happening.

"May I?" He extends a hand and reluctantly I take it.

"Thank you," I say politely as he helps me up.

"My pleasure."

There's silence between us, suddenly filled by music thumping from the tiny dance floor. The DJ must have started his set. Seb looks strained, I decide as I survey him. But that's not surprising, given the ear-bashing he's just had from Briony. If that's who she is.

I should probably make small talk, but I've never been any good at that. So instead I blurt out, more forcefully than I intended, "What are you doing here? You said you never come here. You said it wasn't your scene."

I know I sound antagonistic, but I have good reason. If people say they don't go to places, they shouldn't go to them. And the truth is, seeing Seb is making me all hot and prickly. I've been trying so hard to put on a brave face these last two weeks. I've been making jokes and laughing lightly, spinning the story that Ryan and I were always a temporary fling and I'm not hurt at all. I've even put on the bravest face I can to Hannah.

But Seb knows. He *knows*. He saw me at my most vulnerable, face stricken, world crashing around me. Which is why I would rather not bump into him at clubs.

"I don't usually," says Seb. "And it isn't. This is an exception. What are you doing here?"

"Drinking," I say.

"Ah."

"Drowning my sorrows. We have cocktails," I add, brandishing my glass at him. "You can have one if you like. Only you have to be in our party. D'you want to come to it as my guest? I wouldn't if I were you. It's full of estate agents."

Distantly, I'm aware that I'm not speaking appropriately. But I can't seem to stop myself. Sense has taken a back seat for now. Alcohol is in charge of talking. And Alcohol says, "Woo! Anything goes!"

"Estate agents, huh?" says Seb, his mouth twitching.

"And manufactured-diamond importers," I say, enunciating carefully. "Actually only one of those. He's my brother. Who was that you were with?" I add. "Was it your girlfriend?"

"Yes," he says after a pause. "Her name's—"

"I know her name," I interrupt triumphantly. "I overheard it in the coffee shop. It's . . . Wait . . ." I pause, closing my eyes for a few seconds, letting the music thump through me. "Whiny."

OK, that came out wrong.

"Not Whiny," I say after a moment's thought. "It's something else."

"Briony," corrects Seb, his mouth twitching again.

"*Briony.*" I nod about fifteen times. "Yes. Sorry. *Briony.*" I think for a moment, then add, "You could call her Shouty."

"*What?*" Seb stares at me.

"I saw her having a go at you earlier." I wrinkle my nose. "She looked like . . ." Suddenly it comes to me. "Yes! She looked like a mean newsreader." I put on an exaggerated TV voice. "'Hello. This is the Mean News. You're all rubbish and I despise you.'" I come to a finish and blink at him. "Sorry," I add, as Seb opens his mouth. "I'm very sorry. That's awful. I take it back. I shouldn't be rude about your girlfriend. She's probably really nice."

"No," says Seb evenly. "You shouldn't be rude about my girlfriend."

I swig my drink thoughtfully, then beckon him to lean closer and whisper confidingly in his ear, "She's not nice, though, is she?"

"Are we really going to start assessing each other's love choices?" says Seb tightly. "Is that a game you really want to play?"

"Why not?" I shoot back.

"Fine!" Seb's voice rises with heat. "At least I didn't harness my heart to a bloody *con man*. At least I'm not a gullible mug, making excuses for a total dickhead because I had a crush on him at school."

"*What?*" I gasp so forcefully, I nearly totter over. "How did you know *that*?"

"You said you've known him since you were ten," says Seb, shrugging. "Lucky guess."

I feel a spike of resentment. I should never have given away even a *morsel* of information to this guy. I take a sip of cocktail, swill it round my mouth, and swallow it. Then I glare at him with all the venom I can muster.

"I thought you were polite," I say in icy tones. "I was clearly misinformed."

"I can be polite." Now he looks amused. "When I want to be."

"And by the way, I'm not gullible, I'm *trusting*." I wave my glass vigorously at him for emphasis, spilling a few drops. *"Trusting."*

"D'you want to dance?" His words take me by surprise, and I stare at him blankly, wondering if I heard right.

"Dance?" I echo at last. "You mean . . . *dance*?"

"I like dancing. D'you want to dance?"

"With you?" I peer at him.

"Yes," he says, with elaborate patience. "With me."

"Oh." I take another sip, thinking about it. "No. I don't." That'll teach him.

Although, actually, I like dancing too. And this relentless thumping beat is kind of infectious.

"You don't," says Seb after a pause.

"No," I say, a little defiantly. "I don't."

He's taller than me and as I gaze up at him, the lights seem to halo round his head. His hair is shiny and his cheek-bones are gleaming and his eyes are locked on mine in a way that's kind of disconcerting.

I tell myself to look away, but the truth is, I don't want to look away. I want to be drawn into his gaze.

Which is dumb. And wrong. He belongs to another woman, I remind myself sternly. He likes whiny, shouty, newsreadery-type women.

"But you owe me one," he says, and pulls the coffee sleeve

out of his jacket pocket. He flicks it thoughtfully a couple of times, then proffers it. "See?"

I glance dismissively at my own writing. "That doesn't say anything about dancing."

"Maybe dancing is what I want." His eyes are still fixed on mine. "Maybe it's all I want."

"That's all you want." I force a skeptical tone. "A dance."

The music is thudding through my bones. My blood is pulsing. My feet are twitching. The more we talk about dancing, the more I want to dance.

"That's what I want," says Seb, and there's something about his voice and the way he's looking at me that sends a sudden tremor through me.

"Fine," I say at last, as though bestowing the hugest favor on him. *"Fine."*

I follow him to the dance floor and we start to move. We don't say a word. We don't smile or even look at anyone else. Our eyes are locked on each other and our bodies seem naturally in synch from the minute we start.

I mean, here's the thing. He can dance.

Song blends into song and still we keep on dancing. Lights are playing over us, turning Seb's face into a multicolored whirl. The constant thump feels like a heartbeat. Jake and Leila come onto the dance floor and I glance over briefly, nodding hello, but I can't disengage. I can't shake the spell of dancing with Seb.

The longer I dance, the more I'm transfixed by him, by the intensity of his eyes, by the hint of his body under his shirt as he moves. He's fluid and grounded all at once. Strong and lithe but not pumped up, not an extrovert, not constantly glancing around for approval like Ryan would be. Seb is focused. He's honest. Everything he does seems natural, even the way he wipes the sweat off his brow.

I wipe my own face, mirroring his action. It *is* hot. We're dancing to Calvin Harris now and I'm reflexively mouthing, *How deep is your love,* over and over along with the song. I can't stop moving, I can't stop responding to the music, but at the same time I'm aware of something that's not quite right. The colors are blurring even more than they were before. I'm feeling pretty dizzy. I feel . . . not sick, exactly, but . . .

My stomach gives a heave. OK, I definitely feel weird.

I try to anchor myself by gazing at Seb's face, but it's splintering like a kaleidoscope. And my stomach is protesting about something—did I eat some bad food earlier? Why do I feel so—

Oh God.

OK, *really* not feeling good.

Although . . . does it matter?

My legs suddenly seem to be giving way beneath me, but then I don't mind lying on the dance floor. I'm not fussy. I feel quite blissful, really, lying here under the lights. Leila's face looms above me and I give her a beatific smile.

"Happy birthday," I say, but she doesn't seem to understand.

"Fixie! Oh my God, look at you!"

"Hi!" I try to wave cheerfully but my hand isn't working. Where *is* my hand? Oh my God, someone stole my hand.

"I don't know!" I hear Seb's voice above me. "She was fine. I mean, obviously she'd had a few—"

"Fixie!" Leila seems to be shouting from a great distance. "Fixie, are you OK? How many cocktails did you— Oh God, Jake? Jakey? I need some help here. . . ."

If there's anything worse than waking up to a hangover, it's waking up to a hangover at your brother's flat and hearing how you ruined his girlfriend's birthday and embarrassed him in front of all his friends.

My head is crashing with pain, but I can't even take a paracetamol until Jake has stopped his tirade. Eventually he snaps, "I've got a meeting to go to," as though that's my fault too, and strides out.

"Oh, Fixie," says Leila, giving me a glass of water and two tablets. "Don't listen to Jake. It was quite funny, actually. D'you want some coffee?"

I totter into the living room, sink into the leather sofa (the Conran Shop one? I have no idea), and stare blankly at the massive TV screen which Jake bought last year. This whole flat is glossy and modern, with hi-tech everything. It's in a block called Grosvenor Heights in Shepherd's Bush (he calls it "West Holland Park"). Jake offered on it as soon as he'd landed his nude-knickers deal, and I'm sure he chose it because the word *Grosvenor* sounds posh.

Leila brings me in a cup of coffee, sits down next to me in her silky kimono, and starts opening birthday cards with her sharp nails.

"It was a fun evening, though, wasn't it?" she says in her gentle voice. "Jakey spoils me, he really does. Those cocktails were lush."

"Don't talk about cocktails." I wince.

"Sorry." She laughs her rippling laugh, then puts down the card she's holding and gives me an interested look.

"Who was the man?"

"The man?" I try to look blank.

"The man, silly! The one you were dancing with all that time. He's nice." She waggles her eyebrows at me. "Handsome."

"Well, he's taken," I say quickly, before she gets any ideas.

He was carrying the coffee sleeve in his pocket, a small voice in my head points out.

But another one instantly answers: *So what? He was there with his girlfriend.*

"Oh." Leila deflates. "Shame. Well, he was very concerned about you. He wanted to come and make sure you were all right, but we said don't worry, we're family, we'll look after her."

The way she says, "We're family," gets under my skin and makes me blink. I love Leila. She *is* family.

"Oh, Leila." Impulsively, I throw my arms around her. "Thank you. And I'm sorry I spoiled everything."

"You didn't!" She hugs me back with her bony arms. "If I blame anyone, it's Ryan. I said to Jakey, 'No wonder! I'd be in a state too if the love of my life disappeared like that!'"

"Ryan's not the love of my life," I say firmly. "He's really not."

"He'll be back," says Leila wisely, and pats my knee.

I have to get it into Leila's head that I don't *want* Ryan back. But I'll leave that for another time. I sink onto the buttery leather, cradling my coffee, and watch in a slight trance as Leila slits open each envelope, smiles at the card, puts it down, and reaches for the next one.

"Oh," she says suddenly. "That reminds me. He left this for you."

"Who?"

The man, silly!"

She hands me a 6 Folds Place envelope and I stare at it blankly. There's the sound of a timer from the kitchen, and Leila gets to her feet.

"That's my egg," she says. "D'you want an egg, Fixie?"

"No," I say hurriedly, my stomach heaving at the thought. "Thanks, though."

As she leaves the room, I slowly open the envelope. There's no note inside, just the coffee sleeve. I pull it out and stare at it. It's been written on, in Seb's writing:

Paid in full. With thanks.

And, underneath, his signature.

As I read his words, I feel a deep wrench of—what, exactly? I'm not sure. Wistfulness? Longing? My brain keeps flashing back to dancing with him last night. The lights playing over his face; the pounding music. His eyes on mine. The connection we had. I want somehow to go back there, to that place, to him.

But let's get real. That's never going to happen.

Giving myself a mental shakedown, I slide the coffee sleeve back into the envelope. It's a souvenir, I tell myself as I fold down the flap. A fun memento. I'll never see him again and he'll probably marry Whiny and that's . . . you know. Fine. His choice.

"Is it something interesting?" says Leila, coming back in with her egg and looking at the envelope.

"No." I shake my head with a wry smile.

"Shall I chuck it for you, then?" she says helpfully.

She holds out her hand, and before I can stop myself I exclaim sharply, "No!"

My fingers have tightened around it. I'm not giving it up. I'm not throwing it away. Even if that doesn't make any sense.

"I mean . . . don't worry," I add, seeing Leila's taken-aback expression. "I think I'll hold on to it. Just in case. You know."

"Of course!" says Leila in her easy, unquestioning way. "Come on, share my egg with me, Fixie," she says cozily, sitting back down beside me. "You need some food inside you. And then . . ." Her eyes sparkle at me. "*Then* we'll do your nails."

Fourteen

*H*annah's house is like a John Lewis catalog. All the furniture is from John Lewis, plus most of the curtains and cushions. Her wedding list was half at John Lewis and half at Farrs, and, actually, all the things blend together pretty well. They're good quality, nothing too way out . . . all very *tasteful*.

And usually I think Hannah's house represents her perfectly. John Lewis is such a calm, reassuring place, and Hannah's such a calm, reassuring person. But the Hannah in front of me now is totally different. She's on edge. Her brows are knitted. She's pacing around her tidy white kitchen, nibbling on a carrot stick.

"He doesn't want to know," she's saying. "He doesn't want to know. I've tried talking to him, but it's like he just doesn't want to know."

"Hannah, why don't you sit down?" I say, because she's a bit unnerving, pacing around like that. But she doesn't even seem to hear me. She's lost in her own thoughts.

"I mean, what happened to 'for the procreation of children and their nurture'?" she suddenly says. "What happened to *that*?"

"Huh?" I stare at her.

"It's from our wedding!" she says impatiently. "Marriage is, quote, 'for the procreation of children and their nurture.' I said that to Tim. I said, 'Weren't you listening to that bit, Tim?'"

"You quoted your *wedding vows*?" I say in disbelief.

"I have to get through to him somehow! What's *wrong* with him?" Hannah finally sinks down at the kitchen table. "Tell me again what he said."

"He said he's stressed out by it all," I say warily. "He seemed a bit overwhelmed. He said having a baby was going to be . . . er . . ."

Do not say "a nightmare."

"What?" demands Hannah.

"Tough," I say after a pause. "He thought it was going to be tough."

"Well, it will be, I guess," says Hannah, sounding upset. "But won't it be worth it?"

"Er . . . I suppose so." I bite my lip, remembering Tim's beleaguered look. "By the way, what's Le Mahs?"

"What?"

"Le Mahs. Or La Mars."

"Oh, *Lamaze*," says Hannah. "It's, like, a baby system. There are Lamaze births, Lamaze toys . . ."

"Right. And who's Annabel Karmel?"

"She's the baby-puree guru," says Hannah at once. "You need to start at six months. Ice-cube trays."

OK, the gibberish has started again. *Ice-cube trays?* What's she *on* about?

"Hannah," I say carefully. "You're not even pregnant.

Why are you talking about what happens when the baby's six months old?"

"I'm thinking ahead," she says, as though it's perfectly obvious. "You have to be prepared."

"You don't have to be *that* prepared. Shouldn't you cross each bridge as you come to it?"

"No." Hannah shakes her head adamantly. "You have to *plan*. You have to *research*. You have to start your to-do lists."

To-do lists? Plural?

"How many lists do you have?" I ask lightly.

"Seven."

"*Seven?*" I drop my coffee mug down on the table with a crash. "Hannah, you cannot have seven to-do lists for a baby that hasn't been conceived yet! It's insane!"

"It's not insane!" she says defensively. "You know I like to get everything in order."

"Show them to me," I demand. "I want to see."

"Fine," says Hannah, after a pause. "They're upstairs."

I follow her upstairs, along her immaculate landing, to the room that I've always assumed will be the nursery. We enter, and my hand goes to my mouth. Oh my *God*.

It looks like the control center of some crime inquiry. There's a massive pinboard on the wall, covered with file cards on which I see phrases like *Research baby yoga* and *Second name if it's a boy* and *Investigate epidural risks*. Next to it are blu-tacked three dense typed-out lists, the first headed, *Postpartum—to-do*, the second, *Education—to-do*, the third, *Health checks/issues—to-do*.

"I mean, the main lists are on the computer," says Hannah as she switches on the light. "This is extra stuff."

"The main lists are . . . on the computer?" I echo faintly.

No wonder Tim feels overwhelmed. *I* feel overwhelmed. I don't know anything about having babies, but this *can't* be right.

"Hannah," I begin—then stop, because I don't know how to proceed. "Hannah . . . *Why?*"

"Why what?" she retorts in a snappy way that isn't her, and I know that at last I've got under her skin. I take her hands and hold them firmly in mine, waiting until she meets my eye. She looks tired. And stressed. My strong, calm, super-brain friend looks vulnerable, I realize. When did she last laugh?

"Have you made to-do lists for up until the baby leaves home?" I say in gentle, teasing tones. "Have you worked out every family holiday you'll take?" I give a sudden overdramatic gasp. "Oh my God, where will you hold its eighteenth-birthday party? Quick! Let's google venues!"

A tinge of color comes to Hannah's cheeks.

"You know I like breaking things down into tasks," she mutters.

"I know you do." I nod. "You're kind of addicted to it."

"I'm not *addicted.*" Hannah looks scandalized at the word. I can practically see her thoughts: *I'm a professional woman with furniture from John Lewis! How can I be an addict?*

"You kind of are," I say, undeterred. "And this is not good for you. It's not good for Tim." I let go of her hands as I gesture around. "And it's certainly not good for the baby, because at this rate, the baby's never going to get born!"

"It's just . . . challenging." Hannah sinks down onto the bed, looking worn out. "I don't know how people do it."

"They've been doing it for centuries," I say, sinking down beside her. "They didn't have to-do lists in caveman times, did they?"

"They probably did," returns Hannah, her eyes glinting. "Cave drawings are probably all to-do lists. *Pick up supper. Kill mammoth. Make bearskin.*"

I grin back and for a moment we're quiet. Then I look up.

"Hannah, do you actually *know* anyone with a baby?"

"Well . . . not really," admits Hannah after a pause. "I mean, a couple of people at work have had them. I held one once."

"You held one baby once?" I say incredulously. "That's it? So where did you get all this from?" I wave at the file cards.

"Online. And books. It is on my to-do list to meet real mums," she adds defensively.

"OK," I say. "Well, Nicole has a million friends with babies. Why don't you meet one and ask her what it's like? Maybe Tim could come along too. And you could both think about having an actual *baby,* instead of a to-do list."

"Yes," says Hannah. She heaves a heavy sigh and I can see her eyes traveling about the little room as though seeing it for the first time. "Yes. That would be good. That would be great, in fact. Thanks, Fixie. I'll call Nicole."

"I can talk to her," I volunteer. "If that's easier?"

"No, I'll do it," says Hannah, as I knew she would, because she's like me—she does things for herself.

"Come here." I pull her in for a hug. "I want you to relax. Both you *and* Tim. And you will."

"What about you?" asks Hannah as we eventually draw apart. "I haven't even *asked* about—"

"Oh, you know," I cut her off hurriedly. "Nothing to see. All over."

It's nearly two weeks since that mortifying night at 6 Folds Place. I haven't seen Jake or Leila since the morning after and I certainly haven't heard anything from Ryan.

"Well, you know what I think," says Hannah. And I nod because I do, and we've said it all, both of us.

I know Tim's on his way home from work and I suspect Hannah wants to have a long talk with him, so I don't stay for supper, even though she offers. As I step outside her front door, the air is so freezing, I gasp. It's the coldest October on record and they're talking about snow.

Greg loves it. He kept going outside today to survey the gray sky knowingly and using the word *Snowpocalypse*. I had to turn down suggestions from him that Farrs should stock balaclavas, sleds, and urine bottles (*urine bottles?*) from some activewear catalog that he adores.

"People are going to need this stuff," he said about twenty times. "You wait."

The more he pestered me, the firmer my resolve became: I am never, ever stocking a urine bottle. I don't care if it *is* the Snowpocalypse. I don't care if they *were* used on a genuine polar expedition, I *don't want to know*.

(I must admit, I did wonder: *What about girls?* And I

would have asked Greg, except he would have given me some frank and terrible answer which would have lodged in my brain forever.)

I walk briskly through the streets of Hammersmith and I'm nearing the tube station when I get an incoming call from Drew. I haven't heard from him for a while.

"Drew!" I exclaim. "How are you?"

"Oh, I'm good, thanks," he says, sounding preoccupied. "Is Nicole with you, by any chance?"

"No," I say in surprise.

"It's just that I keep trying her phone, but she's not picking up."

"Oh," I say warily. "Well, maybe her phone's broken or something."

"Yeah, maybe. Maybe." Drew exhales and there's a short silence. Quite an expensive silence, I can't help thinking, what with him being in Abu Dhabi.

"Drew," I venture, "is everything OK?"

"Well, not really," says Drew heavily. "Here's the thing. Nicole keeps saying she'll come out and visit me here in Abu Dhabi. She promises she'll get a flight. But then she doesn't. Has she mentioned it to you at all?"

"No," I admit. "But then, we don't talk that much."

"I know she's really busy, being the face of Farrs and doing her yoga and all that," he says. "And I respect that, Fixie, I do. I'm proud of her. But when I first came out here, we planned that she'd come over soon for a visit. Well, that was months ago!"

"Maybe she's making plans I don't know about," I say evasively.

"Fair enough." He sighs. "Well, sorry to bother you."

He rings off and I walk for a while, my brow crinkled. Nicole's never even mentioned going to Abu Dhabi. Which is pretty weird, now I think about it. Why wouldn't she go and visit her own husband who she misses so much?

I'm just reminding myself that other people's relationships are a mystery and there's no point speculating about them, when my phone bleeps with a text. I look down, expecting it to be Hannah or maybe Drew again—but it's from him. Seb. And it's just one word:

Help.

Help?

I stare at it, disconcerted, then ring his number. It rings and rings and I'm expecting it to go to voicemail, but then suddenly his voice is in my ear.

"Oh, hello," he says, sounding taken aback and kind of strained. "I wasn't expecting to hear from you. D'you mind— I'm slightly in the middle of something—"

"Are you OK?" I say, a bit bewildered. "You texted me **Help.**"

"I texted *you*?" He curses. "I'm so sorry. I meant to text my assistant, Fred. Must have pressed the wrong number. I hope I haven't disturbed you."

"Of course not," I say, my brow creasing. "Of course you haven't." But I feel a bit perplexed. Why would he text his assistant **Help**? "Are you sure you're OK?" I add impulsively.

"I've . . . I've been better," says Seb after a pause, and now he sounds breathless. "Been attacked, actually. My fault for cutting behind the Horizon. It's always been a dodgy alley."

"*Attacked?*" I nearly drop my phone in horror. "Are you— What *happened*?"

"It's really nothing," he says at once. "Some guys decided they wanted my wallet, that's all. Only I seem to have done in my ankle, and I can't move and I'm a bit out of the way here. Thankfully they were too repelled by my ancient phone to take that."

He's lying in an alley and he's been mugged and he's making jokes about his phone. I half want to smile and half want to yell, "Take this seriously!"

"Have you dialed 999?" I ask. "What have you done?"

"Dialed 999?" Seb sounds horrified at the idea. "Of course not. Don't be ridiculous. I just need to get to a hospital. Fred will come and pick me up; he lives in Southwark. It's two minutes from Bermondsey. That's where I am," he adds as an afterthought.

"So why haven't you called him?" I demand, sounding almost aggressive in my worry.

"I tried," says Seb patiently. "Then I texted him, or so I thought. If I can't get through to Fred, I have a lot of other willing colleagues and friends I can easily reach, if you could kindly get off the line—"

"Oh," I say. "Yes. Of course. Sorry."

But I don't want to get off the line. I don't feel happy about this. What if he can't get through to Fred?

"You should dial 999," I say.

"The 999 service is overstretched," says Seb, his voice coming in little fits and jerks. "Don't you read the papers?

It's for *real* emergencies. I'm not dying; I'm not having a baby; I'm not stuck up a tree. But I would quite like to get through to my assistant, so I'm going to ring off now. Bye."

The line goes dead and I stare at my phone, my heart thumping and thoughts jostling in my head.

I mean, it's his life.

And I'm sure he's right: He's got loads of friends who will pop straight round in their car, scoop him up, and take him to hospital. He'll be on the phone by now. They'll be getting in their car. It'll all be fine.

Do not interfere, Fixie. Do not interfere.

I put my phone in my pocket, exhale loudly, walk three steps—then stop dead. My fingers are drumming against each other. Now my feet start pacing: *forward-across-back, forward-across-back.*

I can't not do something, I can't, I *can't.*

Hurriedly, I find Google Maps, search *the Horizon in Bermondsey*—it turns out to be a cinema—and locate the alley Seb must be in. Hook Alley, that has to be it. Then I dial 999, and wait to be connected. Just the act of dialing reminds me of when Mum collapsed, and I feel fresh shoots of anxiety.

"Hello," I say, as soon as I hear an operator's voice. "I need ambulance and police. The address is Hook Alley, Bermondsey. There's an injured person and he needs help and he was mugged and . . . please hurry. Please."

They keep me on the line for what seems like ages, asking me questions I can't possibly answer. But at last they tell me to please keep this phone with me and that the services have been alerted. I ring off, then frantically flag down a taxi. I

can't risk the tube—no signal—and I need to get to Hook
Alley.

As we set off, I call Seb's number, but it goes straight to
busy. What's he busy doing? Being rescued?

Will he be furious that I called 999?

Well, I don't care. Let him be furious.

It takes forty-five minutes to reach Bermondsey, and I sit
tensely for the whole journey. As I scramble out at Hook
Alley, I'm half expecting to see blue lights, but there's no ambulance in sight. There's crime tape, though, and a few people loitering about, gawking even despite the cold, plus a
couple of police officers guarding the scene. As I try to get
near, I feel a horrible dread looming.

"Hi," I say to the nearest police officer, who seems engrossed in his walkie-talkie. "I made the call; it was me. . . ."
My voice is disintegrating breathlessly, but for once it's not
because of Jake; it's because of fear. "Is he OK?"

"Excuse me," says the police officer, not seeming to hear
me, and heads off to consult his partner. I'm desperate to
clamber under the crime tape, but I've seen enough TV shows
to know what happens if you do that. The scene gets con-
taminated and the court throws out the case, and there's no
justice, and grieving families yell at you.

So instead I stand there, almost hyperventilating, needing
to know: Where is he? How is he? What *happened*?

Abruptly, I realize I've been muttering aloud, and a nearby
man has heard me. He's a broad gray-haired guy in a massive
puffer jacket and seems to be standing there for no other reason except to watch.

"Beat him up, they did," he says in an accent which reminds me so strongly of Dad, I feel a sudden visceral pang. "He was out like a light. Wheeled him off on a stretcher. I saw it."

Tears of shock start to my eyes. Out like a *light*?

"But he was conscious!" I say. "I was talking to him! How could he— What happened?"

The man shrugs. "He had rubbish all over him too. They emptied a bin on him, I guess. They're animals, they are. If I had my way they'd get what's coming to 'em. Forget parole, for a start," he adds, warming to his theme. "None of this nancy-boy treatment. Send 'em all on National Service, that'd sort 'em out—"

"Sorry," I interrupt desperately. "Sorry. I just really need to know where they've taken him. Which hospital. Do *you* have any idea?"

The man's mouth twitches. He doesn't say anything but takes a few paces to the corner and swivels his head meaningfully. I follow him, then turn my own head—and find myself staring at the top of a building. Distinctive metal letters are illuminated against the evening sky and they read: NEW LONDON HOSPITAL.

Of course. I'm so *stupid*.

"Won't have taken him nowhere else, will they?" says the man. "Emergency's round the back. Don't even try to get a cab," he adds. "The one-way round here's a shocker. Quicker to walk."

"Thanks," I gasp, already hurrying away. "Thanks so much. Thanks."

I sprint through the back streets, panting in the freezing air, not stopping until my heart feels it will explode. Then I walk for a bit, then run again, then get lost under a railway arch. But finally I make it to the bright lights and bustle of the New London Hospital's emergency room.

As I step inside, the hospital smell hits me first. Then the noise. I know emergency rooms are always busy, but . . . bloody hell. This is mayhem. Far worse than when we took Mum in. There are people everywhere. All the plastic chairs are full, and a guy with a gash on his forehead is sitting on the floor nearby. About three babies are howling, and a man with vomit on his jacket is drunkenly berating his . . . Is that gray-haired, anxious-looking woman his *mother*?

Averting my eyes, I head to the desk and wait for what seems like an eternity before a brisk woman says, "Can I help?"

"Hi, I'm here for Sebastian Marlowe. Has he been admitted?"

The woman types at her computer, then raises her head and gives me a suspicious look.

"He was admitted earlier," she says. "He's been sent for tests."

"What kind of tests?" I ask anxiously. "I mean, is he . . . Will he be . . ."

"You'll have to speak to a doctor," she says. "Are you family?"

"I . . . Not exactly . . . I know him, though. I made the 999 call."

"Hmm. Well, if you wait, you can speak to the doctor who— Oh, you're in luck. Lily!"

She beckons over a pretty Asian-looking doctor, who seems so rushed off her feet, I can hardly bear to hold her up. But I have to know.

"Hello, can I help?" she says charmingly.

"Sorry to delay you," I say in a rush. "I'm here about Sebastian Marlowe. I'm the one who called 999. I just need to know, will he be OK? I mean, is he—"

"Please don't worry," she says, gently cutting me off. "He regained consciousness soon after arrival. We're giving him a CAT scan, though, as a precaution, and taking a couple of X-rays. He's in good hands and I suggest you go home. Tomorrow he'll be on a ward, and if you want to, you can visit then. He's very lucky that you phoned 999," she adds. "Good job."

She smiles again and is moving off, when something else occurs to me.

"Wait!" I say, hurrying after her. "Am I the only person who knows he's here? Do his next of kin . . . does anyone else *know*?"

He doesn't have any family, I've suddenly remembered, and the thought makes my throat constrict. Here he is, beaten up in hospital, with no family, no one at all—

"I'm fairly sure one of the nurses made a call for him," says the doctor, crinkling her brow in thought. "She spoke to his . . . girlfriend?"

The word stops me short. *Girlfriend*.

I mean, of course. His girlfriend. Whiny. He has her. She'll be the one he wants to see.

"Great!" I say a little heartily. "Perfect. His girlfriend. That's—yes. Well. So. My work is done. I'll just—so. I'll go home, then."

"As I say, he'll be on a ward tomorrow," she says kindly. "Why not come back then?"

As she meets my gaze with her wise doctor's eyes, I have a weird conviction that she gets it. She somehow understands that I *have* to know how Seb is, because I feel this strange, inextricable link to him. Which isn't a *relationship*—God, of course not. We're not even friends, really. It's just . . . it's a different kind of thing. A yearning. A tugging in my heart. A need to be with him and know that he's OK. I mean, what would you call that?

I blink and meet the doctor's patient gaze again. *Does* she understand it all?

Or am I projecting?

OK, I'm projecting. She's just waiting for me to go away. *God, Fixie, get a grip.*

"Thanks," I say for a final time. "Thanks so much." And I head out of the hospital before I can catch a superbug.

He's safe. That's all I needed to know. And Whiny will visit him tomorrow. Or his friends will, or whatever. So, really, there's no need for me to. That's the end. Job done.

Fifteen

*E*xcept that at five the next morning I'm wide awake, knowing only one thing: I have to go and see him.

I don't care if Briony's by his side. I don't care if a whole army of friends turn to stare and say, "Who are *you*?" I don't even care if his colleagues whisper to each other, "It's that awful girl who introduced Ryan to the company! Yes, her!"

By 6:00 A.M. I've conjured up about a million possible scenarios, each more embarrassing than the last, but I'm still resolved. I'm going. No one can stop me. I know I don't have any actual relationship with Seb. I know I can't even claim to be a friend. But the thing is, until I see him with my own eyes, all I can picture is crime tape and police officers and my own lurid visions of him lying on a stretcher, hovering between life and death.

I text Greg, telling him that a medical emergency has come up (true), then spend two hours agonizing over what to take. Flowers? Do guys like flowers? They might *say* they do, but do they *actually*?

No. I don't think they do. I think guys *actually* like cans of beer and expensive remote controls and football games. But I can't take any of those to a hospital bed.

Chocolates? Sweets?

But what if his mouth got bashed and he can't eat?

My stomach gives a nasty twinge at the thought, and I shake my head to dispel my worst fears. I'll see him soon enough. I'll know the full picture.

Then the answer hits me: a plant! It's uplifting and natural like flowers but not quite as frilly. And it'll last longer. There's bound to be a plant shop somewhere on the way.

I check the hospital website for visiting times, phone Greg to make sure he's opened up, change my outfit three times, google *plant shops*, spray myself with scent, then stare at myself in the mirror. I'm wearing nothing fancy: just jeans and a nice top.

OK, my best jeans. And my nicest top. It's chiffony and a bit dressy, with sheer sleeves. But it's not too dressy, definitely not, it's simply . . . nice. It's a nice top.

Which is of course totally irrelevant. In sudden shame, I realize I've been looking at my reflection for three minutes and hastily turn away. As if what I look like matters. Come on. Time to go.

The nearest florist to the hospital is called Plants and Petals, and as I arrive I feel it should be hauled up for misrepresentation. There are no plants, only flowers. And those are mostly of the frilly pink variety.

"Oh, hi," I say to the girl behind the counter. "I'm after a plant. Quite a *plain* plant. For a man," I clarify. "It needs to be masculine-looking. Strong-looking."

I'm hoping she might say, "Step this way, the masculine

plants are in the back," but she just sweeps an aimless hand around and says, "Help yourself. Carnations are half price."

"Yes," I say patiently, "but I don't want carnations, I want a plant. A masculine plant."

The girl looks blankly at me as though she has no idea what a masculine plant is. I mean, come on. Masculine plants are definitely a thing. And if they're not, then they should be.

"Don't you do any yuccas?" I ask. "Or really plain spider plants? You're called Plants and Petals," I add, almost accusingly. "Where are the plants?"

"Yeah, we don't really do plants no more," she says with a shrug. "Except the orchids. Very popular, the orchids."

She points at a row of pots on a nearby shelf, each containing a single orchid. Each beautiful flower is tethered to a little wooden stake, and they look quite cool and minimal.

A guy might like an orchid. Mightn't he?

"OK, I'll take this one," I say, grabbing the most minimal orchid of the lot. It has only two white blooms, with large, shell-shaped petals.

"Gift wrap?" asks the girl, beginning to pull out a sheet of iridescent pink cellophane. "You get a free ribbon," she adds. "Pink or purple?"

"No, thanks!" I say hastily. "No gift wrap. It's fine as it is. Thanks. Although I would like a card."

I choose the least garish *Get Well* option and write:

Dear Seb
Wishing you a speedy recovery

Fixie

Then I pay for the orchid and hurry along the streets to the hospital, wishing I'd remembered my gloves. It's bloody freezing, even though the Snowpocalypse hasn't hit. As I reach the hospital entrance, a few shell-shaped orchid petals blow away in the breeze, and I curse myself for not asking if there was any plain cellophane.

Anyway, never mind. I'm here now.

Clutching the orchid, I head to the main desk and eventually discover that Seb is on Nelson Ward on the fourth floor. As I rise up in the crowded lift, my heart starts thudding and my hands suddenly feel a little damp.

I mean, this is a good idea, isn't it?

"Noah!" exclaims a woman. "Leave the lady's flower alone!"

I turn my head and to my horror see a toddler in his mother's arms, triumphantly clutching a fistful of orchid petals.

Shit. What's he *done?* There are only about six petals left on the plant now.

I whisk the orchid away out of danger and survey it anxiously. It still looks OK. It just looks even more minimal. Super-minimal.

"I'm so sorry," says the mother, and I notice that the toddler has a cast on his foot and, really, am I going to make a fuss in a hospital? So I smile and say, "Not to worry," and cradle the precious orchid with both arms until we reach the fourth floor.

As I reach Nelson Ward, I'm starting to lose confidence. My throat is tight with apprehension. My legs have lost their bounce. *What if— What if he's— Oh God, what if—* My head is looping around all kinds of disastrous possibilities, and a large part of me wants to run away and forget it.

But somehow I force myself to walk forward, ask a nurse for Sebastian Marlowe, and make my way to his cubicle. He's in a ward of four beds, and his is at the far end. As I approach, it's fully screened by a printed curtain.

"Knock knock," I say, my voice a bit shaky. "Are you there, Seb? It's Fixie."

There's no reply, so I peep round the curtain, and there he is. Alone. And asleep.

I survey him silently, my heart thumping in reflexive terror, which gradually subsides. His face is bruised. His hair has been shaved a little at the temple, and he's got a dressing there that makes me wince. One of his ankles is strapped up in a bandage, I notice. But he doesn't seem to be on life support or anything like that. My stomach gives the most almighty lurch of relief, and without meaning to, I exhale hugely. He's OK. He's alive.

There's another reason for my relief, I realize: He's asleep. I don't have to talk to him. Because suddenly I feel incredibly nervous and I'm not sure what I would say. Maybe my best plan is: Leave the orchid and card—then back out of his life altogether. Yes.

Trying to be absolutely soundless, I tiptoe around his bed to his nightstand. I prop the card against the wall—then as it slips, I grab at it, bumping against his water jug, which tilts. In silent dismay, I grab for the jug to right it, then realize I've knocked his plastic glass, *shit.* . . .

Desperately I grab for the glass, then realize I'm dropping my orchid and grasp for that too, at which point the glass falls on the floor with a loud clatter, and Seb opens his eyes.

Shit.

He stares at me for about twenty seconds as though he can't compute anything, and I stare back, agonized, wondering where to start.

"Your name is Sebastian," I say at last, in slow, careful tones.

"I know that!" he says. His eyes travel down the hospital bed, taking in his injured ankle, and I see the click of remembrance in his face. "Right," he says. "Right. Yes." He's silent for a moment, then his eyes meet mine again. "Was it you? Who called 999?"

"Yes," I admit. "It was me. I know you didn't want me to, but . . . well, I told you, I can't help fixing things!" I give a high, fake laugh, trying to mask my awkwardness. "Usually turns out badly, but . . ."

"It didn't turn out badly," he says slowly. "It would have turned out badly, if . . ." He halts again, and his woodland eyes turn dark as though with thoughts he's not going to share.

"Well. I did." I give another awkward laugh.

"Yes." His eyes fix on me again, then his face jerks. "I'm so sorry!" he says. "Where are my manners? Sit down, please."

"Thanks," I say, a little shyly, and sit on the plastic visitor's chair. "Oh. This is for you."

I proffer the orchid, which I've been holding all this while. But as he takes it, I realize in horror that my hand has been wrapped tightly around the remaining delicate petals, and they've all come off in my hand.

I've basically given him a bare twig in a pot.

"Wow," says Seb, surveying the twig confusedly. "That's . . . lovely."

And now he's being *nice* about it. I can't bear it.

"It's supposed to have these on it," I say quickly, opening my hand to show him the crumpled white petals. "It was an orchid, but it had a few accidents. This is what it looked like. . . ."

I try to demonstrate where the petals should go, but I keep dropping them, and at last I look up to see Seb clamping his lips together as though he's trying not to laugh.

"No, it's great," he says hurriedly as he catches my eye. "It *was* great. I can see that."

"Maybe they'll grow back," I say in lame hope.

"Yes, definitely. I'll keep watering it." He pats it, his eyes distant for a moment, then adds matter-of-factly, "You saved my life."

I stare at him, jolted. I mean, yes, I called 999. But saved his *life*?

"I'm sure I didn't," I say.

"You saved my life," he repeats. "And I want to thank you."

"I didn't save your *life*!" I say, totally embarrassed. "Honestly! All I did was . . . You know. I made one call. I thought you should have medical attention. That's all. It was nothing. If I hadn't called, someone else would have— Can I pour you a glass of water?"

"What they said to me," Seb continues, ignoring my attempt to deflect him, "was that if you hadn't called, no one might have noticed me in that alley. Apparently I was covered in a mound of litter, behind a bin. I might not have regained consciousness. It was one of the coldest nights of the year. Hypothermia. Kills people every winter." He meets my gaze again, his eyes unreadable. "So. Life. Saved. And again: Thank you."

"Well." I feel a tingle rise up my cheeks. "I just . . . Anyone would have . . . What *happened*, though?" I can't help asking. "You were fine. You were talking. And then you were out cold."

"The guys who'd had a go at me came back," says Seb, his face twisting up as though with a memory he doesn't want to have. "Or maybe it was a different lot. As they say, didn't see them coming. Knocked me out."

I don't know how to reply. I survey Seb's injuries anew and feel tears of anger coming to my eyes. Seb is a good guy. He should not be hurt by *anyone*.

"Anyway, I owe you one," Seb adds with a wry smile.

"You really don't." I smile back, relieved that he's not looking quite so grave anymore.

"I really do," he contradicts me. "Although how I ever pay *that* one back, God only knows."

"Buy me a drink." I shrug. "I'm a cheap date." As soon as I say the words I realize with horror how they might sound. "I mean . . . Not . . ." I flounder hopelessly. "Not *date*. I meant . . ."

"I know what you meant," says Seb, looking amused.

"How's Briony?" I add quickly, to send the message: *I*

know you have a girlfriend. "I expect she's on her way. I'll leave as soon as . . . She must have been shocked."

"She's in Amsterdam on a business trip," says Seb. "Gets back tomorrow. We talked about her getting a flight today," he adds, as though reading my mind, "but there's no need for her to cut her trip short. I'm fine here, and it's a pretty important conference for her."

"Right," I say, nodding. "Absolutely. Makes more sense."

I'm not going to judge Whiny. I'm not.

But *really*? A conference? When he nearly *died*?

"Fair enough," I add for good measure, to make it plain that I'm not casting any aspersions. "Let me pour you that water."

As I hand him the glass, Seb has a quizzical look to his eyes and I have a horrible feeling he's remembering all the rude things I said about Briony that night at 6 Folds Place. Quick, let's move on to another topic.

"Anyway, the police were there," I say. "So let's hope they catch whoever did this."

"Unlikely," says Seb. "But, yes, let's hope." Then his expression changes. "Wait, you *went* there? To the alley itself?"

"Oh," I say, flustered. I hadn't intended to let that slip out. "Well . . . yes. Just to check the ambulance had got there. It was practically on my way," I add quickly.

"No, it wasn't," says Seb, his face crinkling with some emotion I can't read. "You really are my guardian angel."

"Hardly! So . . . how long will you have to stay in?"

"Only a day or two," says Seb. "It was the head injury they were worried about. But as you see, I'm completely all there, totally normal." He suddenly pulls a grotesque face and I can't help giggling.

There's silence for a while, and we listen to the visitors in the next cubicle, who are saying things like, "You can hardly tell," and "It's not much of a scar," and "You'll soon be right as rain, Geoff!" in eager, overlapping voices.

"That guy was mugged too," says Seb conversationally, gesturing at the curtain, and I wince. "You know, I'm a liberal kind of guy, but I find myself feeling . . . what would I call it? Vengeful." He smiles enough that I know he's joking, but his voice is dry enough that I know he's kind of not joking too.

"I'm not surprised," I say lightly, determined to keep the conversation upbeat. "Will you turn into a vigilante?"

"Maybe," says Seb, giving a bark of laughter. "You'll see me on the evening news, wearing my tights and mask, brandishing—what? Lead piping?"

"A candlestick," I suggest, and we both smile again.

"Are you a vengeful person?" Seb asks, taking a sip of water. "You seem like a person who doesn't bear grudges."

"I guess I don't, really," I say after a moment's thought. "Except once, and that was two years ago and I *still* bear the grudge."

"Tell me," says Seb, his eyes lighting up with interest.

"It's a stupid story," I say, feeling embarrassed.

"I love stupid stories," says Seb firmly. "And I'm an invalid and I need entertaining. Tell."

"Well . . . OK. Two years ago I set up this catering firm, and I had a girl who did the admin. Sarah Bates-Wilson."

"She sounds like a villainess," says Seb obligingly.

"Good. Because she is. She was always helping herself to stuff on my desk. Like, pens or whatever. And one day she borrowed my hairbrush."

"Heinous!" says Seb.

"Stop it!" I say, laughing. "I haven't finished yet. It was this really nice tortoiseshell brush from a set that my mum and dad gave me. You know. Brush, comb, mirror. It *went* together."

"And she never gave you the brush back," suggests Seb.

"Exactly. First she said she hadn't taken it, then she said she'd given it back. . . . Anyway, one day I went round to her house."

"For a hairbrush?"

"I really wanted it!" I say defensively. "It was a matching set! She lived in a ground-floor flat, so first of all I crept round the back and I looked in her bedroom window and I could see it. I could actually see it on her chest of drawers!" My voice rises with indignation.

"So what happened?" demands Seb.

"I rang the bell and she answered in her PJs and said she hadn't got it and told me to leave. So I had to go."

"No!" exclaims Seb, sounding genuinely outraged.

"Exactly! So then I thought, *I'll take a picture of it through the window and* prove *it's there.* But by the time I got back, it had gone. She must have hidden it."

"OK, that's creepy," says Seb firmly. "Really creepy. Was she still working for you?"

"No, not by then."

"Thank God. She sounds like a sociopath."

"I wouldn't have *minded,* except it was a present from

Mum and Dad, and since Dad was gone . . ." I trail away. "You don't want to lose stuff like that."

"Of course." Seb's eyes soften. "I'm only teasing. I'd have been livid. And you don't need to explain about the matching set either. We always had this wonderful family story that my great-great-grandfather had an antique chess set. One Christmas Eve, a queen was stolen and a ransom note was left in its place."

"A *ransom* note?" I can't help a giggle.

"It demanded two pounds, to be left inside the grandfather clock. I guess that was a pretty big sum back then. The only people in the house were my great-great-grandfather, his wife, and their four sons, aged between twelve and twenty-three. It could have been any of them."

"So what happened?" I ask, agog.

"Apparently my great-great-grandfather paid the ransom, the piece reappeared, and no one ever said anything about it."

"What?" I stare at him. "OK, that is *so* not what would have happened in our family. Didn't your great-great-granddad want to know who it was? Didn't he want to catch them? Didn't he want to find out *why* they were kidnapping chess pieces?"

Seb thinks for a moment, then shakes his head. "I think he just really wanted his chess piece back."

"Wow," I say incredulously. "Families are the weirdest—" I stop as I suddenly remember. "Sorry." I bite my lip. "Sorry."

"What for?"

"I know about—" I swallow, searching for words. "Your family. What happened."

I have no idea how to put it and I know I'm messing up, but Seb lets me off the hook.

"I've been unlucky," he says, in his straightforward, honest way. "Unlucky. At least, when it comes to my family." He breathes out and I catch a fleeting pain in his eyes. "But please don't apologize."

"Hey, Seb! Man! What did they *do* to you?"

The curtain swishes back and the face of a guy in his twenties peers in.

"Andy!" exclaims Seb, his face lighting up.

"Oh," says Andy, looking at me. "Sorry to interrupt. I'm here with the guys," he adds to Seb. "You like *all* varieties of Krispy Kreme, right? Because we had a row in the shop."

"I should be going," I say hurriedly.

"Don't on our account," says Andy with a friendly smile. "Have a Krispy Kreme."

"No, I need to go. Thanks, though."

"We'll let you say goodbye, then," says Andy, withdrawing from the cubicle, and I get to my feet.

"So . . . get well," I say to Seb, feeling suddenly awkward.

"Thanks for coming." His eyes crinkle at me in a smile. "Thanks for *everything*." Then a thought seems to strike him. "Hey. Have you still got the coffee sleeve? Because I need to make a new entry."

"You don't." I shake my head, laughing.

"I do! I want to record my debt of gratitude. Have you still got it?"

"I *think* so," I say, wrinkling my brow as though I'm not sure. "I think it's somewhere around. I could come and see you again tomorrow, maybe?" I add casually. "Bring it in?"

"I'd like that." He nods. "In fact, I'd love that. If you're not too busy."

"Of course not." I pick up my bag. "So I'll see you tomorrow."

"With the coffee sleeve," he insists.

"OK." I nod, rolling my eyes with a smile. "If I can find it."

Of course I can find it. It's on my dressing table, right where I can look at it every day.

The three guys waiting patiently outside the cubicle smile at me politely, clearly wondering who I am. I recognize one of them from Seb's office and fervently hope he doesn't recognize me.

I walk away through the ward, listening to their voices as they greet Seb:

"Oh my *God*."

"Man! They really got to you."

"Yeah, but you should see how *they* look. Right, Seb?"

They sound so easy and affectionate, I can't help smiling inwardly. And as I'm traveling back down in the lift, I remember all the stories I read online about Seb building up his company, cooking pasta for his staff, creating the amazing atmosphere that he's got. He needed to make a family, I realize. And that's what his company is, his family.

The next day I wake at 5:00 A.M. again. I really need to break this habit. My eyes instantly swivel to the coffee sleeve, propped up on my dressing table, and I feel a little flutter inside. The kind of light, excited flutter I haven't felt since . . .

Oh God. Since Ryan, now I come to think of it. I feel about sixteen years old. This is kind of mortifying.

As I'm showering, I give myself a stern talking-to. This guy is *taken*. He's simply being friendly in a platonic way. There's absolutely no hint that . . . I mean, if there *is* any hint, it's me reading too much into things. . . . And anyway, he's taken. He's *taken*.

I step out of the shower, wrap myself in a towel, and look at my reflection, trying to find some inner resolve. What I should do now is quietly bow out. I should phone up the ward with a friendly excuse, wishing him well and saying goodbye. *Certainly* not prolonging this back-and-forth IOU game we seem to be in. It's inappropriate. It's gone on for long enough. What I need to do is nix it. Throw the coffee sleeve away. Get on with my life. That's what I should do.

And as I look into my own alert, exhilarated eyes, I know that's pretty much exactly what I'm *not* going to do.

After breakfast I get ready with care, putting on a dress I got in a cheap and cheerful Acton boutique the other day. It's navy with a print of dachshunds all over it, and it makes me smile. I was going to keep it for parties, but suddenly that seems boring. Why not wear it now? Today? I do my makeup, text Greg to make sure he's on the case, and pick up my bag to go.

Then I pick up the coffee sleeve. I run my eyes down the entries. His writing . . . mine . . . his . . . For a moment I hesitate. Then, almost defiantly, I pop it into my bag and head out.

Seb is awake as I arrive and greets me with a smile. He already looks a million times better than yesterday, with more color in his cheeks—although some of his bruises are turning lurid. He sees me eyeing them and laughs.

"Don't worry. They'll go."

"How are you feeling?" I say as I sit down.

"Great!" he says. "I'm out of here tomorrow. And I get free crutches, so it's not all bad. Did you bring the coffee sleeve?" he adds. "Tell me you did."

"I did." I can't help smiling at his enthusiasm and produce it from my handbag. Seb takes a pen from the nightstand and writes carefully on the coffee sleeve, then hands it to me with a grin.

"Read it when you get home."

I'm dying to read it now, but obediently I put the coffee sleeve away in my handbag. Then I reach into my canvas tote, produce a flat box, and hand it to him, feeling a little nervous.

"I brought you something, in case you get bored. It's a chess set," I add idiotically, as though he can't read *Chess Set*. "I mean, it's nothing special, it's only cheap. . . ."

"This is great." Seb's face glows. "Thank you! Can you play?"

"No," I admit. "No idea."

"OK, I'll teach you. We'd better clear these away," he adds, gesturing at the newspapers littering his bed. "A nurse kindly procured them for me, but there's only so many articles you can read about aliens."

"Isn't it extraordinary?" I agree, with a laugh, as I start folding the newspapers up. The whole media has exploded over some guy who "saw a UFO" in his garden last night and videoed it.

"D'you think when presidents get elected, one of the first things they do is write their speech for when aliens land?" muses Seb as he unpacks the chessboard.

"Yes!" I say, delighted by this idea. "Of course they do. And they practice it in the mirror. 'My fellow humans, on this epic day, as I stand here, humble yet brave . . . '"

"I bet Obama had a great one prepared," says Seb. "I almost wish we'd been invaded by Martians, just so I could have heard it." He looks at the piece in his hand. "OK. So, introduction to chess."

Seb lays out all the chess pieces and starts explaining how one type goes forward and another goes diagonally and another hops around. And I *do* try to concentrate, but I'm fairly distracted by . . . well, by him. By his focused expression. His strong hands moving the pieces around. The passion he clearly feels for the game. "*This* is an interesting maneuver," he keeps telling me, and I can't admit that I've lost all track of everything he's told me.

"So," he says at last. "Shall we play?"

"Yes!" I say, because what's the worst that can happen, I lose? "You go first."

Seb puts the pieces in order again and moves a pawn. Promptly I copy what he did with one of mine. Then he moves a something-else, and I make a mirror-image move.

"So basically I can keep copying you," I say.

"No, no!" Seb shakes his head. "You should experiment! Like, that knight?" He points to the horse. "That could go to all sorts of places." I pick up the knight and he puts his hand over mine. "So it could go there . . . or there. . . ."

I'm feeling a bit breathless as he moves my hand around

the board, and I'm about to ask him, "What about the queen?" when there's a jangle of curtain rings and a resounding, confident voice exclaims, "Seb!" and my heart stops.

It's her. Briony.

I yank my hand out of Seb's so quickly I send half the chess pieces flying, and Seb looks a little flustered and says, "Briony! I thought you weren't back till— Hi!"

Briony takes a couple of steps toward the bed and I can see her eyes moving over us rapidly, zooming in on every detail.

"I was just—" I begin, as Seb says, "This is Fixie. The one who made the 999 call. Saved my bacon."

"Oh, you're *that* girl," says Briony, and her demeanor instantly changes. "Thank you *so* much. We're *so* grateful. God, Seb, your *face*," she adds, with a *moue* of distaste. "Will it scar?"

"No," says Seb easily, "shouldn't do," and I see something instantly relax in Briony's expression.

Is that what she was worried about? Whether his *face* would scar?

"We need to get *this* better, though," she says, patting his ankle. "What about Klosters?"

"I know!" Seb shakes his head ruefully. "The *one* year we're organized and book ahead— Skiing," he adds to me.

"Of course!" I nod heartily.

"Got you a card," Briony says, handing him a postcard— and as he reads it he bursts into laughter. I can't see what it says. Maybe it's some private joke or whatever.

I'm feeling waves of disappointment and I'm hating myself for it. I mean, what was I hoping? That they wouldn't get on? Of course they get on. Maybe they have the odd row, but they're both tall and sporty and joke around and make one of those great couples you see in the street and say, "What a great couple."

"So," I say, scrabbling for my bag. "I ought to be going. . . ."

"Chess!" exclaims Briony, her eyes lighting upon the board. "Excellent!"

"Fixie brought that too," says Seb.

"*So* kind," says Briony. "How did she know we're both mad about chess?"

"Lucky guess," I say with an awkward laugh. "Anyway, get well soon, Seb. Bye."

I grasp his hand briefly in a weird kind of half shake, avoiding his gaze, then get to my feet.

"Thanks again, Fixie," says Seb, and I mumble something indistinct in reply.

"Yes, thank you *so* much," says Briony in her penetrating, confident voice. She's not being Mean Newsreader anymore; she's being Elegant Duchess. "We're both *incredibly* grateful. Let me see you out," she adds in a hostess-like manner, as though she owns the ward and the hospital and, in fact, everything.

We both walk to the door of the ward, whereupon Briony says again, "We're *so* grateful," and I murmur, "Honestly, it was nothing."

As we reach the double doors, her eye falls on my dog-print dress and she says with interest, "That's Aura Fortuna, isn't it?"

"What?" I say blankly.

"The iconic print," she says, as though it's obvious. "Except . . . shouldn't the dogs have hats on?" She looks even more closely at the fabric. "Oh, wait. It's a knockoff, isn't it?"

"Er . . . dunno," I say, confused. I've never heard of Aura Fortuna. Or any iconic print. I just saw the dress and I liked the dogs.

"Hmm," says Briony in kind, pitying tones. "I kind of think if you're not going to do it properly, you shouldn't even try?"

Her words are like a stinging slap. I can't even think of how to respond.

"Right," I say at last. "Well . . . nice to meet you."

"You too." Briony clasps both my hands with a final, wide smile, which clearly reads: "Go away and stay away." She closes with, "And as I say, thank you *so* much. You did a *wonderful* job and we're both *so* grateful to you."

My face is burning with mortification all the way down in the lift. But by the time I'm pushing my way out into the freezing air, I'm seeing the funny side of it.

Kind of.

I mean, you have to see the funny side of things, otherwise . . . what? You start brooding morosely on why he's with someone so blinkered, and what does he see in her, and how can anyone be that rude, and . . .

Oh God. I *am* brooding morosely. *Stop* it, Fixie.

A thought suddenly occurs to me and I pull out the coffee sleeve. I know it's only a silly game, I know it's meaningless, but I might as well see what he wrote. I pause in the street, breathing out steam in the cold air and reading his handwritten words:

You saved my life, Fixie. To repay you that is impossible. Just know that from now on I owe you everything.

And underneath is his signature.

I read the words twice over, hearing his voice in my head, seeing his warm, honest smile in my mind's eye. My eyes become a little hot. Then I shove the coffee sleeve back in my bag and stride on, down the pavement, shaking my head almost angrily. Enough. It's all stupid. I need to forget about it.

Sixteen

*A*nd I do. I manage to put him out of my mind. At least, most of the time. It's easy enough to throw myself into the shop, what with Christmas heading toward us like a high-speed train and Stacey wanting to sell "Fifty Shades of Farrs" stockings, each containing a spatula, two clamps, and a rolling pin. (I don't want to know.)

Mum's been away for nearly three months, I realize one morning, with a jolt. It's already November. She's got to come home soon, surely? She loves the run-up to Christmas and all our traditions. We'd normally be making our Christmas cake around now, but I don't want to do it without her, so I haven't even bought the ingredients.

I'm at the shop one morning, watching Nicole put away her yoga stuff after an early-morning class, feeling pinpricks of frustration. She *still* doesn't do it properly. The customers will arrive and she'll be putting all the wrong things on the wrong display tables. We had to sell a toaster for a fiver the other day because she'd put it on the £5 table. It's *so* annoying. And it's even worse now we have all our Christmas displays up, because if you keep moving them, they start to look shabby. The gingerbread house on the front table already looks a bit disheveled. We'll have to make another one.

I spray "Yuletide scent" around the place to give it some atmosphere (£4.99 and easily as good as a posh brand) and tidy up the display of festive napkins. Nicole is wandering over, clutching three yoga mats, and I'm about to say something to her about being more careful with the stock—but to my surprise she looks twitchy and worried. If she's any animal right now, it's Anxious Rabbit. I thought yoga was supposed to calm you down?

"Nicole, are you OK?" I say at last, and she jumps about a mile.

"Oh yeah," she says. "Yeah."

She's not, though. She leans against the counter and chews a nail and I notice that it's red and raw already. It's not as if Nicole and I are the kind of sisters who share confidences—or anything, in fact—but she looks strained and Mum's not here and I have to say *something*.

"Nicole, what's up?" I persist. "Come on. Tell me."

"Well, OK," she says at last. "Drew wants me to go to Abu Dhabi." She throws the words out in a tremulous voice, as though saying, "Drew's having an affair." Then she adds, "He wants me to *visit* him."

"Right," I say carefully. "I mean . . . that seems like a good idea, doesn't it? In fact, I spoke to him about it recently."

"He basically gave me an ultimatum!" Nicole seems astounded. "He was like, 'Nicole, I've had enough. I want to see you.'"

"Well, isn't that natural? I think he just misses you."

"He's so *judgmental,*" she continues as though she didn't hear me. "He was like, 'We're married, Nicole.' And 'You promised to come out.' I was like, 'Stop *criticizing* me, Drew. You're so *negative.*'"

I look at her beautiful brow, all creased up with distress. I've wondered about a million times in my life what it's like to be Nicole—and now I'm getting a bit of an inkling. When you've been adored and admired and praised your whole life, maybe any tiny altercation feels like criticism.

"I'm sure he doesn't mean to criticize you," I say. "I'm sure he just wants to see you. I think you should go!" I add encouragingly. "I bet it's amazing out there. And warm. Go for a week. Or two weeks!"

"But what about my *yoga*?" says Nicole. "What about my *business*?"

Immediately my empathy turns to frustration. For God's sake. Her business? Five women lying on mats? "What about your *husband*?" I want to retort. "What about your *relationship*? Don't you value those things?"

I draw breath to say all this—then suddenly lose my nerve. That's never been how we talk to each other. Nicole might bite my head off. And, anyway, is this the right place? Greg's just opened the doors and three customers have come in.

"I'm sure you'll work it out," I say vaguely, then blink in surprise, because Jake is coming through the doors too, dressed in a sharp suit and eyeing the customers with his usual supercilious displeasure.

"Is Bob here?" he demands as he approaches, and I catch a heavy waft of aftershave.

"Bob? No. Don't think so. He'll be here tomorrow. Why?"

"I was trying to get through to him yesterday." Jake frowns. "I thought I'd swing by on the off chance."

"Why do you need to speak to Bob?" I say in surprise.

"Oh, something I noticed in the accounts."

"What did you notice in the accounts?" I ask at once.

"Shit, Fixie!" he says impatiently. "Does it matter? Whatever!"

"Right," I say warily, because I sense he's not in the mood for conversation. He looks fairly shocking this morning. His face is pale, with purple shadows under his eyes. And he seems more lined, somehow.

"Heavy night last night?" I try teasing him. Usually Jake would grin and tell me how many bottles of champagne he got through and what they cost, but today he glowers at me.

"Just lay off, OK?"

"Oh, excuse me," says a pleasant-looking woman, approaching us. "Do you have baskets? To put things in?" she adds. "Shopping baskets," she clarifies, as though the phrase has just occurred to her. "You know what I mean?"

Jake eyes her silently for a moment. Then he goes over to the stack of red plastic baskets, picks one up, and proffers it to the woman with elaborate care.

"Here," he says. "They were in that pile. That pile there, by the door where you walk in? Right where you can see them? That one?"

I stare at him in utter horror. You can't speak to customers like that. Dad would *kill* him.

It's only because of his affected drawl that he gets away with it. The woman stares at him uncertainly, clearly not sure whether he's being sarcastic or not, then gives him the benefit of the doubt and says brightly, "Thank you!"

"Jake, you can't—" I begin, as soon as she's walked off. "That wasn't— You could have offended her—"

Oh God, I'm stuttering again. *Why* can't I sound as confident in actual speech as I do inside my head?

"Well, for fuck's sake," says Jake defensively. "What kind of moron can't see the baskets?"

He heads off to the back room and I count to ten, telling myself that this time I have to confront him. He can't jeopardize our relationship with customers, even if he *has* got a sore head.

I make my way to the back room and push open the door, expecting to see Jake on his phone, or striding around, or being Jake-ish—but to my astonishment he's sitting on one of the foam chairs, his head back, his eyes closed. Is he asleep? Whether or not he is, he looks exhausted. Backing away, I close the door quietly and return to the shop floor. "Now, young lady," comes a stern voice, and I glance up to see a gray-haired woman in a tweed coat approaching me. "Where's all your plastic storage gone?"

"Oh, right," I say. "We do stock storage containers, actually. That aisle." I gesture helpfully, but the woman doesn't seem impressed.

"I've checked! There's nothing there! I want the jumbo size for my mince pies." She eyes me with a gimlet gaze. "Where are *they*?"

"Oh, right," I say again, playing for time.

I had a row with Jake over the jumbo containers. He said they were bulky and tragic-looking and cluttered the place up. So we returned some and the rest are in our storage facility in Willesden.

"I can get you some in," I say. "I can have them by this afternoon—"

"That's no good! I want them now!" the woman huffs angrily. "I'll go to Robert Dyas. But it's out of my way."

She walks off before I can say anything more, and I feel a wave of frustration. I *knew* we shouldn't cut the stock so drastically; I *knew* we should play to our strengths—

"Bye, then, Fixie," says Nicole, who's been drifting around, fiddling with the displays, noticing nothing.

"Wait," I say. "Jake's asleep in the back room. He looks really rough. Not just night-out rough. Worse than that."

"He's probably burned out," says Nicole sagely. "He needs to learn to self-care. He should come to my yoga class."

"Right," I say doubtfully. "I can't really see Jake doing yoga."

"Exactly! And *that's* the problem," says Nicole, as though she's solved everything. "See you."

She wafts out before I can respond, and I stare after her. Maybe she's right; maybe Jake *is* burned out. He's always been about *more,* Jake, his whole life. More money, more status, more stuff for him, more stuff for Leila . . . But how's he paying for it all? With his health?

Maybe I should talk to him. I wanted to have it out with him about the food storage department—but this is more important.

I leave it for an hour, telling all the staff to stay away from the back room. Then I cautiously push open the door and survey Jake. He opens his eyes a chink and peers back at me blearily.

"Hi," I say. "You fell asleep. You must have been tired."

Jake rubs his face, checks his watch, and says irritably, "Jesus." He pulls his phone out of his pocket and starts scrolling down his messages, wincing as he does so.

A few ravens begin to flap around my head, because Jake sometimes bites your head off if you ask him personal questions. But I can't just let this go by. I have to say something.

"Jake," I venture, "you look exhausted. Are you working too hard? Are you burned out?"

"Burned out!" Jake echoes with a short laugh, looking up from his phone for a nanosecond. He turns his eyes back to his screen and I watch as tension creeps up on his face. I've never thought of Jake as vulnerable before. But right now he looks anxious and beleaguered and weary, even though he's just had a nap.

"Are you doing too many deals?" I try again. "Are you overwhelmed?"

"You know what's overwhelming?" says Jake, and there's a sudden edge to his voice which makes me wince. "Life. Just life."

"Well, why don't you slow down a bit? Why don't you have a break?"

Jake puts down his phone and stares at me silently for a moment. His face is strained but his eyes are unreadable. Yet again, I realize I don't know my brother very well.

"You've got a good heart," he says. "Dad used to say that about you. D'you remember?"

"*Dad?*" I stare at him. "No."

"When you were little. Nicole and I used to push you around in the wheelbarrow. And you fell out the whole time, but you always laughed. You never whinged."

"The wheelbarrow!" A memory comes to me—an old wheelbarrow with red handles on our scrubby lawn—and I almost laugh in delight. "Yes!"

"You were cute." A smile passes across Jake's face and I think I can see genuine affection there, a nostalgia for the past. I smile timidly back, hoping we might talk like this for a while longer.

But already Jake is preoccupied by his phone again. "I've got to go," he says, standing up.

"Wait," I say eagerly. "Could we just have a word about storage containers?"

"Storage containers? *Jesus,* Fixie."

All the softness disappears from his face. He's back to impatient, scornful Jake again.

"What's wrong with storage containers?" I retort before I can stop myself, but Jake just rolls his eyes.

"I do *not* have time for this," he says, and strides out of the room.

I stare after him, prickling with stress, thinking, *How did that go so wrong?* when a text bleeps from my phone. I haul it out of my pocket, half-thinking it might be from Jake—but as I see the name, my stomach flips over. It's from Seb.

It's been ten days since his accident, and I thought I'd never hear from him again. I thought he was recuperating with Briony, playing chess and laughing uproariously at all their private jokes.

I wonder what he wants. I mean, it's probably nothing. . . . It's probably another mistake. . . .

Despising my fingers for trembling, I press on the text and read it.

Hello, guardian angel. I have a thank-you gift for you. Are you around this evening? Seb

For the rest of the day I try not to obsess. It's no big deal. It's nothing. We've made an arrangement to meet; he'll give me a box of chocolates or whatever and we'll say goodbye. End of.

But I can't help it: My heart is jumpy. And I keep glancing in the mirror. And I keep thinking of witty things to say. All in all, I'm hugely relieved when at around four o'clock Hannah appears through the doors. Thank God: distraction.

"What are you doing here?" I ask in surprise, whereupon Hannah goes a bit pink around the ears and says, "We took the afternoon off. We're doing what you said. Here they are."

She turns to the doors and I follow her gaze to see Tim entering, followed by a girl with a baby in a sling. I recognize her as one of Nicole's friends, although I can't remember her name. She has long, greasy curly hair and is wearing a hoody spattered with orange stains.

"So, like, it's really easy with one of these," the girl says, gesturing at the sling. "You can, like, take the baby anywhere, feed anywhere. . . . Hi, Fixie. I need, like, a wipe-clean tablecloth."

"Absolutely!" I say. "We've got a whole range."

I point them out and the girl heads over in that direction.
At once I turn to Hannah.

"So . . . ?" I say in an undertone. "And, quick, remind me
of her name?"

"Iona," says Hannah discreetly.

"*Iona.*" I nod. "Yes, of course."

"Nicole put us in touch. We've spent the whole afternoon
with her. Shadowing her. Seeing what having a baby is like."

"Wow!" I say. "And how's it going?"

"Really informative," says Tim.

"*Really* informative," agrees Hannah.

There's a weird undertone to their voices, but I can't quite
tell what it is. I'm about to ask more, but just then Iona
comes back holding a tablecloth and puts it on the counter.
Her baby is adorable, and we all take turns to coo over him
and hold his little chubby hand.

"Like I say," says Iona to Hannah, "parenting is a breeze,
as long as you go with the flow, you know? Don't *stress*. And
you don't need to buy a crib or any of that crap. I sleep with
Blade and his two older brothers, all in the same bed. It's the
natural way."

"What about your . . . partner?" says Tim, taken aback.

"Yeah, he has to put up with it," says Iona with a laugh.

"I see," says Hannah, equally taken aback. "So in terms
of sleeping . . ."

"*Sleeping?*" Iona laughs again. "That doesn't happen!
My God, sleeping! We don't remember what that is, do we,
monster? Nighttime is playtime! I mean, he still feeds, like,
ten times a night? But he's only seven months, so." She
shrugs. "Early days."

"Wow," says Hannah, looking unnerved. "OK. The thing is, I was talking to my doctor once, and he was saying that sleep is really important for—"

"Your doctor," Iona interrupts. "Like an NHS doctor? A mainstream doctor?"

"Well . . . yes," says Hannah, sounding puzzled. "Of course."

"I'm not even registered with a mainstream doctor." Iona gives her a pitying look. "My biggest piece of advice: Don't trust mainstream doctors. They have an *agenda,* you know? They want to get you on their system. The minute you get pregnant, if you do," she adds to Hannah, "go to my nutritionist. I'll give you the number. She specializes in baby health. She's like, 'What are people *doing,* putting drugs into *babies?*'"

I can't help glancing at Hannah and Tim. They both seem frozen.

"But what if the baby's ill?" says Tim at last. "What if the baby needs medication?"

"'Ill,'" says Iona, making quote marks in the air. "You know how many babies are addicted to drugs because the doctors *want* them to be?"

I have to bite my lip. Tim looks like he wants to erupt, and I've never seen Hannah's eyes so goggly.

"Right!" says Tim. "Well. It was great to spend the afternoon with you, Iona. Thank you so much for sparing the time."

"No worries," says Iona easily. She fist-bumps him, then kisses Hannah. "And remember—there *are* no rules."

"Except the rules of science," says Tim under his breath, and I stifle a giggle.

We all watch in silence as Iona saunters out, whereupon Tim and Hannah explode simultaneously.

"Oh my *God*."

"Jesus, what a *nutter*."

"We are never doing it like that. Never. *Never*."

"I couldn't *live* like that."

"Did you see that *kitchen*? The *mess*!"

They're speaking with a common passion, a fervor, a united spirit. It's actually really touching.

"Hannah, your to-do lists are a work of art," says Tim suddenly. He takes her by the shoulders and gazes at her as though he's fallen in love with her all over again. "They're stupendous. I'll do everything on them. Just please don't make me sleep in a bed with six children and ignore medical research."

"Never!" says Hannah, laughing. "Although I could lighten up a little. I guess I am a bit of a . . . What did Iona call me? Controllagirl. All I did was wash up a couple of mugs for her," she adds to me. "There was literally not *one* clean mug in her kitchen."

"I love you, Controllagirl," says Tim, kissing her, and I see Hannah's face turn a happy, rosy pink.

"Right back at you, Controllaguy."

"OK now, garlic press," says Tim, abruptly changing gear. "We mustn't forget. I'll go and get one."

He strides off in his determined way and I beam at Hannah.

"So! Everything's OK again? Tim's not freaked out anymore?"

"I'll tell you what *really* freaked him out," she responds. "The idea that someone could name their children Journey, Wisdom, and Blade."

She catches my eye and starts giggling, and that sets me off, and soon the pair of us are in total fits. And I wasn't planning to tell her, but as we're both calming down I find myself saying, "So guess what? I'm seeing that guy later. The one who gave Ryan the job. Who had the accident. He wants to give me a present to say thank you."

"Oh, him," says Hannah, and I feel her eyes zoom in on me. "That's nice."

"Yes," I say, trying to sound casual. "That's what I thought. He didn't need to."

"But it's not—" She hesitates. "He's attached, right?"

"Oh, totally!" I say quickly. "Totally."

I can tell Hannah's slightly intrigued but isn't going to push it. "Where are you meeting him?" she asks, and I give a wry laugh, because this *is* funny.

"Well. You'll never guess."

Seventeen

I have no idea why Seb has chosen Somerset House skating rink for our meeting. His ankle is injured. He can't skate, surely. But that's what he said, so that's where I am. And I've got here early because . . . Well. Just to watch and enjoy.

It's got to be the most Christmassy bit of London, this ice rink, surrounded by the grand, elegant façade of Somerset House. A spectacular Christmas tree is towering over everything and music is pounding through the air and people are laughing and calling to each other.

I'm sipping a hot chocolate, shivering slightly in the wintry breeze, mesmerized by the ice. I'm remembering what it felt like to sweep out on the rink to start a competition routine, all alone, chin up, heart pounding, and the smell of hairspray in my nostrils. (Mum always overdid the hairspray.) I mean, it's madness when you think about it, trying to dance and jump on two perilous knife-edges. But when it goes right, when you land a big jump safely . . . it's the most exhilarating feeling in the world.

A group of people are making their way onto the ice, laughing and pushing each other and taking selfies, and after a moment I realize that one of them is Briony. Which means

Seb must be here. I swivel my head, looking all around, and suddenly spot him, wrapped up in a dark coat and checked scarf, sitting on a chair and watching the skaters with a pair of crutches at his side. I walk swiftly toward him and wave to attract his attention.

"Hi!" I say, and his face creases into a delighted smile.

"Hi!" he says, and starts struggling to his feet.

"Don't be silly," I say, gesturing at him to stay and crouching down beside him. "How are you? Your face looks a *lot* better," I add, eyeing his cheeks and temple. The swelling has gone right down and he practically looks normal.

"Fun, this," he says, nodding at the rink. "You ever do it?"

"I have done," I say after a pause.

"Well, thanks for coming. I thought it would be a nice Christmassy place to meet."

"Definitely!" I nod.

"You're doing great!" Seb calls out to his friends, and they all wave back. For a few moments I watch Briony on the rink. She's wearing a short white twirly skirt and a fur hat and she *looks* amazing, but her skating is abysmal. It's actually worse than average, I decide, after watching her critically for a few minutes. She needs to slow down and stop flailing her arms, for a start.

Do her boots not fit? Or is she simply showing off too much? As soon as I've had this thought, I realize I've got it. She isn't even thinking about what she's doing; she's posing in front of her friends, most of whom are guys, I notice. They're all well dressed and calling out names like "Archie!" to each other. Jake would *love* them.

"So, I wanted somewhere nice to give you this," says Seb,

interrupting my thoughts. He hesitates, then reaches into a Tesco canvas bag and pulls out a parcel. It's medium-sized, quite light, quite nondescript. No branding or gift bag or anything like that—just plain brown paper. I have *no* idea what it is.

"Open it!" says Seb. "Just my little thank-you," he adds casually.

"Well, you didn't need to," I say, smiling with mock disapproval as I tear open the wrapping paper. "There was really *no* need. But I'm very—"

My words dry up on my lips as the paper comes off. I'm staring at the object in my hands, my head spinning in disbelief.

"My *hairbrush*?" I manage at last.

"Safe and sound," says Seb, looking satisfied. "Restored to its rightful owner."

I turn it over in my hands, my throat tight. I'm flashing back to the day Mum and Dad gave it to me, on my sixteenth birthday. The way it looked in its presentation box, all smart and new.

"I thought I'd never see this again," I say dazedly. "I thought I'd— Wait." A new thought grips me. "How? *How* did you get this?"

"Good vigilantes never tell," says Seb in mysterious tones. "This will go with me to the grave."

"No. No." I shake my head vigorously. "You can't turn up with this, with *this*"—I brandish the hairbrush at him—"and not tell."

"OK." Seb capitulates at once. "Actually, I'm *longing* to tell. Our story begins when you let slip the name of your hairbrush's abductor," he says in dramatic tones. "Sarah Bates-Wilson. At once I knew I could track this villain down. She still lives in a ground-floor flat," he adds more conversationally. "Which was handy."

"Did you break-and-enter?" I stare at him, aghast. "Oh my God." My gaze drops to his foot. "But you couldn't have!"

"I knew my injury would hamper me," Seb continues in his dramatic voice. "I therefore enlisted an accomplice: my faithful sidekick Andy. We hatched a plot in which I would distract Sarah B-W at the door, asking her questions about her political views, while he crept round the back. Her bedroom window was open; the hairbrush was on the chest of drawers. It was a matter of mere seconds for him to reach in and pinch it," he ends with a flourish.

I'm silent for a moment, digesting this.

"What if the window hadn't been open?"

"We would have tried again another day. We were lucky," adds Seb, in his normal voice. "We'd only gone along to case the joint. Getting the hairbrush first go was a bonus."

"I don't know. . . ." I stare at the hairbrush, feeling suddenly conflicted. "I mean, this is amazing, but . . . you broke the law."

"She broke the law first," points out Seb. "She stole your hairbrush."

"Yes, but . . . you *broke the law*!"

I'm clutching stolen goods in my hand, it occurs to me. Oh my God. If Dad taught us anything besides *Family first*, it was *Stay on the right side of the law*.

"I didn't break the *natural* law," says Seb with assurance. "Think about it, Fixie. All those companies legally siphoning off money offshore to avoid paying tax. All those executives legally awarding themselves mammoth pensions while their workers get nothing. All abhorrent. I go to jail for restoring your hairbrush to you—and they don't?"

He sounds so certain, so honest, so *good*, that I feel a bit of confidence seeping back into me.

"The law doesn't always know what it's doing," he adds for good measure. "Humans have a far greater instinct for what's right in life than lawyers do."

"The law is an ass," I volunteer. I heard that once, and I'm not sure where it comes from but it seems appropriate.

"The law is a *wuss,* if you ask me," counters Seb, "but that's another story. Or maybe it's politicians who are wusses." He grins at me disarmingly, his green-brown eyes shining. "Don't let me get onto my hobbyhorse. You'll die with boredom."

"I won't!" I laugh.

"Oh, you will," he assures me. "Many have."

"Well, anyway . . . thank you," I say, giving the hairbrush a loving pat. "Thank you for breaking the law for me."

"Anytime." He grins. "It was fun."

A thought occurs to me and I reach into my bag. I pull out the coffee sleeve, and Seb laughs with appreciation. I take out my pen and start to write *Paid,* but Seb puts a hand on mine.

"Paid in part," he says. "Only in part."

"Don't be silly." I roll my eyes.

"No, I mean it. I haven't even *begun* to pay you back," he says, and now there's a serious tone to his voice. "What you did—"

"I told you. It was nothing."

"You saved my life," contradicts Seb. "In some cultures we'd be bound together forever now," he adds lightly. "Bonded for life."

And I know it's a joke, but my stomach stupidly flips over—and suddenly I've lost my cool. I can't find a witty answer. I gaze back at him, at his honest handsome face, and he's silent too, but unreadable. And I'm thinking desperately, *Say something, Fixie, for God's sake, say something*—when there's a cry from the rink: "Yoo-hoo!"

We both turn our heads and there's Briony, waving to catch Seb's attention. She sees me and her face instantly tightens and Seb calls out easily, "Remember Fixie?"

"Of course! How's it going?" says Briony, her smile dazzling and her voice so acid it could strip paint.

"Fine!" I say. "I should leave," I add automatically to Seb.

"Don't leave! You want to skate?" he adds, bringing a ticket out of his pocket. "I can't use mine, obviously. Go on, have a go!"

I stare at the ticket silently, all kinds of thoughts shimmering around my brain. The music is thudding and the lights are twinkling and Seb is asking me if I want to skate.

It's kind of irresistible.

"Sure," I say at last. "Sure. I'll have a go."

. . .

The first few laps I make are like taking out an old musical instrument, tuning it up, playing the notes slowly, alert for defects and flaws. My body's older than it was, but it's still strong and taut. I still have muscle memory. You don't train for that many hours and not know what you're doing.

As I cut across the white surface, I try not to think longingly of my old skates, hanging up at home, and instead make the best of what I have: a crowded public rink, strange skates, and ice that's already getting wet from people falling over on it.

I don't care. I'm loving this.

I whiz past Briony, turn round, and see her gawping at me as I skate backward. I turn again, make sure I have enough space, then lift a leg in an arabesque. And I'm stiff—really stiff—but my leg still obeys, even if it's screaming, "Whaaat? Seriously? But we don't *do* this anymore!"

Poor legs. I send them a quick message, saying, *Do this for me and we'll have a hot bath later.*

I head into the center of the ice and do a simple spin. Then a faster, flashier spin, ignoring the tremble that begins halfway through. *Come on, legs, you can do it. . . .* Then, for the first time, I dart a look at Seb. He's gaping at me in such openmouthed astonishment that I can't help laughing and doing a few dance steps. I feel so *light* out here; I feel so *happy. . . .*

And suddenly it hits me: I'm performing. I'm blossoming. Because there's someone I want to perform to.

All the other skaters have moved to the sides of the rink, giving me space, nudging each other and applauding. I'm aware of the staff conferring and pointing in a group and I know they'll come and chuck me off any moment. And I'm not going to hog the ice, I'm really not, that would be obnoxious . . . but there's room enough now to spread my wings. To jump. To do a big jump.

"Dancing Queen" is playing through the speakers, and it's not the music I did my junior free program to—but even so, I find myself falling into its familiar patterns. The intricate footwork sequence I practiced, what, a thousand times? My feet are performing it without my brain even switching on. And now I'm out of that sequence and building up momentum for the jump. I'm sweeping in more powerful circles, focusing my mind, remembering the calm voice of Jimmy, my coach.

My thighs are burning and my heart is thudding as I prepare, and even as I'm taking off I'm thinking, *This is crazy! I'm going to break my ankle, my neck. . . .*

As I'm rotating in the air, I feel a moment of sheer terror. I can hear the silence. I can feel the drawn-in breaths. I catch a glimpse of the staff, all turned to watch. And then, like a miracle, my skate lands cleanly, and the whole place erupts in applause. My leg is shaking horrendously, my ankle feels like putty, and every muscle in my body is protesting—but I've done it, I've nailed it, only fourteen years too late. Everyone is still clapping and cheering me and I've never felt like such a show-off in my life.

And I've never felt so good in my life.

I make a little curtsy to the crowd and skate off, unable to wipe the ecstatic smile off my face, replying, "Thank you!" again and again as people say, "Well done!" As I reach the gate to leave, I suddenly come across Briony, standing in her twirly skirt, clinging tightly to the barrier.

"Nice skating," she says, shooting me daggers. "Didn't know you were such a pro."

And I *know* I shouldn't, I *know* I shouldn't . . . but I can't help myself.

"Yeah, well," I say, and give Briony exactly the same pitying look that she gave me in the hospital. "I kind of think if you're not going to do it properly, you shouldn't even try?"

Eighteen

I'm still in my surreal glow as I return my skates, put on my everyday boots, and go to find Seb. As I approach him, he's clapping and nodding, an astounded grin at his lips.

"Well," he says as I get near. "So *that* wasn't what I was expecting."

"Oh yeah," I say nonchalantly. "Did I mention that I used to skate?" I meet his eye and we both start laughing, and then I wince and rub my thighs ruefully. "I'm going to pay for this tomorrow."

"I have some crutches you can borrow," says Seb, and I grin, then pick up the hairbrush.

"I'll go now. But thank you again. You have no idea how precious this is."

"What is it?" comes a familiar foghorn voice behind me, and I turn to see Briony approaching. She must have given up on the skating. She peers at the hairbrush with a frown. "What's this?"

"It's the present I told you about," says Seb. "The thank-you for Fixie."

"When you said 'hairbrush,' I expected something *nice,*"

says Briony, wrinkling her nose. "Not this. I mean, Seb, where did you get this from, Oxfam?"

He didn't tell her the whole story, I register. And I'm about to explain that it has sentimental value, when Seb exclaims, "Can't you for once in your bloody life say something *nice*, Briony!"

Immediately he looks a bit shocked at himself—as though he hadn't been planning to say anything at all, and then that came out.

"Nice?" Briony lashes back at him. "What nice thing am I supposed to say about this? It's hideous!"

"It's not hideous!" I say furiously, before I can stop myself.

"This is too much," says Seb, his face white and taut. "Briony, I think you should apologize to Fixie."

"Apologize?" echoes Briony incredulously. "Apologize to her? Are you *nuts*?" She comes close and stares at him, breathing hard, her face flushed and actually quite beautiful-looking. "You know what, Seb? I don't know *who* this girl is . . . or *how* she came into your life . . . but you're welcome to her. Enjoy!" She makes an exaggerated, sarcastic gesture at the pair of us, then swivels on her heel.

Shit. She's going. She's actually leaving.

"I'm so sorry," says Seb, as she stalks away. "That was—"

"No, it's fine," I say quickly.

"You saw the worst of her." His brow wrinkles. "She has this temper . . . but she can be really fun, really entertaining. I mean, she's *very* bright, and she does a lot of charity work through her job—"

"It's fine," I say again, cutting him off. "Really."

I know what he's doing: He's justifying why he's with her. Or *was* with her, I'm not sure which. But I don't need to hear the list of "Briony's hitherto-unsuspected good qualities."

"So," I say after a long pause. "Is that . . . Are you two . . . ?" I can't bring myself to say the word *over*, but it's hanging there in the air.

"I think that was me getting fired," says Seb with a wry grin. "Don't you?"

"Yeah." I bite my lip, then add, "Sorry. That was my fault."

"No. No, no." He shakes his head adamantly. "I would have walked, anyway."

"Right," I say, trying to sound neutral, because the *biggest* mistake I could make right now would be to criticize Briony.

For a while we're silent, watching the skaters whirling and floundering round the ice. Then Seb draws breath.

"It's funny," he says, his eyes distant. "You get into a relationship. And you *know* that person has flaws, everyone does . . . but you can get so used to them that you . . . you forget. You forget that there's another way. Sorry, I'm not making sense—"

"You are," I say fervently, because what he's describing is exactly Ryan and me. "You forgive the person and you endlessly rationalize and you forget . . ."

"That there are other people out there," says Seb softly, and as he meets my eyes, I feel a sudden tightening in my stomach. *Other people.* What does he mean? Me?

No, don't be stupid, I scold myself at once. *Of course he doesn't mean me. He probably means, like, there are loads of people on Tinder.*

"On Tinder?" I hear myself saying idiotically, and a flicker of amusement passes over his face.

"I wasn't thinking of Tinder."

His warm green-brown eyes are traveling questioningly over my face and I gaze back helplessly, my throat too clenched up with nerves to speak, my thoughts a chaotic whirl: *This is it, this is it. . . . Wait, is this it?*

A bleep suddenly sounds from Seb's phone and we both glance down automatically. I see the name *Briony* flash onto the screen and feel a sudden qualm. Maybe this is her apologizing and wanting to make up.

"You should probably . . ." I gesture awkwardly at the screen. "It might be . . . Don't mind me."

Wordlessly, Seb opens the text and reads it. It's quite long and I can see lots of capitals and exclamation marks.

"Right," he says at last, wryly. "Well, I have been fired. Quite conclusively."

"I'm sorry," I say again. "Really."

I try to look as heartfelt and sorry as I can, but I'm not sure I'm doing a very good job, because there's a twinkle in Seb's gaze. He puts his phone away and there's a breathless beat.

"So, I was wondering," he says at last. "Would you—maybe—like to have dinner sometime?"

Nineteen

*F*orty-eight hours later I'm sitting with Seb in an Italian restaurant, and I don't quite know how I've got through the last two days. I've worked in the shop and started some Christmas shopping and mended the loo when it broke (Dad taught us all elementary plumbing when we were children). Outwardly I've appeared normal. Relaxed, even. But all the time I've been thinking, *Dinner with Seb . . . oh my God . . . Dinner with Seb . . . oh my God . . .*

Then I went the other way and worried that I'd suddenly, inexplicably, find him unattractive. But here we are at last, sitting at a table in the golden glow of an overhead light, and I can't take my gaze off him. Seb's eyes are fixed on mine too. And it's so obvious what both of us want, I don't know how I ever doubted it for a moment. We've both ordered linguine with clams and discussed wine a bit and even the weather, but that's felt like the subtext to a different, silent, much more charged communication.

As the wine arrives, though, Seb clearly decides to become more talkative.

"Tell me about yourself," he says, as the waiter disappears. "Tell me about Fixie." He toasts me and I clink back and sip. The wine is crisp and delicious and I feel like having quite a lot of it.

"What do you want to know?" I laugh, mentally putting together my brief, official "Fixie Farr's life so far" paragraph.

"Everything," says Seb emphatically. "Everything. Clearly you're an Olympic skating champion, for a start. Your family must be really proud of you."

And I know he didn't mean to, but he's already skewered me. He's hit my sore spot. Skating isn't in my official paragraph—usually I edit it right out.

"Kind of," I say, and I shoot him a bright smile, but I know it's not convincing.

"Kind of," echoes Seb slowly.

"Let's talk about you," I parry, and I see him digest the fact that I'm batting him away. He takes a few gulps of wine, his eyes flickering with thought.

"I have an idea," he says at last. "Shall we be honest with each other? Shall we tell each other the Stuff?"

"The Stuff?" I echo blankly.

"You know what I mean." He looks directly at me. "The Stuff. The stuff inside your heart that's made you who you are, that you think about at night. Good *and* bad. Between ourselves."

"Oh, *that* stuff," I say with a light laugh, because I'm suddenly afraid of baring my soul. What if he doesn't like my soul? What if he thinks, *Sheesh! Never expected her soul to be like* that!

"Yes, that stuff." He plants his elbows on the table, his face lit up with that eager, interested expression I've come to know. "Who *is* Fixie Farr? Tell me."

So I take a deep breath—and I tell him. In between mouthfuls of linguine, I tell him about Dad. And Farrs. And Mum. I tell him about my catering company collapsing; how I've never paid Mum back; what a failure I've felt ever since. I tell him a little bit about how Jake makes me feel. (Not everything. Not about my skating fall, because I don't want to cast a shadow over this evening. And definitely not about the ravens. There's "honest" and then there's "too much information.")

Then I tell him all about Ryan, and he listens nicely and doesn't say a single scathing thing about him, even though I can see the antagonism mounting in his eyes.

"I was in love with a girl called Astrid at school," he says, when I've finished. "If she'd come breezing back into my life, I think I would have lost all sense. So I get it."

I even tell him how I got the nickname "Fixie": that when I was three, I used to walk around determinedly, saying, "Got to *fix* it. Got to *fix* it." (Although I could never explain exactly *what* I had to fix.)

"So what's your real name?" Seb asks, and I hesitate, then lower my voice and practically whisper, "Fawn." I know it's my name, but Fawn doesn't sound like me. It sounds like an animal.

"Fawn?" Seb regards me critically. "No. I prefer Fixie."

"Pretend I never told you," I beg him.

"It's forgotten."

The lights in the restaurant have been dimmed by now, and candlelight is flickering on our faces. The waiter clears our plates and we read the dessert menus, like you do, but only order coffee. And then I lean forward.

"Now. Your turn."

He starts with his work. He tells me about how he set up his company and what a struggle it was but fun too—and how it's all about finding the right people. As he describes his colleagues, his enthusiasm pours out, and his eyes shine with what I can only call love. He tells me how he can't stand injustice and arrogance and that's what drove him into ethical investment. He gives me a small lecture on which are the worst executive practices, in his opinion, and how companies *should* be run, before breaking off and saying, "Sorry. Boring. Boring." (It wasn't.)

Then, when our coffee cups are both drained, he tells me about his family's deaths, in more measured tones. He tells me how they all survived his dad's death pretty well and thought, *We've had our bad luck,* and got on with life, but then his mum died while he was at uni and then his brother was killed. . . . Then he notices my eyes swimming with tears and breaks off.

"Fixie, it happened," he says, grabbing my hand and squeezing it. "It happened. That's all you can say about it."

"I suppose," I say after a pause. "But, oh, Seb . . ."

"I'm fine. I'm *fine.* I've moved on, I'm at peace with it, I appreciate what I have. . . . Sorry," he adds, as though noticing for the first time where his hand is.

"No, that's OK," I say, my voice a little husky. I blink away my tears, determined to get a grip. If Seb can be so positive about it, then I should be too.

I squeeze his hand back, and he looks at me with a kind of cryptic, quizzical expression, and with a sudden lurch I realize where we are in the evening. We've talked. We've shared a bottle of wine. We're holding hands.

"So, I was thinking," I say, my gaze fixed on a distant point. "Shall I . . . uh . . . see you back home? You know, with your ankle and everything. You might need a hand up the . . . uh . . . steps. If you have steps. Do you have steps?"

My nervous gabble comes to an end and I wait breathlessly for his reply.

"I do have steps," says Seb. "And that would be very kind of you." His eyes meet mine, and something about his expression starts a pulse inside me.

"Right." I try to sound casual. "Well."

Seb gestures for the bill, then gives me another look, which makes my insides melt. "Shall we get out of here?"

We find a cab and Seb gives the address, and as the cab travels through the lit-up Christmassy London streets, neither of us says much. My breathing is shallow; my whole body feels taut. I'm super-aware of every move Seb makes but grateful he's not one of those guys who lunges at you in the taxi. I want it to be private. I don't want the driver watching in the mirror.

Seb lives in a 1930s-looking block in Islington, and as we get out of the taxi I can't help laughing, because he was totally fibbing.

"There's a ramp, look," I point out. "As well as steps."

"Ah yes." Seb nods. "What I meant was, it would be very kind if you could help me up the ramp."

He strides up the ramp—without my aid—and I follow him, giggling, and then we're in the lift and rising up to the fourth floor, where he ushers me through a gray-painted front door.

"Here we are," he says as the door closes behind us. "Home."

He gestures around, and I'm vaguely aware of a pale wooden floor with white walls, but to be honest, his flat is the last thing I'm interested in. I put my arms around his neck, which is something I've been longing to do all evening, and close my eyes, inhaling him.

His shoulders are the right height. He smells good. He feels good. His lips brush against mine and I give a little whimper, because I really, *really* want this. Does he *realize* this? Does he *realize* it?

Yes, of course he does. (I may actually be a little drunk.)

As his mouth meets mine properly, warmly, I press up against him hard and he makes a deep, indistinct sound.

"Wait, your ankle," I say, suddenly breaking away.

"What does my ankle have to do with it?" Seb looks confused.

"Dunno," I admit, and I start to giggle. "Health and safety?"

"You're delicious," says Seb, drawing back to survey me. "And as you know, I still owe you big time. *Big time.*"

He kisses the side of my neck and I feel the light brush of his teeth. And the thought that we have all night ahead of us makes me dizzy with lust.

"So . . . this is you paying off what you owe?" I manage, my breath coming in short pants.

"This is me chipping away at it," he says, slowly unbuttoning my shirt. "Little by little. I know it'll take a while. . . . Oh my *God*." His eyes darken at the sight of my breasts.

"How long will it take to work off my debt? Forever, I hope."

"I'll let you know when you're there," I murmur as his lips gently meet my collarbone. My head is thrown back in bliss and I never want this to end either. "I'll let you know."

The night is a blur of sex and sleep and sex again. Some time in the early hours of the morning, I find myself staring at him in the dim bedroom light, at the strong, lithe form of him. His back has a curve to it like the sweep of a boat. I steal out a hand to stroke it, wondering whether he's awake, when he turns and his eyes glint at me.

"Do you sail?" I say, half sleepily.

"No. Used to row, though."

"Huh." I nod my head: That makes sense. Then I hear myself saying, "Do you believe in the one? Do you believe in fate?"

I'm not expecting him to take me seriously—in fact, almost at once I regret saying something so needy. Ryan would have said, "Totally, babe," without even listening properly, but Seb is silent. He's staring up at the ceiling. He seems to be thinking.

"The rational part of my brain," he says at last, "understands that everything is random. There are a million possibilities in the universe. Us meeting is just one of those possibilities, and just as meaningless."

He sounds so matter-of-fact, I feel my heart droop a little. But then he carries on, in the same tone:

"The thing is, though, I can't imagine a world that *didn't* bring us together. We were meant to be. Don't you feel it? You were meant to walk into Café Allegro. The water molecules were meant to fall though the ceiling. It's been event on event on event. Your parents bought a shop in Acton. Mine didn't move to France."

"Were they going to?" I say in surprise.

"They thought about it when I was eight. Imagine—I wouldn't even have lived in this country. It's all been coming toward this moment." He rests his head on his hand to gaze at me, a shaft of moonlight falling on his cheekbone.

"This exact moment," I echo, teasing him.

"This precise moment right here."

"So this is pretty epic." I gesture, rumpling the duvet with a smile. It seems quite mundane, for an epic moment.

Although, actually, what more-momentous instant is there in life than being in bed with the person you feel is right? Really, really right? As these thoughts pass through my head, I suddenly feel light-headed, almost scared. Because he is right for me. He is, he *is*.

"So . . . this is it?" I say lightly. "This is what it's all been heading for? This is as good as it gets?"

"No. It's only going to get better." He pulls me toward him, his mouth gently finding the crease of my neck, his body warm and safe. "It's only going to get better."

Twenty

The light dazzles my eyelids and I feel a mouth softly kissing mine, and I find myself looking dazedly up at Seb's face.

Seb . . . Oh my God . . . The whole thing rushes back into my disbelieving, joyful brain.

"Sorry," he says. "I didn't know what time you wanted to wake up. . . ."

"Yes," I say, rubbing my face. "No. I . . . Thank you. What time *is* it?"

"Eight."

"Right." I think for a moment, then find my phone in the tangle of clothes on the floor and text Greg to take charge of opening up.

"OK." I flop back on the pillows. "I'm off the hook."

"So am I," admits Seb. "I've called into the office, told them I'll be late. I didn't want to rush away." He sits on the bed and looks down at me. "Right now I don't want to go anywhere."

We're silent for a while, just looking at each other. Memories of last night are flickering through my head and, I'm pretty sure, his too. As though reading my mind, he reaches for the coffee sleeve, which is lying discarded on the floor.

We scribbled a bit on that last night. It was a bit of a thing. It was fun.

"How's my debt payment coming along?" he says, tracing his finger down the entries. "I can't *quite* tell from this. . . ."

"Oh, you're doing well." I grin at him. "You did me a few favors, remember?"

"I think we were about even on that score." His eyes widen as he reads the scrawled writing, and he looks up. "Miss Farr, you have a dirty mind."

"You can talk!" I grab the coffee sleeve off him and feign shock as I read it. "This is X-rated." I jab at his last entry. "And I don't even know what *that* means. . . ."

"I'll illuminate." His eyes gleam at me. "Later. Breakfast?"

As I follow him out of the bedroom, I glance around curiously. I didn't get much of a look at his flat yesterday. There's a big main reception room with a kitchen off it, where Seb is filling the kettle. It has wooden floors and some modern art on the walls and two low sofas, covered in gray felt. It's impressive. It's cool. Although, weirdly, it doesn't seem very *him*.

It's not as nice as his office, I realize. His office is full of books and ornaments and character. This is a bit sad-looking. A bit hotel-like. The only hint of character in the place is a massive stack of magazines piled against one wall. I mean, *massive*. In fact, it's lots of stacks. They stretch nearly all the way along the wall, and are at least three feet high.

As I wander over to them, I realize that some of the magazines are still in their plastic—in fact, most of them are—and they're all titles about music: *Total Guitar. Vintage*

Rock. Country Music. Some are quite old, but the newest ones are from last week. Does he play the guitar? He never mentioned it.

"Cup of tea?" Seb says, bringing one out. "Or I can do coffee if you prefer?"

"Tea is great." I smile back at him. "Thanks. Nice flat! Swanky!"

It suddenly occurs to me that he probably inherited some money or whatever when his mother died. Shit. It's probably really tactless to say how nice his flat is.

"So . . . music!" I say, changing the subject. I gesture at the piles of magazines. "I had no idea."

"Oh no." Seb follows my gaze. "That's not me. James was the music nut. My brother."

"Right," I say after a pause. "Of course." I have no idea where to go next with this conversation, because my head is full of questions but I don't want to ask any of them aloud. *Why have you got so many magazines stacked up? Why are you still subscribing to magazines you're not interested in? Isn't this a bit . . . weird?*

"I should cancel the subscriptions, I guess," says Seb easily. "I'll do it one of these days."

"Right," I say again, and his voice is so relaxed, I find myself relaxing too. It's only a quirk of his. We all have quirks.

"I know you're a professional chef," says Seb, interrupting my thoughts, "so I hardly dare suggest this, but I could make you some pancakes, if you like. Or waffles?"

"Waffles?" I say, impressed. "Homemade waffles?"

"I like cooking. Although I might have to go and buy some ingredients—"

"Don't buy anything," I say firmly. "Let's have whatever you've got. Toast. Or nothing. Just tea is fine."

We make toast and take it back to bed, and breakfast turns into more sex and then lying in each other's arms, neither of us speaking. And I want to stay here forever.

"I can't," I groan at last. "I can't. I must go."

"Same." Seb sighs.

"*And* I'll have to go home for some clothes," I say, in sinking realization. "I *must* get up."

I have a quick shower; then, while Seb's in the bathroom, I get dressed and roam around his flat. I notice the good knives in the kitchen—he obviously really does like cooking—and look through his DVDs. Then I venture down the hall and come to another door. I can't resist trying the handle, but it won't open. It's locked.

At once I feel guilty and intrusive for even trying to open it, and I hastily return to the living room. As Seb appears, his hair still damp, smelling of Molton Brown shower gel, I say casually, "So how big is the flat altogether?"

"It's this, really," says Seb, gesturing at the big room. "What you see."

"Uh-huh." I nod, but I can feel a tiny cord of tension in my chest. Why hasn't he mentioned the other room?

And I know I should leave it, it's none of my business . . . but I just can't. I can't leave things.

"Nice big living room for a one-bedroom flat," I say conversationally. "It's massive!"

"Oh, well, there is another room," says Seb after a pause. "It was James's."

He flashes me a brief smile, and I wince in sympathy, because I'd already guessed. I suddenly remember that first conversation I heard in the coffee shop. Briony wanted to turn a room into a home gym, didn't she? It must have been that room.

"It's hard," I say in a gentle voice. "I remember my mum clearing out my dad's stuff."

"Yes," says Seb noncommittally, and his face closes up a little. And now I regret even bringing up the subject when everything's so bright and perfect.

"Well . . . thank you," I say, more lightheartedly. "Thank you for my hairbrush. Thank you for dinner. Thank you for . . ." I trail away, not needing to continue. He knows what I mean.

"Thank *you*." Seb comes close and kisses my hair, playing with the strands, winding them round his fingers. "I always wanted to date an Olympic skater," he adds. "You're pretty sexy on the ice, did I mention that?"

"I shouldn't have showed off," I say, shaking my head. "I feel bad now. I was rude to Briony."

"You feel bad?" says Seb incredulously. "Do *not* feel bad about her." He swivels round so that we're both facing a massive wall mirror, and he looks at my reflection, his eyes glinting, his chin resting on my head. "I don't know *who* this girl is or *how* she came into my life," he says, his voice deadpan, and I can't help smiling.

"No idea." I echo his tone. "It's a mystery."

There's silence, and Seb's expression becomes more serious.

"You *are* in my life?" he says.

"Yes," I say, and my voice suddenly falters. "I hope so."

"Well, me too." He strokes my hair and his eyes crinkle at mine in the mirror. And right now his life is the only place I want to be.

Twenty-One

*D*ays turn into a week, then two . . . and it seems as if I've always been in Seb's life. I stay every night at his place, popping back now and then for another supply of clothes. I'm barely at home anymore. I'm barely conscious of the world. I'm intoxicated by Seb. By his body and his mind. His voice and his laugh. The touch of him in the morning; the sound of his breathing at night.

When I'm not with him, I'm yearning for him. Everything else has receded. All the problems I used to have seem a little blurry—nothing except Seb seems that important anymore.

I smile at customers who put items back in the wrong place. I laugh when Stacey arrives at work late. I find Greg's idiosyncrasies funny. Why *shouldn't* he show off his double-jointed thumbs to customers when they're trying to pay? The world is a wonderful place. I skive off a little—not much, just the odd afternoon or morning—so I can meet Seb out of work, or cook for him, or lie in bed with him for a delicious half hour longer.

The more I get to know him, the better I like him. His thoughts are straightforward. His take on life is wry but optimistic. We've talked for hours, and I haven't once winced or frowned or thought, *He thinks what?* So many guys *seem* great until you actually find out what's inside their brain, whereupon you run for cover, panting, "Oh my God, lucky escape!" to yourself. But I've spent two weeks exploring Seb's brain and I haven't stumbled on any gnarly knots of anger or walls of arrogance. Nor has he told any tasteless jokes and expected me to fall about in hysterics.

The only trip wire—the *only* one—is his brother's stuff. His brother's room. That whole situation. A couple of times I've suggested helping him sort out the magazines and he's batted me away. Once or twice I've mentioned James's room in passing and he's changed the subject.

Then one day, when he was out, I took the key—it's on a hook in the kitchen; it's not hidden away—and very quickly opened the door and peeped inside.

I think I'd imagined a neatly kept bedroom with a few pieces of memorabilia around the place. I hadn't imagined what I saw: a shambolically untidy, dusty room, with a screensaver still alive on the computer screen and a wizened apple core on the desk and a recycling bin overflowing with empty water bottles and the duvet rumpled as though it hadn't been touched since—

Then I realized the truth. It hasn't been touched since.

I stood there for a while, very still, my head teeming with thoughts. Then I locked the door again and put the key back in the kitchen. I was remembering Seb's resolutely calm, almost upbeat demeanor when he talked about his family. The words he said, almost like a mantra: "I'm fine. I'm *fine*. I've moved on, I'm at peace with it."

At peace? With a dusty room that hasn't been touched for two years and is locked away from view?

That evening I plucked up courage and ventured, "Seb, about your brother. You said you were at peace with . . . what happened."

"I am," he said, so convincingly that he would fool anyone. Except a girl who can't leave things alone.

"Right. Great!" I hesitated, then forced myself to press on: "I mean, maybe one day you should clear up those magazines. And . . . will that room stay locked forever?"

For a few moments Seb was silent, turned away from me, but when at last he glanced over his shoulder it was with a sunny smile.

"I know. I'm going to do it. It's not a big deal, really, just haven't got round to it. So, more important, what are we going to have with this fish?"

Not a big deal?

Part of me longed to push him even further, but a wiser part told myself to leave it for now. So I moved on to the subject of salad, and I could see Seb relaxing.

Now I know him better, I've realized that he gets a look when you talk about his brother. Not stressed exactly but alert, like an anxious dog on the lookout for danger. And it breaks my heart a little—but I know that if I go blundering in too roughly, I'll ruin everything.

So, for the first time in my life, I'm *not* rushing in. I'm *not* trying to fix it all straightaway. I'm biding my time. It's nearly killing me, but I'm doing it.

And this is the only issue that bothers me. Apart from that, I'm walking around in a bubble of dazed, wondering bliss. Every morning I wake up and it's the opposite of realizing I have the dentist. It's realizing I *don't* have the dentist but I *do* have the best guy in the world sleeping next to me. Nothing else matters.

Until one morning, as I'm arriving at the shop, my electronic calendar sends me an alert—*Family Meeting*—and I realize with a jolt that it's tonight. I stare at the words, blinking back into reality, looking around the shop as though for the first time. Shit. I've been asleep on the job. There were things I planned to do for this meeting. I've been so swept up, I've let my concentration lapse. I've let *everything* lapse.

My thoughts swoop guiltily to Mum. I missed a call from her yesterday and I meant to call back, but I never did. Hastily I dial her number, but it goes to voicemail.

"Hi, Mum!" I say. "It's Fixie calling you back; hope everything's good . . . we're all well . . . I'll try you again soon. Take care, love you."

I'm not going to tell her about Seb yet. And certainly not on voicemail.

As I tap my code into the till, I'm cursing myself. There was so much I was going to do before this meeting. I was going to read through all Bob's emails, for a start. He sends us regular financial summaries, and I wanted to have all that information up my sleeve. I was going to research competitors' websites. I was going to get exact sales figures on all of Jake's new stock.

I'm humming with frustration at myself as Morag approaches me, tucking her hair nervously behind her ear.

"Fixie," she says. "Can I have a word before we open?"

"Oh," I say. "Yes, of course!"

I turn toward her, but for a few moments she doesn't speak. She's looking over my shoulder, her cheeks turning pink.

"I've been interviewing for other jobs," she says at last. "I've had an offer from that big homewares place in Kew. Suttons. And I'm thinking of taking it."

For a full half minute I can't speak.

Morag wants to *leave*?

"Morag . . ." I falter at last. I'm so shocked, I can't even frame any words.

"It's not what I wanted." Her mouth is tight, as though she's trying not to show that she's upset. "You know I love Farrs, you *know* that, Fixie. But . . ." She trails off, and I can hear that there are about a million unsaid words in that *but*.

"Can you tell me what . . ." I rub my face, trying to keep my breath steady. But now that my initial shock has died down, panic is swooping in. I can't lose Morag, I *can't*. "Could you tell me your main issues?"

"Oh, Fixie, love, you know the issues." She exhales unsteadily. "This place has changed. Half the displays have disappeared, I don't know what we're supposed to be selling, all the customers are complaining. . . ." She shakes her head. "The Christmas-cookie promotion day was a disaster! There simply wasn't enough stock!"

"I know," I say with a flash of painful remembrance. "Jake wanted to promote those neon novelty lamps."

I don't even want to think about the neon lamps. Jake landed them on us and we've only sold one—and it's already been returned.

"Yes, well." Morag's expression tells me what she thinks

of that. "And I've just had to cancel Cake Club for the third time—"

"The *third* time?" I stare at her. "Wait. I've missed this. What happened?"

"Nicole, of course! It's always Nicole. A mindfulness session it was, this time. Well, all I'll say is, do her 'mindfulness' friends ever come and buy so much as a whisk? *Do* they?" There are little red spots on Morag's cheeks, and I realize how angry and offended she is and how I've been sleepwalking my way into a total disaster.

Mum, I suddenly think. *What's Mum going to say?* And my stomach spasms with fresh terror, mixed with fury at myself.

"Morag," I say desperately. "We love you. Please don't go."

"Suttons have said they'll give me a regular space for the Cake Club," says Morag, not meeting my eye. "They want to make it bigger, serve drinks, do live Internet events, whatever that is. . . . I don't *want* to leave," she says, her voice sharpening with distress. "None of us do. But—"

"None of us?" I echo stupidly. "What—"

"All the Cake Club members have said they'll come with me. They'll come to events at Suttons. It's not too far."

There's a prickling silence. The subtext is obvious: They'll do all their shopping at Suttons too.

Fear is knotting round my throat. Mum trusted us with the shop and we've lost our best member of staff, plus our core customers. And I know Mum put us all in charge, but I can't help feeling responsible. I swallow hard a few times, trying to get my thoughts straight.

"You haven't accepted Suttons yet?"

"I've told them I need to think." She finally meets my gaze, her eyes sorrowful yet resolute. "But, Fixie, there's not much to think about."

"Morag, let me fix this." My words come tumbling out. "Please. Let me at least come to you with a proposal. Give me forty-eight hours to . . . to sort it out."

"All right," says Morag, and she pats my arm before she walks away. But I can see she hasn't changed her mind.

For the rest of the morning I'm in a kind of internal frenzy. I deal with customers pleasantly—but inside I'm churning. I keep thinking, *How did I let this happen?* I keep looking around the shop, trying to see it through Mum's eyes. And when I do, a slightly cold feeling comes over me. It doesn't look right. It doesn't look *Farrs*.

I'm going to have it out with Nicole tonight. *And* Jake. I'm going to insist on a few things. Those garden lanterns have got to go. We need all our display tables back. Nicole needs to realize we're not a yoga center, we're a *shop*. I'm going to be stern, implacable. . . .

But, oh *God*.

Even as I'm having these thoughts, I know I'll let myself down. My voice will shake. I'll stutter and flush. The ravens will flap and I'll crumble.

On impulse, I head to the back room and dial Seb's number. When he answers, I launch straight in: "Seb, I don't know what to do, I have to read the riot act to Jake and Nicole tonight, but I always let myself down, I get so nervous I can't even speak, but I *have* to speak—"

I break off, realizing I don't even know what I want; I just needed to share all this with him.

"Hey!" says Seb gently. "Fixie, don't worry. You've got this." And he sounds so sure, my confidence zooms up again. Maybe I *have* got this. "You want me to come over for lunch? Have a sandwich, talk it through?"

It hadn't occurred to me that no one at Farrs has met Seb yet. As he walks into the shop in his smart coat and kisses me, right in front of everyone, I'm aware of all the staff turning to gawp at us, in a totally unprofessional way, and I can't help feeling proud. He looks properly handsome, his face all flushed from the cold.

"So, this is Farrs," he says, looking around. "It's fantastic!"

I want to say, "It's not; it's underperforming and it's all my fault," but that can wait till lunch.

"Hello, welcome to Farrs," says Stacey, sidling up and batting her eyelashes at Seb. "Any . . . *needs* I can help you with?"

I hide a spark of frustration. Stacey must *not* pause suggestively before saying the word *needs*. I've told her that before. And has she unbuttoned her top?

"I'm fine," says Seb, smiling at her. "Thanks."

"Funny story," says Greg, coming forward and surveying Seb with his prominent eyes. "Fixie once brought a boyfriend here and he was trying to show off with the knives and he chopped his finger off."

There's a stunned silence. I glance at Seb, and I can see he's trying to think of a reply.

Oh God, if Morag leaves, how am I going to stay *sane*, even?

"That's not really a funny story, is it, Greg?" I say, trying to sound relaxed while killing him with my eyes. "And it was only a tiny slice. He hardly needed to go to hospital."

"Well, we all laughed," says Greg with a shrug. "Didn't last," he says to Seb. "Don't even remember his name now. Oh yeah, I do—Matthew McConnell."

"OK!" I say shrilly. "Well, we'd better get going; see you later, guys. . . ."

I grab Seb, hustle him out of the shop, and only breathe out once we're safely on the pavement. "Sorry," I say. "*Sorry.*"

"Don't be silly." His eyes crinkle in amusement. "They're great."

"They're all deranged."

"They watch out for you. I like that." He squeezes my hand. "Now, come on. Let me buy you lunch."

There's a sandwich shop opposite Farrs, and it's too freezing to venture any farther, so we duck in there and find a tiny table at the back, where no one can overhear us.

"So." Seb spreads his hands once we're sitting down with our paninis. "You need to take charge. Sounds like a good idea to me. What's the problem?"

"It's Jake," I say miserably. "He just . . . I just . . . He affects me. I need to make my case really strongly and I'm afraid that when it comes to it, I won't." I tug at the corner of my panini and nibble at the piece of bread.

"OK," says Seb. "Let's go back to the beginning. Why does Jake freak you out so much, and how?"

He looks like he really wants to know, and I'm tired of only telling half the story. So this time I go right back to our childhood, to Jake's personality, to the way I always felt inferior to both my siblings. I talk about how my skating sucked up Mum's attention, how my failed business sucked up Mum's money, and how bad I felt about both of those.

And then I talk about how I feel today. The guilt. The inadequacy. My faltering voice. The ravens that flap about my face.

Seb listens silently. Occasionally his face flinches, but he doesn't interrupt.

"I *have* thoughts," I conclude despairingly. "I *have* arguments. I can see them there, as if they're in a thought bubble. But I can't get them out of the thought bubble and into the air."

Seb's eyebrows are knitted together in a thoughtful frown. Then he looks directly at me and says, "You're being too gentle. You need to punch through the bubble. Are you angry with your brother?"

"I am," I say after a pause. "But I feel guilty too. I mean, he *can* be nice when he wants to be—"

"That wasn't the question," says Seb, cutting me off. "Are you *angry* with him?"

"Yes," I admit. "Yes, I am. I'm angry."

"Well, use that anger." He leans forward, his face animated. "Feel it. Punch your way out of the bubble like a . . . a ninja."

"A ninja?" I can't help laughing.

"Yes! You have the words, you have the ideas; I know you do. You're bright and dynamic and basically the best person I know, and to be honest the idea that some *brother* of yours is making you feel the way you do makes me feel pretty livid myself. I've only met the guy briefly, but . . ."

Seb smiles, but his jaw is tight and his hand has clenched hard around his panini.

"OK, I'll be a ninja." I stir my coffee round, gazing into the whirlpool, trying to find some strength. "I get so *nervous,* though. How do you do it?"

"How do I do what?" Seb seems surprised.

"You speak up at shareholders' meetings and people shout at you and you don't seem to care."

"I guess I think about why I'm speaking," says Seb thoughtfully. "Who I'm speaking for. Who I represent. I'm speaking for people who don't have a voice, and that inspires me. That powers me along."

He bites into his panini, then nods at me. "Eat," he says. "Ninjas need strength."

I take a bite of my panini, and as I'm chewing, I feel a backbone growing inside me. I'm going to speak up for Mum. She's the one I represent. She's the one who doesn't have a voice right now. And that's going to power *me* along.

For the rest of the lunch, we talk about general stuff, but as we're saying goodbye, Seb holds me by both arms and looks directly into my face.

"Ninja Fixie," he says. "You can do it."

He kisses me and walks away, his breath a trail of steam in the winter's air, and I tell myself firmly, *I can do this, I can do this. I can.*

All afternoon, my jaw is firm. My mind is set. I'm going to do it. I'm going to have my say.

I stay late, wandering around the displays when everyone

else has gone, remembering how I used to come to Farrs when I was a little girl and it seemed enormous. I remember hiding in cardboard boxes in the back room, and Dad "finding" me. I remember trips to the storage facility being the most exciting thing in the world. I remember breaking a plate when I was seven and being terrified and trying to mend it with Sellotape—until Mum found me, crouched behind a display, and scooped me in for a hug.

This place is my life.

There's a sound at the door and I look up in surprise to see Bob coming in, wrapped up against the cold in his usual beige anorak, plus a scarf and woolly hat.

"Fixie!" he says. "I hoped you'd still be around. I left my pullover here yesterday." He clicks his tongue in mild self-reproach. "I'm seeing my sister tonight, and she gave it to me for my birthday, so I want to wear it, of course. We always give each other M&S pullovers," he adds. "You can't go wrong, can you?"

"No," I agree. "You can't go wrong."

I wait for him to pop into the back room and retrieve the pullover. Then, as he's walking toward me, I say impulsively, "Bob, are we OK?"

"OK?" Bob instinctively glances around, as though I meant, "Bob, are we facing imminent attack?"

"OK," I repeat. "Financially. I know you send me figures all the time, but I don't always . . . I mean, recently . . ." I stop feebly, not wanting to admit the truth, which is: "I've been too wrapped up in my new love affair to look at any figures."

Bob puffs out air, as though considering what to say, and I feel a sudden pang of dread.

"We're OK," he says at last. "Not bad. It's not a disaster."

It's not a disaster?

I stare at him, trying not to look as stricken as I feel. I was hoping for better than "It's not a disaster."

"Sales aren't as good as last year, no one can deny that, but there's a while before Christmas, so it's still all to play for. I'm sure you've got lots up your sleeve," Bob adds encouragingly, and his optimism makes me feel warm with shame. "What we *really* need," he adds, as though getting to the nub of the issue, "is a bit of an upswing."

We need a bit of an upswing. How are we going to get an upswing?

"Thanks, Bob." I try to sound breezy, as though getting worrying news is something I deal with in my stride. "Great. Good to know. So. We'll . . . work on that."

"One thing I *was* wondering about, though . . ." Bob takes a few steps toward me, with an odd expression I can't quite read. "These loans we've been making. Will this be a regular thing?"

"What loans?"

"These loans to Jake."

The world seems to slide beneath my feet.

"What . . . loans to Jake?" I manage to say lightly. "I don't . . . I don't know about those, I don't think."

"Ah," says Bob after a pause. "I wondered. Three bank transfers I've made to him since your mum left. Quite big sums." Bob gives an awkward laugh, but his eyes are troubled. "I know your mum okayed the first one, but the last two have just been on Jake's say-so."

"*Jake's* say-so?" I echo incredulously.

"Well, your uncle Ned confirmed it and told me not to bother your mum about it. He was quite firm on that. And obviously it's none of my beeswax, it's a family thing, it's not for me to . . ." He takes a step backward, his eyes raised to the ceiling as though emphasizing his position, not in the family. "But like I say, it's *quite* a lot of money, so I'd have thought you'd be in the loop, Fixie."

I can't reply. My head feels like it's imploding. Jake's been borrowing money from Farrs *without even telling Mum*? I suddenly remember him coming into the shop that time. Asking where Bob was but not telling me why. Obsessed by his phone. I remember thinking that he's always been about *more,* Jake. I wondered how he was paying for it all. Well, now I know.

"Only there hasn't been any talk of repayment, so to speak," Bob adds distantly. "If this happens every month, it'll make quite a hole in the books. And if your mum *was* looking to sell, then . . . Well. It's not the best time to be losing all this cash. Although as I say, none of my beeswax."

Finally he lowers his gaze to meet mine. I've known Bob a long time and I know what his kindly eyes are saying. They're saying, "This isn't right." They're saying, "Do something."

"Right," I manage. "Well . . . thanks, Bob. Thanks." I start to walk away, then come back as a thought hits me. "Why didn't Uncle Ned want to bother Mum?"

"Oh . . ." Bob's eyes slide away again to the ceiling. "Your uncle likes feeling he's got the power, I think. Some people are like that."

This is so daring and disloyal a thing for Bob to say that I stare at him.

"He helped out with the lease," I say automatically, because that's what we always say about Uncle Ned. "He got us good terms."

There's a long silence. I can see a kind of ripple effect on Bob's face. As if he's trying to hold something back. Oh my God.

"Didn't he?" I whisper.

"Your mum was touched that your uncle stepped in," says Bob at last. "She kept saying, 'Oh, Bob, he's such a rock.' I wasn't going to mess that up." His gentle eyes meet mine in a smile. "I'm fond of your mum."

I feel like everything's shifting in my brain.

"Bob," I say bluntly. "Tell me the truth. Who really negotiated the lease?"

"Your uncle made a call or two," says Bob after a pause. "Didn't really help things along." He gives a gentle, reminiscent laugh. "He put his foot in it, to tell you the truth. Insulted the lady at the property company."

"So it was *you* who got us that great deal."

"They were good terms, yes," says Bob, with the barest hint of pride. "It was the least I could do for your dad."

I rub my head, feeling suddenly almost tearful. "Bob . . . I don't know what to say."

"Nothing to say," Bob replies in his mild way. "I was pleased to do it. If you *do* speak to your mum," he adds, "give her my regards."

I watch as he makes his way out of the shop, his shoes squeaking on the floor. I half want to run after him and beg for more advice—but he's done more than enough. He's gone the extra mile. Now it's *my* turn to go the extra mile. But in which direction?

My brain is boiling over with new information. With worry. With indecision. At last I start dialing Mum's number, then stop, then start again. *Not* because I'm going to rat on Jake, but because I need to know, I need facts. What's going on?

"Hello! Fixie?" a cheery familiar voice answers. "That you, love?"

"Hi, Aunty Karen," I say, trying to sound relaxed and calm. "Is Mum there, by any chance?"

"Oh, darling, she's fast asleep. Feeling a bit poorly. She's come down with a virus or something. Overdid it with our trip to Granada, probably. We only got back last night. Oh, Fixie, it's fabulous! The tiles!"

"What about Mum?" I say anxiously. "Is she OK?"

"I'll take her to the doctor tomorrow," says Aunty Karen reassuringly. "If they don't give her any medication, I know where I can get some, dirt cheap. Now, love, I'm trying to persuade your mum to stay with me for Christmas. You wouldn't mind, would you? You're all grown-ups. Probably off doing your own thing!"

I stare at the phone, dismayed. Christmas without Mum? *Without* Mum?

I've always assumed she'll be home by then. I've always had that thought there in my mind, like an anchor: *Mum'll be home.*

"Oh," I say, trying not to sound as hollow as I feel. "Well . . . you know. Mum should do what she wants."

"That's what I said!" cries Aunty Karen triumphantly. "I said, 'You relax, Joanne! I'll cook, and it's eggnog all the way!'"

"Well, give her my love," I say, forcing a bright tone. "I hope she gets better soon. Keep me posted. And let us know if there's anything we can do."

"Of course," says Aunty Karen comfortably. "And are you all OK? Jake? Nicole?"

"Yes, we're fine."

"Oh, and how's the shop?" she adds. "I know your mum'll ask me. She'll say, 'Didn't you ask about the shop, Karen? How could you not ask about the shop?' She loves that shop like another child!"

Aunty Karen hoots with laughter and I look around at the shop that Mum loves so much, feeling even more hollow.

"It's . . . great!" I say. "All good."

"Marvelous. Well, take care, Fixie!"

"You too," I say, and ring off feeling like I always do after conversations with Aunty Karen: as though a tornado has blown away.

So that road is closed. I'm not bothering Mum about Jake, not when she's ill. I'm going to have to do this on my own.

Come on, Fixie. Come on.

I catch sight of my own reflection in the shop-front glass and do a sudden impulsive front kick, punching the air like a kickboxer. Then I do another, then another, moving forward, panting a little with the effort. My chin is jutting out and my expression is fierce and I probably look like an idiot—but I don't care. I feel stronger with every kick. I can do this.

Ninja Fixie. Bring it on.

Twenty-Two

*U*ncle Ned has booked yet another grand restaurant for our meeting, this one on Piccadilly. As I'm on the way there, I cut through a shopping arcade to get out of the freezing cold and am immediately hit by warmth and light and a smell of cinnamon. The marble-floored atrium is filled with pop-up stalls selling scented candles and seasonal goods. Christmas songs are blaring through the sound system. A full-sized snowman is wandering around, making children laugh. It's all very festive, only I don't feel in a festive mood. I feel jagged and angry.

I'm striding along, practicing what I'll say to Jake, ignoring invitations to try out smoothies and massage chairs—when a familiar voice hits my ears and I stop dead. No way. No *way*.

"I'm a makeup artist," he's saying. "And you have a really interesting face, did you know that?"

I swivel slowly on my heel, and there he is. Ryan Chalker. As handsome as ever, wearing a black shirt and trousers, standing next to a pop-up stall covered in pots of face cream.

I wait for the familiar reaction to hit me. I wait for my breath to shorten and my heart to swoop. But the magic has gone. After all these years, the magic has gone. All I can see is a smooth-faced chancer. He's addressing a frowsy-looking woman in a parka, and I can tell he's getting through to her.

"You remind me of this model I used to work with on magazine shoots," he says brazenly, and I breathe in sharply with indignation. Since when did Ryan work on magazine shoots as a makeup artist?

"Really?" I can see the woman blossoming under his compliments.

"You have beautiful skin," he assures her. "But I bet your husband tells you that every day."

God, he's good. Of course the husband never says a word to her, and now this woman is putty in Ryan's hands.

"Who does your eyebrows?" he demands now.

"I do," she admits.

"*No.*" Ryan's eyes widen. "They're amazing! Don't let anyone touch them. Are you over thirty-five?"

"A bit." The woman flushes.

I mean, she's about fifty. Even I can tell that.

"Not by much," says Ryan firmly. "So tell me, darling, do you use eye cream?"

"A bit." Her eyes swivel evasively. "Sometimes."

"*Sometimes?*" Ryan looks devastated. "Sweetheart, look after your skin. I don't care whose products you use, but for me, start using eye cream, yeah? I'm going to give you a free sample. . . ." He's swiftly undoing a little pot. "Can I put this on you? You don't mind?"

He smears some goo on the woman's face, then brandishes a mirror at her. "Can you see that? Can you *see* the transformation? And that's on one use! It's not surgical, but it's surgical."

It's not surgical, but it's surgical? Is he even allowed to say that?

I'm bristling with outrage as I watch. That woman has *so* not been transformed, but she's gazing at herself, transfixed. I don't know what Ryan's doing with angles or lights or simply the power of suggestion, but it's working.

"And we're doing two pots for the price of one today," he says smoothly. "You know what an eye lift costs? You know how many thousands? This is a tenth of the price."

He shows the woman a price list and she blanches. At once Ryan says, lowering his voice, "You know what? I shouldn't do this, but just for you, let's knock ten percent off. I'll get in trouble, but . . . hey. It's Christmas."

"Really?" The woman looks at him so trustingly that I can't bear it any longer.

"Hi there!" I say brightly, striding up to them, and Ryan gives such a startled jump, I grin inwardly.

"Oh, hello," says the woman, looking disconcerted.

"Sorry to interrupt, but I'd hold off if I were you," I say pleasantly. "I once bought some eye cream from some random person in a mall and it gave me hives. I'm sure this nice man will give you some samples and you can try them properly at home. Maybe get another opinion from a friend before you lash out all that money?" I smile sweetly at Ryan. "Wouldn't you agree, sir? With all your experience as a 'makeup artist'?"

"Actually, I should be going," says the woman, looking

flustered. "Thanks anyway," she says over her shoulder to Ryan as she hurries off.

"'Makeup artist,'" I say scathingly. "You're evil."

Ryan stares at me consideringly for a moment, then throws his head back and laughs.

"Fixie," he says. "You've got such a good conscience. You make me feel like a better person." And he smiles at me, his eyes as devastatingly blue as ever.

Once upon a time, that smile would have made my heart flutter. My doubts would have receded; I would have run back to him. But not today.

"Well, you make me feel like a worse person," I say coldly, and Ryan laughs again.

"I've missed you," he says, and I stare at him in disbelief. He's *missed* me? I feel a sudden furious urge to yell at him, to hit him, to make him suffer.

But almost at once it subsides. Ryan's pathological, I've realized. He says anything to anyone to get out of whatever situation he's in. Truth doesn't count, integrity doesn't count, love doesn't even figure. Yelling at him would be like yelling at a rock. It's never going to change.

I'm just glad the magic has gone. I'm free of him. About bloody time.

"I'm not going to say, 'See you,'" I inform him politely. "Because I don't want to see you, ever again. Goodbye."

As I walk off I can hear him laughing again, only the sound is a little more forced, and I briefly wonder if there's any kind of regret or understanding in his eyes. But I honestly can't be bothered to look.

. . .

And then I've reached the entrance to the restaurant and my heart is pounding. Because standing up to Ryan was like a warm-up, but this is the real deal.

The maître d' shows me to our table, where I find Uncle Ned lounging on a banquette, holding what looks like a gin and tonic. Jake is holding one too, and Nicole has a glass of what I'm sure is champagne.

"Fixie!" Uncle Ned greets me. "Take a seat. Have a drink, m'dear." His face is nearly as red as the velvet seat. Did he start early? Looking around at the flushed faces, I wonder: Did they *all* start early? Jake's eyes are bloodshot, I notice, and he still has those shadows under them.

"*What?*" he says defensively, as he feels my eyes on him. "Oh, by the way, I've got some good news for you. Ryan's back in London."

"I've just seen him," I say shortly as I take a chair. "And it's not good news."

"Now, I rather like the look of the porterhouse steak," says Uncle Ned, squinting at a big leather menu.

I bet he bloody does, I think—but force myself to stay calm. I'm a ninja, sizing up my opponents, slow and focused, before I strike.

"Would you like a drink?" a waiter asks me.

"No, thanks," I say politely, and wait till he's gone before adding, "I won't spend Farrs' money here. This is totally inappropriate. *Totally* inappropriate," I repeat for emphasis, and jab at all their expensive drinks with my finger.

"What?" says Nicole blankly.

"Inappropriate?" splutters Uncle Ned.

"What exactly are we achieving here, except spending money?" I look from face to face. "Nothing."

"Now, really." Uncle Ned's face becomes puce. "Here I am, giving freely of my time and advice—"

"Do you even *know* how our sales are doing?" I cut him off, sweeping my gaze around the table. "Do any of you? But here you all are, ordering cocktails and steak. It's freeloading and it's revolting and I'm not doing it."

"What the *fuck*!" exclaims Jake, staring at me. "What's got *into* you?"

"It's her new boyfriend," says Nicole, in sudden inspiration. "That's what it is. He's put her up to it."

"What new boyfriend?" Jake swivels to face her.

"Sebastian Whatsit. The guy who was Ryan's boss? She's, like, practically living with him."

"You're going out with *him*?" says Jake incredulously. "The investment guy?"

"That's irrelevant," I say shortly. "And I have some other things to say."

My words are hovering in a thought bubble, like they always are, all neatly formed. *Come on, Ninja Fixie. Say them.*

I draw breath—then make the mistake of glancing at Jake. His face is so aggressive that for a moment I can feel the old feelings resurfacing. *Inadequate. Guilty. Inferior. Rubbish.*

But I have to punch through those feelings. *Go, Fixie, go.*

"Nicole, you have to cancel all your yoga," I say firmly. "It's disruptive and it hasn't attracted any new customers;

it's just made problems. It has to stop and I'm restocking the shop, *my* way."

Pow.

"Disruptive?" says Nicole, sounding offended.

"Yes, disruptive. And, Jake, for you I have a question." I turn to him, forcing my voice to stay steady. "Why are you borrowing so much money from Farrs and when are you paying it back and why wasn't it mentioned at the last meeting?"

Bam.

I can see the light of shock in Jake's eyes, but almost at once he's regained his swaggering demeanor.

"It's an inter-business loan," he drawls, taking a sip of his drink. "Really, Fixie, you *are* getting your knickers in a twist."

"I didn't know we could take out loans," says Nicole with interest. "That's cool."

"We can't!" I practically shout. "Why do you need loans from Farrs, anyway, Jake?" I say in a calmer, more diplomatic voice. "What's going on? Why didn't you just *say* to us this was happening? And why keep it from Mum?"

I lean forward, trying to get through to the man I saw the other day. The one who talked to me with respect and affection, who felt like a real brother.

But that Jake has vanished. This one won't even meet my eye.

"Nothing's 'going on,'" he says with elaborate sarcasm. "I've had a holdup in Asia. It's simply a cash-flow thing." He sounds dismissive, although I can see his fingers clenching the menu tightly and a vein throbbing at his temple. "You're really quite unsophisticated, Fixie. Do you have *any* idea about global export deals? No. So take it from me, there's nothing to worry about. Now, are we going to order some food?"

"Yes," says Uncle Ned emphatically.

Is that all they can think about? Food? My attempt at calmness instantly vanishes. I'm going to punch and kick as hard as I can.

"You're all users!" I spit. "You're only interested in how much expensive food you can eat. Porterhouse steak? At . . ." I grab the menu, to check the price. "At thirty quid? This is Mum's business! Not a piggy bank!"

"And this is a business dinner!" says Jake.

"You treat the business like a joke!" I retort. "You don't care about it! How many times have you been to the shop since Mum went away, Uncle Ned? Once?"

"After all I've done for you!" huffs Uncle Ned, looking livid. "After your father died—"

"Oh, that's right, you negotiated our lease," I cut in scathingly. "Did you really, Uncle Ned? Or did Bob have anything to do with it?"

"I have never been so offended in my life!" Uncle Ned's voice is trembling with fury. He thumps down his drink and shoots a glare at me. "I don't have to be here, you know. I'm giving up my time, simply out of the goodness of my heart, simply because your mother asked me to, because every organization needs a Man of the House—"

"Not us," I cut him off. "Mum was mistaken. We don't need a Man of the House." And I stare at him silently, steel in my eyes.

Kapow.

"I'm going!" says Uncle Ned, his fleshy neck wobbling as he gets to his feet. "I won't take this anymore. *Never* been so offended," he mutters as he heads toward the exit. "*Never* been so insulted."

"Oh my God," says Nicole, as she watches him leave. "You've started something now, Fixie."

"Good," I say, unrepentant. "I wanted to start something."

"Fixie, cut it out," says Jake, sounding properly irate. "You're embarrassing yourself and us."

"I'm not. I just want a few answers. Why *are* you borrowing all that money, Jake? What's it for? When will you pay it back? What exactly have you told Mum?"

"For God's sake!" Jake almost shouts, as though I've scalded him. "Why are you so obsessed? The business will be ours one day. What's the difference?"

"Mum might want to sell it! That's her retirement fund! We have to keep it safe!" I swivel to Nicole. "Did *you* know Jake was taking so much money out of the business?"

"No," says Nicole with a shrug. "I mean, like, that's really . . ."

"As I say, it's a business-to-business loan," says Jake tightly, and takes another swig of his drink. "It's perfectly standard."

"But why can't you go to the bank?" I persist. "Why do you need to keep raiding Farrs? I mean, once I get, but *three* times?"

For a moment Jake looks as though he wants to hit me, almost. But he reins it in and even manages a taut smile, though his eyes are incandescent with fury.

"You really don't understand anything, do you?" he says. "Poor naïve little Fixie. Have a drink. Calm down."

"No, thanks." I meet his gaze evenly. "I'm not drinking overpriced cocktails on Mum's expense. And I'm not 'Little Fixie.' If you won't talk about it properly, I'll leave. But I haven't finished," I add, looking from face to face. "This isn't over."

Bam. Kapow. Crunch.

As I stride out of the restaurant, adrenaline is rushing through me, and I'm breathing hard. I don't quite know what to think. Did I achieve anything just now, except offend Uncle Ned and make a fool of myself? Was that a success or a fail?

I stand on the pavement for a while, the icy wind in my face, trying to sort out my jumbled thoughts and make a plan for what to do next. Go back to Seb's is the obvious one. Have some food. Relax. I've said my piece; what more can I do right now?

But for some reason I don't move. And gradually I become aware that my fingers are drumming in the way they do. My feet have started pacing: *forward-across-back, forward-across-back.*

Something's bugging me. What's bugging me?

It's Jake, I suddenly realize. His strained face. That vein throbbing at his temple. His raw anger. The way he batted me away, again and again.

I'm used to Jake being impatient and sarcastic. But I'm not used to him looking like a cornered tiger. He looked evasive. He looked on the edge. Amid the flashes of anger, I realize, I saw flashes of fear.

A bad feeling is coming over me. I think for a few moments, then pull out my phone and dial a number.

"Oh, hi," I say when it's answered. "Is that you, Leila?"

As Leila opens the front door, my heart drops. She looks shrunken and there are shadows under her eyes too.

"Hi, Leila!" I clasp her warmly, and I swear she's lost half a stone. "It's been ages! I just fancied a manicure."

"I thought you were having dinner with Jakey?" she says, looking anxiously past me as though expecting to see Jake too.

"I left them to it," I say easily. "You know what they're like. Six bottles of wine each."

"I've *told* Jake to stop drinking," says Leila, and her face becomes even more drawn and I feel a swell of panic, because none of this feels good. I follow Leila into the living room and stop dead at the sight of the big empty wall in front of me, wires trailing from four points.

"What's happened to the telly?" I blurt out before I can stop myself. "Are you getting a new one?"

The words are out before I have a horrible, sinking suspicion.

"It went," says Leila, after a pause. She picks up a plastic bowl from the coffee table and gestures to the sofa. "Sit down. I'll get some warm water."

"It 'went'?"

"They took it away." She flashes me a smile, which I don't believe in for a moment. "It's fine, I watch all the soaps on my laptop."

I sit down warily, looking around at Jake's flash pad, full

of leather and glass and glossy magazines. It always seemed like the pinnacle of achievement, this flat. Now it all seems kind of . . . perilous.

As Leila sits down and instructs me to put my hands in the bowl of water, I eye her closely. She looks on edge. Frail, almost. I don't want to freak her out by firing questions at her, but I have to know. I *have* to know.

"Leila," I say, in my quietest voice. "Is Jake in trouble?"

For a long time, Leila doesn't answer. She's washing my hands, rhythmically, her gaze distant. Then she raises her head.

"Oh, Fixie," she says in a trembling voice, and the look in her huge eyes makes me suddenly fearful. "Of course he is. But he won't admit it. He won't talk about it. I only hear bits and pieces. I've said to him, 'Jakey, what's going *on?*' But he gets so angry. . . ." She adds, more calmly, "If you could place your right hand on the towel?"

As she starts on my cuticles, I say, "He's been taking money from Farrs."

"Taking money?" Leila's eyes widen. "Stealing?"

"No, not stealing," I hastily assure her. "Just loans. But what I don't get is, why does he need them?"

"He can't get finance." Leila's hands quiver as she dunks my fingers back in the bowl. "That's all he talks about, getting finance. If you could please place your other hand on the towel?"

"But I thought everything was going well? I thought he was doing something with manufactured diamonds?"

At once Leila starts. Her hands quiver even more and her eyelids flutter.

"Would you like me to clip or file?" she says, her voice jumpy.

"Er . . . don't mind. You choose."

I wait while she gets out her manicure implements and lays them carefully on the towel, side by side, as though trying to impose order on the world. Then finally she meets my eye.

"He doesn't know I know this," she practically whispers. "But the diamonds were a scam."

"A *scam*?"

Leila nods, and for a moment we stare at each other. My mind is processing what a scam might mean. How damaging it might have been. How humiliating.

"Did he lose . . ." I can't even say it.

"Loads," she says, her voice not working properly. "He's in big trouble. But he won't see it, he won't stop spending money, taking people out for lunch, trying to be flash. . . ." Her eyes fill with tears and I stare at her, aghast. "Oh. We haven't chosen you a color yet. I've got a lovely new amber shade. I think it would really suit you."

She pulls her case of nail polishes onto her knee and a tear drips down onto it.

"Oh, Leila . . ." I put a hand on her arm, but she shoots me a bright smile.

"Or lilac," she says, opening the lid. "With your lovely dark eyes. Or classic red?"

"Leila . . ." I squeeze her. "He's so lucky to have you."

"Oh, I don't do anything," says Leila, patting at her eyes. "I just do my nails and keep my head down. That's it. Nails. That's my life. But I *understand* nails," she adds, looking up with a sudden passion. "I understand how I'm earning my wage. I give you a manicure; you pay me. That makes sense. Whereas what Jakey does . . ."

"What *does* he do?" I ask, because it's something I've often wondered. "I mean, his MBA course, obviously. . . ."

"Oh, he dropped out of that months ago," says Leila. "He said the tutors were all useless."

I should feel shocked, but somehow I don't. Not now.

"He talks as though he's still doing it," I say. "Mum thinks he's still doing it. Everyone does."

"I know." Leila bites her lip. "I've said to him, 'Jakey, you should *tell* your family.' "

He dropped out of his MBA but he didn't volunteer to do any more work at the shop, I silently register. Yet he's taken all these loans from it.

"So what *does* he do all day?" I persist. "How does he make all his money?"

"He made a lot out of those nude knickers," says Leila, her brows winged anxiously. "That was a good deal. They were a good product. I wear them myself!" she adds, with a brief show of brightness. "But ever since then . . ." She trails into silence.

"But that was two years ago." I stare at her. "Hasn't he done any more deals since then? I thought . . ."

Jake talks as though he's made a million deals, each more profitable than the last. He drops constant references to "export" and "my latest venture" and deals which are "on the horizon." We've never questioned him, we've only listened, awed.

Leila still hasn't replied. She's busying herself with bottles of topcoat.

"Leila?" I say more urgently. "Has he?"

"I don't think so," she whispers at last. "He just has lunch with people. That's what I don't get. How does having lunch earn you money?" she says in sudden bewilderment. "I like a job I can *see*." She pats her manicure case. "I like *work*. So, if you give me your right hand again . . ." she adds, in her manicurist's voice.

I watch silently as she starts filing my nails. The rhythmic action of her file is kind of mesmerizing and soothing. It's reassuring. For both of us, I suspect.

"I knew he was stressed out," I say after a while. "But I had no idea . . ."

"He's secretive," says Leila. "He doesn't even tell me everything. He wants everyone to think he's . . ." She pauses as though thinking how to put it. "Winning. Master of the universe."

"I thought maybe he was burned out from too many deals."

"It's the opposite!" Leila replies, her voice wavering between a sob and a laugh. "It's not enough deals! It's no income! Nothing to pay the mortgage!"

"But you're still with him?" I blurt out the question before I can stop myself. For a moment Leila stops filing my nails and I worry that I've offended her. But when she looks up, her gaze is nothing but wistful.

"Jake's been good to me. I'm not going to abandon him, just because . . ." She hesitates, her eyes dimming slightly. "I know some people find him a bit . . . much. But he's got a softer side, you know."

"I know." I nod.

"Jakey talks about life. He has interesting ideas. He's fun. He wants to *do* things, you know? Some men, they don't want to do anything or go anywhere."

"Jake's never had that problem," I say in wry tones, and Leila smiles, then wipes her wet eyes and resumes filing.

When both my hands are done, she pats them dry and starts to apply a base coat.

"Did you choose a color yet?" she asks, and I point randomly to the lilac nail polish.

"Lovely choice!" says Leila, and she starts to unscrew the pot. And we're both so calm and peaceful now, I almost don't want to ruin the atmosphere, but I have to ask one more question.

"So what's Jake going to do now?"

Leila exhales in a shuddery breath and stares down at the nail-polish pot, blinking hard.

"Get some money from somewhere," she says at last. "I said to him, 'Jakey, get a job! A *job*!' But you know what he's like. . . ."

"Where will he get more money?" I say bluntly.

Slowly, Leila's skinny arms and shoulders rise up in the most hopeless shrug I've ever seen. For a few moments we're both silent, because what is there to say? Then Leila's eyes brighten.

"I could put a shimmer on top of the lilac," she says. "I've got a lovely new product, shall I show you?"

I know displacement when I see it. Her hands are trembling as she reaches for the pot and her eyes are shadowy and I decide we've talked enough about Jake.

"That sounds amazing," I say, as warmly as I can. "Leila, you're brilliant."

And she *is* brilliant. As I'm heading to Seb's later, I keep staring at my immaculate shimmery lilac nails and thinking, *I should get Leila to do this every week.*

But that's only about 5 percent of my brain. The rest is remembering Jake's angry bravado. And Leila's shadowy eyes. And that bare wall with wires hanging out of it. All my adrenaline from earlier on has seeped away, leaving me flatter than I've been for ages. I feel pale and washed out and strained.

Seb buzzes me in and I travel up in the lift to his flat. He's waiting there, the front door flung open.

"So, did you do it?" he asks at once, his face bright and expectant. "Were you Ninja Fixie?"

I stare at him for a moment, rewinding to the restaurant. Yes, I was assertive. I said what I thought. I was Ninja Fixie. But that all seems dwarfed now by my discoveries about Jake.

"Yes!" I say. "Kind of. Uncle Ned was offended. He stormed out."

"Excellent!" Seb grins. "Every good shareholders' meeting needs someone storming out in dudgeon. Come on, sit down and relax. You look knackered." He kisses me and ushers me in, and I follow, my head still trying to make sense of the evening.

"Oh, you'll never guess what," I say, suddenly remembering. "I saw Ryan."

"*Ryan?*" Seb echoes, his face instantly tightening, and I immediately regret mentioning him.

"Only for, like, a nanosecond," I say quickly. "I definitely put *him* straight."

"Good," says Seb, after a pause. "Glad to hear it. So, a good evening?"

I sink down at his little kitchen table, feeling my last vestiges of energy slip away. "Actually, no. It was awful."

I fight an urge to burst into tears. I think a kind of delayed shock is hitting me. Shock at Jake's aggression toward me. Shock at the truth behind it.

"*Awful?*" Seb hands me a glass of wine. "Why?"

"Thanks," I say. "It's . . . well, it's Jake."

"What about Jake?"

I hesitate, sipping the wine, trying to work out what to say. I can't blurt out that Jake's in debt. Leila told me in confidence and he's family and it might not be as bad as she thinks and . . . I just can't, not even to Seb.

"He's got some issues," I say at last. "Work issues. It's all quite worrying."

"Right," says Seb carefully. "But that's his problem, isn't it? Not yours?"

"But it involves Mum," I say despairingly. "I have to do something, but I don't know what. . . ." I rub my face. "Everything's got worse than I thought."

"Oh, sweetheart." Seb peers at me anxiously for a moment, then reaches for a plate on the counter. "Have some fudge."

I stare incredulously at the crumbly, delicious-looking cubes. "Is that *homemade fudge?*"

"I thought you might like a treat when you got back. I like making fudge," Seb adds with a shrug. "It's easy. I've been making it since I was seven."

I take a piece and put it in my mouth and it's like a burst of comfort. Sweet, rich, total indulgence.

"Thank you," I say, after a few moments of chewing. "Thank you for making me fudge."

"Well, you did save my life," says Seb, glancing at the coffee sleeve, which is just visible in my tote bag. "Fudge is the very least I owe you." He shoots me a teasing grin, but this time I don't smile back. I don't know why, but his words have flicked me on the raw. I can't smile. I can't joke. I don't find the coffee sleeve charming or amusing anymore; I find it grating.

I finish my piece of fudge, then say, without looking at him, "Are we going to do this forever?"

"Do what?" Seb sounds confused.

"Tit for tat. I owe you. You owe me. Would you have made me fudge if I hadn't saved your life?"

"Of course!" Seb gives a shocked laugh. "It's only a joke!"

"Well, maybe I'm tired of the joke," I say, still staring down at the table. "Is it never going to end? You scratch my back and I'll scratch yours? Backward and forward, totting up what we owe each other, and we'd better settle up or else?"

I'm speaking faster and faster, and my face is getting hot. I don't feel totally in control of myself.

"Fixie," says Seb. "What are you talking about?"

"I don't *know* exactly," I say miserably. "But I wish you'd just said, 'I've made you some fudge.' The end."

"I think you're overreacting," says Seb, a hint of impatience in his voice. "All friends do favors for each other."

"Maybe they do, but they're not counted out. They're not itemized. They're not presented on a spreadsheet."

"No one's got a spreadsheet, for God's sake!" exclaims Seb angrily.

"What's *this*?" Getting to my feet, I take the coffee sleeve out of my tote bag and brandish it at him.

"For fuck's sake!" Seb sounds hurt. "I thought it was *fun*."

"Well, I thought so too," I say, my voice trembling. "But it doesn't feel like fun anymore."

"Why *not*?" he demands, almost furiously.

"Because I want to love you!"

My words spill out before I can stop them, and at once I catch my breath. I'm about to say hurriedly, "I didn't mean it," but that would be a lie. Because I did mean it. So I just stand there, panting slightly, my face turning deep crimson.

"Well, I want to love you," says Seb, after what seems like an endless pause. "Is there a problem with that?"

My stomach starts turning over painfully. We hadn't ever used the word *love,* and now we've both said it. Seb's eyes meet mine, infinitely affectionate and warm, and I know this is my cue to run into his arms and forget everything else . . . but I can't. I have to make my point.

"There's a problem with this!" I jab despairingly at the coffee sleeve. "Love isn't transactional! It's not about what can you do for each other." I gaze at him, desperate for him to understand. "Love means all debts are off."

"Well, they *are* off!"

"They're not! Even if I get rid of this"—I thrust the coffee sleeve back into my tote bag, then jab my head—"they're here!"

For a moment we're silent. The air between us is crackling with tension. I feel like love is on the other side of an invisible wall and neither of us knows how to get there.

"What do you want from me, Fixie?" says Seb at last, sounding a little weary, and I swallow hard, my head racing with thoughts.

"I wish we could go back to that coffee shop," I say at last. "And we'd meet. And you'd say, 'Hi. I'm Sebastian.' And I'd say, 'Hi. I'm Fixie.' And there wouldn't be any favors or owing or receipts or tallies or anything."

"Yes. Well." Seb shrugs unsmilingly. "You can't go back in time and do life a different way. That's not how it works."

"I *know*." I feel a prickle of irritation. "I was just saying. You asked."

"Have another piece of fudge," says Seb pleasantly, but with an edge to his voice. "With no debt or obligation attached whatsoever."

"Thanks." I match his sarcastic tone.

He passes me the plate and I take a piece and for a few moments we're silent, until Seb suddenly draws breath, his face working with thoughts I can't guess.

"You think love isn't transactional?" he says. "That's what you're telling me? Then I have a question. Why do you run around, constantly doing too much for your family?"

"What?" I give a shocked, incredulous laugh. "No, I don't!"

"Is it because of love?" he continues, ignoring me. "Or is it because you feel you owe them? Or is it guilt? Because that's a toxic, subprime, never-ending debt, and you need to get rid of it."

Everything he's saying is touching a nerve. But I can't admit it.

"I *don't* do too much for my family." I glower at him.

"All I hear about is what can you do for your mother, your family, the business. You work harder than any of them. You clear up their messes. Your brother has problems and you want to sort them out! Why should you? Let him sort it out!"

I can't help it; I'm starting to bristle. If people attack my family, I defend them. It's how I'm made.

"Look, you wouldn't understand," I say tightly.

"Because I don't have a family?" he shoots back, equally tightly, and I blink in shock.

"No! Of course not! I only meant . . . We're very close. We have a motto—"

"I know," he cuts me off. "*Family first.* When did they last put *you* first, Fixie?"

I stare at him, my face prickling. I feel like he's taking each of my most hidden, most painful feelings and holding them up to the light to brush them down—and it *hurts*. I want him to *stop*.

"My family may be a distant memory," says Seb, "but what I do remember about them is that love isn't acting like a doormat. Love can be tough. Sometimes love *has* to be tough."

"You think I'm a *doormat*?" I say, breathing hard.

"I didn't say that. But I think you need to start thinking

less about what you owe other people and more about what you owe yourself."

I know what he's saying makes sense. But at the same time, he's making me feel so stupid. Such a mug. And I can't bear it.

"So, what, just stop caring?" I lash back.

"It's not that!" he says hotly. "But you have to care for yourself! You have to be strong. Don't let them make you feel bad about yourself. Try to . . . I don't know. Block them out."

"Oh, right." I hear my stream of hostile words before I can stop them. "Easy. Block out my family. Like you block out your brother? Shut the door and turn the key and look away? Just because you can't see a bin full of bottles doesn't mean it's not there—"

I break off into monumental, terrible silence. Seb looks like I've bludgeoned him.

"How do you know what's in that room?" he says at last, and his voice has lost all its volume and spirit.

"I'm sorry." I rub my face. "I . . . I took the key. I looked."

The atmosphere has disintegrated. I take a step forward, trying to be conciliatory, but Seb doesn't react. His face is pale and distant, as though I'm not even here. I look at the plate of fudge and suddenly realize that if he's been making it since he was seven, he probably made it with his brother.

"Seb—"

"It's fine," he says, looking at me as though I'm a stranger. "It's fine. Really."

"It's not fine."

"It's fine," he repeats. "Let's not talk about it."

His face is all closed up and his voice has lost all its warmth. I feel like I've been excommunicated.

"You don't have to look at me like that," I say in a defensive rush.

"Like what?"

"Like I *meant* to hurt you. I didn't *mean* to hurt you."

"You pried into my dead brother's room behind my back." His tone is unforgiving. "What *were* you meaning to do?"

"I didn't 'pry'!" I say in horror, even though a small voice is whispering, *Yes, I did pry.* "Seb," I begin again, trying to reconnect, "I know you're sensitive, I know this has been awful for you, but I'm sure James would—"

"You have no idea!" he cuts me off furiously, then pauses, regaining control. "You have no idea about James. None."

His gaze is so hostile, it brings tears to my eyes. I've had a hell of a day, and I came here for comfort and instead I've messed up. I shouldn't have invaded Seb's privacy. I shouldn't have blurted it out. But can't he forgive me?

"It seems like neither of us can say anything without hurting the other," I say, my voice trembling. "Maybe I should go."

I'm so desperately hoping that Seb's face will change, that he'll sweep me into his arms and we can say sorry to each other six hundred times and make it better in bed.

But he doesn't. He's silent for a few moments, then says, "If you think so."

So I gather my things with shaking hands, my breaths coming short and shallow. And I go.

I travel home in a daze, sitting on the tube, staring at my distorted reflection. I can't quite comprehend what just happened, how we went so far and so badly so quickly. And it's only when I get home, to my own bedroom, that I bury my face in my pillow and start to sob.

Twenty-Three

I wake up with a splitting headache and only one thought: *Seb. I must contact Seb.* The entirety of last night is in my head, as clearly as though it happened five minutes ago. I still can't believe how we veered off track. I have to talk to him, apologize; we have to make this right.

It was only a spat, I tell myself. All couples have spats. We were both tired and stressed and said stuff we didn't mean. We can fix this.

I grab my phone and send a text to him:

Are we OK?

Then I flop back on my pillow and stare at the ceiling, trying to self-heal my headache. I've seen a book in Nicole's room called *Meditate Your Way to Health,* but what are you supposed to do when your head hurts too much to meditate?

I try to focus on a beach, but the only beach I can visualize is dry and scorching and kind of dystopian-looking, with blinding white sand and harsh cliffs and a vulture trying to peck bits out of my eyes while it screeches in my ear. So in the end I get up, wrap my robe around myself, and stagger down the stairs to find some aspirin. I'll follow the *Drug*

Your Way to Health regime, I decide. Just for this morning. And I'm on the bottom step when a new text pings into my phone, making my heart lurch with nerves. It's from Seb.

I don't know, are we?

I gaze at it, my temples throbbing. I don't know how to reply. If I say *yes,* do I sound too complacent? Obviously I'm not going to say *no.* What I really want to say is, *I don't know, are we?* but that sounds like I'm copying him.

The main thing, I tell myself, is that he replied. Within two minutes. So he's thinking about me too. And maybe the best thing is not to text again yet but to call him later, only I *must* have an aspirin first. . . .

I push open the door of the kitchen and nearly die of shock. Ryan is sitting at the kitchen table, scooping cereal into his mouth.

"What are *you* doing here?" I clutch the doorframe.

"Morning." He shoots me a dazzling smile, but I don't return it.

"What are you *doing* here?" I try again. "What— How—" I feel like I might be going mad. Is Ryan part of my dystopian fantasy? Have I conjured him up to torture myself?

"Jake gave me a key, said I could stay over in his old room." Ryan winks suggestively. "He told me you wouldn't be here; otherwise, I would have come visiting."

"You're vile." I glare at him. "I want you out."

"Give me a chance!" says Ryan, gesturing at his breakfast. "I haven't finished! Although these cornflakes are pretty gross," he adds, wrinkling his nose.

"They're Nicole's," I say. "They're spelt flakes."

"You moron," I want to add. "Can't you read the packet?" But that would be engaging with him, when what I want is not to engage with him, ever again.

"Spelt," he says thoughtfully, finishing his last mouthful. "Huh. Figures."

"Go," I say sternly. "Now."

"So, how have you been?" He leans back in his chair, running his eyes over me in a way that would have had me melting on the floor once upon a time. "I've been hoping you might call me."

He's been *hoping I might call him*? I open my mouth, about six furious responses on my lips, then stop myself. *Do not engage, Fixie. It's what he wants.*

"Go," I repeat. "Just go."

"I'm going!" He lifts his hands, looking amused. "Make me a coffee first, though."

Make him coffee? Is he for real?

"Go! Leave! Vamoose!"

"Oh, I took some chewing gum out of your bag," he adds, pointing to where my tote bag is hanging on a chair. "You don't mind, do you?"

"*Go!*" I say, and now I really am feeling enraged. I look around wildly, see the broom propped up against the wall, and pick it up. "Go! Out!" I start prodding it at him, trying to make him stand up. "Out!"

"Fixie, you're hilarious," says Ryan, finally standing up. "I'll see you soon, babe."

Babe? That's the final straw.

Lifting up the broom like a jousting pole, I charge fiercely at him with a kind of war cry, and he gives a jump of surprise, then half-walks, half-runs, as I prod him bodily down the hall.

"Go!" I'm shouting. "Leave and never come back! You are not allowed in this house!"

"Looking good, Fixie," he says, as I shove him out of the door. "I'll call you."

"Please don't! Ever!"

I slam the door shut. Then I lean against it, panting slightly and even starting to laugh as I remember his expression when I charged at him. He was actually a bit freaked out.

At last I head back into the kitchen, take my aspirin, and sit for a bit, letting all the events of yesterday swirl round my brain. Leila, weeping into her manicure set. Uncle Ned, spluttering at me in rage. *Morag,* I suddenly think. Oh God. I need to sort out Morag. And Jake . . . and is Mum OK?

I'm still sitting there, in a bit of a trance, when the door opens and Jake strides in. I gape at him, feeling I must be in a dream. First Ryan, then Jake? He's dressed as smartly as ever, in a well-cut suit and tie, but his face is shocking. He looks drawn and pale and there's an angry jut about his chin, as though he wants to smash the whole world.

"Where's Ryan?" he says.

"Gone." I'm not going to admit I threw Ryan out, because Jake looks like he wants to lay into someone and he might take it out on me. "So, if you wanted to see him—"

"I don't," he cuts me off. He paces over to the window and I watch in silence. His whole body is twitchy, I notice. He pushes a trembling hand through his hair, then turns to face me and just looks at me, and I know what he means. He means: "You know."

"I saw Leila last night," I say, to get it out in the open.

He nods briefly. "She told me."

"Jake—"

"It's all fucking bollocks. It's all—" He breaks off, breathing hard. It makes me remember him kicking the can around the street when he was a teenager, railing at everything.

"Jake . . ." I close my eyes briefly, trying to marshal my thoughts and get rid of my remaining headache. "How much trouble *are* you in?"

For a while Jake doesn't answer. He pours himself a glass of water and drains it, his head tilted back. I watch him, mesmerized by his Adam's apple moving up and down, wondering what on earth he's going to say next.

"You don't need to know," he says finally.

"Maybe I do! Jake, maybe this is the whole problem, that you're not sharing this stuff!" My words tumble out in my eagerness to help. "We're your family. We're here for you. Whatever it takes, we'll help you. Maybe go to see a debt expert, maybe get counseling—"

"I don't need *counseling*," he lashes back, and I bite my lip. "I need *money*."

"You look knackered," I say, with a wince. "You look like what you need most is sleep."

"Sleep!" He gives a short angry laugh, and I see a vein throbbing at his temple again. Everything I say is making him cross, but I can't stop.

"Why don't you go and have a nap?" I venture. "And I'll make some soup. And then we'll sit down and make a plan."

Just for a split second I think he might agree. There's a flash of some deep-down emotion in his eyes and I feel as though I've got somewhere. But almost at once it's gone. His guard is back up and he's striding around the room again.

"I don't need soup, or a plan, or any bullshit like that. I need cash." He turns to me again, his face alive and urgent. "So here's what you do. You go and see your rich boyfriend and you find me some money. Or a new business contact. Something."

"*What?*" I'm so shocked, I actually laugh. "I can't do that!"

"I need it."

"Jake, I can't."

"I need it," he repeats harshly. "If I can't get some money soon, I'll have to go to the guys who break your legs."

I feel a stab of terror, and the ravens start to bat their wings as hard as they ever have, but I force myself not to cave in. Tough love. That's what Seb advised. Block him out.

"There has to be another way."

"I've *tried* every way!" he erupts. "You know what every businessperson needs, Fixie? A bit of luck. One little nugget of luck. Well, you're going out with this guy Seb, and that's my nugget of luck."

"Seb and I had a row last night," I contradict him. "I'm not even sure if we're going out."

"He owes you, though, doesn't he?" Jake comes back instantly. "You saved his life or whatever? Leila told me the whole thing," he adds, and I curse myself for blabbing about Seb last night, while Leila was finishing off my topcoat.

"He's not rich," I say. "He's not. He manages money, that's all. He's not some flash guy; he's not like all your millionaire friends."

"He has access to money," says Jake. "He knows people. And I'm desperate." He comes over and brings his face close to mine. "*Family first,* Fixie. Do this for me. Or do you want to break up the family?"

"What do you mean, break up the family?" I say in horror.

"If you don't do this for me, that's it," he says nastily. "The family's broken. What, you're going to watch your own brother sink? You think we can play happy family after that?"

He swings away and I breathe out, my head spinning, close to tears. I know what Seb said: tough love. But I'm not tough enough. I can't block out Jake's energy, his aggression.

I have a sudden memory of Mum's voice: "Just don't lose the shop, Fixie. Or let the family break up." And I promised her. I pointed at the gateleg oak table in the dining room and said, "When you get back, we'll be sitting around that very table to celebrate. The shop will be in great shape. And we'll be a happy family."

A wave of despair crashes over me. I've failed on every front. Morag's threatening to leave. Profits are shaky. And now Jake's going to break up the family. He'll turn Nicole against me. Mum will come back to split-up, warring factions and she'll be devastated.

I can't be tough. Not that tough. I can't.

And, anyway, what's Jake actually asking for? He only wants me to request some help from Seb. It's not such a huge deal.

"Fine," I mutter at last.

"What, you'll do it?" Jake's face lights up.

In answer, I reach for my phone and compose a text to Seb:

Can I come to see you? Lunchtime?

I send it and almost at once get a response:

Of course!

"OK, it's on," I say, putting my phone down. "I'm seeing him at lunch."

"Yes!" says Jake, giving an energetic fist pump. "Fixie, you're a star."

"I can't *promise* anything," I say, wanting to make this clear. "I can't *promise* anything. All I can do is ask him for help."

"Oh, he'll help you," says Jake, and all his confident swagger seems to have returned. "He'll help you, Fixie."

As I walk to work, I keep looking at Seb's text on my phone and trying to analyze it. It's only two words—**Of course!**—but I think I can tell a lot from them. He sounds keen. He put an exclamation mark, which he didn't have to. He doesn't sound angry. Or . . . does he?

I try to picture him saying, "Of course!" with a furious scowl, but it doesn't work. I *think* he wants to see me. I hope he does. And of course we'll have to talk about last night, and I'll apologize for looking in his brother's room and it might be a bit prickly . . . but we'll be OK.

Won't we?

At last I shove my phone away. I can't speculate anymore;

it's doing my head in. I enter the shop and at once see Morag at the other end. She's lecturing Stacey about something—I can't hear what exactly, but Morag's pointing to a display—and I feel a sudden wave of love for her. She's planning to leave, but she's still taking the time to do that? She still cares about Farrs; I know she does.

A bleep comes from my pocket and I yank out my phone again, thinking, *Seb?* But it's a text from Mum:

Sorry I missed you, Fixie, feeling a lot better today. Hope all OK. Love, Mum xxx

I glance up at Morag, who is now gesturing at a saucepan, then read Mum's words again: **Hope all OK.**

I hope so too. I really do.

When Morag's finished, I wave to get her attention, and as she approaches, I say, "Morag, could we have a chat?"

I usher her into the back room, my head a mishmash of thoughts. I don't know what I'm going to say or where I'm going to start. But I know that I have to reach out to Morag, urgently. I have to turn things around.

"Morag . . ." I begin, once we're both sitting down with the door closed and cups of tea. "Everything's been a bit of a mess since Mum went off to Spain."

"Yes, love," says Morag, in her sensible, unvarnished way. "It has."

"But I'm going to change that. We're going to cancel all the yoga, we're going to make Cake Club a priority, we're going to restock the shop. . . ."

"Good," says Morag. "Because it needs it."

"I want to look at our online business again. And we need

a really big push before Christmas. We need to turn things around. We *can* turn things around."

"Yes," says Morag. "I think you can."

You. Not *we.*

Has she mentally left already?

There's a pause and I sip my tea, not quite knowing what I'm going to say next. Morag is so sensible, I think, as I stare at her practical hands with their transparent nail polish. She knows the customers. She knows buying. She knows pricing. *She's* the one who should have been sitting round the table all this time, making decisions with me. Not Nicole. Not Jake. Not Uncle Ned.

"Morag, if we can persuade you to stay with us," I hear myself saying, "I'd like you to be a director."

The words are out before I've even stopped to consider them. But the minute I've uttered them, I know they're right. Morag makes this place what it is. She should have ownership.

"A *director*?" Morag peers at me, startled.

"We haven't valued you nearly enough," I say. "And I'm sorry. Morag, please stay."

"So this is a bribe," she says at once.

"It's not." I shake my head vigorously. "At least, it's not meant that way. It's recognition. Of everything that you do."

"A director," says Morag slowly, as though getting used to the idea. Then she looks at me suspiciously. "Is your mum in agreement with this? Your mum's big on family. I'm not family."

Family first runs through my mind. *Family bloody first.* I'm not saying Dad was wrong, I'll never say that, but maybe

I'm starting to see "family" differently. It's not just the people you share genes with; it's the people you share loyalty and friendship and respect with. It's the people you love.

"You're part of the Farrs family," I say. "And that's what counts."

"Fixie, you didn't answer the question," says Morag sharply, and I think, *That's why we need her: She doesn't miss a trick.* "Does your mum even know you're offering me this?"

"I haven't asked Mum, but I don't need to." I look at Morag resolutely. "I know she'll agree."

I've never felt so positive in my life. I *know* this is the right thing. Mum charged me with keeping this shop safe, and that's what I'm doing.

"Well, I'll think about it," says Morag, finishing her tea. "I'd better get back to the shop floor."

And she's so calm, so unruffled, so impressive, that I cross my fingers all the way back to the cash desk and think, *Please stay, please stay, please stay.*

I think she will.

For some reason we get a group of Japanese tourists in that morning, looking for Union Jack memorabilia. Morag, Stacey, and I sell twelve mugs, sixteen cushion covers, and a calendar to them, while Greg attempts to "speak Japanese" in phrases he's picked up off manga cartoons. Although none of the Japanese people seem to understand a word.

"What were you *saying*?" I demand, as soon as they've all left.

"Not sure," he admits. "*Kill,* probably."

"*Kill?*" I stare at him. "You were saying *kill* in Japanese?"

"It might not have been," he says after a moment's thought. "It might have been *decapitate.*"

"*Decapitate?*" I echo in horror. "You greeted a group of customers with the word *decapitate?*"

"They didn't understand," Stacey chimes in. "They just thought he was an idiot. How's your boyfriend, Fixie?" she adds seamlessly, blinking at me.

"Oh," I say, taken off-balance. "He's . . . Um. Yes."

Trust Stacey to catch me off guard. Avoiding her curious eyes—Greg looks pretty interested too—I glance at my watch.

"All good," I add briskly. "In fact, I have to go. And, new rule," I add over my shoulder as I head off to get my coat. "Anyone who says *decapitate* to a customer gets fired."

"Well, *that's* unfair," I can hear Greg grumbling behind my back. "What if it comes up in normal conversation?"

"Normal conversation?" says Stacey mockingly. "What kind of sicko are you, Greg? I've never even *said* the word *decapitate.*"

"You just did!" points out Greg triumphantly. "Just did!" And I can't help biting my lip, trying not to smile. They might be a bit dysfunctional . . . but I do love our staff.

Seb and I haven't actually fixed up a time to meet, so as I leave the shop, I text him:

On way to you now. Is that OK?

Almost immediately he fires back a reply:

Fine.

I compose another text—**Great, see you soon**—and am hesitating over whether to add a kiss when another text pings into my phone. It's from Seb again, and as I read it, I feel a bolt of shock.

Why do you want to meet?

I'm so disconcerted, I stop dead on the pavement. Why do I want to meet?

Why?

For a few moments I don't know how to reply. What does that even *mean*? Isn't it obvious why I want to meet? Pitching Jake's request is the last of my priorities. I want to see Seb. I want to wrap my arms around him. I want to say how sorry I am that I crossed the boundary of his brother's room. I want to tell him that I've *tried* to take his advice, I've *tried* to be tough with Jake, but sometimes I just don't feel strong enough.

I want him. That's all. I want him.

I walk forward, trying to get my head straight, trying to work out what to say, and as I do, I feel more and more upset. **Why do you want to meet?** That's not a friendly question. That's not a kissing-and-making-up question. Does he *not* want to kiss and make up?

As the thought hits me, I feel suddenly empty and scared and a bit stupid. Have I read this all wrong? Have I assumed . . .

Oh God. Does he see everything differently from me?

Are we *over*?

The thought sends unbearable pain ricocheting around me. Over. We can't be over. I need him. I close my eyes, trying to breathe steadily, willing it not to be true. It can't be. It can't be what he wants. But why else would he send such a formal, distancing text?

I read the words yet again—**Why do you want to meet?**—and they're plain hurtful. Where's the intimacy? Where's the affection? What are we, business associates?

My head is throbbing and I think I might start crying if I let myself. But I'm not going to. I'm Ninja Fixie. I'm tough. If he wants to be businesslike, I can be businesslike.

I type a new text, my thumbs jabbing the keys so hard I keep misfiring, but I don't care, I have to let out some of my hurt.

There's a business thing I wanted to ask you about.

I send the text, then wait breathlessly. Two can send hurtful messages. Two can play at being distant and formal. A moment later my phone pings:

Fine.

I stare at the single word, feeling a fresh stabbing in my heart. Why is he like this? Why has he given up on us? We had a row last night. A row. Couples have rows. Is he really going to throw it all away because I made one stupid mistake?

As I scroll backward and forward on my phone, reading all the texts we've exchanged today, I just don't get it. He sounded OK this morning. Not exactly ebullient, but not cold either. He sounded like he wanted to see me.

Now, however, he sounds cold and detached and not the Seb I know. Let alone the Seb I'm in love with. What's happened? Why?

But I can't answer any of these questions standing here, motionless. So at last I force myself onward, my feet feeling heavy. I was so looking forward to seeing him. But now I'm dreading it.

I arrive at the building and Seb greets me himself at the lift and I instantly know: It's worse than I expected.

"So," he says. "Hi." He extends a hand, but he doesn't kiss me. His face is taut. His eyes are dark and ominous and keep looking past me. I shake his hand, feeling a bit surreal.

"Hi," I say. "Thanks for seeing me."

"No problem."

He ushers me into his office as though I'm a stranger, asking politely if I'd like a coffee. All the time, his body language is wretched: stiff and tense, keeping his distance, swiveling away from me at every chance. And I keep thinking, *Is this a joke? Are we really acting like this?* But it doesn't seem to be a joke.

As I'm waiting for him to return with my coffee, I look around his office. It's so much more characterful than his flat. So much more homey, with all the books and photos and the colorful rug.

This *is* his home, I suddenly realize. So his flat is . . . what?

Limbo. The word comes to me, unbidden. His flat is limbo. Empty and unloved and kind of waiting. And suddenly I'm desperate to talk to him about this. But how can I when we're as stiff as two cats preparing to fight?

He comes back in with two mugs, and I look up, hoping that maybe now things will relax—but if anything he looks less friendly than before.

"What can I do for you?" he says, sitting down, and I feel a surge of fresh hurt. Fine. If he wants to play it like that, then fine.

"I'm here for a favor," I say shortly. "Not for me, for someone else. For—"

"Yes, I can guess," he cuts me off.

He sounds so hostile, I flinch. He looks as though he's bubbling with outrage. Hatred even. And, OK, I *know* he told me to be tough with Jake. I *know* I'm doing the opposite of what he advised, coming here for a bailout. But does he have to be so sanctimonious?

"I don't expect you to understand," I say.

"No. Frankly, I don't."

"Well, I guess I'm just not as strong as you thought," I snap miserably. "Sorry."

"Oh, you don't have to apologize." His eyes are so hard and unforgiving, I wince. "Your life. Do what you want."

Do what I want? How can he *be* like this?

"Seb . . ." I stare at him, tears hot behind my eyes. "Look. I know you're angry. I know I hurt you, and I'm sorry. But let me tell you why I'm here."

"*Really?*" he shoots back, so viciously that I inhale in shock. "I have a better idea, Fixie. Let's not talk about it. What do you want? Money?"

I stare at him, stung. *Money?* And I'm about to retort, "Don't be silly, all I want is a bit of advice for Jake or maybe a contact, or even just a hug would do. . . ." when something in me snaps. If we don't love each other, then why am I even hesitating?

"Well, you do owe me," I retort, slapping the words down between us. And instantly Seb's face goes blank and kind of scary-looking.

For a few moments neither of us speaks. The air feels hazy with tension. I feel like I'm in a bad dream and I need to wake up. I need to start again. Say different things. Make things go another way.

But I can't. This is life.

"Yes. I owe you," Seb says at last, his voice sounding like it belongs to someone else. "How much? Wait, I'll find a checkbook."

He gets up without looking at me, heads to a filing cabinet, and roots round in a low drawer. I watch him, motionless, faint with misery. I've achieved what I came here to do. So why do I feel so hollow?

Why am I here, anyway? What am I *doing*?

Trying to keep a grip on things, I remind myself of the facts. Jake. Debt. Family.

Except, sitting here, the facts seem to be taking a different path in my head. I'm thinking this all through in a way I haven't before. Suppose Seb gives Jake a lump of cash. What then? What have I achieved? He'll only spend it on a load of expensive lunches and tell us lots of bullshit about "deals" and we'll be back to square one.

As Seb opens and shuts drawers, I'm light-headed with confusion. I feel like everything is out of my grasp. I can't remember why I thought it was a good idea to come here. I don't have a plan. I don't have anything. Except the knowledge that I've destroyed any hopes of being with Seb.

I feel a dart of anguish, so painful that I drop my head into my hands. Random thoughts are running through my head, in such a bewildering stream that I can't keep track. *Family first. Tough love. Block them out.* That's what Seb said: *Block them out.* But how can I block out Jake? He said he'd break up the family. He looked like he meant it. And I love my family, I love them, despite everything. . . .

And then it comes to me in a kind of flash.

Love. It's all about love.

Love isn't blocking people out; it's the opposite. If you love someone, you engage with them. You don't block them out; you *talk* to them.

When did I last properly talk to Jake? When did Mum? He doesn't let us in. He bats us away with his smart cars and drawling accent, with his lies and threats. But who is he underneath?

My head feels like it's exploding. Everything is becoming clear. I don't need to love Jake less; I need to love him *more.* We all do. Me. Mum. Leila. He needs the kind of tough, unconditional love that means we actually, properly, help him sort himself out.

Tough love. The toughest love. The lovingest love there is.

"OK." I hear Seb's voice and I lift my head to see him sitting back at his desk. "What do I owe you?"

A shaft of light from the window is catching his eyes, turning them a shiny green-brown again. I look at his face and find myself thinking, *I love you.* But what good is that now?

"Nothing." I gather up my bag. "Actually, I don't need any money, after all. Or any help. Thank you. Sorry to bother you."

"That's quite the *volte-face*," says Seb expressionlessly.

"Yes, well. I've realized something. And, actually, it was you who helped me realize it." My voice wavers slightly, and I clear my throat. "So . . . thanks."

"Oh yes?" says Seb with stony indifference.

"Yes. You did." His expression could not be less encouraging, but I force myself to press on. "When you talked about tough love. You helped me realize that if you really love someone, you don't just shove cash at them. You help them become the person they're meant to be. And *that's* what unconditional love is."

I gaze at him, desperate for some reaction, some warmth, *something*. . . .

"Unconditional love," Seb echoes at last, in an odd voice. His eyes look kind of scorched, as though I've dealt him some blow. "Well, I'm glad if you've worked that all out for yourself. But I have a busy day. So." He pushes his chair back, as though to wrap up things.

I stare at him, feeling winded. That's it? That's his reaction?

"Why aren't you more pleased?" My words tumble out before I can stop them, and to my horror, two tears spill over onto my cheeks. "I listened to you! I took your advice!"

"I am pleased," he says. "I'm super-pleased. Good luck with your project. Goodbye," he adds, standing up, and with trembling legs I rise too.

"Goodbye," I echo him with miserable sarcasm. "Nice knowing you."

I stalk out, my head in a daze, my eyes filling with fresh tears. As I do so, I think I catch sight of the IOU coffee sleeve resting on a shelf—and something seems to tug at my mind.

But I'm in too much turmoil to dwell on it or think about anything beyond the fact that Seb looked at me like I was a stranger. And everything's worse than before. And I just don't *get* it.

Twenty-Four

get back to the shop to find Jake waiting outside, looking tense and coiled, like a snake about to strike.

"So?" he says, walking to meet me. "So? So?"

I draw breath, trying to overcome my nerves, trying to ignore the ravens. *Unconditional love,* I remind myself. *I can do this. If I talk honestly and from the heart, maybe I'll get through to him.*

"I didn't get you any money," I say.

"Great." Jake swings away, looking murderous. "Just fucking . . . great."

"I didn't get you any," I continue, my voice shaking desperately, "because you shouldn't be borrowing any more. You're only going to get into more and more trouble. Jake, couldn't you make some changes to your life?" I follow him to where he's leaning against the shop front and look earnestly into his face, trying to meet his eye. "Couldn't you stop taking people out for flash lunches? Stop chasing gazillion-pound deals that aren't going to happen? Do some solid work. Guaranteed work. Wouldn't that make you happier—"

I break off, gazing up at him with a hope which instantly

crumbles. If I was hoping to get through to him, I was an idiot. He doesn't look transformed. He doesn't exclaim, "My God, but you're right." He doesn't give me a heartfelt hug and say, "Thanks. I see it all so clearly now."

"Fuck you, Fixie," he snarls, and stomps off down the street. My heart is beating like a rabbit's, and the ravens are batting round my head, and part of me wants to run after him, apologize, even grovel. But the other part knows better. I have to hold firm. This is just stage one.

I wait till he's disappeared round the corner, then pull out my phone and compose a text.

Hi, Leila. Can we talk? Fixie xxx

I send it, then breathe out long and hard, shaking his voice out of my ears. That's all I can do for now. I have other things to think about.

I spend the rest of the day working on plans for Farrs. Plans we can action *now*. By the end of the day I've made an itemized list of Christmas promotions, price cuts, events, and sales. I've ordered more stock. I've replanned the front of the store. I haven't deferred once to Jake, Nicole, or Uncle Ned. I've made decisions all alone, mentally channeling Mum and occasionally consulting with Morag. No one else. I'm in charge of this. Me, Fixie.

I get home exhausted and find Nicole lolling against the kitchen doorframe, lost in her phone as she always is.

"Oh, hi, Fixie," she says, glancing up. "God, Jake was *mad* with you last night."

"I know," I say shortly. "And I wasn't too impressed by him. So we're quits."

I wait for her to say something else about last night, but her brow is furrowed as she peers at her screen.

"I'm so stressed," she sighs gustily. "I'm so, like . . . All my hormones are shot. I need to see someone."

"Why are you stressed?" I say out of politeness.

"It's Drew. He's booked me a ticket, for the twenty-third. He's, like, 'You *have* to come to Abu Dhabi.'" She blinks at me. "He just, like, *paid* for it."

"What's wrong with that?"

"It's so passive-aggressive!" She opens her eyes wide. "It's so controlling! He knows I'm stressed out, but he just *does* that! It's like . . ." She trails off in her usual way, and I feel a shaft of impatience.

"I thought you were stressed out because you were missing your husband," I point out. "He's bought you a plane ticket to see him, so surely now you should be *less* stressed out?"

"You don't understand." Nicole shoots me a glare. "God, I'm dying for a coffee. Make me a coffee, Fixie."

I count to three, then say clearly, "Make it yourself."

"What?" Nicole blinks at me.

"We've got a coffee machine." I gesture at it. "Make it yourself."

"Oh, but you know I can't do it," says Nicole at once, as though proclaiming a law of nature.

"So learn," I say. "I'll teach you."

"My head can't learn that kind of stuff." Nicole wrinkles her nose. "It's, like, I get a mental block? Go on, you do it, Fixie. You're so brilliant at the coffee machine."

And there's something about her lazy, drifty, entitled voice that suddenly makes me flip out.

"Stop telling me I'm brilliant at things you don't want to do!" I yell, and her head jerks up in surprise. "Stop pretending to be incompetent to get out of things!"

"*What?*" Nicole's staring at me as though she's never heard me speak before and didn't even realize I had a voice. Which maybe she didn't.

"You *can* learn the coffee machine! Of course you can. You just don't want to! You avoid everything, Nicole! Everything! Including your own husband!"

Shit. That popped out before I could stop it.

"What are you *talking* about?" Nicole's hand flutters defensively to her mouth, and I feel my face flame. That was going too far. Or was it?

I swallow a few times, my mind working furiously. I could backtrack. Apologize. Close the conversation down. But I'm not in the mood for backtracking, or apologizing, or closing the conversation down. Maybe it's time for us to be the kind of sisters Mum always wanted us to be. The kind who actually know something meaningful about each other's lives.

"I know it's none of my business," I say, more calmly. "But you never talk to him on the phone. You don't seem to care when he's ill. And now you don't want to go to Abu Dhabi to see him. Nicole . . . do you actually *love* Drew?"

There's a massive silence. Nicole's beautiful face is swiveled away from me, but I can see a tightness at the corner of her mouth. Her fingers are fiddling with her tassely belt and I notice her chewed-up nails. Then at last she turns her head, and to my shock, her eyes are full of tears.

"I don't know," she says in a whisper. "I don't know. I don't bloody *know*."

"Right," I say, trying to hide my shock. "Well . . . did you love him when you married him?"

"I don't *know*." Nicole looks desperate. "I thought I did. But I might have made a massive mistake. Don't tell Mum," she adds quickly, and she sounds so like she did when she was fifteen years old and I found her swigging from a bottle of vodka that I can't help a snort of laughter.

"I thought you were dying from separation anxiety," I say, and Nicole's nostrils flare.

"I *have* been really stressed out, *actually*," she says, returning to her haughty self. "My yoga teacher says she's concerned about me."

I roll my eyes. Nicole will never not take herself seriously. But at least she's sounding a bit more real.

"So, what went wrong?" I can't help asking. "You seemed so happy at the wedding."

"The wedding was great." Nicole's eyes soften with the memory. "And the honeymoon was great. But then I was a bit, 'Is this it?' There wasn't anything to *plan* for anymore, you know? All the excitement was gone. It was so, I dunno, *flat*."

"Couldn't you have gone to Abu Dhabi with Drew?" I suggest. "Couldn't you have planned for that? Why *didn't* you go, anyway? Don't tell me there aren't yoga courses out there."

"I panicked," admits Nicole after a pause. "We'd had a couple of rows, and I thought, *Drew and me on our own in Abu Dhabi in some expat flat? What if it all goes pearshaped? What if we have more rows?* I thought it would be easier this way. You know. It'd be . . ." She trails off in her usual unfinished way.

"You thought it would be easier to completely avoid your husband than to have a few rows." I stare at her. "Yup. That makes sense."

"It was stressful!" says Nicole defensively. "I thought, *I'll sit it out in England and it'll work out one way or another.*"

"You don't work out a relationship by burying your head in the sand!" I exclaim incredulously. "All relationships are stressful! All relationships have rows! Do you *love* him?"

There's a long silence. Nicole is twisting her hair round her fingers, her face turned away.

"Sometimes I think yes," she says finally. "But sometimes I look at him and I think . . ." She flinches expressively. "But I mean, I haven't seen him for, like, so long. . . ."

I wait for her to continue—then realize that she's finished. Even by Nicole standards, it's a pretty inconclusive answer.

"Nicole, you have to go to Abu Dhabi," I say firmly. "And then maybe you'll find out whether you love Drew or not."

"Yeah," says Nicole, looking uncertain. "I suppose."

"You *have* to," I impress on her. "You need to spend time together. You need to confront this. Otherwise you don't even know if you want to be married or not."

"Maybe. But what if I get out there and . . ." Nicole trails off in her irritating way—but for once I know what she means. She means, "What if I realize I don't love Drew?" And she looks pretty freaked out.

I mean, fair enough. I'd be freaked out too.

"I guess you have to face up to that possibility," I say, with a sympathy I've never felt for Nicole before. "I mean, what else were you planning to do? Did you *have* a plan?"

"I don't know! I thought . . ." She hesitates, chewing her nails. "I thought maybe Drew would meet someone else out there and it would all be decided for me." And this is so ridiculous that I burst into real, proper laughter.

At once Nicole frowns, as though not sure whether to get offended or not—but then her face cracks into a smile. And I grin back. I feel like for the first time in our life, the two of us have connected. We were always like some electric circuit which didn't work and was about to be chucked away in the bin. But now the bulb is flickering. There's hope.

"For what it's worth, I think Drew's a great guy," I say. "But that's kind of irrelevant. The point is if he's the *right* guy. For you."

"Well, you know, either we stay married or we divorce," replies Nicole, with a rare flash of comedy. "Win-win." She pulls such a wry face I can't help smiling. And now this connection has been made between us, I feel like I want to say everything I have to, very quickly.

"Nicole, there's something else I need to say," I blurt out. "It's on a different topic, but it's important. I was serious last night. You *have* to stop your yoga classes. We need to get back on track. Otherwise Morag will leave and Farrs will go bust and we'll lose the house and Mum will never speak to us again."

"You always exaggerate, Fixie." Nicole gives me one of her dismissive eye rolls.

"I'm not exaggerating! We're really in trouble! Bob said so," I add for good measure. "Yesterday."

This is a slight lie: Bob didn't actually say we were in trouble. But everyone respects Bob. Sure enough, Nicole looks alarmed.

"Bob said we're in trouble?"

"Yes."

"What exactly did he say?"

"He said . . ." I cross my fingers behind my back. "He said, 'You're in trouble.' And it's true!" I try to impress the facts on her. "Basically, we've messed up the shop while Mum's been away and we need to put it right."

"I haven't messed up anything," counters Nicole in her customary lordly manner. "Have you seen the Instagram page?" She tosses her hair back and glances at her reflection in a glass-fronted cupboard. "It's *transformed*. Everyone agrees. The images are *amazing*."

"Yes, but it's only pictures of you!" I retort in exasperation. "And the only comments are people asking you for dates!"

"It's increased our profile," says Nicole at once, but she sounds defensive and I can tell I'm getting through.

"We need a big Christmas push," I say. "I have a ton of ideas but you need to help me. Proper practical help in the store."

"Oh, I can't," she says at once. "I'm not available. I'm going to Abu Dhabi."

Is she for *real*?

"You're not going until the twenty-third." I give her a flinty look. "You're free till then. And you're helping. And you're doing it my way. OK? You owe it to Farrs," I add, as she draws breath. "You owe it to Mum. You owe it to *me*."

Nicole is silent for a while, her eyes narrowing. I stare at her, unblinking, realizing that this is probably the first time I've ever asserted myself against her.

"*Fine,*" she says finally, huffing loudly. "Only I'm not lugging stock about. My yoga teacher says I shouldn't be lifting heavy items. My arms are exceptionally slender."

"I'll bear that in mind," I say, lifting my eyes skyward. "And now, welcome to the coffee machine, your new best friend."

Shooting me a resentful look, Nicole walks over to the coffee machine and stares at it dubiously. "It's so *complicated,*" she says at last.

"Yes," I agree. "And?"

Nicole prods at the display and jumps as it lights up. Then she turns to frown suspiciously at me.

"You've changed, Fixie," she says.

"Yeah." I nod matter-of-factly. "Yeah, I have."

"How's your new boyfriend?" she asks, light dawning on her face, as though this might explain everything.

"He's not," I say succinctly. "We broke up."

"Oh." Nicole's face crumples a little in sympathy. "Shit. That didn't last long."

"No. Well." I shrug.

We look at each other silently and I feel like we have more in common right now than I can ever remember. We met guys and we fell in love and everything seemed to work out. Until it didn't.

My eyes are starting to shimmer. My throat is thick. I fiercely blink my tears away, but Nicole notices. She peers at me expressionlessly—then suddenly holds out her arms. For a moment I don't even know what she means . . . then I realize and my ears turn warm and I go to her, feeling almost self-conscious.

Her arms wrap around me and my eyes leak hot tears onto her shoulder and I exhale as though I've been holding my breath for a long time. It must be years since my big sister hugged me. She smells of some Nicole-ish perfume, and her earrings make gentle clinky sounds as she pats my back.

"Make me a coffee," she says wheedlingly as we draw apart. "Go on."

"No!" I can't help erupting with outraged laughter, tears still edging my voice. "I'm not doing it! You're going to *learn*!"

It takes over half an hour to teach her. God, she's frustrating. Her brain just slides away when it sees something it doesn't like. But at last she's clutching a latte and looking proudly down at it.

"See?" I say. "And next you can learn how to dehumidify the toaster."

"Dehumidify the toaster?" echoes Nicole, looking aghast, and I bite my lip, giggling. I'm about to tell her I invented "dehumidify the toaster" to freak her out, when my phone beeps with a text.

Hi. Jake's in a real mood. What happened? Can you talk now? Leila xxx

All at once my mind is wrenched away from the coffee machine, away from Nicole, away from easy problems like how to clean the milk frother . . . back to Jake. I see his cold, furious eyes this morning, and my stomach flips with nerves.

Swiftly I type a reply to Leila:

I'll call in 5 xxx

I send the text, then stare at the screen, feeling daunted. I know what I think should happen. And I want to make it happen. But I can't do it alone.

"Nicole," I say at last. "There's something else."

"Yeah?" She's peering at the coffee machine again. "Wait, it does a macchiato?"

"There's something else I need your help with. Something big." I wait until she turns, then add, "It's to do with Jake."

It takes us two days to arrange everything. About half of that is spent explaining it all to Nicole, who starts off by saying, "Honestly, Fixie. Do you have to interfere in *everything*?"

But then she talks to Leila and sees the TV wrenched off Jake's wall. Then we have a meeting with Bob in the back room at the shop and he shows us the withdrawals Jake has been making from the company—and even Nicole looks jolted out of her usual bubble.

"But what does he *spend* it on?" she says, leafing through the printouts that Bob has made for us. "It can't all have gone on the scam," she adds with a wince—I've already filled her in on that.

"You know." I shrug. "Jake stuff. Networking. If you asked him, he'd say he was entertaining clients or softening up prospects or something. But you can't soften up prospects forever. You have to land the deal."

"And how come Mum let him take out that first loan, any-way?" Nicole lifts her eyes to Bob.

Bob looks around as though to check we're not being overheard and sips his instant coffee with three sugars. (We have a filter machine, but he prefers instant.)

"Here's the thing," he says apologetically. "Your mother's always had a soft spot for Jake. No one's perfect, and that's her foible, and she knows it. She says, 'Oh, Bob, I shouldn't,' but she can't help herself. She's bailed him out plenty over the years. I did wonder if you girls knew," he adds, reaching for a rich tea biscuit. "But I reckon you're all in the business now, so to speak."

She's bailed him out? She's bailed out *Jake*?

As I stare at Bob, my head is whirling. I feel a bit weak. All this time, I've felt mortified because *I* was the one who used Mum's money. *I* was the one who failed. Jake made me feel guilty and inferior because he'd done everything on his own, with no help, like the business star that he was.

Only he hadn't, had he? It was all lies.

Or at least . . . I draw myself up short, thinking furiously, trying to remember. Did anyone ever actually lie to me? Or did I simply assume?

I'm waiting to feel a surge of fury with Mum, but it doesn't come. I can't blame her. It's her money. I can't even feel angry with Jake. I just feel kind of rueful. Because how much of my life have I spent comparing myself to Jake? And how utterly pointless was that?

"As for your uncle Ned, I reckon Jake pulled the wool over his eyes," says Bob thoughtfully. "I should think Jake threw his big words around and they drank their gins and Ned didn't ask any questions. But here's the thing: If you're responsible for someone's money, you've got to be able to ask questions. Doesn't matter if you sound stupid." His face breaks into a rare smile. "I'm never afraid of sounding stupid. Just ask, is what I say. Can't hurt to ask."

"You're never stupid, Bob," I say warmly. "You're a star."

"Ah well," says Bob, looking mortified. "That's going a bit far. Just do the job, is what I do."

"OK, well, Fixie, you're right," says Nicole, putting the printouts down. "As *usual*." She shoots me a little grin, and I grin back and decide I won't mention that she left the kitchen in a total tip this morning.

By the following afternoon we're all set—and at six o'clock we're waiting on the steps of Grosvenor Heights, all three of us: Leila, Nicole, and me. We're standing in a row, under the lights of the smart entrance porch, and I'm shivering slightly with cold. Nerves too. Jake's texted Leila to say he's on his way home; he shouldn't be long now. I glance at the others, and Nicole's jaw is tense. Leila looks, frankly, terrified. But at least she's going through with it. She's tougher than she seems, Leila.

And then suddenly there he is, walking toward the building, looking at his phone, and we all stiffen. As he notices us, his face jerks with shock, and his pace speeds up.

"What's going on?" he demands as he gets near. "Why are you all here? Is it Mum?"

"No," says Nicole. "It's you."

"What?" Jake stares from face to face, his phone dangling from his hand. "What are you talking about?"

Nicole and I glance at Leila and she steps forward, her face trembling but brave. "Jakey, we're moving out. We're letting the flat. We can't afford to live here anymore. We'll get a good price."

Jake's eyes darken. "You have to be kidding. She's kidding." He looks at Nicole and me. "She's gone nuts, right?"

"My dad and I put a new TV on the wall," Leila presses on resolutely. "A cheap one. It looks OK. The agent's bringing a professional couple round in an hour. Three more tomorrow. He thinks if we price it right, it'll go quickly."

Jake's face has gone almost rubbery with shock. He stares blankly at Leila, then makes a visible effort to pull himself together.

"This is bollocks," he says, pushing past her. "Excuse me, could I please get through to my own home?"

"I've changed the locks," Leila calls after him, and Jake slowly wheels round.

"You've *what*?" he says ominously.

"I've changed the locks. Just to . . . to make things clear."

"You've locked me out of my own home? You can't *do* that!" he bellows, erupting, and Leila looks like she might collapse.

"Well, she did it," I say, putting an arm around Leila. "Jake, you can't go on like this."

"What the hell are you two doing here, anyway?" He turns on us like a riled tiger.

"We're moral support," says Nicole. " 'If you want to go

fast, go alone,'" she adds wisely, glancing at me. "'If you want to go far, go together.'"

I'm fairly sure she got that quote off a cushion, but I nod gratefully at her. The thing about all Nicole's quotes is that some of them are actually pretty good. Especially the wooden sign she gave me yesterday, which reads, YOU'RE STRONGER THAN YOU THINK. I've looked at it quite a lot—and it *does* make me feel stronger.

"Jakey, do you have any money coming in?" Leila says, her hands twisting anxiously. "Any *actual money*?"

"I have . . . I have a stack of potential deals," says Jake, his face evasive. "There's a guy in Northampton who deals in wine. I have irons in the fire—"

"You don't have any irons in the fire," Leila cuts him off sorrowfully. "You don't."

A police siren blares in the next street and for a moment no one speaks, and I suddenly find myself thinking of Ryan. Jake's too much like Ryan. It's as if he's still trying to *be* Ryan. Just like he always has done, since they were teenagers. All big names and swagger. It was Ryan who made living like a millionaire seem normal to Jake. Of course, Jake was always ambitious; he always wanted money. But even so, I wish he'd never met Ryan. That neither of us had.

"My dad's here to take me home," says Leila, raising her chin. Her skinny legs are encased in tight jeans and high-heeled boots and her nails are works of iridescent art. She looks so dignified, I want to hug her. "All your stuff's in the van. Dad says you're welcome to come and live with us for a bit."

"You've moved out my *stuff*?" Jake reels, as though under a fresh blow.

"We're renting the flat out, Jake," Leila says, as though explaining to someone very stupid. "I had to."

"All right, love? I've had to move the van, bloody traffic wardens." We all look up as a gruff voice hails Leila. It's her dad, Tony. I've met him a few times; he has a building firm in Northwood. He's a big, strong guy with callused hands, and he runs his eyes up and down Jake's smart suit with barely concealed contempt. I'm not sure they've ever really got on. "If you're in trouble, I can give you a job on the site," he adds to Jake in short tones. "You're unskilled, so it would be basic pay."

"Thanks, Dad," says Leila. Her eyes fix on Jake like lamps, and I can see her message: "Thank my dad."

"Thanks, Tony," says Jake, sounding as though the words are choking him.

"Right. Well." Tony strides away and Leila totters after him.

"Wait, Dad. I'll come. Give me a sec." She turns to Jake again on her clippy-cloppy heel, her delicate face full of a strength that makes it even more beautiful than usual. "We'll be in the van for ten minutes, OK? You can come to ours—or we can deliver your stuff somewhere else. But if you come with me, you've got to want to come. You've got to *want* it, Jakey. You and me . . ." Her voice begins to tremble. "We can be something. It's not about you buying me stuff or being a hero or how many clubs we go to. It's about you and me making plans and enjoying life together and . . . and being us. But you've got to want to *be us,* Jakey." She points at him and then herself with her slender fingers. "You've got to want to *be us.*"

She finishes and there's a breathless beat. Then she turns back and hurries toward her dad, who links his arm in hers and together they disappear around the corner, while I resist the urge to shout, "Go, Leila!"

I risk a look at Jake—and feel a pang of shock. He looks ill. He's sunk onto his haunches and his head is bent and his shoulders are heaving. At last he raises his head, and he's not crying but he looks close.

"You fucking ganged up on me," he says, his voice muffled. "You're *family.*"

"That's *why* we ganged up on you," I say. "*Because* we're family. *Because* we care about you."

I used to yearn so hard for the sunshine of Jake's approval. But now I'm feeling a different kind of glow. Conviction that we're doing the right thing.

"So, what, you think I should work on a *building site*?" he says with a miserable glare. "That's what you think of me?"

"Why shouldn't you work on a building site?" I say, in sudden fury. "Who do you think you *are*? Jake, stop trying to be posh. Be proud of where you came from. Leila's right, you've got to want to be who you are. And you're Jake Farr. Be proud of that."

For a moment Jake just stares ahead as though he hasn't heard me.

"Be proud of being Jake Farr," he says at last, his voice empty. "Proud of what? I have nothing."

He buries his head in his hands again, looking desolate,

and I have a flashback to my own desolation when Farr's Food went under. The grief I used to feel when I looked at my green aprons under the bed. I felt as though life would never be good again.

But maybe I was lucky, I find myself thinking. We've all got to have some kind of failure in life, and I had mine early. I got back on my feet. I learned that failing doesn't mean you *are* a failure; it just means you're a human being.

"You have Leila, who's *awesome,*" I say robustly. "You have us. And you have Farrs. *Not* the 'Notting Hill Family Deli.' " I can't help adding a little dig. "Farrs."

Jake doesn't even move, and I hunker down beside him, trying to think how else to get through to him.

"Dad was so proud of you, Jake," I say, more gently. "He didn't care about being smart or having designer suits or making more money than anyone else. D'you remember what he used to say? 'Do an honest day's work, sleep an honest night's sleep.' "

"I haven't slept properly for weeks," says Jake after a pause. He turns his head and I don't know if it's the light, but he looks more haggard than I've ever seen him.

"Oh, sleep is vital," says Nicole at once. "*Vital.* Like, I haven't been sleeping well either, and it's been really bad for me? I have some essential oils I can give you," she adds.

"There you go," I say to Jake. "Essential oils. That'll cure everything." I'm trying to lighten the mood, and I *think* his mouth twitches a bit. Just a bit. "Will you be able to pay off your debts now?" I add more seriously.

"Yes," says Jake, looking away. "Pretty much. Although if I clear them it doesn't leave me with anything to do business with." I sense he can't stand discussing his finances with his little sister but realizes he has no choice.

"So actually you're not in bad shape." I shrug. "You only owe Farrs, and you can pay that back, easy."

"How?" Jake demands, as though I'm playing a trick on him. "How can I do that?"

"Work," I say simply. "You work it off."

As I say the words, I suddenly realize a weird thing. My voice is steady. My words are clear. And there aren't any ravens flapping around my head.

Maybe they've flown away.

Twenty-Five

Jake's on Gingerbread Man duty. Ten hours a day, he stands outside Farrs, dressed in a Gingerbread Man suit, calling, "Come on in! Gingerbread houses at Farrs! Christmas decorations at Farrs! Biscuit cutters at Farrs! Ho ho ho!" He has flyers to hand out and samples of gingerbread and special-offer coupons.

He wasn't supposed to be doing it all day—I originally planned for us to do shifts. But we were trying to sort it out at a staff meeting, and everyone was arguing about what times they wanted, when Jake suddenly said, "OK, enough. I'm Gingerbread Guy. End of."

We all stared at him and I said, "All day long?" Whereupon he said, deadpan, "Beats hanging around in store with you lot." And after a moment (when we were sure he was joking), we all laughed.

Now that Jake's relaxed a bit, now that he's not chasing millions and just working at Farrs every day, he's actually quite cheerful. He's funny. He and Stacey have a good line in banter, and Greg keeps trying to get him to start a Staff Mixed Martial Arts Group, with a membership of two: Jake and Greg. (Bob said no.)

"So you basically want to beat me up, Greg," Jake said at last, and Greg got all bulgy-eyed and said that was a *complete* misunderstanding of the skills and artistry of MMA, while Jake winked at me.

As for his Gingerbread Man skills, it turns out they're great! The promotion is working better than I could have dreamed: The gingerbread houses are flying off the shelves, along with all the Christmas baking equipment. Morag—our new director—sat down with me one evening and we completely refreshed our stock. We went out on a limb on a few festive items that we both felt instinctively were right—and they've totally outperformed. The mixing bowl decorated with gingerbread men sells out as soon as we put it on the shelves, and the holly-leaf version is nearly as popular. In fact, we've had to start waiting lists.

It's three weeks since Bob's gloomy assessment, and even he blinked in surprise as he came in last Saturday. The place was buzzing. Jake was calling out, "Get your gingerbread house! Three for two on gift wrap!" Nicole was assisting Morag with a children's table decoration activity, while their parents all browsed the shop. There was a happy hum of chatter and the tills were bleeping nonstop. We won't know till January how everything's shaken down, but it's looking OK. It's looking better.

To be fair, Nicole and Jake have both worked their socks off. We've run as many late-night shopping events as we can, with different themes and promotions. It's been pretty exhausting, and we've had to reprioritize a bit. The house is a mess, the kitchen is a tip, we haven't even *thought* about our own Christmas, and we're all a bit frazzled . . . but it's worth it.

Jake even managed to be polite to the customers last night at our first-ever seniors' event. He appeared truly delighted to see my lovely shuffly brown-mug customer, whose name turns out to be Stanley. He was also über-charming to Sheila *and* Sheila's mother, aged ninety-eight, who told Jake about six times how handsome he was and how she'd always wanted a toyboy.

Morag has never looked happier—she's got completely free rein now and is making loads of plans for the New Year. I've made a few plans of my own too. I'm going to launch cooking lessons for customers, once a month. I'll call it the Dinner Party Club, to go alongside the Cake Club, and I'm already working on menus. I've even wondered if I might get back into a bit of catering, for customers, as a sideline. I mean, why not? Suddenly everything is feeling possible.

Meanwhile, the Farrs Instagram page has changed from pictures of Nicole to photos of customers and cakes and—my idea—Farrs' items in funny locations around London. There's a food mixer in a phone box and a chopping board balanced on top of a red pillar box, and Vanessa even posted a picture of a Jell-O mold on her judge's chair in court.

As I head outside to give Jake a cup of tea, he greets me with "Five days till Christmas! Ho ho ho!" We had a small staff debate about whether *ho ho ho* was quite right for a gingerbread man, with Greg claiming it was copyright Santa Claus. But I thought *ho ho ho* sounded festive and jolly. And these days, what I say tends to go. (Then Stacey wanted to join in and found a Gingerbread Girl costume online. Oh my God. *Totally* inappropriate. Plus she would have got hypothermia standing out there in stockings and suspenders.)

"Here you are, Gingerbread Man," I say, handing Jake his cup of tea.

"Gingerbread *Guy*," Jake corrects me, as he always does, and I roll my eyes at him. I think *Gingerbread Guy* is un-Christmassy—but if he wants to be Gingerbread Guy in his own head, let him.

"Oh, I've got a message from Leila," he adds. "Everyone's invited over for drinks on Christmas Eve. Six o'clock; bring a bottle."

A year ago, Jake would never have hosted a "bring a bottle" party. He would have been all grand and served champagne and boasted about the canapés. He's a different person these days. Kind of chastened—but also more relaxed, as though he doesn't need to pretend anymore. His eyes aren't strained. He laughs more. I think Leila's dad treats him pretty brusquely, and a few times Jake has said maybe he and Leila should move into our place.

But I think it's great. I think Leila's dad is exactly what Jake needs right now.

"Wonderful," I say. "Tell Leila I'll be there."

"She said, if you want to bring anyone . . ." Jake trails off cautiously and shoots me a questioning look.

"No." I force myself to smile. "Just me."

I haven't confided in Jake about Seb—our relationship hasn't changed *that* much. But from his expression I'm pretty sure that Leila has filled him in.

So he'll know that I was with Seb . . . and then somehow I wasn't anymore. He'll know how devastated I've been. What he won't know is that I've replayed our last couple of days over in my mind almost obsessively, and I still can't work out quite how everything disintegrated.

What *happened*? One minute Seb and I were happy, the next we were shouting, the next we couldn't even look each other in the eye. All in a blink. And if I could go back, if I could only go back . . .

No, I tell myself furiously. *Don't think that.* Seb said it himself: "You can't go back in time and do life a different way."

I take a piece of gingerbread from Jake's basket and munch it, trying to get a grip on myself, but it's not easy. Thinking about Seb and what might have been fills me with such pain I can barely breathe.

Which is why I try not to do it. But I can't help myself.

He's back with Briony. Which shouldn't have shocked me but did. I discovered it from looking on Facebook a couple of weeks ago. She'd posted a picture of the pair of them, smiling at the camera, captioned: *Back together after a blip, all good now!!*

And my heart kind of caved in on itself.

I was the blip.

I didn't feel like a blip. I felt like more than a blip. But there it is in black-and-white: *blip*. And there's no reason whatsoever for me ever to run into Seb again—London's a big city—so that's it. The end. I'll never quite know why we broke up. Or how you can be the happiest you've ever felt with someone and then the saddest.

"Fixie?" Jake's voice interrupts my thoughts, and I realize my damp eyes are giving me away.

"Right. Yes. Christmas Eve! It'll be fun!" I say, my voice a little shrill, blinking furiously. "Although I've got nowhere with my Christmas shopping; is there anything you want?"

We talk for a bit more, then I head back inside to the familiar colorful buzz of the shop. Morag has just found a new source of picnicware, all printed with daffodils and perfect for summer, and we're both oohing-and-aahing over the catalog when I hear a loud, hideously familiar voice: "Can I get some service?"

My stomach plummets to the floor. For a moment I can't even move for horror—then, very slowly, I turn my head, knowing exactly who I'm going to see.

It's her. Whiny.

She looks spectacular. She's in a white cable-knit turtleneck with a faux-fur vest over the top and shiny riding boots. Her skin is glowing with fake tan and her black jeans fit her snugly and her hair is all glossy under the lights.

"Oh, hi, I'd forgotten this was your place," she drawls, her eyes running over me with gratification.

She hadn't forgotten. I know what this is: It's payback for the skating.

"Welcome to Farrs," I say, feeling like a robot. "What can I get for you?"

"Oh, I'm not sure," she says carelessly. "I'll just browse all your little things. I haven't even *thought* about Christmas yet. Seb's such a great chef and it's the first Christmas we're spending together, just the two of us . . . so the pressure's on!" She laughs merrily. "Seb's so sweet, though; he keeps saying he'll cook everything. He's an angel." Her eyes slide to mine. "As you know."

As I know. Is she *trying* to torture me? Well, yes, of course she is.

"Stacey," I call out, my voice husky because I'm actually finding this really difficult. "Could you . . . This customer needs . . ."

But my voice doesn't rise above the hubbub strongly enough. Stacey's head doesn't turn.

"So, I'm *finally* moving in with him," Briony says, as though we're having a cozy girls' chat over coffee. "About bloody time! I said to him, 'Seb, we're a couple! Let's *behave* like one!' And he agreed. He was like, 'I've been a bit mad these last few weeks. I don't know what got into me.' And we're off to Klosters on Boxing Day, so, you know. Back to normal."

"Right," I manage. My head is pounding as though I'm about to vomit, but I force my lips into a smile.

"Hi, Lucia!" Briony suddenly waves at a girl I'm sure I've seen in here before, with glossy blond hair to match Briony's and a navy coat. They kiss each other and Lucia brandishes a basket cheerfully at Briony.

"I'm going to go mad," she says. "I *love* this place. I come in for cling film and leave with ten bags of stuff. But why did you suggest meeting here?" she adds curiously. "I know about it, but I'm local."

"Oh, I just heard about it," says Briony, her eyes sliding again to mine and away again.

"If I can help you with anything, please let me know," I say, still with my stiff, pleasant smile, then turn away.

And I know I should leave—but I can't bring myself to. I head to a nearby display, pointlessly rearranging a row of eggcups, my ears straining to hear their conversation.

"You should have brought Seb," Lucia is saying as she looks at serving dishes. "He's the real chef, isn't he? You're *so* lucky."

"Oh, he's *amazing*," agrees Briony smugly. "Makes me breakfast in bed all the time. I'm going to put on twenty pounds!"

She's speaking far more loudly than she needs to, and, again, I know I should walk away; I need to save myself from this. But my legs just won't do it.

"Oh well, wait till you've got your home gym," says Lucia easily. "You'll both be so buff! By the way, I *can* come round and help clear out that room, after all. The removers are coming at ten tomorrow, aren't they? Will they bring boxes?"

My hand freezes over an eggcup. *Removers?* Are they finally clearing out that second bedroom, then? Has Briony managed to get through to Seb? Is she more sensitive than I realized? Did she succeed where I failed? I can't help feeling a twinge of envy, which is unworthy of me. If Sebastian is moving forward, then that's good, *whoever* achieved it.

"Oh, right," says Briony, sounding a bit discomfited. "Yeah. Shall we look around?" She seems to be trying to move away, but Lucia doesn't notice.

"Definitely," she replies vaguely, examining a serving dish. "So, are you having a treadmill or a cross-trainer in the end? Because apparently there's this *new* kind of cross-trainer . . ."

As Lucia babbles on, my head is churning with thoughts and questions. How did Seb come to terms with clearing out the room? Is he all right? I *have* to know, even if it means going through Briony to find out.

"Sorry," I hear myself blurting out, swiveling round to face Briony. "Sorry. But I couldn't help overhearing. Is Seb OK, then? Has he come to terms with . . . everything?"

The look on Lucia's face is priceless.

"Do you two *know* each other?" she exclaims.

"I know Seb," I say shortly, then address Briony again. "So he's . . . he's OK? About clearing his brother's room?"

"He has no idea it's happening, does he?" says Lucia, sounding surprised. "Isn't that the whole point? He'll arrive back and it'll be done?"

"He has no *idea*?" I echo, shocked. Briony's cheeks have the slightest tinge of pink, but her jaw is defiant.

"What else am I supposed to do?" she says. "That place is a hazard!"

"He'll never do it for himself," chimes in Lucia knowledgeably. "Briony's doing him a favor. Sometimes you have to be cruel to be kind, you know. I had to smuggle three pairs of my husband's manky old trousers out of the house once," she adds gaily. "Three pairs! I *literally* hid them in a black bin bag. He would never have got rid of them otherwise!"

I can't find an answer. I'm quivering with distress. I want to yell, "You think this has any resemblance to three pairs of manky old trousers? Has Briony told you the actual *truth* about this?"

"He'll thank me for it in the end," says Briony, still with that edge of defiance. "Short, sharp shock. It's the only way."

I'm dazed by her callousness. I think of Seb arriving back to find his brother's room cleared, with no warning. I think of him standing there, his honest warm face draining of blood . . . and I can't bear it. I feel as though I'm getting a short, sharp shock myself. Except it's not short and sharp; it's deep and damaging and can never be undone.

And now, as I survey Briony's beautiful, selfish face, my fingers are drumming like they've never drummed before. My feet are itching. There's a weird buzzing in my head. A tension rising through me. I know it's not my life. I know he's not with me. I know it's their business. But I *can't* stand by. I *can't*.

"Right," I manage at last, trying to sound unconcerned. "Fair enough. Good for you. Actually . . . I need to go. Sorry, I've just remembered I have a . . . meeting. Enjoy the shop. Stacey!" I call, so piercingly that she turns round this time.

"Hi," she says, sauntering over, looking Briony and Lucia up and down.

"Please show these customers around. They want to see the whole shop. The *whole* shop," I add for emphasis, and I see Stacey's sharp eyes receive the message.

"Sure thing. Let's start with glassware; that's at the *back* of the shop. . . ." she says, leading them away.

I grab my coat from behind the cash desk, pick up my bag, and hurry outside into the wintry street, almost bumping into Gingerbread Jake.

"Jake," I say breathlessly. "I have to go. Take over. Please?"

"Fine," he says, looking taken aback. "Go. Do what you have to do." He hesitates, then adds, "You OK?"

"Of course I'm OK, why shouldn't I be?" I retort, and Jake gives me an odd look.

"Well, you're crying."

I'm *crying*? I reach up in shock and feel the streams of tears, wet on my cheeks.

"Busted." I manage to grin, rubbing at my face. "I'm not really OK. But I just have to . . . I have to do this thing."

Jake lifts a hand in its gingerbread glove and squeezes my shoulder, tight.

"Go for it," he says. And I nod gratefully, before turning and breaking into a run.

The journey is at once too long and too short. As I arrive at Seb's office, I feel almost sick with nerves. But the thought of Briony crashing into the most sensitive part of Seb's life makes me feel even sicker, so I steel myself and march in.

"Hi," I say to the receptionist without preamble. "I need to see Seb. It's urgent."

There must be something about my face, because she hesitates, then gets up and knocks on his door, and within thirty seconds he's coming out himself. And my legs weaken underneath me because I can't cope with this. I thought I could, but I can't.

I was hoping I'd see him and think, *Ah, he's not so great after all,* but it's the opposite. He's as tall and strong and handsome as ever, his woodland eyes wary as they meet mine. I have that weird thought, just as I did in the coffee shop when I first saw him: *I know you.*

But I can't know him, can I? Or I'd know why we've ended up like this, meeting like two stilted strangers. Didn't he feel what I was feeling? Didn't he feel the joy? What happened between us—what *happened*?

My head is tumbling with anguish, with questions . . . but somehow I force myself to focus. I can't keep tormenting myself. He's with Briony. It's over. It's done. *You can't go back in time and do life a different way.*

And, anyway, I'm not here because of us. I'm here because of him.

"Hi, Seb," I say, and my voice trembles, but I carry on resolutely. "There's something . . . Could we talk?"

"Of course," says Seb, after a pause. "Come on in."

He ushers me in and I sit down and for a beat there's silence.

"Are you . . . How are you?" says Seb, and I can see by the way he's sitting bolt upright, his hands making a tense pyramid on his desk, that he's thrown off-balance.

"Fine, thanks. You?"

"Yes, I'm good."

"Good."

The air seems thin between us. Our words are thin. I don't know how to proceed, how to bring up the subject. But I need to—it's in me like a ticking time bomb—so in the end I just blurt out:

"James."

"What?" Seb jolts as though I've scalded him.

"You . . . you never told me about James."

I'm thinking that maybe Seb can tell me about his brother and we can move on to the subject that way—but it doesn't work. Seb's body language immediately crackles with tension.

"*Told* you about him? Why should I tell you about him?"

"No!" I backtrack. "No reason. I just meant . . ." I rub

my nose, trying to find a different tack. "You always say that you've moved on and you've dealt with his death and you're at peace."

"Yes," says Seb, his voice dangerously even. "I have. And I am. Your point is?"

"You say that clearing out his room isn't a big deal. You say you 'just haven't got round to it.' But I wondered . . ." I swallow several times. "I just wondered . . . if maybe it *was* quite a big deal. After all. And if you'd like some help. That's all. That's what I— That's it."

I break off into a terrible silence. Seb looks as though some sort of volcano is building inside, and I stare at him, in agonized, half-terrified dread.

"You just can't leave things alone, can you?" he finally erupts in an explosion of fury. "You have to 'fix' them. Jeez, I can see how you got your name now. No, I *don't* need any help, thank you. I know you were always itching to get your mitts on that room, but it's fine; it doesn't need your interference or anybody's. I will clear it out in my *own* time, in my *own* way. Now please get the hell out of here."

He's shaking with anger, and his voice is thundering around the office, and he's such an intimidating sight, I automatically scrabble to my feet, my legs almost buckling underneath me. But he has to know. He has to.

"She's going to clear the room," I say desperately. "Whiny. She's making it into a home gym. She's booked the removers. They're coming at ten A.M. tomorrow, and she says she's going to chuck the lot."

If Seb looked like a bubbling volcano a moment ago, he's suddenly a pit. He's empty. Hollow.

"No," he says, as though he can't compute what I'm saying.

"Yes. She told me."

"She . . . wouldn't . . ." But his voice is uncertain. As his eyes meet mine, his antagonism has gone; I can see panic growing in them. Childlike panic. And I can feel tears rising again, because doesn't she *realize*?

"I know you're with Briony," I say hastily, my voice thick and jerky, my eyes fixed on the carpet. "I know you're a happy couple. I'm not trying to come between you; I'm really not. And you're right: I shouldn't interfere. I try to fix everything and it's my stupid flaw and I'm really sorry. I just couldn't bear for you to come home and—" I swallow hard, unable to say it. "I just thought you should know."

I finally dare to raise my head and Seb is staring out of the window, his jaw tight, his gaze transfixed.

"Yes," he says tonelessly, and I don't know what he means, but I don't dare ask. He wraps his arms around his body as if trying to soothe himself, and I'm longing so hard to go over there, to soothe him myself. . . .

But I have to stop thinking like that. He's *with* someone. Briony's the girlfriend. I'm the blip.

I stand motionless, my legs feeling a little firmer, watching him, hardly daring to breathe, trying to guess what's going on in his head. I'm in no hurry. Time feels like it's suspended.

At last he turns his head, breathes out sharply, and pushes a hand through his hair. Then he says unsteadily, "I think maybe it's time for me to clear out my brother's room. Today. This afternoon."

I feel an almighty spike of shock but try to hide it. "Right," I say. "Yes. I mean . . . yes. That's a good . . . Yes."

There's another pause. My hands are clenched by my sides, my brain circling uncertainly. I can't— I *can't* offer— After everything he said, I *can't* interfere—

Oh God, but it's bigger than me. I can't help myself.

"Would you—" I begin, my feet pacing awkwardly on the spot. "No. I shouldn't even— I mean . . ." I clear my throat. "Would you like some— No." I cut myself off. "Sorry."

"Yes, please." Seb's voice takes me by surprise and he looks at me, his eyes so dark and vulnerable I catch my breath. "Yes. Please. I would."

I never knew Seb's brother, James. I never will know him. But as we sit in his room together, passing things backward and forward, trying to sort and organize, I feel I'm getting a sense of him. He was like Seb in some ways, but more idio-syncratic. He worked from home in graphic design and was super-talented. From the few things Seb says, I think he could get quite ratty when his work wasn't going well, but he told the best jokes too.

Everything I touch tells me something about him. His hasty handwriting, barely legible, on Post-its to himself. His bags of jelly babies, piled up in the bottom drawer of his desk. Doodles that he drew with Sharpies on computer paper. One portrait of Seb makes me gasp, it's so succinct and accurate.

"You should keep this," I say. "You should frame it." And Seb nods silently and puts it into the "precious pile." We have a precious pile for the things he knows he's going to keep (notes, drawings, James's ancient teddy bear). And a rubbish pile for the things he knows he's going to get rid of (socks, old bills, all those empty water bottles).

And then there's the stuff he stares at and can't decide. I can see it in his face—just the *thought* of having to decide is overwhelming. So we're going to put that in storage bags and he can have a look in three months and see what he thinks.

That's what Mum did. Every few months after Dad died, she processed another batch of stuff. And each time she cried a little but felt a little stronger. There wasn't any point in her rushing it. And there's no point in Seb rushing it.

The rest of the world has receded. Everything has shrunk to this room, with its dust motes dancing in the air and smell of the past. We both have bloodshot eyes. Each of us occasionally reaches for a tissue. Seb was first to break down, when he found a photo of him and James that he'd never seen before. He gave one almighty heartrending sob and then furiously apologized, then sobbed again. Whereupon tears rose to my eyes too and I furiously apologized. And he apologized for upsetting me. Until at last I put a hand on his arm and said, "Shall we just not apologize?"

And so we didn't anymore.

Now I sit back on my heels and take a massive breath, sweeping my hands through my hair.

"I think we've done most of it. At least, you know, we've sorted it. Except the magazines . . ."

"Right." Seb's face twists a little. "Those. Recycling, I guess."

"Or you could sell them? Like . . . an archive?"

I don't ask if he's going to cancel the subscriptions. I'm fairly sure I know the answer.

"We need some storage bags, or whatever," I add, looking at the piles of stuff.

"There's a shop round the corner." Seb nods. "It sells those tartan ones."

"You should have come to Farrs," I say automatically. "We have lovely storage bags in amazing prints—" I break off, with an abashed smile. "Sorry. Can't stop selling."

Seb returns my smile. Then his brow suddenly crumples. "Fixie," he says, as though only just realizing the situation. "You've done enough. You must surely need to go. It's a busy time for you."

"Come on," I say. "Let's get the bags. Then I'll go."

As we step out of the building, the cold air feels refreshing, and we fall easily into step, side by side.

"Well . . . thank you," says Seb, after we've walked for a couple of minutes. "Thank you so much. What you did today is above and beyond."

"Don't be silly," I say at once. "I wanted to. As a . . ." I hesitate. "As a friend."

"As a friend," Seb echoes after a beat. "Right."

We walk on a while longer, until we're in a little arcade of shops, all decorated with lights and tinsel. A group of children is singing carols and we stop to listen for a bit. Then, against the background of *tra-la-las,* Seb says, his eyes firmly fixed forward, "So, how's the unconditional love going?"

At once my stomach flips over. My mind swoops back to

his office, to that horrible row we had about Jake. Is *that* his issue? That I won't give up on my brother? That I ignored his advice and stuck by my family?

"Fine," I say.

"Good," he says, but his voice is tight and when I glance at him, his face is studiously blank.

I can feel the tension between us rising again, and I need to burst it, because what's happened with Jake and me and the whole family is good. It's *good*.

"People can change, you know," I say, slightly more passionately than I intended, and I see Seb's jawline twitch, as though this isn't something he wants to hear. But at last he turns his head to look at me, his face pink and blue from the glow of the nearby Christmas lights.

"I'm sure. And I'm glad for you." His face creases with some emotion I can't read, and for an instant his eyes seem to shimmer again. "You're . . . you're quite a woman." He takes hold of my hands and squeezes them, and I stare back breathlessly, my eyes hot again too. I can't help it—I'm lost in his gaze.

Then the carol-singing stops and ragged applause breaks out and we both seem to snap back into reality.

"So." Seb gives me a wry smile and releases my hands, and suddenly I can't bear being near him anymore. I can't bear seeing his generous, brave face, his woodland eyes, his *everything* . . . and knowing that they can't be mine.

"So," I say, my voice a bit gruff. "Actually, I do have some things to get done. I ought to—"

"Of course," says Seb at once, his tone more formal, and he actually takes a step back, as though wanting to put space between us. "Of course. You've done far too much. Thank you a thousand times."

"It was nothing."

"It wasn't nothing." He shakes his head. "You've . . . I don't think I'd realized . . ." He meets my eyes frankly. "I can go forward now."

"Well, good. That's all I wanted." I smile brightly, trying to mask the pain which I can feel coming for me like a tsunami. "Good luck with everything. With Briony, and life, and . . . everything."

There's only so long you can smile brightly at the man who has your heart but loves someone else. Already my mouth is starting to tremble.

"So . . . goodbye," I say, and I'm making to leave when Seb calls out, "Wait!"

I look back and he's reaching into his pocket and somehow I'm not surprised when he produces the coffee sleeve.

I take a step back toward him and we stand there in the street, the two of us gazing at it. The original IOU. It's crumpled and creased now, the writing indistinct and blurred in places where we spilled wine on it in bed, and I have a sudden memory of him giving it to me in the first place.

"Stupid thing." I try to laugh.

"Yes." Seb nods, suddenly grave. "It is. Because if I really wrote down all the reasons I owe you, it would fill a book."

His words take me by surprise, and for a moment I can't answer.

"No, it wouldn't." I say at last, trying to be flippant but not really succeeding.

"It would. You know it would."

"Well . . . me too." My throat is tight. "I owe you too."

"But we're not keeping score anymore."

"No, we're not."

I take the coffee sleeve from him and look at our melded scrawled writings, feeling such pangs of loss I can't bear it. Then, on impulse, I start to rip. Once through. Twice through. I need quite a lot of force to tear the cardboard—it's stronger than it looks—but at last it's in pieces and I look up.

"We're done," I say, and Seb nods, with such a wry, sad expression I want to cry again, but I mustn't.

"Done," he echoes.

I run my gaze over his face one last time. Then I take a deep breath as though plunging underwater, turn, and walk swiftly away, dumping the pieces in a recycling bin as I go.

Twenty-Six

Sometimes life gives you what you need. Sometimes it gives you what you don't need. What I *really* don't need in my life right now is Ryan Chalker—but as soon as I get within view of Farrs, I see him, standing on the pavement, talking to Jake.

Great. Just bloody . . . great.

I'm feeling so sore right now, I can barely face anyone, let alone him. But I can't run away; I need to get into the shop. Which means I'm forced to approach him, with my chin as stiff as possible, wishing my face wasn't all blotchy from wiping away tears but equally thinking: *So I've got a blotchy face, so what, it's my face, fuck off.*

I'm braced for him to say something offensive—but to my surprise, as I get near them, he seems to be arguing with Jake.

"Not happening," Jake is saying. "No. I'm working." He gestures at his Gingerbread Man suit.

"It's two days!" Ryan says dismissively. "You can easily take two days off, the flights are, like, *nothing,* and we'll have a blast. You and me, partying like the old days. Drinks on me," he adds with a twinkle.

Ryan is as cajoling as I've ever seen him, and for an instant I see Jake waver. I see him weaken. I see the old appetite growing in his face.

But then it closes up.

"I'm working," he repeats doggedly. "And I can't afford a trip to Prague. So as I say, it's not happening."

"For God's sake, Jake! What happened to you? Hi, Fixie," Ryan adds brazenly, as though the last time we saw each other I wasn't quite literally sweeping him out of the house.

"Nothing happened," says Jake evenly. "But my priority right now is work."

"Work!" Ryan gives a scornful laugh, which makes me cringe. "What, dressing up as a gingerbread man? Do you know how tragic you look, mate?"

I stare at him, incensed. How *dare* he come around and insult my family?

"Shouldn't you be getting back to Hollywood now, Ryan?" I say sweetly. "Doesn't Tom Cruise want to have lunch with you at Nobu?" Ryan shoots me a look of dislike and I gaze coolly back. "You're cluttering the pavement. So either come in and buy something or move along."

"Yes, just go," says Jake. "Go, Ryan. We've had enough of you."

"Oh, you've had enough of me!" Ryan retorts at once, with another scornful laugh.

"Yes," says Jake steadfastly. "We have."

In silence, Ryan looks from Jake's face to mine and back again. I've never felt such solidarity with my brother. Ryan's eyes flicker uncertainly as he surveys us, and just for an instant I feel sorry for him. Just an instant.

"Well, fuck off, then," he snarls at last, then turns and strides away.

"Merry Christmas!" Jake calls after him. "I hope Santa's good to you!"

"Santa will *not* be good to him," I say, and I start giggling uncontrollably, letting out some of my painful tension. "Are you kidding? Santa will give him a turnip and a lump of coal."

"He doesn't even deserve a turnip. Remember one year Dad put a turnip in my stocking?" Jake suddenly adds reminiscently. "When I was about eleven. He thought I needed a fright. The toys were in the corner of the room and I didn't see them at first—so I thought that was it. A turnip."

"I don't remember that." I stare at him incredulously. "*Did* you get a fright?"

"Oh yeah." Jake grins. "I nearly had a heart attack. Dad thought it'd make me calm down a bit." He pauses, then adds with a kind of rueful glint in his eye, "Guess a turnip wasn't enough. I was still a little bastard."

"You weren't so bad," I say easily.

"Oh, I was. I was a toe-rag. That day I laid into you about your skating? That was pretty low." He hesitates. "But, I mean, you were about to give up anyway, weren't you?"

I'm so stunned I can't respond at once. I was about to *give up*? Is that how he's rationalized it all this time? Does he have *any* idea . . . ? My chest is burning with all the things I could say, all the accusations I could hurl at him.

But then . . . why would I? It's done. It happened. What are we going to do, start a tally of who did what when?

"Oh well," I manage. "Think how much worse you *could*

have been." And Jake smiles at me in the way he often does these days—as though he's consciously trying to get on with his family, he only needs a bit of practice. Then he turns to look down the street, where Ryan is still just about visible.

"He's an arse," he says matter-of-factly, and I nod.

"You got rid of him, anyway."

There's silence as we both watch Ryan finally disappear from view. Ryan, who blinded both of us with his dazzle, who led us both astray. I'm sure both of us are rewinding our lives and thinking how they might have been different with no Ryan Chalker in them.

But what can you do about mistakes except think, *Won't do that again,* and move forward?

"I wonder what Dad would think of us," says Jake, breaking the silence. "Now. If he could see us."

His voice is casual, but his eyes seem to have a genuine question in them. As if it matters.

Well, of course it matters. Jake always cared desperately what Dad thought of him, even when he was yelling. We all did.

"I hope he'd realize we're doing our best," I say, after a moment's thought. On a whim I look up at the sky and call out softly, "Dad, we're doing our best, OK?"

"He says, 'No you're not, the stock room's a mess, and what's happened to the licorice allsorts?'" shoots back Jake, deadpan, and I burst into a giggle.

"I have to go," I say. "The stock room *is* a mess."

"Hannah's in there, by the way," says Jake, jerking his head toward the shop. "Christmas shopping."

I feel a sudden swell of love for Hannah. She's the most loyal friend in the world. All her family must be sick to death of Farrs stock, but she supports us every year. She even schedules a Farrs shopping session on her calendar.

"Thanks," I say, and squeeze him on the arm. "Don't get too cold out here."

"Oh, I'm fine," says Jake, and brandishes his stack of flyers. "Come on in!" he resumes shouting, winking at me. "Gingerbread houses at Farrs! Christmas decorations at Farrs! Ho ho ho!"

Inside the shop, I find Hannah loading up her basket with ceramic rolling pins decorated with gingerbread men.

"I'm on the waiting list for one of those mixing bowls," she greets me without any preamble. "Morag says they'll be in tomorrow?"

She looks radiant these days, even though she's not pregnant yet (I'll be first to know, after her mum and Tim). She and Tim have "started again"—her words—and they're really blissful and she's thrown away all her to-do lists.

Or at least put them away somewhere secret. She's a bit cagey on that point.

"So where were you?" she asks now. "Jake said you rushed off somewhere."

For a few moments I can't reply. I will tell her everything, of course I will—but not in this bright bustle of Christmas cheer.

"Just . . . something," I say. "I was with Seb."

"*Seb?*" Her eyes light up questioningly and I shake my head.

"No. No. Not that. Tell you later. So what else do you need?" I force a bright Christmas-shopping manner. And she's just showing me the list on her phone, when I feel a tap on my shoulder.

"Hey, Fixie, you dropped this." It's Jake in his gingerbread outfit, holding out my scarf.

"Oh, thanks," I say as I wind it back around my neck. "I guess I was distracted by Ryan."

"*Ryan?*" says Hannah, looking scandalized. "Was that him outside? I *thought* I saw him, but then I thought, *No, that can't be him, he wouldn't dare.* . . . "

"He has no shame," I say. "None."

"He's an arse," Jake repeats firmly. "You know, Fixie, I meant to tell you, and you *really* won't believe this, he actually went and asked your guy for money."

"What?" I say, frowning, not quite following.

"You know, what's-his-name. Seb. Ryan went to his office and tried to get him to invest in some scheme or other. The guy who *fired* him. Can you believe it?"

"The nerve of him!" exclaims Hannah. "You know, I think he has a chip missing. It's the only explanation."

Something weird is buzzing in my head. This doesn't make sense. Ryan went to see Seb? Why didn't Seb ever mention it?

"I'm sorry," I say, sounding brusque in my need to get this clear. "I'm sorry, explain again, what did Ryan do? When was this?"

"About three weeks ago?" says Jake, creasing his brow in thought. Then his eyes widen. "I know exactly. It was the day after he spent the night at ours. He went there first thing in the morning. He wanted me to come too, but I said not a chance. I knew Seb would throw him out."

Ryan went to see Seb. But Seb never mentioned it to me. Why?

Because he thought I knew already?

But why—

Hang on. Oh God. No. *No*. Seb's prickliness . . . Seb's hurt, scorched eyes . . .

My head is churning. The pieces are slotting together, and they're terrible, disastrous pieces. Ryan went to see Seb just before I did. He asked him for money. So did Seb think . . . ? My stomach heaves in horror. Did Seb think that when I came and asked him for money it was for *Ryan*?

No. He *couldn't* have, surely?

I flash back to Seb's tight, strained face. His expression today when he asked how the "unconditional love" was going. And now I feel almost faint. It's obvious. Seb thinks I went back to Ryan. He thinks I love Ryan. I can hear my own blithe voice in his office: "If you really love someone, you don't just shove cash at them. You help them become the person they're meant to be." Seb had no idea I meant Jake. I'd never told him Jake was in debt. So he thought—

But how could he ever believe I'd go back to Ryan? *How?*

"Fixie, are you OK?" Hannah is peering at me.

"I . . . Maybe I need a cup of tea," I falter.

"You look shocking," says Jake bluntly. "I'd have a whiskey."

"OK, come on." Hannah grasps my arm and leads me to the back room. Nicole is in there, unpacking a box of Christmas decorations, and she looks up in surprise to see us. Hannah shuts the door and flips on the kettle, then says, "Fixie, I know you're in a state, and you don't have to tell us everything, but—"

"The coffee sleeve," I interrupt her in a despairing gasp, because it's come to me, in a final, horrible burst of comprehension. *That's* how.

I remember registering the coffee sleeve in Seb's office that awful day and not quite understanding why it was there. I'd thought it was in my tote bag. It seemed a bit weird.

I brushed it away at the time; it felt like an unimportant detail. But it's the key to everything. Ryan must have taken it. Used it. Brandished it at Seb. God alone knows what lies he told—but whatever he said, it convinced Seb that we were together again.

Blood is pulsing through my ears as I imagine Ryan, the practiced pathological liar, spinning some vile story. I recall his easy voice that morning: "Oh, I took some chewing gum out of your bag. You don't mind, do you?" But chewing gum wasn't the only thing he took.

He is a toxic, terrible, bad, bad man. I'm shaking all over, with rage at Ryan, rage at myself. . . .

"Fixie?" Hannah has knelt down before me and taken my hands. "Fixie, we're getting worried here. What's *happened*?"

I look at her kind, familiar face and I can't be strong anymore. I know we're busy on the shop floor. I know it's five days till Christmas. I know I should put this aside for now. But it's too big. It's burning a hole in me.

So I take a deep breath and I tell her and Nicole everything. I start right from the beginning, right from that first meeting in the coffee shop, although they already know some of it. Because that way I feel like I'm in control of *something*, even if it's just my own story.

It takes a while and they listen in pin-drop silence. When I get to my new theory about Ryan, they both exclaim, "No!" in simultaneous horror, and I half-smile, despite everything.

"So what do you do now?" says Hannah, who is always practical and forward-looking and has already got a pen out of her bag.

"Tell him," says Nicole.

"You *have* to tell him," agrees Hannah.

"Go and see him—"

"Explain there's been a misunderstanding—"

"But he's taken!" I say despairingly. "He's with someone! I don't take other women's men, I just don't. It's the rule. It's the sisterhood."

There's silence and I sip my cup of tea, which has gone lukewarm but is still comforting.

"I mean, what if the other woman is a total bitch?" says Hannah at last, casually. "Because then I think that rule doesn't apply."

"She's not a bitch." I can't believe I'm coming to the defense of Whiny, but there you go. "At least, she's not terrible. She's bright and she makes him laugh and they go skiing together. . . ."

"Oh, well, *skiing*," says Hannah sardonically. "Fixie, anyone can ski with someone! You and Seb, you have something amazing. And you can't let it slip away."

"I don't know." I try to imagine calling up Seb, broaching the subject . . . and I quail. What if I'm wrong? What if there's a million other reasons he doesn't want to be with me?

"I need to get back to work." I change the subject. "It's not fair on the others. Friday afternoons always get frantic."

"OK," says Hannah, rising to her feet. "But you *have* to do something."

"Maybe." I bite my lip. "I dunno. I need to think. Really think."

"All right, go home tonight," says Hannah firmly. "Have a long, peaceful bath. Really think about it." She pauses. "And then call him."

I put my cup down and get to my feet. As I do so, my phone bleeps with a text, and my chest stiffens in hope.

"Is that him?" says Nicole at once.

"Have a look!" says Hannah. "I bet you *anything* it's him."

"I had a psychic feeling he was going to text." Nicole nods. "I just had this feeling."

"I'm *sure* it's not him," I say, pulling my phone out of my pocket with trembling fingers. "I'm *sure* it's not— There, you see, it's from Mum."

I click on the text—and stop dead. For a brief moment, Seb has been swept from my mind. I'm staring at the words in disbelief. I'm not sure I can take this in.

"What?" demands Nicole. "What does she say?"

In silence, I hold out the phone so everyone can see the words:

Coming home for Christmas after all! Can't wait to see you! Arriving Sunday morning in time for lunch! All my love, Mum xxx

"The house," whispers Nicole in horror.

"The kitchen." I gulp.

"The shop." And now both our eyes are widening as the full scope of the situation hits us.

"*Christmas.*"

Twenty-Seven

*B*y ten on Sunday morning I've had approximately two and a half hours' sleep and I'm wired, but I'm on it. I'm *so* on it.

We got back on Friday night and tackled the house, all of us—me, Nicole, Jake, and Leila, who insisted on bringing her Dustbuster over. Jake was on bathrooms, and I take my hat off to him—he volunteered for it. I was on the kitchen. Nicole was on dusting and Hoovering and *not* saying, "I don't understand the vacuum cleaner." (She did open her mouth when I said, "Can you do the stairs with the nozzle attachment?" Then she closed it again and I saw her looking up *nozzle attachment* on Google.)

Saturday was a massive day in the shop, with two events and customers streaming in constantly. We didn't shut till ten, after which I insisted we stay and go over the place, checking there weren't any bare spots or clumsy displays or signs not looking their best.

We'll need to be in again this afternoon, but meanwhile Morag's opening up and we're getting lunch ready. I've organized the menu, and Nicole popped to the shops yesterday, and now she's chopping broccoli while Jake crushes biscuits for the cheesecake and Leila lays the table. We're all in my green Farr's Food aprons, which was Jake's idea. We look like a team. We *feel* like a team.

"OK." I put my lamb casserole back into the oven. "It's all on track. The table looks *great*, Leila," I call into the dining room through the serving hatch.

"The Cava's cold," says Jake, looking in the fridge, and I shoot an affectionate glance at his back, because not so long ago he wouldn't have been seen dead drinking Cava.

It's weird: I'm getting on with Jake better and better. I never really *knew* him before, but we're both quite similar. We're punchy when it comes to the shop. We have the same kinds of ideas. We think big.

Which I suppose was always the case, but Jake was only thinking big for himself before.

"So, where are we?" I say, consulting my to-do list. (I'm not Hannah's best friend for nothing.) "Nibbles, tick. Lamb, tick; broccoli's nearly there; potatoes are in. . . ." I check my phone. "Mum says forty minutes. OK, what else?"

"Fixie." Leila comes into the kitchen and surveys me anxiously. "Why don't you sit down for a moment?"

"I don't need to sit down!"

"How are you *feeling*?" she adds delicately.

Nicole has filled in the entire family on the situation with Seb. Which means about every five minutes someone asks me if I'm OK or what I'm going to do or whether I want to "talk." Even Jake asked last night if I wanted to "talk." And when I said no, thanks, he proceeded to tell me, for about an hour, what a bastard Ryan was. Which didn't particularly help me. Although it might have helped Jake.

So, no, I don't want to "talk" and I don't *know* what I'm going to do now. Break up Seb and Briony? Put him on the spot and wait to see if he wants me? Make all sort of assumptions about him that might be wrong?

Just thinking about it gives me an achy head and an achy heart and an achy all-over. So I'm not going to, at least not today. I'm going to make Mum's homecoming perfect, that's what I'm going to do.

"The only thing is the coffee," says Nicole, looking up from the machine. "We're out of beans."

"Out?" I stare at her. "How can we be out? It was half full yesterday."

"Dunno." Nicole gives one of her trademark vague shrugs. "But it's saying *Refill bean tray*."

For God's sake.

I head over to the coffee machine and stare at it impatiently. I *know* it had beans yesterday.

"It's temperamental," says Nicole, following my gaze. "You know? It's needy. Never mind, Café Allegro is open. Someone can pop out and buy more beans?"

"I'm in the middle of this," says Jake, looking up from the cheesecake. "Leila'll go."

"Jakey, you know I've hurt my toe," says Leila, sounding hurt. "You know it's all swollen up."

"Nicole, you go," I command, but Nicole looks affronted.

"I can't go!" she says. "I'm talking to Drew in a moment. It's all been arranged. God, Fixie, you could go yourself, you know. It's only ten minutes' walk."

"I thought you were supposed to have *changed*." I glare at her. "Fine, I'll go."

"Have a coffee!" calls Nicole mollifyingly. "There's no rush!"

As I head out, my bag swinging on my shoulder, I feel indignant with both my siblings. Why should I have to go? It's *so* typical.

But as I walk along, my anger abates, and I start feeling glad of the fresh air, grateful for the time out. It's been a pretty intense couple of days, and I woke this morning with my heart hammering. I'm not *nervous* about Mum returning, exactly, but . . .

Well. Maybe I am nervous. I so don't want her to be disappointed in us.

I round the corner and head toward Café Allegro and my heart starts beating hard again—but not because of Mum. I've been in here for coffee a few times since Seb and I broke up, and it's always been difficult. Now I'm getting impatient with myself. Am I going to feel like this *every* time I go to Café Allegro? Am I going to replay every instant of our meeting? The laptop . . . the ceiling crashing down . . . the coffee sleeve . . .

It's ridiculous, I tell myself firmly as I push open the door. *I'm here for coffee beans. I'm not even going to* think *about him.* A few people are sitting around with coffees, but there's no queue and I walk straight up to the counter. I order the beans and order myself a takeaway cappuccino, then turn to go.

And everything seems to go wobbly.

Am I . . .

Is this *real*?

He's sitting by the window in the same seat. He's working

on his laptop. And there's a spare seat opposite. As though he can feel my gaze on him, Seb looks up briefly, and I see everything in his eyes that I want to see.

I don't know what magic has brought him here. My brain can't function well enough; I can't make sense of it. But he's here. And his eyes are telling me that they love me.

Hardly able to breathe, I make my way over to the table and sit down. Seb doesn't look up from his laptop but keeps typing, and I look out of the window as though I don't know him.

You can't go back in time and do life a different way.

Well, maybe you can.

Seb's phone buzzes with a call and I watch, prickling like a cat, as he answers it. I feel so taut, so wound up, I could scream. I have to get this right. We have to get this right.

"Oh, hi, Fred. Yes, it's me." Seb listens for a bit to the voice at the other end, then gets to his feet.

"Excuse me," he says politely to me in a stranger's voice. "I'm just stepping out to take a phone call. Could you watch my laptop?"

"Sure," I manage, my voice hardly working. I watch him threading his way between the tables, already back on the phone, saying, "Thanks, mate. Yup."

He stands outside, exactly as he did before, and I take a sip of cappuccino, but I can't taste it. All my senses are on high alert. Now is the cue for the ceiling to collapse, but the ceiling's been mended; I saw the workmen doing it last month. It's different, all different.

And now Seb's coming back into the shop, and I'm not clutching his laptop while water drips from me; it's there, safe on the table. But he still stops before he reaches the table and meets my eyes as though something seismic has happened.

Or maybe is happening.

"Hi," he says. "I'm Sebastian."

"I'm Fixie," I say.

"Thanks for looking after my laptop."

And this is where he should add, "I owe you one," and we should start down the inexorable path toward shouting and tears and splitting up—but this time the words don't come. All that comes is his warm gaze. Loving and kind of questioning.

"Anytime," I say, and he nods, and I can sense us both breathing out.

We did it. We did it differently.

"Can I buy you a coffee?" he says, still in über-polite tones. "Or a cup of tea? A juice?"

"Actually, I must be going," I say, remembering my script. "I have a family party I need to get back for." Seb's face falls and I see doubt creep in, and just for a *moment* I let him suffer . . . before I add with a tentative smile, "Would you like to come?"

Mum looks amazing. I mean, *amazing*. She's not only tanned and fit-looking, with a new red sweater and dangling pearl earrings, she has a new spring in her step. She's energetic. As we greet her taxi, she cries out in delight and hugs us all, over and over, and then we bundle her luggage into the house while she tells us about Christmas in Spain and how Aunty Karen was planning to serve lobster.

"I was all set to do it," she says. "I really was. But then, do you know what it was? It was watching *White Christmas* one evening. Oh, it got to me! My eyes filled with tears and I looked at your Aunty Karen and she said, 'You're going home, aren't you?' And I said, 'Oh, Karen.' And I booked the flight the next day. I couldn't have Christmas away from home, just couldn't do it. I *had* to be here with you all—Jake, Nicole, and Fixie, and Leila, of course, and—" Her eyes fall confusedly on Seb, as though for the first time. Well, in fact, exactly for the first time, I realize.

"Right," I say hastily. "Er . . . this is Seb."

"Seb!" cries Mum, as though she'd known all the time, his name had just slipped her mind. "Oh, it's wonderful to be back. You all look so well, and the house looks lovely. . . ."

She's picked up a bit of Aunty Karen's zest for life, I decide as we troop into the kitchen, and that's no bad thing.

"Are you hungry?" I ask.

"Would you like some coffee?" chimes in Nicole. "I can do you a macchiato, a latte, flat white. . . ."

"I'm opening the Cava," says Jake firmly. "Red-letter day."

"Red-letter day," echoes Seb, drawing me a little way into the hall. His lips brush briefly against mine and he murmurs, "I want you *so* much," in my ear, and I feel an instant pang of lust.

"Later," I murmur back, smiling.

For a while we just gaze silently at each other. I feel as if his woodland eyes are enveloping me and I can't bear to tear myself away—till a sudden clatter from the kitchen makes us both start.

"Come on," I say, my voice a little husky. "We'd better join the others."

As we enter the kitchen, I see Leila nudging Nicole excitedly—and at once my lust is replaced by hope they won't be *too* mortifying over lunch. Leila has already totally embarrassed me by calling out, "It's them! They're together! Yay!" as we approached the house.

Then, when we got inside, it all came out. It wasn't magic that brought Seb to Café Allegro; it was Nicole and Hannah. They contacted Seb secretly on Friday night and filled him in on a few key facts. Apparently Hannah set up a conference call to discuss it, which is *so* her. Apparently she also said directly to Seb, "And *why* did you get back together with Briony?" and Seb said, "Better the devil you know," whereupon Hannah said, "No! Wrong!" as though he was a junior on her team.

I mean, I wish I'd been on the call, now.

It was Hannah's idea to set up our meeting today, and it was Nicole who thought of emptying the coffee machine of beans. I mean, honestly. Since when did she become so *practical*?

"So, is there anything I can do?" I ask, a little too briskly. "We were just . . ."

"We know," says Leila with a sudden gurgle of laughter. Then her expression changes. "Fixie, let me . . ." She adjusts my hair quickly, patting and tweaking it, then gives me one of her sweet smiles. "There. *That's* better!"

"How's Drew?" says Mum as Jake hands out the Cava, and Nicole colors slightly.

"Actually, Mum, there's something I need to tell you. I

won't be here for Christmas. I'm off to Abu Dhabi to see Drew. I'm flying tomorrow."

Mum's sharp eyes survey Nicole as though searching for trouble—but then something in her face relaxes.

"Good idea, Nicole," she says. "Good idea, darling."

"Well, here's to you, Mum," says Jake, lifting a glass. "Welcome back!"

We all take a sip and then Mum says, "Here's to *you,* loves. All of you. You've done so well, keeping the house spotless and everything running so well. The shop looks in marvelous shape! Morag sent me some pictures of you, Jake, all dressed up as a gingerbread man." She smiles at him. "And the events for children are such a good idea. . . ."

"The sales aren't bad either," I say eagerly. "Last week's takings are better than last year's."

I got Bob to pull some figures together for me yesterday, and as he handed them over, he smiled. He actually smiled.

"Mum," I add a little nervously, because I want to get it over with, "there's something I need to tell you too. I've made Morag a director."

I've been plucking up courage to tell her, but first she was ill, and then I was distracted, and then I thought, *Face-to-face is better.* Although now I'm thinking: *No, face-to-face is worse; I should have sent an email in the middle of the night.*

"I know, love." Mum pats my hand kindly. "It was exactly the right thing to do. I should have done it myself. You've brought a fresh eye to the business. All of you," she adds, looking around. "I should have gone away years ago! And was Uncle Ned helpful?" she adds innocently, and there's such a charged silence I think I might explode.

I'm dying to tell Mum everything. I want her to know the truth about Uncle Ned . . . and Bob . . . and all of it. Actually, I want her to become Ninja Mum and see off Uncle Ned for good.

But not now. That's for another day.

"Here's to Farrs!" exclaims Jake, lifting his glass, totally ignoring the question. We drink again, and Seb adds robustly, "Best store in Europe!"

"And here's to you, Jake," says Mum, turning toward him. "Well done for being the head of the family in my place, for keeping everyone together, for stepping in when the shop needed you—" She breaks off as Jake puts a hand on her arm.

"I'd love to take the credit," he says, in his familiar drawl. "But I've got this new annoying habit of being honest. And the truth is . . . it was Fixie."

There's silence and I stare at him, gobsmacked.

"Fixie?" Mum looks taken aback.

"Fixie was the head of the family while you were away," says Jake. "A lot of stuff went on and . . . well . . . Fixie took care of it."

"Fixie was the head," Nicole agrees. "She sorted us all out. She was boss."

"Boss-*y*," amends Jake wryly, and Leila gives a nervous giggle, which she hastily quells.

"I see." Mum looks around at the three of us, as though reappraising things. "Well . . . to Fixie, then."

"To Fixie." Jake raises his glass. "For everything." He meets my eyes gravely and I nod back, unable to speak, my head hot.

"Fixie." Nicole nods, her glass rising too. "Well done."

"You know me," I say, finally finding my voice. "I just have to fix stuff. It's always been my flaw—" I break off as I see Seb shaking his head, his eyes warm and loving.

"It's your strength," he says. "It's what makes you. Don't ever stop fixing stuff."

"We *need* you to fix stuff!" agrees Nicole. "Except the coffee machine," she adds as an afterthought. "I'm totally on that."

"To Fixie," says Leila eagerly, and Seb lifts his glass, his hand tight in mine.

"To Fixie," he says. "To Fixie Farr."

"Well," I say, still flustered. "Thanks very much and . . . and . . . let's have lunch."

Mum goes off to freshen up, and the rest of us crack into catering-team mode, and in a few minutes we're serving up lamb casserole with baked potatoes and broccoli, along with Mum's favorite crusty bread.

"Wait," I say, as she sits down and Jake starts pouring wine. "Wait. We haven't got enough seats. I don't understand. . . ." I look around the table, confused, then realize it's because Seb's here. There's an extra person.

"Use that chair?" Seb suggests, pointing at Dad's empty carver, and I stiffen automatically.

"No, we don't ever use that. It was Dad's. But it's fine—we can bring one in from the kitchen. . . ."

"You sit in it, Fixie," says Nicole suddenly, and I gape at her, stunned that she would even suggest it. "Why not? You wouldn't mind, would you, Mum?"

We're all looking at Dad's chair, and back at Mum, and I

can see her thinking hard, looking at us again, her unfamiliar earrings dangling. I can almost read her mind: *Everything's changed.*

"Yes," she says slowly. "I think it's time to use it again. Fixie, love, you sit in it."

"But . . ." I flounder. Dad's chair? The chair at the head of the table? Me?

"Go on," says Jake, nodding at the chair. "Sit down, or I'll take it. Seriously, you deserve it," he adds in a nicer voice.

"I'll lay an extra place," says Leila quickly. "It'll only take a second."

As Nicole passes broccoli around the table and Seb pours out the wine, I venture toward the big heavy chair. As I pull it out, I'm remembering Dad in this chair. His authority. And just for an instant I think, *I can't sit here, I'm not worthy*— but then I glance up and catch Seb's eye. He gives me a tiny, infinitesimal nod, and I suddenly remember those words he hurled at me in fury: *You need to start thinking less about what you owe other people and more about what you owe yourself.*

He might have been angry, but he was right.

I owe this to myself. I do. I owe it to myself.

I sit down in my place, pull the chair in with more confidence, and shake out the napkin that Leila's set for me, with a smile of thanks. And as I survey the faces that I love so dearly, I feel a kind of contentment. So we're not flash. So we're not moneyed. So we don't have all the answers or know exactly where we're going. We'll still be all right, our family. We'll be all right.

Acknowledgments

I owe one to many, many people.

Francesca at Transworld, Kara and Susan at Penguin Random House NYC, and all my wonderful publishers around the world.

Julia and Becky, Debbie, Jess and Sharon and the whole amazing Team Kinsella, with a special thank-you to Richard Ogle.

My tireless agents, Araminta, Marina, Kim, Nicki, and Sam and all at LAW and ILA.

My writerly friends for cocktails and wise counsel—especially Jojo, Lisa, Jenny, Kirsty, Linda, Joanna, Tom, and the Board.

The very helpful owners and staff of Harts of Stur—a fabulous family store!

My family—I owe you about eleventy billion.

And finally: the nameless American man who asked me to mind his laptop in a Starbucks one time, and instantly triggered my imagination . . .

I definitely owe you one.

SOPHIE KINSELLA is the author of the bestselling Shopaholic series as well as the novels *Can You Keep a Secret?, The Undomestic Goddess, Remember Me?, Twenties Girl, I've Got Your Number, Wedding Night, My Not So Perfect Life,* and, most recently, *Surprise Me.* She lives in the UK.

Sophiekinsella.com
Facebook.com/SophieKinsellaOfficial
Twitter: @KinsellaSophie
Instagram: @sophiekinsellawriter

About the Type

This book was set in Sabon, a typeface designed by the well-known German typographer Jan Tschichold (1902–74). Sabon's design is based upon the original letter forms of sixteenth-century French type designer Claude Garamond and was created specifically to be used for three sources: foundry type for hand composition, Linotype, and Monotype. Tschichold named his typeface for the famous Frankfurt typefounder Jacques Sabon (c. 1520–80).